İnci Birsel
MY COOKING NOTEBOOK
http://www.mycookingnotebook.com
First printing 2005, Istanbul

ISBN 975-00550-0-4

Recipes and Text: İnci Birsel
Editors: İnci Birsel, Selma Yalter
Illustrations: Nevin Kuloğlu
Graphic Design: REKLAM MERKEZİ
Graphic Applications: PARALEL TASARIM
Color Separation: APA Gama Röprodüksiyon A.Ş.
Printing: APA Uniprint Basım Sanayi ve Ticaret A.Ş.
Hadımköy-İstanbul Asfaltı, Ömerli Köyü
34555 Hadımköy, Çatalca Istanbul - Turkey
Tel: +90 212 798 28 40
Binding: Bayındır Ciltevi

MY COOKING NOTEBOOK

FAVORITE RECIPES FROM MY KITCHEN

İNCİ BİRSEL

CONTENTS

INTRODUCTION

If I were asked to define cooking in my own words it would be something like this – cooking is a passionate hobby, a totally absorbing and relaxing experience, a hands on practice on curiosity, courage, patience, and change.

I am a home cook. I'm not a chef. I have not had any formal training in cooking. I feel comfortable in the kitchen and most of what I do in the kitchen is self-taught. Reading cookbooks and magazines is a favorite pass time hobby. I am always curious to find out and learn further about changes in the culinary scene. I try out recipes even those with unusual combinations. I have courage to pair sweet and spicy or hot and cold. I don't give up on a recipe when it doesn't turn out as expected. I try again, changing this and that. I practice patience when improving recipes and when physical drawbacks don't interfere I can gladly spend hours in the kitchen. I am open to everything new in the culinary practice. Improvising on a theme is an integral part of my cooking. I enjoy this practice in the kitchen that works the taste buds and helps develop the educated palate. Thus this collection of recipes exhibits my approach to cuisine of our times.

Very often it pays to be adventurous in the kitchen. The end results may even surprise you. Be ready to embrace the challenge in the kitchen. Trust your senses and experiment with tastes and textures. The aroma, color, taste and, above all, the presentation of food all contribute to a perfect meal, the goal of which is bringing people together so they can enjoy each other's company.

I hope this collection of recipes satisfies that goal. You are the boss in your own kitchen. Carry the recipes to different directions. Add or change ingredients of your own choice. Let the seasons dictate to you which recipe to try and present at your dinner table. I would like this book to be an inspiration rather than a 'cook like this' book. I hope that you'll think I've achieved it. And finally I hope that this book caters to everyone who loves cooking and who makes entertaining less of a chore and more of a pleasure.

DEDICATION

This book is dedicated to my mother, Fatma Erker. She has passed on to me the instinct and interest in cooking. She has instilled in me the importance of food prepared with love and a dinner table set with pride. Her unending energy has been an inspiration.

This book is dedicated to my father, Halim Erker. He has always brought home the best of produce generously. He has always thought of me as a fabulous cook. Moreover, by his many examples of lifelong achievements, he has undoubtedly passed on to me the ability to channel my hobby and interests into creative and productive pieces of work. I share the joy of creating this book with him.

I dedicate this book to my parents in loving gratitude.

STARTERS

STARTERS, TAPAS, MEZES, DIM SUN, or whatever you want to call them

Serve starters on their own or create a collection of starters which in a sense is the harmonious grouping of tastes or textures. They can be the center of an informal meal or a beginning to several courses of a carefully planned meal – versatility and creativity in the kitchen.

STARTERS

Roasted Potatoes with Herb Dip

Cheese Sticks in Olive Dressing

Grilled Cherry Tomatoes

Roasted Beet Relish

Mushroom and Spinach Quiche

Eggplant stuffed with Cheese Polenta

Pumpkin and Ricotta Topping on Bread

Crostini with Onions

Smoked Salmon on Winter Vegetables

Celeriac Carpacio

Pumpkin and Leek Pancakes

Spiced Green Olives

Vegetable Terrine with Beet Sauce

About this and that

Salt, a substance made of sodium and chloride, is an essential ingredient in cooking. Addition of salt brings out the flavors in savory dishes as well as in sweet ones. Salt must be used in moderation because over-consumption has negative impact on health.

Salt is also an excellent preservative for meats, fish, cheese and vegetables (pickles). The most common kind of salt is table salt, which contains iodine. Sea salt, by contrast, has no additives but has more minerals than table salt. Sea salt is naturally evaporated along seashores. Ocean waters flood shallow man-made beds along the coastlines and during the summer the water evaporates leaving large salt crystals. Most sea salt comes from France, England and United States. Fleur du Sel (from Brittany, France) and Maldon Salt (from England) are two brands that are highly prized.

Sea salt is available in coarse and fine grains. A small amount of sea salt has more flavor than the same amount of table salt. It adheres better to foods and dissolves more quickly. Some chefs believe that sea salt has a purer and superior flavor and I go along with this culinary idea and use sea salt in my cooking.

ROASTED POTATOES

ROASTED POTATOES WITH HERB DIP

WITH HERB DIP

This tasty dip replaces ketchup in a sophisticated way. Serve this starter with several other vegetable-based antipasti and enjoy a glass of wine with it. Whenever I prepare starters, I always picture food on the table, friends and family around the table and a good serving of conversation and laughter. I guess this defines the joy of cooking for me.

SERVES 8

• 250 g / 1/2 lb podded peas
• a large handful of fresh coriander or parsley leaves, chopped
• a handful of fresh mint leaves, chopped
• 6 cloves garlic, chopped • 3 tablespoons vinegar
• 1-2 tablespoons Dijon mustard • 1/4 cup olive oil
• 4 spring onions, very finely chopped
• a good squeeze of lemon • sea salt and freshly ground pepper

Cook the peas in salted water until very tender. Drain and rinse to cool quickly. Put the peas, fresh herbs, garlic, vinegar and mustard in food processor. Pulse on and off until well chopped and homogeneous. Then pour the oil in a thin stream into the processor. The dip should have a thick consistency. Add more vinegar if too thick. Squeeze the lemon into the dip. Season with salt and plenty of pepper. Place into a bowl and stir in spring onions. Taste and adjust seasoning if necessary. Cover and refrigerate if prepared ahead of serving time, but bring to room temperature before serving.

ROASTED POTATO

ROASTED POTATO WEDGES

WEDGES

• 500 g / 1 lb potatoes • olive oil • sea salt

Preheat oven 450 °F / 230 °C.
Wash and brush the potatoes clean and pat them dry. First halve each unpeeled potato and then cut into wedges. Brush wedges with oliveoil and sprinkle with sea salt. Roast in the oven until wedges are browned and tender when pierced with a knife. Serve immediately with the sauce.

CUMMIN

About this and that

Cumin is a member of the parsley family. It is an essential spice, which has a sharp and strong flavor and a pronounced smell. It is available ground or whole. Always buy small amounts of ground cumin as the smell and flavor deteriorate easily and quickly. For superior flavor, toast whole seeds before grinding.

Cumin is much used in Latin American, Indian and North African cooking. In Turkey, ground cumin is added to minced meat dishes. In Spain, it is used in stews in combination with other spices. In Texas, it is used in chili con carne. In India, it is an essential part of the spice mixture called garam masala. It flavors sausages, pickles, relishes and a variety of other foods. It is taken as remedy for diarrhea and as well as indigestion.

CHEESE STICKS IN

CHEESE STICKS IN OLIVE DRESSING

OLIVE DRESSING

Paired with Grilled Cherry Tomatoes (p.19) and crusty bread (dip it in the pungent dressing) and beer or wine—this is pure luxury at the table with the simplest of ingredients.

SERVES 6

- **18 sticks of cheese of choice, feta or Halloumi cheese or a mixture of these cheeses**
- **1/2 cup pitted green olives, packed tightly**
- **8 - 10 fresh basil leaves**
- **1/3 cup olive oil** • **juice of 1/2 lemon**
- **1/2 teaspoon cumin**

Soak cheese sticks in water overnight to remove as much of the salt as possible. Or use your choice of unsalted cheese.

Process the olives, basil leaves and the oil in the food processor to a thick sauce. Do not season as cheese and dressing will be salty enough. Add lemon juice and cumin.

Spoon dressing over cheese sticks. Cover and refrigerate. When ready to serve place cheese sticks onto a serving dish. Then thin sauce with a bit more olive oil and lemon juice. Spoon all of sauce on cheese sticks and drizzle with a good squeeze of lemon juice.

Decorate with tiny basil leaves.

G A R L I C

About this and that

Balsamic Vinegar, aceto balsamico, is the gastronomical specialty of the town of Modeno, Italy and is famous throughout the world. Its extraordinary flavor enriches the culinary arts. Authentic balsamic vinegar, made from wine must (unfermented grape juice), ages from one year to 25 years and longer. It acquires a brown color and mellow, sweet taste in wooden casks. The different woods contribute to its flavor. It has an intense flavor and should be used sparingly. Authentic balsamic vinegar is relatively expensive. On the other hand, balsamic aged for a shorter time is widely available. It is used in salad dressings and perks up sauces without the addition of excess sodium and calories. It is superb on strawberries producing an exceptionally pleasing flavor. I think that there should be a place for balsamic vinegar in every kitchen. Inexpensive varieties of balsamic vinegar made from grape must and mixed with good quality vinegar are also widely available and are generally used in salad dressings.

GRILLED CHERRY

GRILLED CHERRY TOMATOES

TOMATOES

Cook the tomatoes a few hours ahead of serving time so that there will be plenty of time for the tomatoes to cool. Serve with other 'mezes' or 'tapas' on a summer dinner table.

SERVES 6

- 750 g / 1 1/2 lb cherry tomatoes
- 4 garlic cloves, peeled and sliced
- 3 - 4 sprigs of fresh thyme
- sea salt and freshly ground pepper
- 1/4 cup olive oil
- 3 tablespoons balsamic vinegar

Preheat oven to 350 °F / 180 °C.

Toss the tomatoes in the olive oil to coat. Season and spread on an ovenproof dish. Drizzle with balsamic vinegar. Sprinkle garlic slices and place thyme sprigs among tomatoes. Season with salt and pepper. Grill for about 10 minutes until beginning to burst and brown. Lower oven temperature to the lowest degree and roast for another hour. Watch carefully. The tomatoes should not char.

P O M E G R A N A T E

About this and that

Pomegranate molasses, also called pomegranate syrup, is a fresh tasting molasses with a fruity tartness. It is an essential ingredient in Mediterranean cuisines. It perks up salad dressings and is used in sauces for grilled fish and chicken. The molasses is made from pomegranate juice by boiling it down to a thick, dark red sauce. It has a long shelf life and I think it is essential to supplement the vinegars in your cupboard with a bottle of this flavorful molasses.

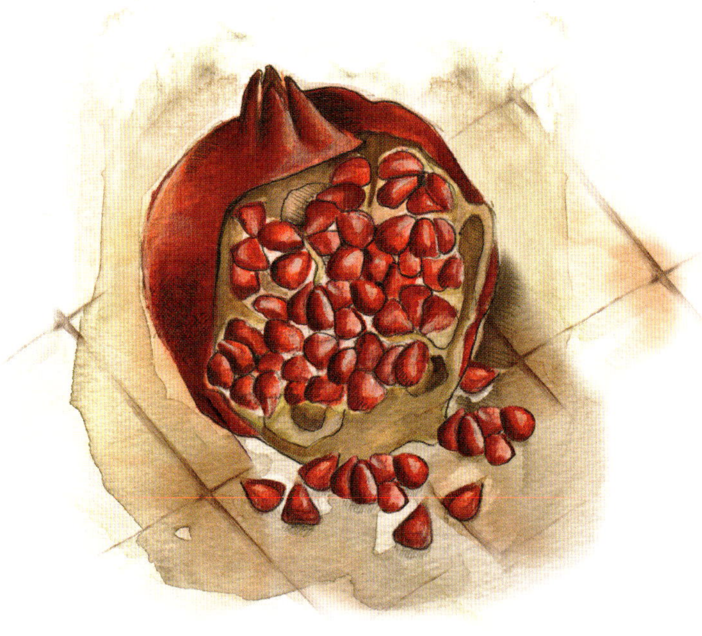

ROASTED BEET RELISH

This easy to assemble relish is very tasty as well as being colorful on the plate. I created the recipe after having a very similar dish at a restaurant in New York several years ago. It is great served with boiled or grilled shrimp.

SERVES 8

• 500 g / 1 lb beets, trimmed and washed
• 3 tablespoons pomegranate molasses • 1/4 cup very finely chopped onion
• 2 cloves garlic, very finely chopped • 1 tablespoon olive oil
• sea salt and freshly ground pepper
• 1/2 cup toasted walnuts, chopped
• 3-4 dried apricots, finely chopped
• a few drops of hot pepper sauce

Preheat oven to 350 °F / 180 °C.
Wrap beets in foil and place on a baking tray. Bake for 1 1/2 to 2 hours until done (poke with a knife; if knife moves in without any resistance then they are done). Unwrap beets and let cool. Peel and chop up in food processor or grate coarsely. Transfer beets to a bowl and add the rest of the ingredients. Mix well to incorporate flavors. Let rest for half an hour. Set a ring mold on each plate and spoon about 1/3 cup or more relish into each mold. Spread evenly and press down to form an even round shape. Carefully lift off the mold. Then decorate each plate to your heart's desire.

MUSHROOMS

MUSHROOM AND SPINACH QUICHE

MUSHROOM AND SPINACH QUICHE

Soluble fiber in oats, a small amount of butter and vegetables - all turn this quiche into a healthy choice. It is perfect for a light lunch or dinner. Serve it with soup and salad of your choice. Spiced Pears (p.197) is a good choice to end the meal.

SERVES 6-8

for the crust:

- **1 1/4 cups oats**
- **1/3 cup oat bran cereal, coarsely crushed**
- **2 1/2 tablespoons butter**
- **3 1/2 tablespoons cold water**
- **sea salt and freshly ground pepper**

for the filling:

- **1 tablespoon olive oil**
- **2 cloves garlic, chopped**
- **1 cup thinly sliced leeks**
- **3 cups tightly packed fresh spinach leaves, chopped coarsely**
- **1 1/4 cups thinly sliced mushrooms**
- **1 1/4 cups milk**
- **3 eggs**
- **1/2 cup grated Parmesan cheese**
- **salt and freshly ground pepper**
- **1/4 teaspoon thyme**
- **1/3 cup grated Gruyere cheese or any other hard cheese**

Preheat oven to 375 0F / 190 °C.

To make the crust combine oats and cereal in a bowl. Cut in butter with 2 knives until mixture turns into coarse meal. Add water and stir until moistened. Season and then press mixture into a ball. Flatten into a circle between two sheets of wax paper to fit and come up sides of a 25-28 cm / 10 inch pie plate. Remove one sheet and fit dough into pie plate. Remove top sheet and use hand to repair any torn bits. Bake in the oven for 10-15 minutes. Then cool completely.

To make the filling heat the oil in a skillet over medium heat. Add garlic, leeks and spinach. Sauté a few minutes until vegetables wilt. Add mushrooms and continue cooking and stirring for 5 or more minutes. Remove from heat.

Meanwhile combine milk and eggs. Add this mixture to vegetables along with the Parmesan cheese. Add thyme and then taste and season accordingly. Pour filling into crust. Sprinkle with grated Gruyere cheese. Bake for about 30 minutes until quiche is set and top browns. Remove from oven and let rest for 5 minutes before serving.

OLIVES

EGGPLANT STUFFED WITH CHEESE POLENTA

EGGPLANT STUFFED WITH CHEESE POLENTA

I take enormous pride in counting the endless variations to preparing eggplant. It is a family favorite and I never tire from serving it. Here is one example to the many variations.

SERVES 4

• 2 eggplants, (Asian long), tips cut off and sliced in half lengthwise
• 6 tablespoons olive oil • 4 cups vegetable broth or more
• 1 cup coarse polenta • 1/2 cup pitted and chopped black olives
• 1/2 - 3/4 cup crumbled Gorgonzola cheese
• 1 medium onion minced
• 1/2 tablespoon thyme (or 1/2 tablespoon fresh thyme leaves)
• 1/2 teaspoon lemon zest • sea salt and freshly ground pepper

Preheat oven to 425 °F / 220 °C.
Place eggplant on a baking dish and make cuts in the pulp of eggplant halves. Sprinkle with salt and pepper. Drizzle with 3 tablespoons of the olive oil and roast for about 20 minutes until pulp is soft. Remove from oven. Cool a bit and spoon out the pulp into a bowl leaving about a half centimetre around the edges of the eggplant boats. Chop up finely. Meanwhile heat 3 cups of the broth in a pot. Just as it boils add polenta in a thin stream, stirring constantly. Reduce heat and continue whisking for 15-20 minutes. Add additional broth if too thick. The polenta should have a thick creamy consistency. It will also thicken a bit more as it cools. Stir in the olives and half of the cheese. Pour polenta into a shallow dish sprinkled with a little water. This will prevent polenta from sticking to the dish. Cool to room temperature. Next sauté onion in 2 tablespoons of the oil until translucent. Add eggplant pulp and continue sautéing for another 5 minutes, stirring to incorporate finely. Taste for seasoning. Crumble polenta into eggplant mixture and mix well. At this point you may add about 1/4 cup cream for a creamier texture.
Add the rest of the cheese. Place the eggplant skins in an oven proof-serving dish and spoon polenta filling generously into each. Drizzle with the remaining 1 tablespoon of the olive oil. Combine lemon zest and thyme. Sprinkle over polenta. Bake in the oven for 15-20 minutes until warmed through and browned on top. Serve with Braised Leaves (p. 97) and slices of tomatoes drizzled with balsamic vinegar.

PUMPKIN AND RICOTTA

PUMPKIN AND RICOTTA TOPPING ON BREAD

TOPPING ON BREAD

The mellow taste of pumpkin paired with the cheeses is just great. Sprinkle a few red-pepper flakes if you like for a slight hint of hot spice.

SERVES 6-8

(Serving size: 2 pieces)

- 4 cups grated pumpkin • a handful of parsley leaves, chopped
- 2 garlic cloves, peeled and grated
- 1 cup Ricotta cheese, crumbled
- 3/4 cup freshly grated Parmesan cheese
- olive oil • sea salt and freshly ground pepper
- a pinch of grated nutmeg
- 16 slices of baguette • grated cheese (optional)

Preheat oven to 400 °F / 200 °C.

Mix pumpkin, parsley leaves and garlic in a bowl. Season to taste with salt and grate some nutmeg.

In another bowl mix the two cheeses.

Spread a generous amount of cheese over each slice of bread. Grind some pepper over the cheese. Top with the pumpkin mixture. Press down gently with fingers. Drizzle with olive oil and bake in oven until golden brown. Grind some pepper on each piece. If you wish sprinkle with grated cheese of your choice. Serve with lemon wedges. A squeeze of lemon enhances the flavors.

O N I O N

About this and that

Crostini are small pieces of bread toasted in the oven. Making crostini is a good way of using stale bread. Stale bread is easier to slice and it also toasts more quickly. Brush pieces of bread cut into quarters with olive oil on both sides. Toast in the oven until crisp (350 °F / 180 °C). Spoon your choice of topping while still hot and serve. Crostini keeps well in an airtight container for a couple of days. If they are kept too long the oil becomes stale. Place in a heated oven for 10 minutes to crisp them up before spooning on your choice of topping.

CROSTINI WITH ONIONS

CROSTINI WITH ONIONS

It is a surprisingly easy to prepare starter which, I'm sure, you'll make over and over again. Crostini is served with many different toppings. It also pairs well with clear soup. Prepare as stated on the previous page and simply float on soup.

Caramelised Onion Topping

SERVES 4

- 6-8 red onions, peeled, halved and sliced thinly
- 2 tablespoons olive oil
- 1-2 tablespoons brown sugar
- sea salt and freshly ground pepper
- 16 slices of baguette

Cook onions in the oil in a saucepan over medium heat, stirring once in a while for a few minutes. Add the sugar, reduce heat and cook stirring until onions are softened completely and are deep brown in color. Season to taste. Cool to room temperature. Prepare crostini as explained on page 28. Top each crostini with one heaped tablespoon of onion. Place an olive on each crostini. Drizzle with olive oil and serve immediately.

If you are not rushed for time, do not add sugar to the onions but sauté them in oil over medium heat long enough (15-20 minutes) for moisture to evaporate and natural sugars to brown. Stir the onions frequently to ensure even browning. The onions may require an additional 20 minutes to become completely caramelized. They should not burn around the edges. Caramelized onions freeze well up to three months and can be used in various other recipes. So it may be worth to prepare a large amount at one time. Of course this will definitely require patience in front of the stove.

M U S T A R D

SMOKED SALMON ON

SMOKED SALMON ON WINTER VEGETABLES

WINTER VEGETABLES

For a long while it was very fashionable to serve smoked salmon on a bed of shredded lettuce. Then it sort of fell out of fashion with the arrival of smoked salmon wrapped around peeled fresh figs. Salmon served in any form is always a favorite of mine. This recipe is a variation on the original theme and one can easily develop more variations.

SERVES 4-6

• 300 g / 10 oz smoked salmon slices
• 2 medium celeriac, peeled, sliced and cut into fine julliene
• 1 small red onion, cut in half and very thinly sliced
• half an apple, cored, and cut into fine julliene
• 1 carrot, coarsely grated • 3-4 dill sprigs, chopped
• 8 tablespoons light mayonnaise
• 2 tablespoons yogurt • 1 tablespoon Dijon mustard
• zest and juice of 1/2 lemon • sea salt and freshly ground pepper

Soak onion slices in cold water for 10 minutes to take away the raw taste. Rub slices with fingers to separate onion into its single layers. Squeeze all excess water out and pat dry between paper towels.

Place all vegetables into a bowl. In another bowl mix the mayonnaise, yogurt, mustard, lemon zest and juice. Season according to your taste. Using a fork work sauce into vegetables. Let rest for 5 minutes.

Divide vegetable onto individual plates. Top with folds of smoked salmon. Place 1/4 of a lemon on each plate and garnish with dill sprigs or a tiny spoonfull of caviar.

CELERY

CELERIAC CARPACIO

Here is a sophisticated vegetarian starter in which the marinated paper-thin slices of celery root stand in for beef. Onions and celery complete each other in both flavor and texture.
Consider using thinly sliced zucchini in place of celeriac for a softer texture.

SERVES 4

• 4 medium celeriac, root ends removed, peeled and cut in half diagonally

for the onion marmalade:
• 3 medium onions, halved and thinly sliced • 1 tablespoon each butter and olive oil
• 1 tablespoon balsamic vinegar • 1 teaspoon brown sugar
• sea salt and freshly ground pepper
• 1/2 cup white wine • extra-virgin olive oil
• Parmesan cheese shavings

First make the onion marmelade. Sweat the onion in oil and butter in a skillet over medium low heat until soft. Stir occasionally. Next add the vinegar, sugar, salt and pepper and continue cooking until onions are caramelized. Be patient as you do this because you may need to stand in front of the stove for a good half hour. Then it is time to add the wine. Stir and cook until most of the liquid evaporates. Spoon the onions into a food processor and purée coarsely. Return marmelade into a pan, taste and add more sugar or salt as needed.
Meanwhile prepare the celeriac. Bring a pot of water to the boil. Add the halved celery roots and cook until crisp on the outside and tender in the middle. Drain and pat dry. When the celeriac is completely cooled, slice into paper thin slices using a mandolin or a vegetable slicer. Squeeze some lemon juice over the slices and season with salt and pepper.
To assemble this starter spoon about 2-3 spoonfuls of onion marmelade onto each plate. Spread it into a flat disk by using back of spoon.
Arrange prepared celery root slices over the marmelade slightly overlapping but forming only one layer. Scatter 4-5 Parmesan cheese shavings and garnish with fresh dill sprigs. Place a piece of lemon on each plate and serve.

LEEKS

PUMPKIN AND

PUMPKIN AND LEEK PANCAKES

LEEK PANCAKES

Serve these pancakes warm with apple sauce and sour cream or jam and cheese or simply with yogurt flavored with mashed garlic. They are great for brunch or for a light lunch.

SERVES 6-8

- **2 cups peeled grated potatoes**
- **2 cups peeled and grated pumpkin**
- **1 1/2 cups very thinly sliced leeks**
- **1/4 cup flour** • **2 eggs**
- **sea salt and freshly ground pepper**
- **1/2 teaspoon ground nutmeg**
- **oil for cooking pancakes**

Mix all ingredients (except oil) in a large bowl. Use a fork and blend everything well. Heat 3 tablespoons oil in a skillet. Drop vegetable mixture by 2 tablespoons onto skillet. Flatten slightly with a spatula. Cook both sides until brown. Remove from skillet and place on paper towels to drain excess oil. Continue making more pancakes and adding spoonfuls of oil to skillet as needed. Serve warm with something sweet (jam) and something salty (cheese) or with sour cream.

ROSEMARY

SPICED GREEN OLIVES

As a rule of the thumb, I like soaking anchovies or any other salt cured ingredient in water to cut down on the salt content. First, rinse each fillet under running water and then soak them in water for fifteen minutes. Drain well and use in recipe.

- **500 g / 1 lb green olives, sliced or with pits**
- **1 teaspoon ground cumin**
- **1 tablespoon chopped fresh rosemary or 1 teaspoon dried rosemary, crushed**
- **1 tablespoon fresh thyme leaves or 1 teaspoon dried thyme, crushed**
- **4 cloves garlic, finely chopped**
- **1/2 cup vinegar**
- **3 anchovy fillets, crushed with a pestle in a mortar into a paste together with 2 tablespoons of olive oil**

Drain olives and rinse once or twice. If using olives with pits crush olives to break open the skin by using a meat mallet and remove pits.
Combine the rest of the ingredients in a bowl. Mix well and add olives. Spoon into a jar. Pour water all the way to the top. Seal and shake jar. Refrigerate olives in marinade at least 4 days before serving. Shake jar occasionally.
To serve, just spoon desired amount into a bowl draining the brine. Drizzle with your best olive oil and sprinkle with thyme. Serve it with crusty fresh bread and a glass of chilled white wine. Yummy!

Tips + Tricks + Techniques

Crème fraîche is a tasty dairy product that can very easily be unavailable in the refrigerator when desperately needed. But then you can just as easily make your own by combining $^1/_2$ cup sour cream and $^1/_2$ cup whipping cream. Cover the mixture and let it rest at room temperature for about 4 hours. Cream will thicken during this time. It can be refrigerated for up to one week.

VEGETABLE TERRINE

VEGETABLE TERRINE WITH BEET SAUCE

WITH BEET SAUCE

This terrine has a delicate, mellow taste and a smooth texture. It pairs well with the Beet Sauce (p.235) making a pleasing color contrast. Bake it in one large dish or individual ramekins.

SERVES 6-8

- **250 g / 1/2 lb cauliflower florets** • **250 g / 1/2 lb broccoli florets**
- **2 medium sized carrots, peeled and cut into cubes**
- **1 cup milk** • **1 cup créme fraîche**
- **sea salt and freshly ground pepper**
- **a pinch of freshly grated nutmeg** • **5 eggs, whisked**

Preheat oven to 325 °F / 160 °C.

Drop the cauliflower florets into boiling water. About 5 minutes later the broccoli florets should join them. Cook until just crisp tender. Drain and rinse with cold water. In another pan cook carrot cubes until crisp tender. Drain and rinse. Vegetables can be prepared one day ahead and refrigerated.

When ready to continue with the recipe, bring to room temperature and.....

Mix together the milk and créme fraîche. Add the whisked eggs. Then season generously. Next place vegetables in buttered terrine form of your choice. I sometimes use a cake pan and it works just as well. Then pour milk and cream mixture over the vegetables and place the form in large pan. Pour hot water to come halfway up the terrine form.

It helps to place a folded newspaper page in the water under the terrine form. This prevents it from sliding every which way when moved around in the oven.

Bake for about 40 minutes until custard is firmly set. Remove from oven and let cool to room temperature. Then run a knife around the adge and unmold on a flat surface. Cut into 3 – 4 cm thick slices. Serve 2 pieces over beet sauce.

Try this: Add 1/2 cup each yellow and red pepper, diced into small pieces. Blanche them with the carrots or mix them raw into the custard for a crunchy texture.

S A L A D S

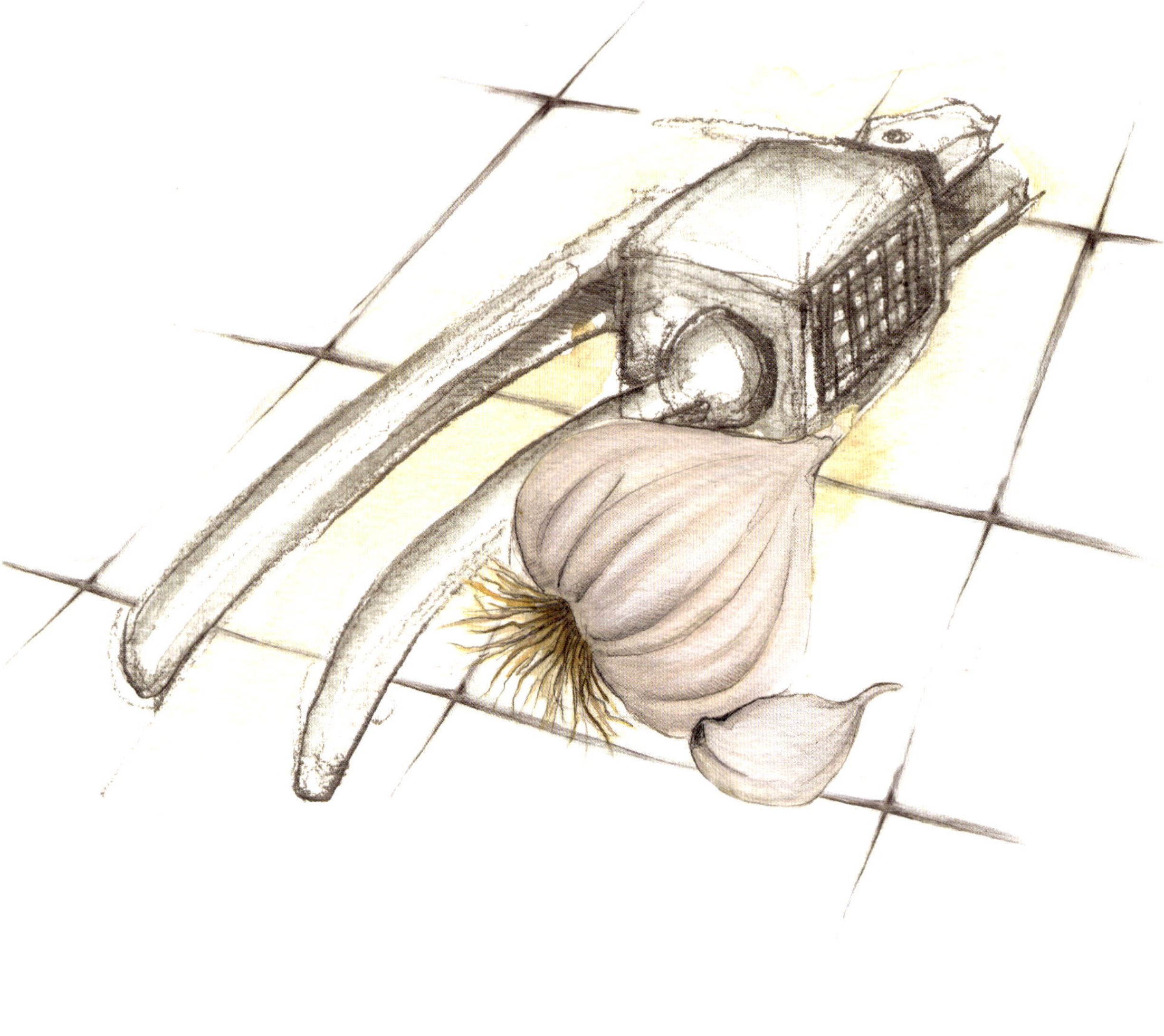

SALADS

I am of the firm opinion that each and every meal deserves a salad. I think no other food can match a salad freshly made only a short time before everyone gathers around the table. Since the simplest of foods demand only the best ingredients, care must be given to the choice of ingredients that go into a salad bowl, including the dressing. Always use the freshest greens and the best olive oil. Stock your cupboard with a couple of different vinegars. There is much choice now. Take care to dress your salad just before its arrival at the table. I hope the choice of ingredients in the following recipes will inspire you to try new combinations of fruits and vegetables in creating salads. Let me know if I have tempted you into trying things you've never thought of tossing into a salad bowl before.

SALADS

Lemon Coleslaw

Arugula and Pear Salad with Roquefort Cheese

Purslane Salad with Peaches and Goat's Cheese

Fennel, Apple and Radish Salad

Broccoli Salad

Poached Chicken Salad with Peaches

Watermelon and Salad Greens

Zucchini Ribbon Salad

C H I L L I E S

Tips + Tricks + Techniques

Chilles or chilies? Both spelling forms are right and both are hot. They have little aroma but vary in taste, from mild to fiery hot. Chillies are members of the capsicum family and come in all shapes and sizes. They are available fresh, dried, crushed, flaked and ground. When buying fresh chilies, choose crisp and unwrinkled ones.

Be very careful when handling chillies. First cut chillies in half lengthwise. Then use a small spoon to scrape away the seeds and the membrane, which holds the capsaicin that gives chillies their kick. They can burn the skin of your hands or parts of your body you touch with your hand- especially do not touch your eyes. You may want to wear rubber gloves and wash hands with WARM water - not hot and not cold- after handling them.

LEMON COLESLAW

LEMON COLESLAW

A delicate blend of flavors combine to make this delicious salad. As a variation add 1/4 cup raisins and 1/2 cup coarsely chopped walnuts. This is a tasty accompaniment to grilled chicken or turkey.

SERVES 6-8

for the dressing:

- 1/2 cup mayonnaise
- 1/2 cup yogurt
- 1/4 cup fresh lemon juice and orange juice
- 2 tablespoons Dijon mustard
- 1 tablespoon olive oil
- 1 tablespoon sugar
- 1 tablespoon vinegar
- sea salt and freshly ground pepper
- 1 hot red chilli, all seeds removed and finely chopped (optional)

for the salad:

- 6 cups shredded cabbage
- 1 large green or red pepper, cut into strips
- 1 red onion, cut into quarters and thinly sliced
- 1 large apple, cut into quarters, cored and thinly sliced
- 1 large carrot, shredded
- a generous handful of parsley leaves, chopped
- 3 teaspoons grated lemon peel

Put all the ingredients for the dressing in a bowl and whisk with a fork. Taste and season well. Refrigerate until ready to use.

Next soak all of the cut up onion in a bowl of water for 5-10 minutes. Drain, rinse and pat dry. This will take away the raw taste of onions.

And finally combine cabbage, pepper, onion, carrot, parsley and lemon peel in a large bowl. Toss with enough dressing just before serving. The vegetables will then retain their crispness. A little squeeze of lemon juice and a generous amount of chopped parsley over the top of the salad should just about do it.

A R U G U L A

About this and that

Arugula is also known as rocket. It has a piquant flavor and adds a sharp, spicy edge to salads. Arugula is a popular salad green in the Mediterranean. It is also used in sandwiches, pasta sauces, and soups as well as on top of pizzas after they are baked in the oven. The American palates often find its flavor too assertive. Arugula is a rich source of iron as well as vitamins A and C. It is best to use arugula immediately upon purchase. These delicate leaves keep only a few days in the refrigerator when wrapped in a damp paper towel and sealed in a plastic bag.

ARUGULA AND PEAR SALAD WITH ROQUEFORT CHEESE

ARUGULA AND PEAR SALAD WITH ROQUEFORT CHEESE

Make this simple and refreshing salad when pears are at their best – tasty and full of aroma. The pairing of greens and fruit may seem unusual but as in this recipe, some unlikely ingredients can easily come together and produce great tastes.

For one serving I use half a pear, two handfulls of arugula. Do not peel pears. Cut in half and remove the core. Slice each half into eights. Rub with lemon to stop discoloration. Wash and pat arugula dry. Place pears and arugula in a bowl. Drizzle with dressing made with your best olive oil, a good squeeze of lemon juice as well as orange juice, a pinch of sugar and a half teaspoon of mustard. Season with sea salt and freshly ground black pepper. Toss together with your fingers.
You may also try Lemon and Garlic Dressing (p. 221) over the salad.
Transfer salad onto a large flat plate. Top with 10 –12 toasted walnut halves and crumbled Roquefort cheese. Serve this salad as a starter or as anaccompaniment to grilled meat.

About this and that

Purslane once grew only in the wild, but it is now widely grown for the market. Its stalks are saturated with water and it has succulent, fleshy leaves. Purslane is a good source of potassium and magnesium. It may be cooked like spinach, can be added to soups and sauces or just sautéed on its own. It is excellent served as a salad with peeled, seeded and chopped tomatoes and thinly sliced red onion. It requires the same selecting and storing methods as of any salad green. It is best to use purslane upon purchase.

PURSLANE SALAD WITH PEACHES AND GOAT'S CHEESE

PURSLANE SALAD WITH PEACHES AND GOAT'S CHEESE

Another great summer salad – can be an antipasto selection or an accompaniment to grilled meat or even to a pasta dish. I like the mellow taste of purslane but do use any mixed greens of choice like mesculine greens or just plain lettuce.

Amount of ingredients will vary according to the number of servings. For one, I use half a peach, peeled and sliced; 2 big handfulls of purslane, leaves picked, washed and spin dried; a generous crumble of goat's cheese (Roquefort or Gorgonzola cheese can be substituted); onion rings. Place sliced peaches and crumbled cheese on a large plate. Slice red onion into thin slices. Separate into rings. Soak in water for 5-10 minutes. Then drain and rinse to take away the raw taste. Pat onion rigs dry between sheets of paper towels.

Mix together zest of half an orange, some orange or grapefruit juice, a reasonable amount of your best olive oil. Add a few drops of balsamic vinegar and 1 teaspoon powdered sugar. Whisk with a fork.

Toss purslane (and some fresh mint leaves) with the dressing you have prepared. Throw greens gracefully on top of peaches and cheese. Top with onion rings. Grind some black pepper over the salad and sprinkle with toasted and chopped walnuts.

F E N N E L

About this and that

Fennel is a Mediterranean native plant, which is both a vegetable and an herb. It has a bulbous base, green stalks and feathery fronds, which can be reserved for garnish. Fennel is a slightly sweet vegetable with a hint of anise flavor. The base of the plant can be eaten raw in salads and raw fennel is an excellent source of potassium. Fennel lends itself to be prepared in a wide variety of ways and loses its anise flavor when cooked. Wrapped tightly in a plastic bag, fennel keeps up to one week in the refrigerator.

Fennel seeds may be used whole or ground in both sweet and savory dishes as well as in some breads. Fennel also has medicinal properties. It has a reputation as colic easier and stomach soother. Babies sleep happily after being fed spoonfuls of fennel tea. It is effective for relieving symptoms of indigestion. A cup of freshly brewed fennel tea may be just the best remedy after a rich evening meal.

FENNEL, APPLE AND RADISH SALAD

FENNEL, APPLE AND RADISH SALAD

You are once more on your own with this light, refreshing salad. The quantities are up to you, but mine go like this – one part radish, two parts each fennel and apple. Dress the salad with the great tasting apple juice dressing. This is a very crunchy salad that requires a good amount of chewing.

Cut the base of the root and excess stalks off the fennel. Remove any tough outer leaves. Cut the bulb in half and cut out the hard core. Slice them thinly along with the radishes. Then to get the vegetables really crisp, soak them in cold water for ten minutes or more. Drain and pat dry. Core one tart apple. Quarter and slice thinly. Squeeze some lemon juice over apples to stop discoloration. Combine sliced fennel, radish and apple in a bowl. Toss with enough dressing to coat evenly. Always use yourhand for a gentle toss. Place vegetables on a flat serving dish. Sprinkle with toasted nuts of your choice – almonds or hazelnuts or pine nuts or even better then all, walnut halves. A small handful of raisins offers the right amount of sweetness to this salad.

Try this for a dressing:

- **1/3 cup apple cider or apple juice**
- **4 tablespoons of your best olive oil**
- **3 tablespoons apple cider vinegar**
- **1-2 teaspoons honey**
- **a pinch of hot red pepper flakes, if you like hot food**

Whisk all ingredients to blend. Season dressing with salt and freshly ground pepper. Add a good squeeze of lemon juice.

Or try this:

- **2 tablespoons Dijon mustard**
- **2 tablespoons pomegranate molasses**
- **1 tablespoon honey**
- **1/3 cup your best olive oil**
- **sea salt and freshly ground pepper**

Whisk together mustard, pomegranate molasses and honey. Season with sea salt and freshly ground black pepper. Gradually whisk in oil until emulsified.

BROCCOLI

BROCCOLI SALAD

I'm always looking for recipes which will help me put more vegetables on the table. This one is a winner. It is low in fat and calories. And we all know very well by now that broccoli is very good for our health! The broccoli, sweet fruit and creamy dressing provide a lively contrast in this salad.

SERVES 6-8

(Serving size: 1 cup)

for the salad:

- **500 g / 1 lb broccoli florets (reserve stalks for another use)**
- **1 cup seedless grapes, halved**
- **1/2 cup canned sweet corn, drained**
- **1/2 cup raisins**
- **1/2 cup toasted pine nuts**

for the dressing:

- **1/2 cup light mayonnaise**
- **1/2 cup fat-free yogurt**
- **1 teaspoon sugar**
- **3 tablespoons vinegar or more**
- **1 tablespoon mustard**
- **1 tablespoon water**
- **1/4 cup extra-virgin olive oil**
- **sea salt and freshly ground black pepper**

Steam broccoli florets until crisp tender. They should retain that fresh crunch. Then whisk the dressing by mixing all of the ingredients.

Next combine all the ingredients for the salad in a shallow bowl.

Spoon the dressing over the vegetables and fruit and let sit for a while for all the tastes to incorporate and the raisins to swell up a bit. Or refrigerate the salad if you have started work in the kitchen ahead of serving time. But then take care to serve the salad at room temperature to bring out all of the flavors.

C O R I A N D E R

About this and that

Coriander, also called cilantro, is a delicate herb resembling parsley but with a strong smell and spicy flavor. Fresh coriander is widely used in Asian cuisines as well as in many other cuisines all over the world such as Mexican, Indian, Caribbean and Chinese to name but a few. Fresh coriander does not cook well, so it is advisable to add it to hot dishes at the last minute of cooking process. Float a few fresh coriander leaves on fruit compotes for an additional depth of flavor. Fresh coriander leaves, when not available, can easily be substituted with the following combinations which duplicate the minty, citrucy flavor of coriander: equal parts of mint and parsley leaves or parsley leaves with very little mint, a squeeze of lemon juice and a dash of ground coriander. The use of the seeds of the plant is more widespread. This aromatic spice is used with seafood and meat as well as in soups and desserts. A little bit of this spice goes a long way.

POACHED CHICKEN SALAD WITH PEACHES

POACHED CHICKEN SALAD WITH PEACHES

Tasty curried dressing teams up with poached chicken, peaches and fresh greens to make this main dish salad. This no-fuss salad was inspired by a recipe I have come across in a cooking magazine. Originally mango chutney was used. Although we can occasionally purchase mangoes in our local markets, I have chosen to substitute peaches which are more easily available.

SERVES 4

for the salad:

- **4 skinless, boneless chicken breast halves, slightly pounded**
  (sea salt and water for poaching)
- **1 large peach, peeled and diced**
- **2 celery stalks, thinly sliced**
- **a handful of fresh coriander or parsley leaves,chopped**
- **2 – 3 tablespoons sliced almonds, toasted**
- **sea salt and freshly ground pepper**

for the dressing:

- **1 teaspoon curry powder, toasted over low heat for one minute**
- **1/3 cup low-fat yogurt**
- **1/4 cup low-fat mayonnaise**
- **2 tablespoons or more peach relish (p. 241)**
- **2 tablespoons lemon juice**

First poach chicken. Place chicken in a saucepan over high heat with water covering all pieces. Sprinkle with salt. Add a few sprigs of thyme. Place a plate over chicken pieces to hold them under the boiling water. Just as soon as the water comes to a boil, lower heat and simmer until chicken pieces are cooked through. Then cool completely in liquid. Drain and cut into small pieces. While the chicken is cooling, prepare the dressing in a bowl by whisking together all the ingredients. If dressing is thicker than you would like, then thin down by adding more lemon juice. And finally toss chicken (cut into cubes), diced peaches, sliced celery stalks, fresh coriander, and dressing. Place lettuce leaves on each individual serving plate and top with chicken salad. Sprinkle almonds and serve with a chilled white wine and warm pita bread.

W A T E R M E L O N

About this and that

Rice vinegar, as the name suggests, is made from fermented rice. It is clear vinegar with a soft mellow taste due to its low acetic content. It has been used in Asian cuisines for centuries. It lends itself to oriental dipping sauces and salad dressings and is especially exceptional in sweet and sour dishes. Japanese rice vinegar is mild, but the Chinese variety has a strong taste, which can be white, red or black, depending on the rice used. A small bottle of rice vinegar will go a long way and I think, it is worth to keep a bottle in the cupboard and experiment with its taste.

WATERMELON AND

WATERMELON AND SALAD GREENS

SALAD GREENS

This is a refreshing salad alongside any grilled meat. Prepare the salad just before you are ready to serve. When cutting cubes of watermelon try to cut them out of pieces closest to the peel. Choose the freshest greens and include baby spinach leaves as well as loads of parsley and mint leaves. The fresh greens, mildly sweet and juicy fruit and tangy sauce provide a lively contrast in this salad—an excellent choice for a summer salad.

SERVES 4

for the dressing:

- **2 tablespoons rice vinegar**
- **1 tablespoon extra-virgin olive oil**
- **grated zest of one lemon**
- **1 garlic clove, minced**
- **2 teaspoons minced peeled fresh ginger (optional)**
- **sea salt and freshly ground pepper**

for the salad:

- **2 cups cubes of water melon**
- **2-3 cups salad greens**
- **1 cucumber**
- **3-4 green onions, thinly sliced**
- **a handful of fresh cilantro or parsley, chopped**

Peel the skin off the cucumber in alternating, lengthways strips, creating a striped effect. Halve it lengthways. Scoop out and discard the seeds. Then slice to desired thickness. Transfer to a sieve suspended over the sink. Sprinkle with salt and let rest for half an hour. Finally rinse, drain and squeeze out the moisture with your hands. Then soak the green onions in ice-cold water to take away the raw taste. Rinse and pat dry.

Make the dressing by whisking all the ingredients in a large salad bowl. Season to taste with salt and pepper. Add watermelon and all remaining ingredients you have prepared. Toss to coat evenly and scatter mint or sage leaves over the salad. Take care to serve immediately so that the greens retain their crisp texture.

P E A N U T S

Tips + Tricks + Techniques

Toasting seeds and nuts.

Preheat oven to 350 °F / 180 °C. Spread nuts or seeds on an ungreased baking sheet and toast for 5-7 minutes or more. Shake baking sheet once in a while and remove when the nuts or seeds have turned to desired color. Another method is to toast nuts in a non-stick pan over medium-high heat for 3-5 minutes. Toast seeds in the same way but only for a shorter time until they are fragrant. Always toss constantly to prevent deep browning. Transfer to a bowl or plate to cool and to stop deep browning. Grind or crush seeds as necessary. Seeds like cumin or coriander toasted and crushed give a depth of flavor to any recipe. Store toasted nuts in an airtight container in the refrigerator. Scatter them over salads and pasta dishes or on bruchetta. In a nutshell, incorporate toasted nuts and seeds into your cooking.

ZUCCHINI

ZUCCHINI RIBBON SALAD

RIBBON SALAD

Served as a starter on its own with crusty bread, this colorful salad could also easily accompany grilled or poached fish. The most important ingredient in this salad is freshness.

SERVES 4

for the dressing:

- **1/3 cup olive oil** • **2 1/2 tablespoons red wine vinegar**
- **2 1/2 tablespoons pomegranate molasses**
- **sea salt and freshly ground pepper**

for the salad:

- **5- 6 medium size firm zucchinis, washed, scrubbed and sliced lengthwise with a mandolin or a vegetable slicer into long, thin shavings**
- **2 large bunches arugula, stems discarded**
- **a generous handful of Parmesan cheese shavings** • **1 tablespoon toasted sesame seeds**
- **1 tablespoon thinly sliced candied orange peels**

Make the dressing in a large bowl by whisking all the ingredients. Season with salt and pepper. Let flavors mingle for 5 – 10 minutes. Add paper thin zucchini slices and toss with fingers. Start assembling the salad by piling zucchini on individual plates as high as they go. Next throw arugula leaves into the bowl containing the dressing and toss gently. Mount on the zucchini. Arrange cheese shavings on the salad, forming the shape of a tent. Scatter the rest around the plate. A sprinkling of sesame seeds and strips of candied orange peel will complete the beautiful presentation. Dizzle any left over dressing on the plate around the salad.

SOUPS

SOUPS

There is hardly any dish that can take the place of a warm bowl of soup on a cold winter day. Soups can start a meal or can be the main course if they are hearty enough. A good stock or broth defines a good soup. Once the stock is available and the freshest of ingredients are used, then turning these into a tasty soup is no chore. Whenever I make soup I always make it for a crowd and freeze the extra. Leave your soup chunky or purée it. Add some cream, milk or for a healthier version, soy milk to give your soup a richer taste and a silky texture. Embellish it with croutons or herbs. Here are some of my favorite soups.

SOUPS

Pumpkin and Pear Soup

Zucchini and Apple Soup

Celery Root and Chestnut Soup

Spicy Corn Chowder

Cream of Fennel Soup

Chickpea Soup with Spinach

Cabbage and Potatoe Soup

Tips + Tricks + Techniques

A French technique of cooking called sweating is used in this recipe. Sweating is simply cooking food – usually vegetables and onions -gently in a small amount of butter or oil on the stovetop or in the oven without browning. Sometimes a piece of aluminum foil cut to the size of pan is placed onto the surface of food. The pan is then covered and set over medium low heat. During the cooking process the vegetables give off steam and release juices. They turn translucent as they are cooked slowly. The vegetables are neither caramelized nor browned. The flavor is concentrated. Sweating is a preferred technique when making soups, sauces, and stocks. The recipe usually starts with these words: "Sweat the onions first." As onion, garlic and other vegetables, such as celery or leeks are cooked, all the flavorful juices are extracted to add great depth of taste to many dishes.

PUMPKIN AND PEAR SOUP

I love pumpkin. So here is a recipe I came across in an old recipe book and have improvised. The pumpkin melts into a smooth background. As this soup sits,the flavors will develop, so feel free to make it a few days before serving. It tastes fantastic and is so easy to prepare.
Feel free to improvise as well. Who knows, you may end up with a better recipe.

SERVES 4-6

- **1 tablespoon butter** • **1 tablespoon olive oil**
- **2 medium onions, chopped**
- **750 g / 1 1/2 lb pumpkin, peeled, seeded and cut into cubes**
- **1 large pear, peeled and chopped**
- **1 medium potato, peeled and chopped**
- **1 celery root, peeled and chopped**
- **2 tomatoes, skinned, seeded and chopped** • **4 cups vegetable broth**
- **1/2 - 1 cup milk** • **sea salt and freshly ground pepper**

for garnish:

chopped parsley.

Sweat the onions in oil and butter in a soup pot over medium low heat for 10 minutes. Stir and shake the pot a few times to avoid browning. Add pear, pumpkin, celery and potato. Cover and simmer for an additional 10 minutes, stirring occasionally. Add tomato and broth. Season with salt and pepper. Simmer steadily for about 20 mimutes.
Purée with a hand blender (or in a food processor, in batches) and then pass through a sieve for a silky texture. Return to pot, stir in milk and heat until hot. Taste and adjust seasoning. If soup is too thick add more milk. Garnish with chopped parsley. Sprinkle Oven-dried Zucchini (p. 215) over soup.

About this and that

Nutmeg is the seed of a tropical evergreen tree. The membrane of the seed becomes the spice known as mace. The inner kernel is the nutmeg. It is best used sparingly. A pinch of freshly grated nutmeg in spinach dishes is definitely the secret ingredient that perks up flavors. Its flavor also complements potatoes, milk products, egg and cheese dishes and hot drinks such as eggnog. Nutmeg quickly loses its flavor when ground. It is best to buy them whole and keep them in airtight containers. Grate nutmeg as required on nutmeg graters, which have tiny rasps that turn this hard spice into ground form.

ZUCCHINI AND APPLE SOUP

ZUCCHINI AND APPLE SOUP

Broths and stocks are basics for soups. I usually make my own chicken stock (p.255) or vegetable broth (p.253) and freeze what is left over to be used later in soups or sauces. Combining a good stock or broth with fresh vegetables produces delicious tasting soups. The simplest of ingredients create great results.

SERVES 6

- **2 1/2 cups chicken stock or vegetable broth**
- **3 medium sized zucchini, cut into small pieces**
- **1 medium onion, chopped** • **garlic cloves, chopped**
- **2 tablespoons butter** • **1 tablespoon olive oil**
- **2 slices dark or white bread, cut into cubes**
- **sea salt and freshly ground pepper** • **1 tart apple, peeled and thinly sliced**
- **1 cup milk or soy milk** • **1/4 cup cream**
- **1/8 teaspoon grated nutmeg**

for garnish:

chopped parsley and grated orange peel.

Bring chicken stock to a boil in a soup pot and add zucchini. Simmer until tender. Meanwhile in another pot sweat the onions and garlic in butter and oil until translucent. Add bread cubes, stir and cook until bread cubes are crisply toasted. Throw in the apples and keep stirring until the apples are slightly cooked. Add the chicken stock and zucchini and cook a bit more. Season with salt and pepper.

Purée in food processor and return to pot. Pour in milk and bring to a slow boil. Lower heat. (Can be prepared up to this stage. Then rewarm and continue cooking.) Add cream and correct seasoning. Ladle into a warmed soup bowl and garnish with parsley and orange peel. Nutmeg Croutons (p. 211) make a tasty garnish as well.

CHESTNUTS

CELERY ROOT AND CHESTNUT SOUP

A soothing winter soup with great flavors which makes the best of the market's bounty. Buy roasted chestnuts to cut down on preparation time.

SERVES 6

• 1/4 cup olive oil • 3 celery roots, peeled and cut into cubes
• 1 small onion, diced • 1 leek, thinly sliced
• 400 g /about 1 lb roasted chestnuts, cut in half, (reserve 4-5 chestnuts for garnish)
• 6 – 8 cups chicken stock • a pinch of ground nutmeg
• sea salt and pepper • a generous pinch of ground cinnamon
• 1 - 2 tablespoons honey

Preheat oven to 350 °F / 180 °C.
Arrange diced celery on a baking sheet and coat with 2 tablespoons of the olive oil. Sprinkle with salt. Roast in preheated oven until tender.
Meanwhile sauté onion and leek in remaining oil until slightly browned. Add roasted celery root and chestnuts. Cook for 5 minutes stirring all the time. Add 6 cups stock and bring to a boil. Lower heat and simmer for 20 minutes or so. Blend mixture in food processor just enough to leave it a bit chunky or blend until it turns into a smooth purée. Add seasoning and spices.
If soup is too thick add rest of stock. For a richer taste fold in some cream. And lastly, add honey. Taste to correct seasoning.
Ladle into a bowl. Garnish with chopped up roasted chestnuts.
For an additional crunch sprinkle a handful of toasted and chopped hazelnuts.

C O R N

SPICY CORN CHOWDER

SPICY CORN CHOWDER

This chunky, robust spicy soup recipe has undergone changes. It is not as spicy as the original but if you prefer spicy food feel free to add more red pepper.What can be better than making this hearty soup on a cold winter day for lunch or dinner? It is also substantial enough to make a meal on its own.

SERVES 4-6

• 1 3/4 cups corn, canned and drained (or frozen and thawed)
• zest of one lemon • juice of 1 large lemon
• 1 tablespoon olive oil • 2 large onions, coarsley chopped • 4 1/2 cups chicken stock
• 1 large potato, peeled and diced
• 1/2 teaspoon hot red pepper flakes • 3/4 teaspoon ground cumin
• 1 large red or green pepper, chopped • 2/3 cup cream
• 1/3 cup milk or soy milk • sea salt and freshly ground pepper
• 1/3 cup chopped fresh parsley

for garnish:

• sprigs of parsley • 1/2 cup yogurt

Mix corn, lemon juice and zest in a bowl. Set aside.

In a pan over medium heat sweat the chopped onion in oil until softened. Add stock and potato. Bring to a boil. Add spices and chopped peppers. Lower heat and simmer until potatoes are soft. Then add the corn and lemon mixture and milk. Simmer gently until soup thickens. And lastly spoon in the cream. Taste and correct seasoning and throw in chopped parsley. Serve soup with a dollop of yogurt and warm crusty bread.

Pass around hot pepper sauce and lemon halves.

F E N N E L

CREAM OF FENNEL SOUP

CREAM OF FENNEL SOUP

A smooth and soft soup with a slight anise flavor that is also deeply satisfying.

SERVES 6

- 1 teaspoon fennel seeds, toasted and ground
- 1 large onion, peeled and diced
- 2 garlic cloves, peeled and chopped
- 2 tablespoons butter
- 2 celery sticks, chopped
- 1 leek, chopped
- 2 large fennel bulbs, chopped
- 6 – 8 cups chicken stock
- 1 cup cream or soy cream
- sea salt and white pepper

Toast fennel seeds in a pan over medium heat for a few minutes. Transfer into a mortar and grind with a pestle. Sweat the onion and garlic in butter for 5 minutes. Stir in the ground seeds. Then add chopped celery, leek and fennel. Season and simmer for 20 minutes. Stir from time to time. Pour in stock and continue simmering for another 10 minutes. Purée soup in food processor.Then pass it through a sieve into a soup pan, pressing with the back of a wooden spoon. Stir in cream and season with white pepper.
Serve grilled cheese sandwiches on the side.

Tips + Tricks + Techniques

Dried beans, peas and lentils are known as legumes. All legumes except lentils and peas require rehydrating before cooking. It is best to soak them overnight, but if you have not preplanned then pour hot water over the beans and soak them for at least 4-5 hours. Whichever method of soaking is used, always drain and rinse beans before proceeding with the recipe. I choose to cook dried beans halfway through before adding salt, sugar or any acidic ingredient. A reasonable amount of salt will only add flavor. Beans are high in fiber and are hard to digest when not cooked well. My motto is to over-cook them a little bit more than necessary. Acquainting the digestive system to well cooked legumes will eventually lessen indigestion and flatulence. Try to incorporate legumes into your diet for their healthy benefits.

CHICKPEA SOUP WITH SPINACH

CHICKPEA SOUP WITH SPINACH

Great tasting winter soup. It's a complete meal served with slices of hearty bread and a crisp green salad. Consider using Swiss chard in place of the spinach.Thinly sliced turkey sausages could also be added into the soup.Let soup sit one or two hours before serving.

SERVES 6-8

• 2 cups dried chickpeas (garbanzo beans), soaked overnight
• 9 cups water • 2 large onions, diced
• 1 large beef bone • 2 whole garlic cloves
• 4 tablespoons olive oil • 3 garlic cloves, minced
• 3 cups lightly packed shredded spinach or Swiss Chard (leaves only)
• 4 cups chicken broth • freshly grated Parmesan cheese
• sea salt and freshly ground pepper

Drain chickpeas and rinse. Place half of chickpeas in a large pan and pour in 5 cups of water. Add half of the onion, bone and garlic cloves. Bring to a boil and simmer until chickpeas are very tender. Remove bone from pan. Purée mixture in food processor until smooth. Return to pot. In another pot, cook the remaining chick peas in 4 cups of water until very tender. Drain and remove skins if you wish. Add to chickpea purée.

Heat oil in a pan and sweat the minced garlic and the remaining onion until translucent. Add chopped up spinach or Swiss chard and stir until wilted. Stir this mixture into chickpeas. Pour in chicken stock, place over medium heat and simmer until heated through. Taste and season with salt and pepper.

For a really spicy version, seed and chop 1 or 2 fresh or dried red chillies and add to soup. Serve with a good drizzling of extra – virgin olive oil and a generous sprinkling of Parmesan cheese.

A dollop of Spinach Pesto (p.209) tastes especially good with this soup.

Happy winter days!

CABBAGE AND POTATO SOUP

CABBAGE AND POTATO SOUP

A hearty soup that tastes even better when served with Roquefort Cheese croutons (p.211).

SERVES 6-8

• 4 cups chicken stock • 3 medium potatoes, peeled and diced
• 3 cups shredded cabbage • 1 tablespoon butter
• 1 cup chopped leek, white and light green parts (dark green parts saved to use in making vegetable broth)
• 3 garlic cloves, chopped • 3 tablespoons flour • 1 1/2 cups milk
• 2 teaspoons mustard of choice
• 3 – 4 drops hot red pepper sauce such as Tabasco
• sea salt and freshly ground pepper
• mixture of 1/2 cup cream and 1/2 cup milk or soy milk

Combine stock, potato and cabbage in a large soup pot. Simmer over medium heat until vegetables are tender.

Meanwhile sauté garlic and leek in butter in another pot over medium high heat until tender. Stir in flour and cook, stirring all the time. Pour in milk and stir to incorporate. Cook until thickened. Add mustard and hot red pepper sauce. Taste and season with salt and pepper. Stir into stock and vegetable mixture. Slowly pour in cream and milk mixture. Cook over low heat for about 10 minutes until very hot. Do not boil or cream may curdle.

Ladle into soup bowls and drop in a few croutons. Pass the rest around.

VEGETABLES

VEGETABLES

Preparing vegetable dishes not only calls for careful shopping for the freshest of produce but also for many hours of LABOR in the kitchen. The quality of the end product is determined by the attention and effort given to these two factors. Vegetables offer an extraordinary range of flavors and textures and can be prepared in a variety of cooking techniques. The results are always satisfying, whether they are roasted, steamed, sautéed, braised or mashed. Providing one or more samples of vegetables on the dinner table regularly helps develop the affinity to eating them. Don't miss out on the taste, flavor and texture of all the newly arriving vegetables in open-market stalls and supermarkets. The vast array of choice is tempting and this excites mc.What follows is a collection of some of my favorite vegetable dishes. They are immensely satisfying and versatile-- serve them on their own, incorporate them into pasta dishes or use them to extend and enrich other foods.

VEGETABLES

Broccoli with Garlic and Lemon Breadcrumbs

Fennel with Mustard Sauce

Stuffed Kohlrabi

Braised Brussels Sprouts,Pearl Onions and Chestnuts

Mascarpone Creamed Spinach

Roasted Vegetables

Layered Spinach, Cheese and Tomato Pie

Sautéed Greens

Leeks in Lemon Sauce

Oven-baked Tomatoes

Grilled Zucchini Slices

Cabbage and Cheese Deep-Dish Pie

Eggplant and Zucchini Baked in the Oven

Tips + Tricks + Techniques

Breadcrumbs are one of the essentials in the kitchen. They are used in meatballs and meatloaf, as topping on casseroles and desserts, or as a coating on pan-fried or oven baked meats and vegetables. Fresh breadcrumbs are easily made at home. It is a good way of using up what is left of bread a few days passed its peak of freshness. One slice of bread makes about 1/2 cup breadcrumbs.

Cut bread into slices and trim off crusts. Break into pieces and place in food processor. Pulse on and off until crumbs reach coarse to fine texture consistency. It is better when crumbs are irregularly shaped. They produce a crunchier coating. Store in the freezer in a tightly covered container. Freshly made bread crumbs can also be seasoned. Toss crumbs with a little olive oil. Bake in the oven (300 °F/150 °C) until crisp and sprinkle with garlic, herbs and spices of your choice. Dried breadcrumbs can be produced by drying out slices of bread in the oven (200 °F/100 °C) for about 1 hour. Do not let the bread brown. Remove from oven, cool only slightly then break into pieces and process.

BROCCOLI WITH GARLIC

BROCCOLI WITH GARLIC AND LEMON BREADCRUMBS

AND LEMON BREADCRUMBS

This winner broccoli recipe is packed with great taste. Serve it with any kind of meat. Perk up the taste of the dish with chopped up fresh chillies or dried chilli flakes.

SERVES 8

- **500 g / 1 lb broccoli (or 2 large heads), separated into florets**
- **1 tablespoon butter**
- **1 tablespoon olive oil**

for the topping:

- **1 cup bread crumbs**
- **2 cloves garlic, grated**
- **grated rind of one lemon**
- **2-3 teaspoons fresh lemon juice**
- **1/2 cup freshly grated Parmesan cheese**
- **sea salt and freshly ground pepper**

Boil unsalted water in a pot and drop in the broccoli florets and cook until CRISP tender, no longer than 5 minutes. Drain and plunge in cold water to stop cooking. Drain well and set aside. Heat only half of butter and oil until hot. Add broccoli and lower heat. Toss gently to coat florets with the oil and butter. Season to taste with salt and pepper. Place broccoli in an ovenproof dish. For the topping which is packed with flavor, return pan to heat and add remaining butter and oil. Immediately add bread crumbs and cook tossing and stirring until golden in color. Mix in grated garlic and toss. Add lemon rind and juice. Taste and season with salt and pepper. Remove from heat and sprinkle the flavored bread crumbs evenly over broccoli. Top with grated Parmesan cheese.

Drizzle with additional olive oil. Bake under the broiler until cheese turns golden brown. Serve straight out of the oven.

FENNEL WITH

FENNEL WITH MUSTARD SAUCE

MUSTARD SAUCE

Fennel is a new-comer in our markets. Look for this vegetable in markets from fall to spring. Fennel has a sweet and delicate anisy flavor and this may not be to everyone's liking. So I think this recipe is one of choice but definitely a good one –light and flavorsome. The anisy flavor of fennel is more elusive when cooked. Give it a try. You may add fennel to your list of healthy vegetables. Serve this dish with any kind of meat or as a vegetarian dish on its own.

SERVES 4

• 3 large or 5 medium fennel bulbs, washed, trimmed and sliced lengthwise thickly into 3 – 4 slices (reserve feathery fonds to scatter over the finished dish)
• 2 tablespoons olive oil • 1/3 – 1/2 cup white wine
• 3/4 cup vegatable broth • 1 heaping tablespoon Dijon mustard
• 1 tablespoon chopped dill
• sea salt and freshly ground pepper

Heat olive oil in a large skillet over low heat. Brown fennel slices in batches on both sides, making sure slices hold their shape. (When fennel is sliced lengthwise layers tend to seperate). Remove all onto a plate and set aside.

Pour wine and broth into skillet and add mustard. Mix and heat until mixture reaches a light boil. Taste and season with salt and pepper. Add fennel slices and any juices that may have accumulated on plate. Cook a little longer over low heat so fennel slices suck up all the lovely flavors in the sauce. Add more stock if necessary.

Transfer to a serving platter and spoon sauce over fennel and sprinkle with dill or scatter reserved feathery fennel fronds which resemble dill.

K O H L R A B I

About this and that

Kohlrabi is a member of the turnip family and is also called cabbage turnip. It has a mild flavor and tastes like a sweet turnip. Unless young, kohlrabi is too fibrous in texture so try to choose a kohlrabi that is heavy for its size. The leaves should be firm and deep green. It is delicious steamed and served with lemon juice and olive oil while still warm. Although it is best steamed kohlrabi can also be added to soups and stews. It stores well in the refrigerator when tightly wrapped up. It is an excellent source of potassium and vitamin C.

STUFFED KOHLRABI

Kohlrabi is another new-comer in the market which I welcome. If you can't get kohlrabi then adapt the recipe and stuff celery root or even tomatoes or zuchini or a medley of these vegatables. If stuffing each single vegetable seems like too much work at the end of a long day or if you are pressed for time, then simply slice kohlrabi into 1 cm thick slices and then cook until crisp tender. Layer vegetable slices and stuffing, ending with a thin layer of stuffing. Great with meat, fish or on its own as an antipasto.

SERVES 4

- **2 large or 4 medium kohlrabies, peeled**
- **6 thick slices of white bread, crusts removed and broken into pieces**
- **1/2 cup milk**
- **1/4 cup olive oil**
- **500 g / 1 lb. mushrooms, minced**
- **1 egg yolk**
- **sea salt and freshly ground pepper**
- **grated nutmeg**
- **3/4 cup grated Parmesan cheese**
- **1/2 cup vegetable broth**
- **a handful of parsley leaves, chopped**

for the topping:

- **1/3 cup bread crumbs**
- **2 tablespoons grated Parmesan cheese**

Preheat oven to 400 °F / 200 °C.

Cul peeled kohlrabies diagonally in half if you arc using large ones. If using medium sized ones then cut a thin slice off bottom of each to stand them flat. Bring a large pot of salted water to the boil and add kohlrabies. Cook until tender. While the kohlrabies are happily boiling in the pot, make the stuffing. Soak bread in cream and milk mixture. Using a fork work into a paste and set aside. I'm sure by this time the kohlrabies have turned tender. Remove from water and let cool a bit. Hollow out each kohlrabi with a spoon, leaving the shell about 1/2 cm thick. Chop the kohlrabi flesh into small pieces and add to bread mixture.

Next sauté minced mushrooms in half of oil over medium heat until all the moisture has evaporated. Season with salt and pepper and bring to room temperature. Add mushrooms, egg yolk, cheese and parsley to bread mixture. Add nutmeg, taste and correct seasoning. Fill hollowed kohlrabies with the stuffing. Place in an oven proof dish. Sprinkle with grated cheese and bread crumbs. Drizzle rest of oil and pour all of broth into dish and bake for about 20 – 25 minutes basting occasionally. When serving spoon sauce over kohlrabi.

BRUSSELS SPROUTS

About this and that

Brussels sprouts are a member of the cabbage family and resemble tiny cabbage heads. Many rows of sprouts grow on a single long stalk. The smaller sprouts are always more tender. Buy small bright green sprouts with compact heads. Brussels sprouts are only eaten cooked and they also freeze well. When stored longer than 3-4 days Brussels sprouts develop a strong flavor. They are a good source of vitamin A and C and are rich in iron and potassium.

BRAISED BRUSSELS SPROUTS, PEARL ONIONS AND CHESTNUTS

This side dish is great with chicken or turkey and can be prepared beforehand. Just reheat slowly when ready to serve. Let me share with you a very helpful tip for saving time and unnecessary labor in the kitchen– soak onions in water for at least 4 – 5 hours or even overnight to make pealing easier. And buy chestnuts from the corner vendor in your neighborhood who roasts them fresh every afternoon or be brave and roast your own. This is a favorite winter dish in our house.

SERVES 6-8

- **a knob of butter**
- **1 tablespoon olive oil**
- **250 g / 1/2 lb pearl onions**
- **1 1/2 cups vegetable broth**
- **2 bay leaves**
- **500 g / 1/2 lb roasted chestnuts, peeled**
- **500 g / 1/2 lb Brussels sprouts, trimmed**
- **sea salt and freshy ground pepper**

Melt butter in a skillet over medium heat. Add olive oil and onions. Cook until golden brown stirring all the while. This will take a while but have patience. Then add broth and bay leaves. Cover and simmer for no more than 10 minutes.

Meanwhile cook trimmed Brussels sprouts in a pot of boiling water until tender. Drain and rinse with cold water and drain again. Set aside.

Add chestnuts to onions and cook slowly for another 10 minutes, until chestnuts are tender. Take care not to over-cook the vegetables as both onions and chestnuts can go mushy easily at this stage of cooking. (Can be prepared ahead up to this stage. Then reheat over low heat and continue as follows.)

Add Brussels sprouts to skillet and simmer gently covered until heated through. The liquid should be syrupy. Correct seasoning according to your taste.

Tips + Tricks + Techniques

The following recipe can easily be substituted for Mascarpone cheese, when it is not easily available.

Blend together:

250 g / 8 oz cream cheese

1/4 cup cream

2 tablespoons yogurt

a knob of softened butter.

MASCARPONE CREAMED SPINACH

This recipe is a variation on creamed spinach which everyone of us has prepared many times. The difference is only the Mascarpone – the fantastically delicious Italian cheese. On previous page you will find a recipe for an equivalent of Mascarpone cheese in case it is not available in your grocery store when you need to use it. It is a useful substitute in other recipes which call for Mascarpone as well.

SERVES 4-6

- **2 tablespoons olive oil**
- **1 large onion, chopped**
- **2 garlic cloves, chopped**
- **500 g / 1 lb spinach leaves, trimmed, washed and drained**
- **1/2 teaspoon ground ginger**
- **1 cup Mascarpone cheese**
- **1/4 cup toasted pine nuts**
- **sea salt and freshly ground pepper**

Heat oil in a large pan. Add onion and garlic and sauté until tender. Toss all of spinach into pot. Stir and mix until wilted. Mix in ginger. Spoon in Mascarpone cheese and lastly throw in the pine nuts. Stir until heated through. Taste and then correct seasoning. Serve immediately.

BELL PEPPERS

ROASTED VEGETABLES

I love vegetables grilled in the oven or on a cast iron grill (or griddle) pan on the stove. The grill marks also offer an attractive finish. Every one has their favorite vegetables and I have chosen my favorites for this recipe. Use fresh herbs and spices to give a fresh aroma to the vegetables. Cut vegetables into almost the same size for even baking. It is so completely effortless to prepare this dish that you may find yourself grilling almost any vegetable you have in your refrigerator. I like to try a variety of herbs and spices— onions with sage; root vegetables and squash or pumpkin with thyme or even cumin; fruits with coriander seeds and so on. Do create your own combinations.

SERVES 4-6

- **2 fennel bulbs,trimmed and quartered**
- **500 g / 1 lb squash or pumpkin, peeled and cut into large chunks**
- **2 – 3 red onions, peeled and quartered**
- **10 Jerusalem artichokes, scrubbed (if large then halved)**
- **1 quince, cored and cut into large chunks**
- **3 – 4 garlic cloves, crushed whole**
- **rosemary sprigs**
- **thyme sprigs**
- **sea salt and freshly ground pepper**
- **3 tablespoons olive oil**
- **red pepper flakes**

Preheat oven to 400 °F / 200 °C.

Brush a large roasting pan lightly with oil. Put all vegetables into pan. Drizzle with the olive oil and mix by hands so all vegetable pieces are evenly coated. Season with salt and pepper. Place sprigs of rosemary and thyme in between the vegetables. Sprinkle with red pepper flakes if you wish. Bake in the oven for 30 – 45 minutes or until vegetables are soft and browned around the edges. Serve luke warm and drizzle with balsamic vinegar if you wish. Or grill a few lemon halves on the griddle pan (until grill marks appear) to squeeze on the vegetables.

LAYERED SPINACH, CHEESE AND TOMATO PIE

Baked without a crust this is a mock pie recipe (fewer calories!) that is full of vitamins and taste. It is one of my favorite recipes which proves the saying " simple and fresh ingredients often produce outstanding results". See if you agree!

SERVES 4-6

- 1 tablespoon olive oil
- 500 g / 1/2 lb spinach leaves, washed and drained
- 4 cloves garlic, chopped
- 3/4 cup ricotta cheese
- grated nutmeg
- sea salt and freshly ground pepper
- 6 – 8 slices mozzarella cheese, water packed
- 2 large tomatoes, thinly sliced
- 4 tablespoons bread crumbs
- 4 tablespoons grated Parmesan cheese
- a knob of butter or 1 tablespoon olive oil

Preheat oven to 350 °F / 180 °C.

Heat oil in a skillet over medium heat. Add garlic and spinach leaves and sautée over medium high heat until spinach leaves wilt and all water evaporates.

Transfer spinach into a bowl and add ricotta, nutmeg, salt and pepper. Mix gently with a fork. Spread this mixture in a round oven-proof serving dish (25 cm/10" in diameter) brushed lightly with oil. Cover spinach mixture with mozzarella slices. Then top with tomato slices. Mix bread crumbs with Parmesan cheese. Sprinkle evenly over tomatoes. Dot with butter. Sprinkle with red pepper if you wish. Bake in oven until top turns light brown. Remove from oven and let rest for 5 minutes before serving.

About this and that

Sprouting broccoli, also called broccoli rabe or raab, grows throughout the summer and early fall. It is easily available in local fresh produce markets. It has a long branching stem with flowering shoots. Choose stems with tightly closed flower shoots and discard any larger outer leaves. Sprouting broccoli is popular in Mediterranean cooking. It may be sautéed, steamed and blanched. It has a mild taste.

SAUTÉED GREENS

A Chinese recipe has inspired me to make this dish over and over again. A mixture of greens makes it a very appealing dish. I think springtime is the right time to try this recipe as all leafy green vegetables are in abundance. Sprouting broccoli hits the markets about this time. It mostly has leaves on a stalk with very tiny florets. Choose your combination of greens such as Swiss chard, spinach, beet greens or any other locally grown greens and leaves -- whatever you fancy. This easy to prepare recipe can be made fairly quickly and is definitely last minute fare.

SERVES 4

- **2 very large handfuls of spinach, tops cut off and discarded, stems and leaves chopped into large pieces**
- **1 very large handful of sprouting broccoli, largely chopped**
- **1 very large handful of beet greens, chopped (use beets in another recipe p.21 or p.235)**
- **3 tablespoons olive oil**
- **3-4 cardamom pods, crushed**
- **4 large garlic cloves, very thinly sliced (use a potato peeler)**
- **sea salt and freshly ground pepper**
- **juice of 1/2 lemon**
- **a handful of toasted peanuts**

Blanch greens in boiling salted water for only 3 – 4 minutes. Drain in colander. Meanwhile heat oil in a pan and add cardamom pods. Then stir fry garlic in oil until lightly colored. Drop in all of the greens and stir with two forks so oil coats all leaves evenly. Continue cooking only a short while until vegetables are heated through. Season with salt and pepper and drizzle lemon juice over vegetables. Scatter a handful of toasted peanuts over the vegetables. Serve immediately with grilled meats or fish. Leftovers taste just as good the next day.

L E M O N S

LEEKS IN LEMON SAUCE

Leeks, one of my favorite vegetables, turn into a sweet and sour dish with this recipe. You may consider slicing leeks thinly instead of cutting them into long pieces. This dish is at its best when served luke warm.

SERVES 4

- 6 leeks, cleaned and dark green ends discarded; cut into 10 cm/4" long pieces and halved lengthwise
- juice of 1/2 lemon
- 1/2 lemon, cut into thin slices
- 3-4 sprigs of fresh thyme or 1/2 teaspoon dried thyme
- 4 tablespoons olive oil
- 1 tablespoon honey
- 1 cup vegetable broth
- 1 tablespoon grainy mustard
- sea salt and freshly ground pepper

Place one layer of leeks into a shallow saucepan. Try to flatten leeks by pressing down with hands. Place half of lemon slices and 2 sprigs of thyme on leeks. Season with salt and pepper. Repeat this once more creating two layers of leeks. Drizzle 3 tablespoons of the oil on the leeks. Meanwhile heat vegetable broth in a pot until luke warm. Mix in the honey, mustard and lemon juice. Pour over the leeks in the saucepan. Cook leeks covered over medium heat until they turn soft Should the liquid evaporate before the vegetables are tender, just keep on adding more warm broth or water as needed. Remove from heat and let cool. Then place leeks onto a serving plate. Boil the sauce in the pan to reduce only a little bit. Taste and correct seasoning by adding more honey or lemon juice. Drizzle with the remaining olive oil and serve at room temperature.

P A R S L E Y

OVEN-BAKED TOMATOES

OVEN–BAKED TOMATOES

These tomatoes adorn any antipasti plate beautifully. They can also be served as a side dish with grilled meats or fish. For a dramatic presentation deep-fry three handfuls of parsley leaves (Be careful! Spatters badly!) and pile them on the baked tomatoes.

SERVES 4

- 4 ripe but firm large tomatoes
- 4 tablespoons olive oil
- 3 tablespoons fine bread crumbs (p. 82)
- 1 garlic clove, peeled and finely chopped
- 2 tablespoons finely chopped parsley
- sea salt and freshly ground pepper
- sprigs of fresh thyme

Preheat oven to 450 °F / 230 °C.
Cut tomatoes in half and remove all seeds. Lightly oil an ovenproof dish and place all of tomatoes cut side up. Meanwhile sauté garlic in 1 tablespoon of the oil and immediately add breadcrumbs. Add parsley and season with salt and pepper. Cover tomato halves with the crumb mixture. Drizzle remaining oil over the tomatoes. Place sprigs of thyme between them. Bake for about 15 minutes until tomatoes turn soft and tops sizzle.

ZUCCHINI

GRILLED ZUCCHINI SLICES

GRILLED ZUCCHINI SLICES

I could not make up my mind whether this dish should go in the salad or the vegetable section. So I tossed a coin and it ended in this section. It doesn't really matter, does it? And then there is already a salad recipe with zucchinis in the salad section. Once more an easy to make, tasty and healthy recipe for which you need to choose small and firm zucchinis.

SERVES 4

- **4 medium size zucchinis**
- **3- 4 tablespoons olive oil**
- **1 clove garlic, peeled and grated**
- **grated zest of one lemon**
- **a handful of parsley leaves, finely chopped**
- **sea salt and freshly grated pepper**
- **very finely chopped 1 red hot chilli (optional)**

Do not peel zucchinis but shave them lengthways with a potato peeler to make very thin slices. Stir the grated garlic into the oil. Season with salt. Spoon olive oil over the slices and use your fingers to toss and coat each slice evenly with the oil. Cook in batches on a very hot griddle pan. Zucchini slices will wilt and will have brown stripes. Remove into a bowl. Season and toss with lemon zest and parsley.

Pile zucchini slices onto a serving plate. Sprinkle chopped chilli over the zucchini and drizzle with your best olive oil.

C A B B A G E

CABBAGE AND CHEESE DEEPDISH PIE

CABBAGE AND CHEESE DEEPDISH PIE

Cabbage doesn't appeal to everyone's taste but this dish is sure to be a winner served with boiled meats or served on its own as a filling vegetarian dish.

SERVES 6-8

- 1 tablespoon olive oil
- 2 tablespoons hot water
- 1 teaspoon sugar
- 3 onions, cut in half and very thinly sliced
- 500 g / 1 lb cabbage leaves, separated, stalks cut out and discarded, each leaf quartered
- grated nutmeg
- sea salt and freshly ground pepper
- 250 g / 8 oz hard cheese of your choice such as Parmesan or Gruyere, sliced into 1/2 cm thick pieces
- 8 – 10 large slices of hearty white bread
- 3 – 4 cup warmed vegetable broth, seasoned with freshly grated pepper

Preheat oven to 350 °F / 180 °C.

Heat oil in a deep saucepan. Sweat the onions in the oil over medium to low heat until translucent. Halfway through add hot water and cook stirring occasionally until the liquid evaporates by half. Then add cabbage leaves. Season with salt and pepper and grate a generous amount of nutmeg. Cover pot and cook until cabbage leaves wilt and all liquid evaporates. Oil a deep ovenproof dish. Start assembling the deep-dish pie. Place half of bread slices to form the bottom layer. Spread half of cabbage leaves and cover with cheese slices, slightly overlapping each other. Repeat layering once more with bread, cabbage and cheese. Press down with fingers. Pour vegetable broth to come all the way up to the top of the dish. Finish by sprinkling the top with red pepper.

Bake in the oven until top browns and it's bubbling on the sides. Remove from oven and allow to rest for 10 or more minutes before serving.

EGGPLANT

EGGPLANT AND ZUCCHINI BAKED IN THE OVEN

This is another version of roasting vegetables that is very easy. Whenever there are some left-over vegetables in your refrigerator, try using them up in this recipe.

SERVES 6-8

- **1 large eggplant, thinly sliced**
- **2 zucchines, thinly sliced** • **16 cherry tomatoes**
- **10 spring potatoes, parboiled with skins and cut in half**
- **10 cloves of garlic, coarsley chopped**
- **2 tablespoons capers** • **fresh thyme and rosemary sprigs**
- **sea salt and freshly ground pepper** • **4 tablespoons olive oil**

Preheat oven to 425 °F / 220 °C.

Drizzle some oil on vegetable slices and salt generously. Layer vegetables in an oiled oven-proof dish. Scatter cherry tomatoes, potatoes, garlic and capers between the layers of vegetable slices. With your fingers or a fork, wiggle the layers so that the garlic can slip in among vegetables. Place fresh thyme and rosemary sprigs on and among vegetables. Season with salt and pepper. Drizzle generously with olive oil.

Bake uncovered until vegetables are done. Tent with foil if top browns quickly and continue cooking until the vegetables are done.

PASTA, RICE, POLENTA

PASTA, RICE, POLENTA

Starchy foods like rice and pasta are called comfort foods becacuce they encourage the body to relax. Let's face it. We all get tired, stressed or sad in the turmoil of our daily lives. This is the food that soothes our souls. A bowl of pasta or rice will give a full-stomach feeling (what can be more soothing than that!) and when eaten in the evening will help produce sleep inducing hormones. So why not try one of the following recipes for dinner tonight. In this section you'll find amazingly easy pasta recipes with variations, several polenta recipes and finally tasty risotto dishes.

PASTA, RICE, POLENTA

PASTA, RICE, POLENTA

M O R T A R

About this and that

A basic pesto recipe calls for fresh basil leaves, pine nuts, garlic, oil, and cheese. Pesto recipes can be used in a variety of ways. Pesto can be thinned with additional oil and cream to be used as a sauce for pasta. It can be mixed into risotto in any chosen consistency. It can be used as a dip by adding cream or cream cheese. And as in the recipe in this book (p.75 /p.209), a dollop of pesto spooned into a bowl of soup can develop additional flavor. Substituting fresh mint, parsley, coriander or spinach in place of basil leaves can create other tasty pesto variations. Walnuts can be substituted for pine nuts. Sun-dried tomato pesto is also worth a try. Coriander pesto accompanies Asian dishes excellently. Pesto of any flavor is sensational served on bruchetta with shavings of Parmesan cheese.

PASTA WITH

PASTA WITH GREEN PESTO

GREEN PESTO

The pesto recipe is a variation to the basic one with the additional taste of peppery arugula and fresh parsley. This pasta recipe is definitely one of my favorite ones because it is healthy as well as being tasty.

SERVES 6

(Serving size: 1 1/2 cups)

for the green pesto:

- **2 cups fresh basil leaves, tightly packed**
- **1 1/2 cups arugula leaves, hard stems discarded**
- **1/3 cup fresh parsley leaves, tightly packed**
- **10 walnut halves**
- **4 garlic cloves, peeled and halved**
- **2 tablespoons olive oil**
- **1/2 cup freshly grated Parmesan cheese**
- **1/4 - 1/2 cup vegetable broth**
- **sea salt and freshly ground pepper**

580 g / 1 lb uncooked pasta of choice, my choice being linguine.

Place the 3 different kinds of green leaves, walnuts, garlic and olive oil in food processor. Mix until mixture turns into a smooth paste. Add cheese and broth. Pulse until combined. Taste and season pesto with salt and pepper.

Throw 2 cloves of peeled garlic into the pot of water and bring to a boil. Cook pasta until al dente or according to package directions. Save about 1/3 cup of pasta water. Drain pasta and combine with pesto in a large bowl. If pasta looks dry add some of reserved warm water. Serve with a salad of sliced tomatoes topped with fresh basil leaves and crumbled feta cheese.

BASIL, ROSEMARY, CHIVES

PASTA WITH OVEN-DRIED

PASTA WITH OVEN-DRIED CHERRY TOMATOES

CHERRY TOMATOES

Slow roasting gives tomatoes an intense flavor. Use them in salads as well as in any other dish. I usually oven dry two large trays of cherry tomatoes and freeze what I don't need. Refer to page 217 for the recipe.

SERVES 4

for the pasta:

- **500g / 1 lb linguine**
- **1 cup packed baby spinach leaves, stemmed and chopped coarsely**
- **1/2 cup freshly grated Parmesan cheese**
- **salt and freshly ground pepper**

for the dressing:

- **1/4 cup olive oil**
- **1 teaspoon each dried rosemary, thyme and basil**
- **2 garlic cloves, quartered**
- **sea salt and freshly ground pepper**
- **2 cups oven-dried cherry tomatoes, lightly packed**

for garnish:

- **10 or more fresh basil leaves, chopped fine just before serving.**

Oven-dry your cherry tomatoes the day before or early in the morning. Then make the dressing. Warm the olive oil over low heat. Add dried herbs and garlic. Continue cooking for 5 minutes. Pour everything into a bowl and cool completely. Soak all of the dried tomatoes in the oil. Let rest until you are busy with other preparations.

Meanwhile boil some water for the pasta and cook until al dente. Drain and transfer to a bowl. Immediately add prepared spinach leaves. The baby spinach leaves will wilt when mixed with the hot pasta but also retain a fresh color and a crisp bite. Drain half the oil from the tomatoes and save for another use. Spoon sauce into pasta along with cheese. Taste and season to your taste. Sprinkle some toasted pine nuts and chopped fresh basil leaves over pasta. Serve immediately passing more freshly grated Parmesan cheese around. What can go better with this dish than a bottle of robust red wine!! Cheers!!

M U S H R O O M S

PASTA AND

PASTA AND TUNA FISH SALAD

TUNA FISH SALAD

This light main–dish pasta salad is a full meal in itself and a perfect one for the summer. Add other fresh vegetables if you like. Very thinly sliced fresh baby zucchinis will always give the additional crunch.

SERVES 4-6

for the pasta sala:

- 250 g / 1/2 lb bow–tie pasta, cooked
- 1 can oil packed tuna (about 200 g/7oz.) drained and broken into chunks
- 12 dried tomato halves, reconstituted and chopped (p. 120)
- 1 cup fresh mushrooms, stems discarded and thinly sliced
- 3/4 cup pitted green olives, sliced

for the dressing:

- 1/4 cup extra virgin olive oil
- 2 tablespoons apple cider vinegar
- 1/4 cup tomato paste
- 2 tablespoons freshly grated Parmesan cheese
- salt and freshly ground pepper
- 1 – 2 drops hot pepper sauce such as Tabasco
- a handful of parsley leaves, finely chopped
- a handful of fresh mint leaves

First make the dressing by whisking everything together. Let rest while you prepare the pasta salad. Flavors will develop and mature if dressing is made an hour or so before tossing everything together.

Next cook pasta in salted boiling water until el dente. Drain and save some of the cooking liquid to mix in the pasta salad in case you think it is not moist enough. Mix in the chunks of tuna, dried tomatoes, mushrooms and olives. Add dressing by spoonfuls to coat ingredients generously and toss just enough to incorporate all ingredients.

Spoon prepared pasta onto a bed of salad greens on each plate.

P E A S

PASTA SALAD WITH PARSLEY PESTO

PASTA SALAD WITH PARSLEY PESTO

Pasta is one of my favorite comfort foods. So I've put together this recipe as a summer salad. I make the pesto in the food processor and it takes no time to assemble this rich tasting salad. As with most pasta dishes it is at its best the very moment it is tossed.

SERVES 8-10

- 500 g / 1 lb penne or bow tie pasta
- 1 red onion, peeled and finely chopped • 1 cup sliced olives (green or black)
- 3/4 cup dried currants, picked • 2/3 cup toasted pine nuts • 1 cup boiled peas

for the pesto:

- 1 large garlic clove, quartered • 1 teaspoon salt
- 1 cup tightly packed fresh parsley leaves
- 1/4 cup fresh lemon juice • 1/4 cup red wine vinegar
- 1 teaspoon curry powder • 1 teaspoon sugar • 3/4 teaspoon ground cumin
- 1/4 teaspoon black pepper • 3/4 -1 cup olive oil

for garnish:

- fresh parsley sprigs • 10 or more cherry tomatoes, cut into quarters

Cook the pasta of your choice al dente in salted boiling water. While the pasta is cooking, whip up the pesto. Chop the garlic and salt in processor. Add all of parsley and mince. Then add all the rest of ingredients up to oil. With machine running, gradually pour oil through feed tube in a steady stream. Making the pesto by hand is just as easy but time consuming. Drain pasta and save some of the cooking liquid. Pour all of dressing over pasta. Add chopped onion, olives, currants, pine nuts, and peas. Season with freshly ground pepper. Add some of the reserved cooking liquid if necessary. Garnish with parsley sprigs and cherry tomatoes. Drizzle your best olive oil all over the pasta salad.

G R E E N O N I O N S

Tips + Tricks + Techniques

Reconstitute dry-packed sun-dried tomatoes by placing them in a bowl and pouring boiling water over them. Soak the tomatoes for about 20 minutes. Drain, rinse and squeeze all water out. Then use whole or chopped according to recipe. The soaking liquid can be saved to be used in soups and sauces after straining. Sun-dried tomatoes can also be purchased oil-packed in jars. Spoon the amount needed into a sieve and rinse with boiling water. Drain and squeeze all water out before using. The oil in the jar, which has a high tomato flavor can be used in salad dressings and pasta sauces or can be brushed on bruchetta and crostini.

RICE SALAD WITH

RICE SALAD WITH SUN-DRIED TOMATO DRESSING

SUN-DRIED TOMATO DRESSING

Simple, easy, and tasty. The dominating taste of sun-dried tomatoes and the spices in the dressing – what a great combo with the mellow taste of rice. I love the tart fruits tossed into rice or pasta salads. Choose unripe apricots, plums, peaches or mangoes. Serve this salad slightly warm accompanied by a big bowl of green salad – a gorgeous idea for a summer dinner around the table with family. And how about sipping a glass of chilled white wine with your dinner? Cheers!

SERVES 4

• 2 cups boiled rice
• 8 sun dried tomato halves, reconstituted and diced if using dried ones (p.120) or drained and diced if using oil packed • 1/3 cup toasted pine nuts
• 4 scallions, minced • sea salt and freshly ground pepper
• 3 unripe apricots or red plums, seeded and cut into small cubes
• 1 bunch of fresh coriander or parsley,chopped up

for the dressing:

• 6 sun dried tomato halves, treated same as stated above and diced tiny, almost minced
• 6 tablespoons extra virgin olive oil • 3 tablespoons balsamic vinegar
• 1 large clove garlic, minced • 1 teaspoon chili powder or flakes, use more or less according to your own taste
• sea salt and freshly ground pepper

Make the dressing first. Whisk ingredients in a bowl and let rest for a quarter of an hour while preparing the rice.

Reconstitute dried tomatoes (p.120) and chop to desired size. Flake rice with a fork and add all other ingredients except fresh coriander or parsley. Add the dressing and mix until well blended. Correct seasoning. Sprinkle in the chopped up greens and mix once more.

W A L N U T S

ORZO WITH

ORZO WITH ROASTED–PUMPKIN

ROASTED-PUMKIN

The orzo turns into a good vegetarian dish when served with mixed vegetables or a green salad – just ideal for lunch. It also tastes delicious cold, so leftovers are welcome.

SERVES 4

- **500 g / 1 lb pumpkin, peeled, seeded and cut into uniform chunks**
- **olive oil** • **sea salt and freshly ground pepper**
- **1-2 tablespoons honey** • **3 tablespoons balsamic vinegar**
- **1 cup vegetable broth** • **1 1/2 cups orzo**
- **extra virgin olive oil**
- **1/3 cup crumbled Roquefort cheese**
- **toasted walnut halves**

Brush the pumpkin pieces with olive oil. Season with salt and pepper. Wrap in foil and roast in the oven until pumpkin is very soft. Cool and then place all of pumpkin along with the honey and balsamic vinegar in the bowl of a food processor. Process into a smooth puree. Pour purée into a pot. Add the vegetable broth and bring to a simmer. Keep warm. Meanwhile boil a pot of water, add salt and orzo. Cook orzo for only 5 minutes. Drain well and add the orzo to the pot of pumpkin purée. Cook over medium heat stirring frequently until the thick broth is absorbed. Taste the orzo for doneness and correct seasoning. If the orzo is too dry add more broth. It should have a soupy consistency much like a risotto. Spoon into warmed individual bowls and crumble cheese over the orzo. Drizzle with olive oil. Scatter toasted walnut halves over each servingof orzo.

Tips + Tricks + Techniques

Blanching is basically submerging food in boiling water to soften texture and preserve color. Young, fresh vegetables, green peas, broccoli and the like as well as vegetables to be frozen, are blanched for a few minutes. At the end of this process they retain their color and crispness. Other vegetables like cauliflower, cabbage, leeks, onions and garlic are blanched to lessen their pungency. Cured meats are blanched to reduce their saltiness. The blanching water is always discarded and the blanched food is refreshed immediately. Refreshing is plunging boiled or blanched vegetables into ice water to stop the cooking process.

Here is an 'easy blanch' tip for spinach and Swiss chard: Put the leaves in a colander set inside a large bowl. Pour hot water over the leaves and lift the colander. Drain and squeeze water out by pressing on the leaves. And here is another tip to eliminate the messy process of squeezing water out of boiled spinach and other green leaves – simply line a salad spinner with paper towels and scatter the leaves on the towels. Spin the leaves until all excess water is removed. NO MESS! Remove the spinach or leaves and throw out the paper towels.

SPINACH AND

SPINACH AND ORZO PIE

ORZO PIE

This dish is an old time favorite, which is very satisfying as well as being very balanced. The spinach, orzo and tomato create a tasty trio. The tomato sauce can be made ahead of time and blended into the orzo when the dish is put together.

SERVES 6-8

**• 2 eggs, lightly beaten with 1 tablespoon of milk
• 2 cups cooked orzo (about 1 1/4 cup uncooked) • 1 1/2 cups Tomato Sauce with Herbs (p.249/251)
• 1/2 cup freshly grated Parmesan cheese • 500 g/1 lb spinach leaves, blanched and drained
• 1/4 cup toasted pine nuts • 1/2 cup ricotta cheese
• 1/2 cup shredded Cheddar cheese or any other hard cheese of choice
• a pinch of nutmeg • sea salt and freshly ground pepper**

Preheat oven to 350 °F / 180 °C
In a large bowl combine cooked orzo, egg and milk mixture, 3/4 cup tomato sauce and Parmesan cheese. Spread mixture evenly into an oiled oven-safe glass dish. Next squeeze all water out of spinach and chop coarsely. Mix spinach with ricotta cheese, pine nuts, and nutmeg. Taste and season with salt and pepper. Spoon everything onto orzo mixture, spreading evenly. Then spread remaining tomato sauce on spinach layer. Bake covered for 30 minutes.
Remove from oven and cover the top of the pie with the shredded cheese. Return to oven and bake uncovered for an additional 6-8 minutes until cheese is bubbly. Allow to rest a few minutes before serving.

BASIL, DILL, PARSLEY

About this and that

Risotto rice is absorbent, round-grain rice. Like all other rice risotto rice also comes in grades. For best results always use the best rice when cooking risotto. The heat should be medium - do not use too high heat because then the liquid evaporates too quickly and the rice does not absorb the liquid and refrain from using low heat because then the rice becomes soggy. It best to use a pan with a heavy base for even distribution of heat. Add seasoning while still cooking and not at the end, so that the rice absorbs the seasoning. Each type of rice absorbs liquid differently. The amount of liquid and duration of cooking will differ accordingly. Use your judgment to produce risotto that is al dente.

BASIC RISOTTO WITH HERBS

Tender yet firm but truly creamy – these words describe a successfully cooked risotto, the Italian rice dish. Sitting at the top of the list of comfort foods, risotto is open to innumerous improvisations. When making risotto the rice is flavored with broth and wine and embellished with herbs, vegetables, meat, poultry and fish. Always choose a mild flavored broth or stock and let the embellishments and cheese develop the final flavor. I have not called for adding butter at the end of cooking time just because I like to streamline my recipes. I think the Parmesan cheese contributes deliciously to a silky finish.

SERVES 4

- **6 – 7 cups vegetable broth**
- **2 teaspoons butter**
- **2 teaspoons olive oil**
- **1 medium onion, finely chopped**
- **1 1/2 cups (Arborio) rice for risotto**
- **1/2 cup dry white wine**
- **2 tablespoons sour cream**
- **1/2 cup freshly grated Parmesan cheese**
- **1/2 cup finely chopped herbs (parsley, dill, basil)**
- **sea salt and freshly ground pepper**

Bring the broth to a simmer in a saucepan over medium high heat. Reduce heat and keep warm. Heat the butter and oil in another pan big enough to cook the risotto. Sweat the onions covered about 5 minutes stirring occasionally until translucent. Keep the heat low and do not brown the onions. Add the rice all at once and cook stirring until the rice is slightly translucent as well. Add the wine. Raise the heat just a bit and cook the rice, stirring until the wine is absorbed. Then lower heat and start ladling the simmering broth into the rice 1/2 cup at a time. Let each addition be absorbed before feeding the rice more liquid. Stir constantly. This will take about 15 – 20 minutes. Taste the risotto. If the rice is still too hard add more broth and continue cooking. The risotto should be slightly soupy. Reserve 1/4 cup of stock to add at the very end. Add the chopped herbs and sour cream when you think the rice is tender and firm at the same time. Give it a good stir. Remove pan from heat and add the grated cheese. Taste and correct seasoning as needed. Cover pan and let rest for a few minutes. And finally add the reserved 1/4 cup warm stock before spooning into warmed individual bowls. Sprinkle with additional Parmesan cheese and finely chopped parsley. Top each risotto with a dollop of sour cream.

ARTICHOKES

RISOTTO WITH ARTICHOKE

RISOTTO WITH ARTICHOKE AND BROCCOLI STALKS

AND BROCCOLI STALKS

You can almost use any kind of vegetable -- pumpkin, peas, asparagus, Swiss chard, leeks, to name but a few. My choice here is artichoke and broccoli. Only the stalks of these vegetables are used and they add the crunchy texture that pairs well with the creamy rice. The light green color of the vegetables gives the risotto a lovely hue. Risotto deserves the best of ingredients and will not disappoint you if only the best are used. Homemade stock is always preferred in making risotto as the finished dish is infused with its flavor.

SERVES 4-6

- **6 – 7 cups reduced vegetable broth (p.253)**
- **2 1/2 tablespoons olive oil**
- **6 (scallions), spring onions, chopped thinly**
- **1 1/2 cups (Arborio) rice for risotto**
- **1/2 cup dry white wine**
- **2 cups artichoke stalks, peeled and cut into small pieces**
- **2 cups broccoli stalks,peeled and cut into small pieces**
- **4 tablespoons very finely chopped dill**
- **1/2 cup freshly grated Parmesan cheese**
- **sea salt and freshly ground pepper**
- **4 tablespoons toasted pinenuts.**

Bring a pot of water to the boil. Add salt and sugar and cook the artichoke and broccoli stalks for 3 minutes until crisp tender. Remove vegetables with a slotted spoon. Reserve cooking liquid. Refresh vegetables in cold water to stop cooking process. Measure reserved broth in pot and add more vegetable broth to make 7 cups. Simmer and keep warm. Heat the oil until warm and add the chopped spring onions. Then immediately add the rice and cook, stirring until rice is thoroughly coated with the oil. Add the wine. Raise the heat and cook, again stirring until it is absorbed. Then lower heat and start ladling the simmering broth 1/2 cup a time. Let each addition be absorbed before feeding the rice more liquid. When half of the broth is used add the sliced vegetables. Then continue with the rest of the broth until the rice is tender and the risotto is slightly soupy. Next add the dill and Parmesan cheese. Taste and season with salt and pepper. Cover pan and let rest for a few minutes before spooning into warmed individual bowls. Sprinkle toasted pine nuts and decorate with dill sprigs and thin spring onions. Drizzle with your best olive oil.

POLENTA WITH MASCARPONE CHEESE

POLENTA WITH MASCARPONE CHEESE

Polenta is the name of the dish and the raw ingredient is cornmeal. The ingredient and the dish are both called by the same name. Polenta is extremely versatile because it can be eaten soft and creamy or allowed to harden and then sliced and served grilled or fried. Coarse cornmeal is best for making polenta. Serve it in place of potatoes or rice as a companion dish to meat and vegetables. To produce good polenta in the kitchen considerable time, care and concentration is needed in front of the stove. If you are short on time or aren't up to manuel labor by stirring polenta then try to bake it unattended in the oven. This method will allow you time to prepare the rest of the meal.

SERVES 6-8

- **4 1/2 cups cold water**
- **1 cup polenta or coarse cornmeal**
- **sea salt**
- **1/2 cup mascarpone cheese (p. 90)**

To cook polenta on the stove-top:

Bring water and salt to a boil in a saucepan. Slowly add the cornmeal in a thin stream, whisking all the while. Use a deep pan and a long wooden spoon because polenta will spatter. Lower heat and stir for 35-45 minutes. Polenta needs to be cooked long enough until its mellow taste developes. Turn the heat off and stir in the cheese. Then keep the polenta warm in a double boiler until needed.

To cook polenta in the oven:

Preheat oven to 350 °F / 180 °C.

Simply combine the cornmeal, salt and cold water (use 1/2 cup less) in a heavy oven proof pan. Bring to a boil on the stove-top and then place in the oven. Bake uncovered for 40 minutes. Remove from oven, stir and bake for another 10 minutes. Then add cheese and serve.

GRATER

POLENTA TRIANGLES WITH PARMESAN CHESSE

POLENTA TRIANGLES WITH PARMESAN CHEESE

Another variation on the polenta theme. This version has a thicker consistency, is cooled until firm and cut into shapes. Each piece can then be baked in the oven or grilled until crisp and brown. Another way of serving oven baked polenta triangles is overlapping them in a buttered oven proof dish and topping them with grated Parmesan and a drizzle of melted butter. For the health conscious, a heathier version is to serve 2 pieces of oven browned polenta triangles with dollops of Tangy Tomato Sauce (p. 251) or Red Bell Pepper Sauce (p. 231).

SERVES 6-8

- **3 1/2 cups water**
- **1 cup polenta or coarse cornmeal**
- **sea salt**
- **1/4 cup freshly grated Parmesan cheese**

Bring water to a boil in a sauce pan over high heat, slowly add the cornmeal in a thin stream, whisking constantly. Lower heat and use a wooden spoon to stir the mixture until it is thickened for at least 35 minutes. Polenta will pull away from the sides of the pan. Remove from heat and stir in the cheese. Pour the cooked cornmeal into a greased shallow dish. Spread it out to an even layer and cool for about 1 hour until firm. Do not refrigerate.

Cut into triangles or any other desired shape with cookie cutters or a round glass moistened with cold water. Remove each piece with a spatula onto an oiled baking sheet and then brown in the oven or grill on a hot griddle pan. Serve on the side of any meat, poultry or vegetable dish you have prepared or simply top with sauce of your choice.

SEAFOOD

SEAFOOD

For those of us who are blessed to be living along the waters of the Aegean Sea there is always the easy possibility of having the freshest of charcoal-grilled seafood (what a luxury!), or seafood prepared in a variety of other ways at any one of the fish restaurants which dots the coastline. For this reason alone preparing fish remains daunting for many home cooks. Many prefer to think of fish only as restaurant food. But I think we need to re-evaluate this in the light of all the research which tells us that fish is an essential component of a healthful diet. Many supermarkets now have great offerings in their seafood departments with the additional service of scaling, boning or filleting your choice of fish. Let us then take the time and make the effort to incorporate fish into our repertoire with the following easy-to-prepare recipes. Most dishes in this chapter are made with my two favorite fish – salmon and sardines (they are also the two fish which are rich in omega-3 fatty acids) as well as with plenty of vegetables. These recipes all reflect the way I try to serve fish.

SEAFOOD

SARDINES

BAKED CRISPY SARDINES

There is something appealing about a crispy topping on food. For that reason, it is a must that everybody is around the dinner table as you remove this dish from the oven. Serve it immediately – crunchy crumb topping over tangy tasting sardines.

SERVES 4

- **1 kg / 2 lb sardines, scaled, gutted and heads removed**
- **sea salt and freshly ground pepper**
- **4 cloves garlic, peeled and minced**
- **1/3 cup very finely chopped parsley**
- **zest and juice of 1 lemon**
- **1/3 cup white wine** • **1/4 cup olive oil**
- **2/3 cup bread crumbs, made from a day-old bread**

Preheat oven to 350 °F / 180 °C.

Rinse and pat the sardines dry. Rub them with salt and pepper, inside and out. Brush a round shallow dish (preferably earthenware) with oil. Fan the sardines out in a circle, all the tails coming together in the middle.

Mix the oil, wine and lemon juice. Pour over the fish.

Then in a separate bowl mix the bread crumbs, parsley,garlic and lemon zest. Scatter evenly over the sardines. Drizzle with more oil if you like.

Bake until the fish are cooked and the crumb topping is golden brown for about 30 minutes. Serve straight from the oven.

LEMONS

SARDINES TOPPED WITH TANGY TOMATO SAUCE

Another great oven baked recipe without a lot of effort. Why sardines? just because they are rich in omega-3 fatty acids (i.e.they are good for us). They are also easily available in every local fish market.

SERVES 2

- **500 g / 1 lb sardines, scaled and gutted**
- **3/4 to 1 cup Tangy Tomato sauce (p.251)**
- **1 Preserved Lemon, sliced (p.243) or one lemon, sliced**
- **extra virgin olive oil**

Arrange sardines in a single layer in an ovenproof dish. Spoon sauce over fish. Top with slices of preserved lemon. Drizzle with olive oil. Roast in the oven uncovered until fish are done. Serve with Braised Leaves (p.97) and Roasted Vegetables (p.93) or very simply, serve with boiled potatoes.

G R E E N B E A N S

SEA BASS STEAKS WITH FRESH BEANS

The combination of ingredients go well together. This is a grand meal in itself. Serve it with boiled or baked potatoes and a green salad of your choice.

SERVES 4

- **500 g / 1 lb fresh green beans, trimmed, and cut into thin strips and blanched, (save 3 tablespoons of the blanching liquid)**
- **1 tablespoon olive oil**
- **4 pieces sea bass steaks on the bone (250-300g / 10 oz each) rinsed and dried**
- **1/2 cup pine nuts, toasted**
- **2 lemons, halved**
- **1/2 cup (or more) garlic bread crumb topping (p. 83)**
- **sea salt and freshly ground pepper**
- **extra–virgin olive oil**

Preheat the oven to 400 °F / 200 °C.

Brush an oven–safe dish with olive oil. Place the blanched beans in the dish, spreading them out evenly. Drizzle the saved blanching liquid and oil all over the green beans. Season lightly. Then set the sea bass steaks in among the beans. Sprinkle with pine nuts and bread crumbs and drizzle a little olive oil over the top. Place the lemon halves in the dish. They will develop a sweet and mellow flavor as they cook,in which case they may even be eaten along with the fish. Slide the dish in the oven.

If the crumbs brown too qiuckly just lay a piece of aluminum foil over the fish but continue cooking until the fish is cooked through, about 30–40 minutes.

S H R I M P

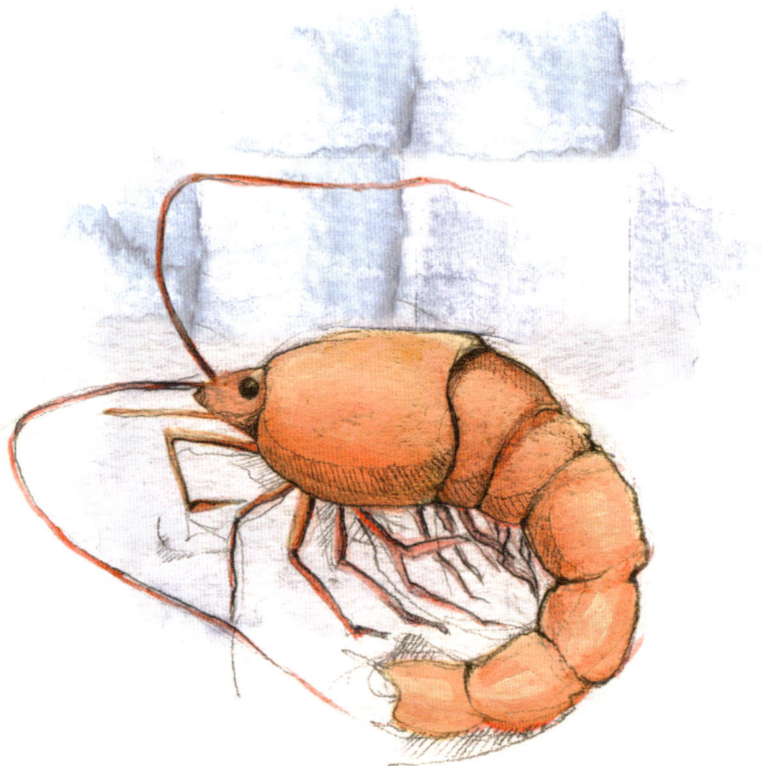

SHRIMP AND PEAS IN ARTICHOKE HEARTS

The convenience of using frozen artichoke hearts, frozen peas and frozen tiny baby shrimp speed up the preparation process of this dish. Needless to say fresh spring artichokes taste ever so great and are worth all the effort if you are willing to trim them. I think peeling artichokes and shelling shrimp are tasks one can chose to avoid. This dish is served chilled and is yummy on a warm summer day served with a glass of chilled white wine or cold beer.

SERVES 4

• 4 frozen artichoke hearts • 5 cups water • juice of 1 lemon • sea salt • 2 teaspoons sugar • 1/2 cup baby peas, cooked • 1 1/2 cups baby shrimp, cooked • 1 cup Avocado Mayonnaise (p.213) • 1/4 cup chopped fresh dill • sea salt and freshly ground pepper • 1-2 tablespoons capers (optional)

Bring the water to the boil. Add the lemon juice, salt and sugar. Drop in the frozen artichoke hearts and cook until the artichokes are soft when poked with a knife. This will not take very long, 10 minutes or so,depending on the size of the artichokes. Remove artichoke hearts with a slotted spoon and refresh them in cold water to stop the cooking. Save some of the cooking liquid. Meanwhile mix the peas and shrimp in a bowl and add the mayonnaise. If the mixture too thick to pile on artichoke hearts then add one or more spoonfuls of the reserved artichoke water. Stir in the dill. If you wish you may add 1-2 tablespoons capers at this stage of preparation. Taste and then season with salt and pepper. Chill artichoke hearts and peas and shrimp mixture separately.

Just before serving place artichoke hearts on a flat serving platter covered with finely shredded lettuce leaves. Fill the hearts with the peas and shrimp mixture. Decorate with dill sprigs and lemon slices.

Have a basket of freshly baked bread ready at the table.

P A R S L E Y

SHRIMP WITH BLACK – EYED PEAS

Black–eyed peas, unlike other legumes, do not need to be presoaked. They cook very quickly, taste great and rank high in nutritional value, and have an affinity with seafood. This main course dish calls for a crisp green salad on the side. I always like beer with dried beans but for the sake of the shrimp one could forsake it for wine.

SERVES 4

• 16 shrimp, deveined, peeled but tails left intact
• extra-virgin olive oil • sea salt • 3 garlic cloves, peeled and quartered
• 1/8 teaspoon dried red chilli flakes • 3 – 4 sprigs fresh thyme
• 1 1/2 cups black eyed peas, picked and rinsed
• a handful each, mint, parsley and basil leaves, coarsely chopped
• 4 handfuls fresh spinach leaves, coarsely chopped
• juice of half a lemon • 3 tablespoons yogurt, thinned down with 1 tablespoon of milk
• 2 green onions, minced finely

Preheat oven to 350 °F / 180 °C

Put the black-eyed peas in a pan, cover with water, bring to a boil and then simmer 5 minutes. Drain and add fresh boiling water. Season with salt and pepper and a pinch of sugar. Cook over medium heat until tender.

Meanwhile place shrimp in an oven proof dish. Drizzle generously with olive oil and season with salt and chilli flakes. Add the garlic and roast shrimp in the oven until shrimp are pink in color and appear translucent.

Drain the black-eyed peas and immediately add the fresh herbs and spinach. The heat will wilt the greens. Season with salt and pepper. Drizzle with lemon juice. Taste and correct seasoning. Spoon black–eyed peas onto a serving platter. Spoon yogurt and milk mixture over black-eyed peas and sprinkle the minced green onions. Arrange shrimp all around and serve immediately.

FRESH ANCHOVIES IN VINEGAR

This is a very quick and simple way of cooking fish for the home cook. The trick is to get the small fish cleaned at the fish market. Just give the fish a quick wash, drain well and pat dry. Then cook according to recipe. But just in case you need to do this on your own, here is what you need to do. Trim the fins of all the anchovies using kitchen scissors. With a sharp knife slit each fish along the belly from head to tail and pull out the entrails and cut out the head. At this point you may want to pull out the spine as well. It certainly makes eating the fish easier and more enjoyable. Rinse the fish once more and fold to preserve shape. Sardines could be substituted in this recipe and they can be cleaned in the same way as described above.

SERVES 2

• 500 g / 1 lb anchovies, gutted and scaled
(it would be easier to eat if head and spine were removed as well)
• 1/4 cup dry white wine
• 2 tablespoons lemon vinegar
• 1/4 cup capers • 2 tablespoons extra-virgin olive oil • lemon wedges

Arrange fish in a skillet large enough to accomodate all in a single layer. Drizzle with wine, vinegar and 1 tablespoon of olive oil. Scatter capers on fish. Cook on top of the stove, covered, over moderate heat, until fish are done. Cool until luke warm. Transfer to a serving dish. Drizzle with another tablespoon of oil and spinkle with finely chopped parsley leaves. Decorate with lemon wedges. Serve with a green salad and some well chilled white wine. Pass around Avocado Mayonnaise (p.215) or Preserved Lemon and Bread Sauce (p.247).

About this and that

Salmon has a flavorful flesh and is rich in heart-beneficial omega-3 oils. Salmon tops the list of most healthful foods. It is high in protein and A and B complex vitamins. Salmon is a meaty and oily fish so it lends itself to a big variety if cooking techniques such as poaching, steaming, baking, grilling, boiling and pan-frying. It is used fresh or canned. Smoked salmon is a delicacy that never fades out of fashion. Salmon is also farmed but the farmed product has a blander flavor and softer texture.

SALMON STEAKS WRAPPED IN FOIL

This is my personal interpretation of combining two ingredients I love to eat – fish and lentils. This dish is very easy to prepare for company or a crowd because foil packages can be prepared ahead and refrigerated until cooking time. Serve each foil packet on individual plates and let everyone cut into their own. A big basket of slices of fresh crusty bread on the table would be great. Pass Avocado Mayonnaise (p.213) on the side to spread on bread. A dollop of this tasty mayonnaise tastes outstanding on fish steaks as well.

SERVES 4

• 4 salmon steaks or fillets of any flat fish such as sea bass
• 2 carrots, peeled and cut into tiny cubes
• 1 celery root, peeled and cut into tiny cubes • 3 tablespoons extra-virgin olive oil
• 4 fresh onions, thinly sliced
• 2 cups tightly packed spinach leaves, washed, drained and chopped
• 1/4 cup white wine • 1 1/4 cup vegetable broth
• 3/4 cup green lentils
• 1 tablespoon lemon zest • 2 tablespoons lemon juice
• sea salt and freshly ground pepper • Preserved Lemon slices (p. 243)

Preheat oven to 350 °F / 180 °C

Sweat the onions, carrot and celery cubes in oil in saucepan over medium low heat. Stir occasionally. Add the wine and cook stirring until it evaporates. Then add the broth and bring to a simmer. Rinse and drain lentils. Add these to the vegetables. Season with salt and pepper. Cook covered until all the liquid is absorbed and the lentils are soft. Next add the spinach and cook stirring until wilted. Then add the lemon zest and juice. Turn heat off and start assembling the foil packages. Cut 4 rectangular pieces of foil big enough to hold vegetables and fish steak. Spoon 1/4 of vegetables onto a foil sheet. Place a fish steak on the vegetables and top with preserved lemon slices. Season lightly. Bring the long ends of foil together and fold. Squeeze short ends tightly like a candy wrap. Place foil packages on a baking tray and bake in the oven about 30 minutes or until fish steaks are done.

MEAT, POULTRY

MEAT, POULTRY

Lamb chops seem such old-fashioned food. And a leg of lamb is hardly ever roasted in the oven anymore. Red meat has fallen out of fashion. It may seem odd then to include a section on red meat especially when it is also no longer in my current repertoire of recipes. Firstly, red meat is a part of our culture – a fact not to be ignored. And secondly, it is worthwhile to prepare a full-fledged meal ONCE IN A WHILE, pushing oneself beyond all the newly and duly acquired boundaries of healthy cooking. At this point, in the interest of health, I can't help but add that red meat should still be consumed in moderation and with plentiful of appealing side dishes which draw the attention away from the meat itself. I like to think that I preach only what I practice. And thus the confession -- the four red meat recipes included in this section serve to satisfy a sense of nostalgia for me. They are all favorites of my family. Poultry, on the other hand, is my favorite meat. It has replaced red meat in my kitchen. Chicken and turkey meat can both be bland but can easily be turned into memorable dishes by paying lavish attention to preparation. So all I ask of you is that you try some of these recipes and see if you agree with me.

MEAT, POULTRY

EGGS

MEATBALLS IN LEMON AND WINE SAUCE

Meatballs – everybody's favorite dish. This one has a tangy taste due to the lemons. I think this recipe works well with ground turkey or chicken meat as well. But then consider using only 2 egg yolks and 1/2 cup additional bread crumbs. This dish received excellent ratings from the tasting panel (i.e. my family).

SERVES 6-8

for the meatballs:

• **500 g / 1 lb ground beef** • **1/2 cup grated Parmesan cheese**
• **1 1/2 cups breadcrumbs** • **1 egg and 1 egg yolk**
• **a handful of parsley leaves, very finely chopped** • **zest of one lemon**
• **2 tablespoons water** • **1 tablespoon olive oil**
• **sea salt and freshly ground pepper** • **1/4 cup flour**
• **1/4 cup olive oil** • **1/2 cup white wine** • **3/4 cup hot water** • **juice of 1 lemon**

for garnish:

half a lemon, very thinly sliced and each slice cut into quarters

Combine the meat, grated cheese, breadcrumbs, egg, egg yolk, parsley and zest in a bowl. Mix with a fork. Then add the water to moisten the mixture and then the olive oil and the seasoning. Use your fingers to incorporate ingredients finely. It is of course much faster to throw everything into the food processor and pulse on and off until a fine mixture forms. Next form small sized balls (smaller than golf balls) out of the mixture. Put flour onto a plate and roll each ball in the flour until lightly coated. Heat the oil in a large skillet over medium heat and fry all of the meatballs on all sides until browned. Next add the wine and let the alcohol burn off for a few minutes before adding the hot water. Scatter bay leaves on the meatballs and cook covered over a gentle heat for 5 – 6 minutes. Remove cover and pour in the lemon juice. Continue cooking for a few minutes more. By this time the sauce should be syrupy. Taste for seasoning and remove bay leaves. Spoon the meatballs into a shallow serving dish and decorate with all of the paper thin lemon slices.

MEAT LOAF WITH SUN-DRIED TOMATOES

No need for an introduction – meat loaf is another favorite. Occasionally it is worth to buy red meat – make sure it's lean enough to be on the healthy side. I have streamlined this recipe by using egg whites as a binder. Serve this dish with your favorite recipe of potatoes or Polenta (p.131) or Roasted Vegetables (p. 93) and a green salad.

SERVES 6

(serving size: 2 slices)

• 12 oil packed sun-dried tomatoes, (drained and chopped into small pieces)
• 1/2 cup ketchup • 1 large onion, finely chopped
• 1 cup breadcrumbs (p.82) • 3 garlic cloves, minced
• a handful of fresh basil leaves, finely chopped
• 1/2 cup of hard cheese of choice, grated • 2 egg whites
• sea salt and freshly ground pepper
• 500 g / 1 lb lean ground meat, (beef or a mixture of equal parts of beef and lean lamb)

Preheat oven to 350 °F / 180 °C.
Throw all the ingredients into a bowl and mix well with a fork. Spoon and spread mixture into a loaf pan coated with olive oil. If you wish, spread about a tablespoon of ketchup on meat – and cook in the oven for 1 hour.
Let rest for 10 minutes before serving. Serve Avocado Mayonnaise (p. 213) on the side.
Try this: Add chopped and sautéed mushrooms (about 10-15) to the meat loaf.

P I S T A C H I O S

About this and that

Pistachio is a nut with a small greenish kernel. The shell around the kernel cracks as the nut ripens. It is easy to shell pistachios only by pressing on the shell with fingers. Pistachios can easily be skinned by blanching. Simply pour boiling water over nuts in a bowl. Let sit for a few minutes and then rinse under cool water and slip the skin off. 1/2 kilo / 1lb of unshelled nuts will yield half the amount of shelled nuts.

Pistachios are used widely in Mediterranean and Asian cuisines from savory dishes to desserts. Pistachios are a good source of potassium and magnesium. They are best used in moderation due to their high content of unsaturated fatty acids and high calorie content.

LAMB CHOPS WITH PISTACHIO PESTO CRUMBS

Pesto means 'pounded' in Italian. Pestos were once worked into a paste using a mortar and pestel. But now life in the kitchen is easier and quicker with the food processor.

SERVES 4

(serving size : 3 lamb chops)

12 bone-in lamb chops, all fat removed and slightly pounded

for pesto:

- **3/4 cup shelled pistachios** • **1/2 cup finely chopped fresh parsley**
- **2 cloves garlic** • **1/2 cup olive oil** • **1 teaspoon cumin**
- **1/8 teaspoon red hot pepper (cayenne pepper)**
- **sea salt** • **1/4 cup grated Parmesan cheese**
- **a generous sqeeze of lemon juice**
- **1 cup bread crumbs, made from fresh bread**

Preheat oven to 350 °F / 180 °C.

Make pesto first by toasting pistachios in preheated oven for about 10 minutes. Shake pan once or twice for even toasting. Cool and remove dried skin. Then put all ingredients in food processor and blend until smooth. The pesto can be prepared ahead and best of all, left over pesto can be frozen for future use. Season lamb chops with salt and pepper.

HEAT your skillet and brush with olive oil. Then sear chops on both sides, approximately 2 - 3 minutes per side. Place chops in an oven proof dish and let them cool. Spread about 1 heaping teaspoon of pesto on each chop. Sprinkle with bread crumbs. Brown in oven for 20 minutes or so until tops of chops are browned.

Serve chops with mashed potatoes and Oven Baked Tomatoes (p.101).

LEG OF LAMB

Tips + Tricks + Techniques

Butterflying is the technique of boning a leg of lamb or other meat with bone, so that it can lie flat with an even thickness. The meat can be opened up to lie relatively flat like a butterfly. If you are not an expert in handling sharp knives, I am sure your butcher will gladly do it for you. Butterflied and flattened chicken with bones is marinated easily and cooks very quickly. Boned meat cooks evenly and is easier to cut into portions at serving time. Butterflying also allows meat to be stuffed and rolled up. This technique can be applied to some vegetables such as bell peppers and even meaty fruits but especially to shrimp and whole chicken.

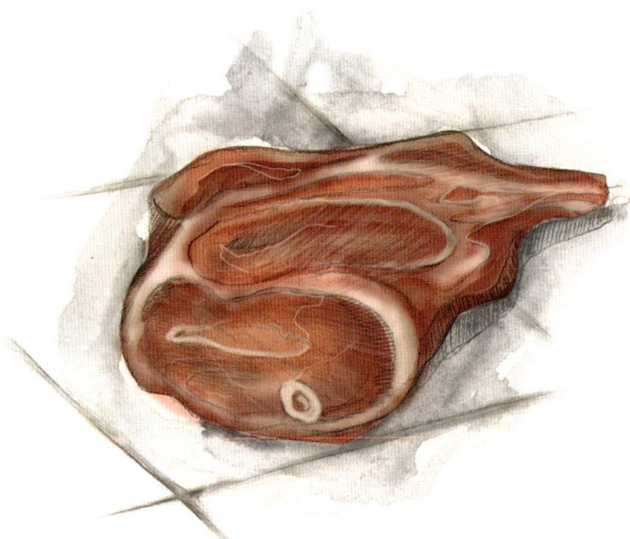

GRILLED LEG OF LAMB

The leg of lamb is one of the most flavorful cuts of meat as well as being one of the leanest cuts from lamb. For this recipe you will need the help of your butcher to butterfly the leg for you – that is to bone, trim, and open it out into a flat piece of meat. The paste helps to soften the meat and makes it very tasty. You can' t really go wrong with it. Needless to say, this piece of meat is also great for a summer barbeque.

SERVES 6

(Serving size: 200 g per person)

• **1.5 kilos / 3 lb leg of lamb,**
(fat removed and butterflied so that it can lie flat with an even thickness)

for the paste:

• **2 tablespoons Dijon mustard** • **2 tablespoons soy sauce**
• **2 sprigs fresh rosemary, snipped from stalles and finely chopped**
• **4 cloves garlic, chopped** • **1 teaspoon toasted cumin seeds,crushed**
• **2 – 3 tablespoons olive oil** • **sea salt and freshly ground pepper**
• **a few drops of chilli sauce like Tabasco**
(vary amount according to how hot you like your food)

Mix all the ingredients for the paste. Use fingers (the best utensils in the kitchen) to cover both sides of meat with the paste. Let rest covered in the refrigerator for 4-6 hours. Remove from refrigerator and bring to room temperature Meanwhile preheat oven grill. Place a rack on an oven tray and brush with oil. Place meat on rack. Grill turning only once until choice of doneness (rare, medium or well-done) is reached. Brush with a bit of olive oil occasionally to attain a deliciously moist piece of meat. Let the leg of lamb rest for 10 minutes before cutting it into slices across the grain.

Serve with Roasted Vegetables (p.93) and bulghur (cracked wheat) or rice. Any lefover meat thinly sliced is exceptionally tasty on a green salad or in a sandwich the following day.

Tips + Tricks + Techniques

Brining means immersing food in brine. Brine is a strong salt-water solution, which can also be flavored with herbs and spices. It preserves and flavors food. Soaking poultry in brine several hours before cooking enhances it juiciness. Whole birds or cut up white meat of poultry benefit greatly from brining. A basic brine calls for 1 1/4 tablespoon of salt to 1 liter of water. Use salt, which is free of additives. Adding 1/2 tablespoon of sugar and 1 tablespoon peppercorns improves taste as well. The size of the bird or pieces of meat to be soaked determines the amount of brine to be prepared. Mix everything until dissolved, place meat in a large pot, and pour brine over it. The brine must cover the food completely. 1 kilo/ 2 lb of chicken meat should brine for 2 hours in the refrigerator. When brining is done pat whole bird or pieces dry and cook immediately. The result is poultry that is just delicious.

STUFFED TURKEY BREAST ROLLS

Turkey meat tends to be dry but this tray-baked recipe is always moist. Brining the meat is the ultimate solution (p.164). Use a small amount of salt in the recipe if you choose to brine the turkey breasts.The sauce in the bottom of the pan also contributes to making this a moist and tasty dish. This recipe works just as well when choice of meat is chicken or beef.

SERVES 4

- **4 boneless, skinless turkey breasts, pounded and flattened**

for the stuffing:

- **1 tablespoon olive oil** • **3 garlic cloves, chopped**
- **2 cups finely chopped spinach leaves (packed tightly)**
- **2 medium potatoes, peeled, diced, boiled and coarsley mashed with a fork**
- **3 green onions, minced** • **sea salt and freshly ground pepper**

for the top:

- **1 tomato, thinly sliced** • **1 small onion, thinly sliced** • **12 fresh basil leaves** • **12 mint leaves**
- **juice of one lemon** • **2 tablespoon olive oil** • **1/2 cup pitted and sliced black olives**
- **1/4 cup capers** • **rosemary sprigs (optional)**

Preheat oven to 375 °F / 190 °C.

Brine the turkey breasts (see page 164).

Start by preparing the stuffing. Sauté garlic and spinach in olive oil on medium-high heat until greens are wilted. Add potatoes and green onions. Give it a good stir and break the potato pieces with fork. Taste the stuffing to season with salt and pepper. Or better yet, refrain from using any salt as brined meat tends to be salty. Freshly ground pepper should be enough for a good taste balance. Let cool completely as you keep yourself busy slicing and measuring ingredients for the topping. Fill turkey breasts with stuffing and roll or wrap. Secure rolls with toothpicks if necessary or use the right size pan to hold the rolls snugly. Place a sprig of rosemary between each roll. Top the turkey rolls with tomato and onion slices, basil and mint leaves. Pour wine and lemon juice over the rolls and top with the olives and capers. Grind some pepper. Drizzle with olive oil. Cover pan and bake for 40 minutes. Remove cover and continue baking for another 10 minutes or so. Remove the rolls to a serving dish and spoon sauce around the meat.

B R E A D

SPICY OVENFRIED CHICKEN

A very healthy and equally tasty dish – try adding other fresh herbs like thyme and chopped rosemary to make the coating as fragrant as possible. Serve with Sautéed Greens (p.97) or just a freshly made green salad and Oven Baked Tomatoes (p.101). The best way to enjoy these ovenfried little birds is to pick them up with your fingers. Provide finger bowls and a good stack of paper napkins. Serve with Oriental Dipping Sauce (p.233).

SERVES 4

- 3 slices of white bread,crusts removed and cut into cubes
- a generous handful of tightly packed parsley leaves
- 2 tablespoons cornmeal
- 2 tablespoons toasted pine nuts
- 2 garlic cloves
- 1 teaspoon cumin
- 1/2 teaspoon oregano
- 1/4 - 1/2 teaspoon hot red pepper
- sea salt and freshly ground pepper
- 1 egg white
- 2 tablespoons mustard of your choice
- 1 tablespoon water
- 2 tablespoons honey
- 4 chicken thighs, skin and fat removed
- 8 chicken drumsticks, skin and fat removed

Preheat oven to 400 °F / 200 °C.

Put all the ingredients up to egg whites in the food processor and pulse on and off until finely crumbled. Then add the egg white and once more pulse on and off until mixture is moist. Place crumb mixture onto a plate.

Mix mustard, water and honey in a bowl. Wash the chicken pieces and pat dry with paper towels. Dip chicken pieces first into mustard mixture and then into crumb mixture. Pat crumbs in place with fingers to form a thin layer. Place chicken pieces on greased oven tray. Bake uncovered for about 45 minutes until crisp and brown.

Provide a small bowl for each guest and pour some dipping sauce into it. Dip chicken pieces in the sauce and enjoy this finger licking good dish.

Tips + Tricks + Techniques

White meat of chicken and turkey fall into the category of meat, which with a little bit of know-how can be transformed from the blandest of foods into a wonderful meal. The taste and texture of both can easily be enhanced by soaking them in milk or in brine (p.164). Soaking white meat of poultry in milk softens it and gives it a mellow taste and a silky texture. Score and soak meat for at least 3 hours (keep in the refrigerator). Then drain, pat dry, season and cook according to recipe. Be very careful not to overcook. Overcooking also dries the meat. Chicken drumsticks and wings lend themselves to marinades. Slash the flesh so that the flavors can penetrate. Refer to page 219 for a tasty marinade.

LEEK–STUFFED CHICKEN WITH WALNUT SAUCE

I always think of this recipe as one of the most luxurious chicken dishes simply because cream (sinful!!) and walnuts give it a rich and satisfying taste and flavor. This dish is not as rich as one might think. It is balanced in its creamy and crunchy texture. Try it and see if you agree with me.

SERVES 4

- **4 large chicken breasts, skinned and flattened or 4 large breaded schnitzel pieces**

for the stuffing:

- **3 leeks, split lengthwise, thinly cut (white and light green parts only)**
- **2 garlic cloves, minced (optional)**
- **1 tablespoon olive oil**
- **2 tablespoons hot water**
- **3 tablespoons cream**
- **1/2 cup toasted walnuts,chopped**
- **1/4 - 1/2 cup fresh parsley, finely chopped**
- **sea salt and freshly ground pepper**

for the sauce:

- **1/2 cup cream**
- **1/3 cup (or more) chicken stock or water**
- **1/3 cup toasted walnuts, chopped**
- **sea salt and freshly ground pepper**
- **what remains of the stuffing**
- **6 – 8 walnut halves for garnish**

Preheat oven to 375 °F / 190 °C.

Cook the leeks and garlic in oil over medium-high heat until softened. Do not brown. Add cream and hot water. Season to your taste with salt and pepper. Cook until some of the liquid evaporates. Cool completely and add the rest of the ingredients. Spoon about 1 tablespoon or more of stuffing onto each chicken piece. Fold in sides and roll up tightly jelly roll fashion. (Reserve the rest of the stuffing for the sauce.) Secure chicken rolls with toothpicks and arrange them in an oven proof pan. Brush with olive oil and bake covered for 20 minutes. Then uncover and continue baking for another 10 – 15 minutes until chicken is cooked. Remove from oven and place chicken rolls on a serving platter. Tent with foil. Add cream, chicken stock and reserved leek stuffing to the pan and place on stove. Scrape and stir over medium heat until very hot. The sauce should have a creamy texture – not too thick. Stir in walnuts. Taste and correct seasoning. Spoon sauce over and around chicken rolls. Garnish with walnut halves.

Enjoy sharing this dish with friends and family – it is one of my favorite recipes.

MEAT MALLET

About this and that

Oats are grains that are rich in soluble fiber and therefore a healthful addition to our diets. Oats decrease food cravings and are an excellent choice of food for breakfast. They also raise mood serotonin levels and are a good example of comfort foods. Oats are a good source of B vitamins and iron. Use oats in cakes, cookies, and muffins. Stir them into soups as a thickener and add them to meatloaf and casserole recipes. Make the best use of its health benefits by maximizing the use of oats in your cooking.

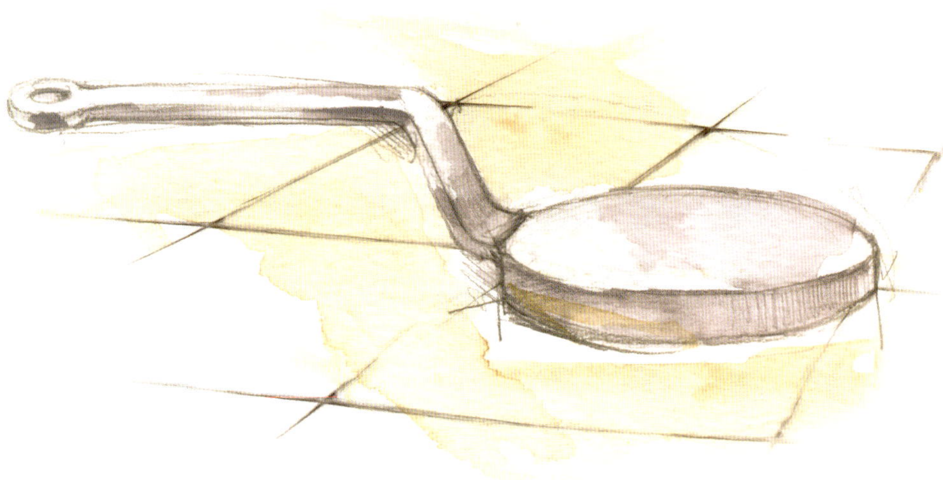

HERB AND OAT CRUSTED CHICKEN WITH POMEGRANATE AND SPINACH

I like to re-invent chicken dishes. In this recipe I have incorporated parts from three different ones and the end product is one of the tastiest chicken recipe I have. The presentation is pleasing to the eye with tones of golden brown, red and green. It is a perfect dish for fall and winter and definitely worthy of a celebration. Don't be put off by the long list of ingredients – it is assembled easily and speedily with a bit of preplanning.

SERVES 6

6 pieces skinless chicken breast halves

for the herb crust:

• 1 cup oats • 2 cloves garlic, grated • 1/4 teaspoon each sage and thyme
• a handful of fresh parsley leaves, roughly chopped
• 1 egg and 1 egg white, ligtly beaten • 1 tablespoon butter, melted

for the vegetable sauce:

• 1 tablespoon olive oil • 2 cloves garlic, peeled and sliced
• 5 large plum tomatoes, peeled,seeded and cut into large chunks
• 1 tomato, seeds removed and grated • 500 g / 1 lb fresh spinach leaves, thoroughly washed and spin dried
• 1/2 cup white wine • seeds of 1/2 pomegranate, skin and pith removed • sea salt and freshly ground pepper

Preheat oven to 400 °F / 200 °C.
Brine your meat (p. 164).
Spread oats on a baking sheet and bake until golden. Stir once in a while for even browning. Combine oats, garlic, parsley leaves, sage and thyme, salt and pepper in the food processor until finely incorporated. Place on a flat dish. Dip chicken pieces first in lightly beaten egg mixture. And then press both sides of chicken breasts in oat mixture. Place chicken pieces in an oven pan coated with oil. Drizzle melted butter over chicken and bake for 35 – 40 minutes until browned. While the chicken is cooking, slowly fry garlic in olive oil. Before it turns brown, add the wine and cook for a few minutes. Then add the chopped tomatoes and the grated one.Simmer for a short while until some of the water has evaporated. Throw in your spinach which will wilt in a minute. Check for seasoning and add a good pinch of sugar. By this time your chicken should be cooked. Spoon sauce on a large serving platter to form a bed for the chicken pieces. Place oat crusted chicken breasts onto the sauce and drizzle with olive oil if you like. Sprinkle with the pomegranate seeds. Bon Appétit.

About this and that

Meat, fish and poultry are flavored and tenderized by soaking them in marinades. Marinade is a seasoned liquid concoction, which contains an acid such as wine, vinegar, lemon juice or yogurt for tenderizing the protein. A blend of spices and herbs are added to marinades for flavoring. Bay leaf, rosemary, thyme are the basic herbs used in marinades. Onion and garlic are also staple ingredients. Addition of oil to marinades keeps meats moist. Always score meat to aid the penetration of marinade. For best results let meat sit in marinade for several hours or overnight. Refrigerate the meat if marinating for more than one hour. As a variation add rice vinegar or sesame oil for an Asian flavor. Use red wine for meat and orange or grapefruit juice with light oil for fish. Lamb lends itself to a marinade that is either spicy or rich in fresh mint. You can easily create your own combination. Baste with the marinade during cooking.

CHICKEN WINGS IN THE OVEN

This dish, another favorite at our dinner table, is very much a part of my repertoire especially in the summer when our son grills the wings on the barbecue. It is best to eat the wings using your fingers. I'm sure you'll lick them clean at the end of the meal.

SERVES 4

for the marinade:

- 4 garlic cloves, chopped
- 2 teaspoons cayenne pepper
- 2 tablespoons brown sugar
- 1/4 cup olive oil
- 1/2 cup soy sauce
- sea salt and black pepper

1 kilo / 2 lb chicken wings, washed, drained and patted dry

Prepare marinade by mixing all ingredients in a bowl. Place chicken wings in the bowl and mix with fingers so all are coated with marinade. Cover and marinate in the refrigerator overnight.

Preheat oven to 400 °F / 200 °C.

Place a rack on an oven pan. Remove chicken wings from marinade and save marinade for basting. Place chicken pieces on rack and cook 6 – 8 minutes.

Then turn wings over. Brush with marinade and cook until done.

Ready in no time at all, this will be a winner recipe. Cold left-overs will be just as good.

ONIONS

CHICKEN BREASTS IN FOIL

Lamb can easily be used in this recipe. Cooking chicken or meat in foils will help the meat retain its juices.

SERVES 4

- **4 medium sized chicken breasts**
- **sea salt and freshly ground pepper**
- **2 large onions, cut into cubes**
- **3 - 4 celery stalks, cut into cubes**
- **mustard**
- **2 tablespoons fresh thyme leaves, snipped from stalks**
- **lemon slices**

Brine your meat first (p.164).
Bring a large pot of water to the boil while you prepare the chicken.
Season chicken on both sides and sear evenly in a pan with olive oil.
Remove chicken from pan and sautée the onions and celery cubes until translucent.
Cut foil in rectangular sheets. Spoon 2 tablespoons or more of onion – celery mixture in the middle of each sheet. Place one piece of chicken on top and spread 1 – 1 1/2 teaspoons mustard of your choice. Sprinkle generously with thyme leaves and place 2 or 3 lemon slices on each chicken breast. Wrap foil around chicken breasts and vegetables to form a tube. Sgueeze ends tightly like a candry wrap. Drop foil packages into boiling water and cook for about 10 minutes. Remove and let cool for a few minutes.
Place one package on each plate and let everyone unwrap their own. Serve with Polenta (p.131) and Sautéed Greens (p.97).

DESSERTS

DESSERTS

Much can be said about desserts especially by someone like me who often has a GOOD mount of craving for them. To be fair on myself, it must be mentioned here and now that I have not yet met one person who doesn't like desserts. There is a mixture of pleasure and guilt involved in enjoying desserts and this in itself is tempting. In my opinion desserts deserve a full-hearted attention at the dinner table. Curb your appetite for something sweet with some of the guilt-free recipes provided in this section.Indulge in moderation and enjoy some of the nontraditional combinations of fruits and cheese desserts embellished with spices and sauces. I hope this selection of recipes will pleasantly increase your repertoire of desserts and will sooth your hunger for something sweet.

DESSERTS

Stuffed Apples with Chocolate Sauce

Coffee and Chocolate Trifle

Broiled Pears in Caramel Sauce

Strawberries in Wine

Baked Fruit

Pumpkin Cheesecake

Bread and Peach Cobbler

Grilled Halloumi Cheese and Nectarines

Spiced Pears

Poached Fruit with Grilled Cake

Spiced Plums

Compote of Autumn Fruit

APPLES

STUFFED APPLES WITH CHOCOLATE SAUCE

STUFFED APPLES WITH CHOCOLATE SAUCE

The presentation of this dessert wins almost the same number of points as the taste.
If you like ice cream with fruit desserts then scoop some on the side and enjoy!

SERVES 4

- 1/4 cup raisins
- 1/4 cup sweet wine
- 4 large apples
- 4 ladyfingers, crumbled
- 1/4 cup blanched almonds, chopped
- 1/4 cup pine nuts, toasted and chopped
- 8 walnut halves, chopped
- 1 teaspoon grated orange peel
- 25 g bittersweet chocolate, broken into pieces
- 1/2 cup cream
- 2 tablespoons confectioner's sugar

Soak raisins in wine for 30 minutes. Drain and set aside.

Cut tops of apples and reserve them as lids. Carve out the apples leaving 1 1/2 cm apple flesh and chop the removed pulp into the crumbled ladyfingers which you have placed in a bowl. Then add chopped almonds, pine nuts, walnuts, raisins and orange peel. Fill hollowed apples with the mixture. Push in with spoon and top with the apple lid.

Place apples in a steamer over boiling water. Cover and steam for 10-12 minutes, until the apples are just tender.

Meanwhile melt chocolate and cream over low heat in a double boiler until chocolate melts. Spoon chocolate sauce onto individual dessert plates and spread with a spoon so sauce forms an even circle on each plate. Sit a stuffed apple on sauce and dust generously with confectioner's sugar.

Enjoy this dessert with a sweet dessert wine. Cheers!

COFFEE AND CHOCOLATE TRIFLE

COFFEE AND CHOCOLATE TRIFLE

The creamy pudding and the crunchy cookies combine to make a great dessert. This is a heart-friendly recipe that calls for low-fat milk but if you can use whole milk instead.

SERVES 8

- 1/2 cup sugar
- 1/4 cup cornstarch
- 1 tablespoon instant coffee granules
- 1 large egg
- 2 1/2 cups low- fat milk
- 1 tablespoon coffee flavored liqueur
- 16 cream filled chocolate sandwich cookies
- 1 1/2 cups whipped cream

Combine sugar, cornstarch, coffee and egg in a bowl. Pour milk into a pan and heat over medium heat. Do not boil. Add hot milk to egg mixture, stirring constantly. Return mixture to pan and cook over medium heat until thickened. Then lower heat and continue cooking a little longer. Remove from heat and add liqueur. Cool pudding immediately, placing pan in a large bowl of ice water.

Break 8 cookies into bite size pieces and fold into cooled pudding. Next fold in 1 cup of whipped cream. Divide pudding evenly among 8 parfait glasses or custard cups. Cover and chill until cold. When you are ready to serve top each with a cookie and a dollop of whipping cream flavored with a few drops of coffee liqueur.

P E A R S

BROILED PEARS IN CARAMEL SAUCE

BROILED PEARS IN CARAMEL SAUCE

The sauce is superb with pears and can be prepared ahead. It tastes great over ice cream or puddings as well. Yummy!

SERVES 6

for the sauce:

• 2/3 cup sugar
• 3 tablespoons water • 3 tablespoons hot water
• 1 1/2 cups cream
• 1 teaspoon vanilla extract • 1 teaspoon chilled butter

for the pears:

• 3 large ripe pears • 1 lemon, halved
• 2 tablespoons butter, melted • sugar

Preheat the broiler on high.

Make the sauce first. Cook sugar and water over low heat in a deep pan until sugar dissolves. Increase heat and bring to a boil. Continue boiling until syrup turns golden brown. Remove from heat and add hot water. Be very careful! Mixture will spatter. Add cream and return to heat. Boil until thickened for about 6–8 minutes. Turn heat off and add vanilla and butter. Pour sauce into a bowl and set aside.

Peel pears, halve lengthwise and remove cores. Rub with lemon to prevent discoloration. Score rounded sides of pears lengthwise (do not cut through).

Now it is time to broil the pears. Place pear halves in a lightly buttered oven proof dish and fan each one out. Brush with butter and sprinkle with sugar.

Broil until golden brown, about 8–10 minutes.

When you are ready to serve spoon enough sauce onto individual dessert dishes. Spread sauce with the backside of a spoon to cover entire bottom of plate. Place fanned out pear half over the sauce and decorate with fresh mint leaves. Pass more sauce separately. Absolutely delicious.

S T R A W B E R R I E S

STRAWBERRIES IN WINE

STRAWBERRIES IN WINE

A wonderful way of presenting fruit desserts. It is so very easy to make. Try this recipe with other fruits like peaches or apricots or sour cherries. (Add more sugar than the recipe calls for if you choose to use sour cherries.)

SERVES 6

- **1 package strawberry flavored jello**
- **1 cup boiling water**
- **3 cups chilled sweet wine or fruit wine (such as strawberry or cranberry)**
- **500 g / 1 lb strawberries, washed, hulled and thinly sliced lengthwise**
- **1/4 cup sugar**

Measure enough strawberry flavor gelatin to set 4 cups of liquid. First dissolve gelatin in 1 cup hot water. Then stir in chilled wine. Pour gelatin mixture into a shallow, large dish and chill until set, preferably overnight. About 1 hour before serving toss strawberries with 1/4 cup sugar. Chill until ready to assemble dessert. It would be a great idea to chill dessert glasses as well. Break gelatin into small flakes with a fork and scramble completely.

Spoon about 3 tablespoons of gelatin into each of the 6 dessert glasses. Top with a layer of strawberry slices. Repeat two or more times with layers of gelatin and fruit. Drizzle a little juice from the berries over the top. Sprinkle with chocolate curls and serve with a dollop of whipped cream.

F I G S

BAKED

BAKED FRUIT

FRUIT

Grilled or baked fruits add a new taste dimension to fruits in season and make a strikingly delicious dessert. The simplicity of this dessert is alluring. Choose your fruits according to the season. Buy some quinces, apples, pears, pumpkin in the winter, and peaches, nectarines, apricots, or fresh figs in the summer. Use firm textured fruits that aren't over ripe and remember that cooking time varies with each fruit.Quince,apples, and pears need a longer time in the oven than other fruits like pumpkin,figs and so on. In this recipe the quantities are up to you, but plan to serve 4-5 pieces of fruit on each plate. This isn't a recipe so much as a few suggestions.

Fruits of your choice

Preheat oven to 475 °F / 250 °C.

Wash, halve, pit or core fruit as necessary but do not peel.If you are grilling fresh figs cut an x on the stem and go only half way into the fruit.

Place fruit, cut side up, in an oven proof dish. Sprinkle sparingly or generously with some fruit liqueur and with sugar—granulated or brown according to your choice.Grill fruit in the oven until edges brown and sugar caramelizes. Remember that winter fruits need more time to bake than summer fruits. To shorten the cooking time for these fruits, cut them into 4 cm/1 1/2 in thick slices and bake as explained above.

Here is a great idea for creating grill marks on the pieces of fruit baked in the oven: Dust baked fruit with a small amount of confectioner's sugar. Heat a skewer on open flame until very hot and place on flesh of fruit to create criss-cross design. Reheat skewer each time you want to repeat the design. Wipe clean before reheating.

Another option with summer fruits is using a griddle pan on the stove top. Heat pan until very hot and grill fruit cut side down long enough to soften, about 5 minutes or longer. By this time sugar in fruit will start to caramelize and brown griddle lines appear on fruit flesh. Serve with whipped cream flavored with drops of liqueur or vanilla ice cream.

Pass your favorite kind of cookies around.

PUMPKIN

PUMPKIN CHEESECAKE

PUMPKIN CHEESECAKE

The irresistable spicy flavor of pumpkin pie turned into a cheese cake and baked without a crust. The top is sprinkled with a praline-like confection.

SERVES 12

• 500 g /1 lb puréed pumpkin (about 700 g with peel)
• 1 cup ricotta cheese
• 2 packages light cream cheese (225 g/ 8 oz each)
• 1 cup brown sugar, packed tightly
• 3 tablespoons flour • 1/4 teaspoon ground cinnamon
• 1/2 teaspoon ground ginger and nutmeg • 1/4 teaspoon ground cloves
• 2 eggs • 4 egg whites • 1/4 cup sugar • 1/4 teaspoon cream of tartar

for praline topping:

• 3 tablespoons sugar

Preheat oven to 300 °F / 150 °C.

First of all prepare pumpkin. Bake pumpkin with its peel in the oven until very soft when pierced with a fork. Then spoon the pulp into a bowl (or peel and steam pumpkin until soft). Then mash with a fork until smooth and measure the amount asked for in the recipe. Next spoon ricotta and cream cheese into food processor. Mix until smooth. Add brown sugar, flour and all of the spices and mix. Spoon mixture into a bowl and stir in the mashed pumpkin and whisk in the eggs. Next beat egg whites and cream of tartar with a mixer until foamy. Slowly add the sugar and beat until stiff but not dry. Gently fold egg whites in parts into pumpkin mixture and incorporate. Pour into a lightly oiled oven proof dish. Bake for 50 minutes or until set. Remove pumpkin cheese cake from the oven and cool for an hour. Then cover top and chill at least 6 hours. Meanwhile prepare praline topping. Caramelize sugar in a pan over medium – high heat until golden. Spread hot mixture onto a baking sheet brushed with oil. Cool completely. Break into small pieces and process in the food processor until pieces turn into crystallized sugar. Sprinkle over cheesecake and serve with dollops of whipped cream and cookies or slices of cake of choice.

S P A T U L A

About this and that

Cinnamon is the dried bark of the cinnamon tree. It can be bought ground or in stick form. Ground cinnamon has a stronger flavor. It is used in both sweet and savory dishes. Cinnamon tastes great when sprinkled over custards and warm milk drinks.

BREAD AND

BREAD AND PEACH COBBLER

PEACH COBBLER

This is a very easy dessert I whip up in minutes. It is actually a variation on an American recipe. Although the recipe calls for peaches you could cut up any fruit combo you fancy – juicy plums with grated pears or apples. Serve this cobbler warm with big spoonfuls of vanilla ice cream sprinkled with toasted nuts.

SERVES 8-10

- **12 large ripe peaches, peeled, pitted and cut into quarters**
- **1 cup sugar**
- **1/3 cup flour**
- **1 teaspoon grated rind of an orange**
- **1/2 cup orange juice**
- **1/4 cup butter, melted**
- **1/4 teaspoon ground cinnamon**
- **3 egg whites**
- **1/3 cup sugar**
- **8 slices or more hearty white bread (a few days old), crusts trimmed and cut into 4 triangles or squares**
- **2 tablespoons sugar mixed with 1/4 teaspoon cinnamon**

Preheat oven to 350 °F / 180 °C.

In a large bowl combine fruit, sugar and flour. Let mixture rest for half an hour. Give it a stir once in a while.Brush a large ovenproof dish lightly with melted butter. Arrange fruit in dish by pushing down with fingers.

Meanwhile whisk together the sugar, orange rind, orange juice, melted butter, cinnamon and egg whites. Dip bread pieces in the juice mixture and arrange them on fruit by overlapping and creating your own design. Spoon any remaining orange juice or more on bread slices. Sprinkle with cinnamon sugar and bake 35 minutes or so until your whole kitchen smells delicious. The topping will turn crisp and golden in color. The juices will bubble up from the sides. Absolutely yummy! Let rest for about 30 minutes before serving.

A L M O N D S

About this and that

Almond, an edible seed, is added to both sweet and savory dishes. It is also used to garnish fish, poultry and vegetables for an elegant presentation. Almond is both delicate and fragrant. Almond paste is used in making candy and cake decorations. Nut milk is made from almonds. Amaretto is produced from the oil of bitter almonds.

Almonds are good for us. They are rich in vitamin E, protein and fiber.

A handful has only 170 calories. Add a handful of almonds to your diet while eliminating some of the carbohydrates or saturated fat to balance the calories.

Use almonds in moderation but definitely try incorporating them into you everyday cooking.

GRILLED HALLOUMI CHEESE AND NECTARINES

GRILLED HALLOUMI CHEESE AND NECTARINES

Here is another cheese and fruit dessert, which is worth trying. Salty and sweet, an unlikely combination of two flavors which compliment each other well. I like to serve this dessert after a light vegetarian meal.

SERVES 4

- **250 g / 8 oz package Halloumi cheese, cut into 8 slices**
- **4 large nectarines, cut in half and pitted**
- **1/3 cup sugar**
- **2 teaspoons ground cinnamon**
- **125 ml / 1/2 cup /4 fl.oz sweet dessert wine of your choice**

for garnish:

- **toasted sliced almonds and sprigs of mint**

Preheat oven to 275 °F / 120 °C.

Mix sugar and cinnamon together in a shallow dish. Dip cheese on both sides and nectarines on cut side in sugar to coat. Heat a ridged grill pan and brush lightly with oil. Grill cheese slices and fruit in batches until brown grill marks appear. Keep warm by placing on a plate in the oven.Pour the wine into a small saucepan and bring to a boil. Allow the alcohol to escape as you reduce wine only a little bit.

Place 2 pieces of cheese and 2 nectarine halves on individual dessert plates and pour 2 tablespoons wine over. Drizzle honey in a thin stream forming a zigzag design. Sprinkle with almonds and garnish with sprigs of mint.

About this and that

Verjuice, verjus or verjus molasses, as it may be called, is the vinegar made from juice of unripe grapes as well as of red ones. Other unripened fruit such as apples, pears and plums have also been used to produce verjus. Verjus in French means 'green juice'. Almost every wine-producing region in France and in the Mediterranean also produces verjus. It has a tart flavor but is less harsh than vinegar. Just a few tablespoons can make a difference in taking flavor of cooked food to another dimension. Sauces, stews, casseroles and some vegetable dished such as okra, acquire the piquant taste by the addition of verjus just before serving.

SPICED

SPICED PEARS

PEARS

The sweetness of the pears is a good foil for the spicy flavor of the sauce. These spiced pears accompany cheese fantastically –especially Brie or Camembert. Prepare individual serving plates of cheese and pears for an effortless yet dramatic ending to any meal instead of serving a cheese platter. Serve chilled Riesling wine with this cheese dessert.

SERVES 6

- **250 ml / 1 cup verjus or any strong vinegar of your choice**
- **1 tablespoons mustard seeds, crushed lightly**
- **3 whole cloves**
- **one stick of cinnamon**
- **1 tablespoon honey**
- **3 tablespoons sugar**
- **1 cup water**
- **3 large pears, peeled, cored and cut into eighths**
- **1/4 teaspoon Dijon mustard**

Boil and then simmer all the ingredients, except the pears and mustard, in a saucepan over medium heat for about 15 minutes. Add the pears and continue simmering until the pears are tender. Remove the pears with a slotted spoon. Continue simmering the liquid until syrupy. Whisk in the mustard. Taste and sweeten further as necessary. Pour syrup over the pears. Cool and refrigerate until ready to serve with an assortment of cheeses of your choice. Accompany dessert with walnut halves.

POACHED FRUIT WITH

POACHED FRUIT WITH GRILLED CAKE

GRILLED CAKE

This is a summer dessert, which is easy to make in no time at all. In the winter consider poaching dried fruits - apricots, figs and plums - and create a richer dessert using the basic idea.

SERVES 6-8

for the poaching liquid:

- **about 3 cups of sugar** • **about 6 cups of water**
- **strips of lemon peel** • **half a handful of fresh mint leaves**
- **3-4 tablespoons fruit liqueur**
- **3 peaches** • **6 apricots** • **3 nectarines**
- **raisin loaf cake, cut into slices (8 or more)**

for the honey cream:

- **1 cup cream, whipped** • **2 tablespoons honey**
- **1 tablespoon lemon juice** • **1 tablespoon lemon zest**

for garnish:

- **toasted nuts of choice, crushed**

Bring water, sugar, lemon peel and mint leaves to a boil in a large saucepan. Score fruit and lower into the syrup. Simmer until tender but firm. Remove fruit with a slotted spoon. Cool and peel carefully. Halve and remove pits.

Meanwhile, add the liqueur to syrup and boil until reduced by half. Cool thickened syrup and then pour over poached fruit. Place in refrigerator until ready to serve.

Next whip up the cream, honey, lemon zest and juice with a whisk. Cover and refrigerate. When ready to serve place two apricot halves and one half each of peach and nectarine on individual dessert plates. Spoon some sauce over fruit. Toast slices of cake in toaster. Place one slice cake on each plate. Spoon dollops of honey cream on the side and sprinkle with nuts.

C A R D A M O M

About this and that

Cardamom is a member of the ginger family. It is one of the most ancient spices as well as one of the most expensive ones like saffron and vanilla. Cardamom has an intensely aromatic flavor. It is used in baked goods, fruit compotes, marinades and wines. Cardamom is the key ingredient in curry dishes. It is also used to flavor coffee. It is valued for its digestive properties and is also a breath freshener. Cardamom is sold either in small pods, which need to be crushed to remove the seeds, or as whole or ground seeds.

SPICED PLUMS

Pile the spiced plums over pound cake slices or serve on individual meringues. Top with whipped cream and plum syrup. This is absolutely delicious.

SERVES 6

- **750 g / 1 1/2 lb. red plums, halved, pitted and each half sliced into 3 pieces**
- **1/2 cup sugar**
- **1 tablespoon lemon juice**
- **1/2 teaspoon ground cardamom**
- **6 slices of pound cake or 6 individual meringues**

Combine all ingredients in a wide saucepan and toss a few times. Cook over medium high heat, stirring until sugar dissolves. Continue cooking until plums are tender but not mushy. Cool and transfer to a covered container and refrigerate until ready to use.

Place one slice of pound cake or a meringue on individual dessert plate. Pile each with plums, dividing evenly. Serve with dollops of whipped cream. Drizzle some of the fruit syrup over the cream.

VANILLA

About this and that

Vanilla is a fruit of a vine, which resembles the green bean. It has a rich perfumed aroma and a fragrant, sweet taste. It may be used in its bean form or as vanilla extract. The bean can be cut lengthwise, the seeds scraped and added with the pod into liquid to be cooked. It adds perfume and a deep nuance to everything it is added to. Vanilla beans are expensive but can be reused several times. Just wash the whole bean after soaking in milk or sauce. Dry and store in a tightly covered container. Or simply stick the used and dried vanilla bean into a bowl of sugar to produce vanilla sugar which can then be used in baking. Culinary uses of vanilla are innumerable. Ice cream, puddings, custards, sauces, cakes, chocolate and candy rely on vanilla for their flavor. Vanilla is also produced synthetically. Imitation vanilla has an inferior taste. Compare the two and you will always favor the real thing.

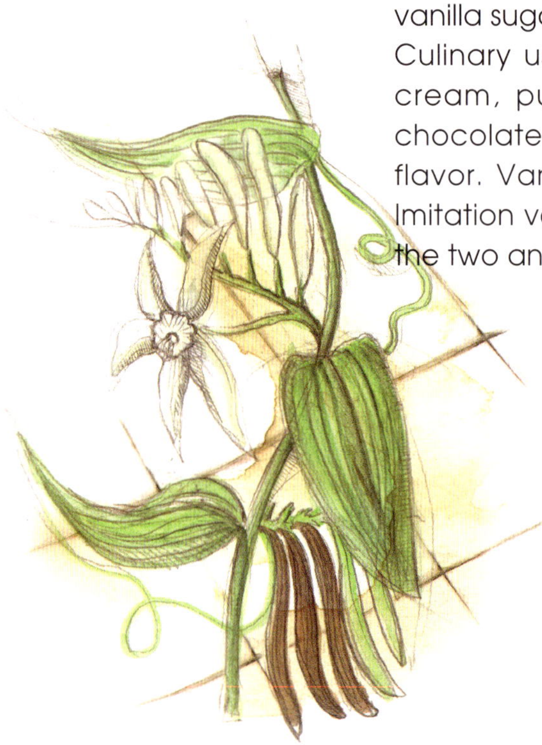

COMPOTE OF AUTUMN FRUITS

COMPOTE OF AUTUMN FRUITS

Two recipes competed to take this space in the collection. My taste buds chose this one because there is a good mixture of fresh and dried fruits with a rich aroma of vanilla.

SERVES 6-8

- **2 tablespoons pomegranate molasses**
- **1 cup + 2 tablespoons water**
- **1/2 cup sugar**
- **2 cups mineral water**
- **1 vanilla pod, split lengthways, and seeds scraped**
- **3-4 pears, peeled, cored and cut into quarters (rub with lemon)**
- **3-4 apples, peeled, cored and cut into quarters (rub with lemon)**
- **12-16 dried apricots**
- **12-16 dried pitted prunes**
- **pomegranate seeds to decorate**

Put the pomegranate molasses, water, sugar and mineral water into a non-aluminium pan. Boil until sugar dissolves. Add the vanilla pod and scraped seeds. First add the pears and cook covered over very low heat for 10-30 minutes depending on how ripe they are. Then drop in the apples and cook uncovered until they are tender. Remove fruit from pan into a bowl with a slotted spoon.

Then boil the syrup until reduced by half. Taste and add some more sugar or a squeeze of lemon juice to adjust the sweetness or tartness. Remove the vanilla pod. Add the apricots and prunes to the bowl of fruit and pour hot syrup over. Cool, cover and chill.

Serve in individual dessert bowls. Sprinkle a handful of pomegranate seeds and serve with dollops of cream.

SAUCES, DIPS ET AL...

All the recipes that a cook cannot survive without SAUCES, DIPS ET AL...

There are no strict parameters to this section. I have included sauces, relishes, dips, dressings, salsas, chutneys, pestos, broths and stocks as well as other very tasty enhancements -- the preparation of which is neither difficult nor time consuming. Most can be prepared ahead with a bit of pre-planning. All of these flavor catalysts are essential in the kitchen. Some are applied to food before cooking, some are used in cooking and others are there to embellish. These powerful additions revive simply prepared foods into complex dishes and transform each into a complete and special dish.

SAUCES, DIPS ET AL...

BASIL

SPINACH PESTO

This pesto is great to serve with any vegetable soup. Ladle soup into bowls and top each with a generous dollop of pesto. This recipe pairs with Chickpea Soup with Spinach (p.75). It is also good on plain toast, crostini or bruchetta.

Makes about 2 cups

- **1/4 cup pine nuts, toasted**
- **1 cup olive oil**
- **3 cups lightly packed spinach leaves**
- **1 cup lightly packed fresh basil leaves**
- **1 cup freshly grated Parmesan cheese**
- **3 small cloves of garlic, cut into quarters**
- **sea salt and freshly ground pepper**

Everything goes into the food processor. Blend until thin mayonnaise texture is obtained. Pour into a jar. Makes about 2 cups and keeps in the refrigerator up to one week. Bring to room temperature before serving.

NUTMEG CROUTONS

These croutons are at their best when they are freshly made.This recipe pairs with Zucchini and Apple Soup (p. 67).

• 4 slices bread, crusts removed, and cut into cubes
• 1/4 cup olive oil • 1/4 teaspoon nutmeg
• 1/4 teaspoon cinnamon • a pinch of allspice • a pinch of black pepper

Place bread cubes on an oven sheet to air-dry overnight. Heat oil in skillet. Throw in bread cubes.Cook until golden brown on all sides, tossing frequently. Mix spices and sprinkle evenly over croutons. Shake and cool.

ROQUEFORT CROUTONS

Spreading the cheese mixture on each crouton is tedious work in the kitchen but it is worth it. These croutons taste fantastic with soup or over salads. Try them with Cabbage and Potato Soup (p. 77).

• 4 slices white bread, crusts removed • 100 g / 4 oz Roquefort cheese, crumbled
• 1 tablespoon butter, room temperature • 1 tablespoon sesame seeds, toasted

Preheat oven to 350 °F / 180 °C.
Cut bread into 2 cm cubes and place on a baking sheet. Bake in preheated oven for 10 minutes or more until beginning to crisp. Shake pan once or twice to ensure even browning. Mix cheese and butter with a fork. Spread one side of each crouton with the cheese mixture. Broil crouton (cheese side up) until cheese melts and browns. Sprinkle with sesame seeds immediately after removing from the oven and serve warm.

AVOCADO

AVOCADO MAYONNAISE

This tasty mayonnaise is great with chicken or turkey burgers. It also pairs well with potato salad. Serve it with grilled asparagus as a starter. The options are numerous. My suggestion was to serve it alongside Meatloaf with Sun-Dried Tomatoes (p.159). Double the recipe when serving more than 4 people. You can make good use of avocados which are slightly over ripe. Cut out any bruised parts and mash the creamy flesh.

Makes about 1 cup

- **half of one ripe avocado, seeded and peeled**
- **1/2 cup mayonnaise, preferably fat-free**
- **1 generous handful of cilantro or parsley leaves, very finely chopped**
- **2 tablespoons juice of grilled lemon**
- **sea salt and freshly ground pepper**
- **a dash of cayenne pepper**

Mash avocado with a fork in a bowl. Add cilantro (or parsley) and mayonnaise. Grill your lemon halves on a hot griddle pan (brushed with olive oil) for a couple minutes until soft and charred. Squeeze juice of the grilled lemon and measure 2 tablespoons. Mix everything vigorously to combine (or use a hand blender). Taste and correct seasoning. Cover and refrigerate until ready to use. It will keep in the refrigerator up to one week.

Z U C C H I N I

OVEN-DRIED ZUCCHINI

The salty crunchy taste of zucchini pairs well especially with neutral to sweet tasting soups. My suggestion is to serve it with Pumpkin and Pear Soup (p.65). Add this as garnish to soups and salad you fancy. Sprinkle over omelettes. Oven-dry a large amount and freeze in airtight containers up to 6 months. Defrost before using

Makes not quite 1 cup

- **1 kilo / 2 lb zucchini**
- **2 teaspoons salt**
- **paprika**

Preheat oven to 275 °F / 120 °C.

Coarsely grate zucchini with peel. Discard the middle part with seeds. Toss grated zucchini with salt in a colander set in the sink. Put a plate on the zucchini and weigh down with a heavy can. Let zucchini drain for at least 20 minutes.

Next squeeze out as much water as possible and blot zucchini dry between paper towels. Spread grated zucchini on a lightly oiled baking sheet separating evenly with fingers. Bake for one hour rotating pan to ensure even drying and browning. It would also help to remove pan from oven once or twice and mix grated zucchini with a fork. Zucchini will reduce in volume by more than half as it dries.

Remove from oven when all has completely dried and the zucchini is crunchy to bite. Cool and transfer to an airtight container.

OVEN-DRIED CHERRY TOMATOES

These tomatoes roasted in the oven explode with flavor – both sweet and tart. Slow roasting gives them an intense flavor. They can also be frozen for up to 2 months. Scatter a generous handful on green salads. Keep this as an essential recipe in your repertoire and as a variation turn the roasted tomatoes into a creamy sauce. It is excellent again with pasta or served on polenta slices. Dollops of it liven up any vegetable soup. Simply place roasted tomatoes in a saucepan. Add some vegetable broth and warm over medium heat. Add some fresh herbs of choice or a tablespoon of balsamic vinegar and some good olive oil. Cook until liquid has evaporated. Pass through a sieve for a smoother texture.

And finally you can enrich the sauce by adding crème fraîche or thick Nut Milk (p.247).

- **1 kg cherry tomatoes, cut in half**
- **2 tablespoons olive oil**
- **1 teaspoon each dried rosemary, thyme and basil**
- **sea salt and a pinch of sugar**

Preheat oven to 200 °F / 100 °C.

Lightly oil an oven rack and place it on a large oven tray.

Cover your pan with foil to catch the drippings to eventually minimize the mess and time spent on cleaning up.

Place tomato halves in a bowl. Sprinkle with dry herbs, salt and sugar. Drizzle olive oil over tomatoes and mix gently with hands to coat all tomatoes evenly.

Try to arrange all tomatoes neatly, facing cut side up, so you have one layer. Bake for 2 hours, rotating rack once in a while to ensure even drying. Reduce oven temperature to lowest possible degree and roast for another hour. Again rotate rack. Turn oven off and let tomatoes cool in the oven completely. Transfer tomato halves into a bowl, cover and refrigerate. Use in any recipe that calls for oven-dried tomatoes.

MORTAR

MARINADE FOR CHICKEN

This is an oriental marinade which makes chicken very soft and tasty. Chicken or turkey breasts especially benefit from this marinade and retain a moist texture. The recipe is just enough to marinate 4 medium chicken breasts.

- **1 tablespoon olive oil or corn oil**
- **1 egg white**
- **1/4 teaspoon sugar**
- **1 teaspoon corn starch**
- **2 teaspoons soy sauce**
- **2 garlic cloves, finely minced**
- **sea salt and freshly ground pepper**
- **1/4 teaspoon chilli flakes**

Mix all ingredients in a bowl. Add chicken pieces and mix with fingers to coat. Cover and marinate in the refrigerator for one hour or more.

Remove chicken from marinade. Drain and use in recipe of your choice.

Tips + Tricks + Techniques

Zest is the aromatic top skin of the citrus fruits. It is used widely in cooking and baking because the oils in the zest intensify and perk up the flavors of food. Be sure to wash and scrub the fruit well to remove any chemicals before removing the zest. The zest can then be removed with a zester or it can be grated or minced. Finely grated zest releases more flavor than larger strips. Grate lemon zest over wax paper to make it easier to gather for measuring. Care must be given to remove only the zest and not the white pith under the zest, which is bitter. When citrus is seasonal it is a great idea to zest the fruits before peeling or juicing them. The zest freezes well and can be used when it is called for in recipes. Frozen zest tastes just like fresh zest.

LEMON AND GARLIC DRESSING

This is an easy make-ahead dressing. Spoon it over steamed vegetables, boiled potatoes or salad of your choice. My choice is Arugula and Pear Salad with Roquefort Cheese (p.47).

- **3 tablespoons olive oil**
- **3 cloves garlic, crushed**
- **1 cup vegetable broth**
- **1/4 cup fresh lemon juice**
- **zest of one lemon**
- **sea salt and freshly ground pepper**
- **a good pinch of sugar**
- **a large handful of parsley leaves**

Sauté garlic in oil over low heat for a few minutes. Increase heat and add broth and simmer until reduced by half. Add lemon juice, zest and season with salt and pepper. Cook a few minutes more and remove from heat. Chop parsley leaves very fine in food processor or with a mezzaluna. Stir into dressing and let cool before spooning over any salad.

P I N E N U T S

Tips + Tricks + Techniques

Emulsifying is a cooking technique used almost every day in the kitchen in which one ingredient is added to another while whisking rapidly. The best example of ingredients that we want to emulsify in making salad dressing are oil and vinegar. They do not naturally dissolve into each other so are called temporary emulsions. When left to sit they separate. Mayonnaise and Hollandaise Sauce, on the other hand, are stable emulsions, which require an emulsifier like eggs, mustard or cream, to hold all other ingredients together. They do not separate. These emulsifiers are used daily in cooking.

PINE NUT, BASIL AND BALSAMIC DRESSING

A crunchy dressing which is great over a green salad or steamed vegetables. We are using the original method of making pesto – pounding and bashing to produce the crunchy texture. It is fun.

- **1 clove garlic, cut in half**
- **a large handful of fresh basil leaves**
- **1/2 cup toasted pine nuts**
- **6 tablespoons extra - virgin olive oil**
- **2 – 3 tablespoons balsamic vinegar**
- **sea salt and freshly ground pepper**

Place garlic in your mortar and sprinkle a pinch of salt. Pound into a pulp with the pestle. Add the basil leaves and press and bash to incorporate. Then do the same with the pine nuts. Spoon this mixture into a bowl and mix in oil and vinegar whisking vigorously until emulsified. Taste and season to your taste.

APPLES

CORNELIAN CHERRY AND APPLE CHUTNEY

Ever since I have been introduced to the sweet and tangy taste of cranberry sauce many years ago, turkey meat is almost unthinkable without it. There is always a craving for it when I prepare turkey for a special celebration meal. Cranberries are not available in our markets. This tangy chutney replaces cranberry sauce in my kitchen. It pairs well not only with turkey but also with quiches. The contrast of flavors is appealing to the palate. Add finely chopped chillies if you prefer a spicier flavor. Sour cherries can easily replace cornelian cherries in this recipe. (Pits need to be removed. A messy process!!) Use frozen cherries when fresh ones are or are not available to save time and work in the kitchen.

Makes about 2 1/2 cups

- **2 tablespoons oil**
- **1 large red onion, chopped**
- **1 cup apple cider vinegar**
- **2 tart green apples, peeled, cored and diced**
- **1 cup cornelian cherries**
- **1 thin slice of ginger, peeled and minced**
- **1/4 teaspoon ground allspice**

Sweat the onions in the oil until they are translucent, for about 10 minutes. Add vinegar, apples, cherries, ginger and allspice. Simmer for 30 minutes. Serve at room temperature.

About this and that

Sesame seeds, which are tiny and flat seeds, come in shades of brown, red and black. The most commonly found ones are a pale grayish-ivory. Sesame seeds have a nutty, slightly sweet flavor that make them versatile for use in baked goods such as breads, pastries, cakes and confections as well as in salads and savory dishes. The seeds are available packaged in supermarkets and can be found in bulk in spice markets. Sesame seeds have high oil content, so they turn rancid quickly. Store them in an airtight container in a cool, dark place for 3 months. They keep longer if refrigerated or frozen. Sesame seeds can be ground into a paste called tahini and the paste is used in many Middle Eastern dishes. The seeds are also crushed to make oil, which is used in Asian dishes.

SESAME SEED SAUCE

This sauce will make any dullish salad leap into life. Use as a sauce for poached chicken or fish as well. Keep in a sealed jar in the refrigerator up to one week. Bring to room temperature before using.

Makes enough to dress 2 large bowls of salad

- **4 tablespoons apple cider vinegar**
- **2 tablespoons soy sauce**
- **1 tablespoon water**
- **1 tablespoon honey**
- **sea salt and freshly ground pepper**
- **5 tablespoons olive oil**
- **1 tablespoon lemon zest**
- **1 garlic clove, minced**
- **2 tablespoons sesame seeds, toasted**
- **1/4 teaspoon sesame oil**

Blend vinegar, soy sauce, water with a fork until well incorporated. Add honey and mix well. Season with salt and pepper. Add olive oil in a thin stream beating all the while. Add lemon zest, minced garlic, sesame seeds and sesame oil. If you prefer a sweeter tasting sauce, then add more honey. Keep at room temperature until ready to dress salad.

G I N G E R

About this and that

Ginger is one of the oldest cultivated spices and is also one of the first to reach the Mediterranean. It is mistakenly called a root but is actually a rhizome or underground stem. It has a fresh, sweet and fragrant flavor. Ginger is a basic ingredient in Asian cuisines and is used all over the world. It adds a fresh note to rich dishes and makes them easily digestible. Fresh ginger is peeled and then grated, sliced or mashed and used accordingly as the recipe calls.

Ginger freezes well and the frozen ginger can easily be sliced into pieces as needed. Sometimes it is best to sauté thin slice of peeled ginger in oil to extract the flavor instead of using the fresh ginger, which may have too pungent a flavor for many.

Pickled ginger is served with sushi as a palate cleanser.

Crystallized ginger adds a sweet and spicy flavor to ice creams, cakes fruit salads and puddings. Ground ginger is added to breads cookies and cakes.

PEANUT SAUCE

A new taste worth trying. It is great served as a dip with carrot sticks or as an accompaniment to spring rolls and grilled chicken on skewers.

Makes about 1 cup

- 225 g / 8 oz raw peanuts
- 1 garlic clove, chopped
- a small handful of parsley leaves, chopped
- 1-2 chillies, chopped or a couple of drops of hot pepper sauce
- 1 tablespoon soy sauce
- 1 teaspoon ground ginger or 1 tablespoon or less freshly grated ginger
- 1 teaspoon honey
- a pinch of cumin
- hot water

Place peanuts in food processor and pulse on and off until they turn into a chunky paste. Then add the rest of the ingredients and whisk to incorporate thoroughly. And finally pour in hot water, one tablespoon at a time until mixture reaches dropping consistency.

B E L L P E P P E R

About this and that

Bruchetta is a traditional Italian antipasto. In its most naked form bruchetta is grilled or toasted (preferably char grilled) bread rubbed with garlic and drizzled with extra-virgin olive oil while still warm. Bruchetta is best made with slightly stale bread. Crisp crusted sourdough bread is the best choice. Toast the bread as close to serving time as possible. Bruchetta toppings are innumerable. Let imagination take over for the topping you would want to serve on each bruchetta.

RED BELL PEPPER SAUCE

There are only two ingredients in this sauce –peppers and onions – but it is an experience on the taste buds.This is a tasty sauce to accompany Polenta Triangles (p.133) or any other dish. The sauce can also be used as a topping for bruchetta (or crostini). Spread generously over prepared bruchetta and top with anything you fancy --- olives, toasted pine nuts, prosciutto, parmesan, ricotta, mozzarella, grilled vegetables, (and the list goes on and on).

SERVES 6

- **5 large red bell peppers or 10 long red peppers, seeded**
- **olive oil**
- **a few drops of hot pepper sauce (such as Tabasco)**
- **1 medium onion, peeled and chopped**
- **sea salt and freshly ground pepper**
- **a pinch of sugar or more**
- **a splash of vinegar (optional)**

Cut the peppers into large pieces. Smear an oven tray with olive oil and lay the peppers on the tray. Cover and bake until peppers are soft. When the peppers are cool, place them in a food processor with all of the rest of the ingredients. Process until smooth. Scrape the sauce into a bowl. Taste and correct seasoning if necessary. Keep refrigerated until ready to use. Return to room temperature before serving.

KITCHEN TOOLS

ORIENTAL DIPPING SAUCE

ORIENTAL DIPPING SAUCE

Serve this as a dipping sauce with Spicy Ovenfried Chickens (p.167) or with spring rolls or Chunky Roasted Potatoes (p.15) replacing the Herb Dip.

SERVES 4

Makes about 1 cup

- **1/4 cup soy sauce**
- **2 tablespoons sugar**
- **3-4 tablespoons tomato ketchup or sun–dried tomato ketchup**
- **1/4 cup + 1 tablespoon Worcestershire sauce**
- **1-2 teaspoons Dijon mustard**
- **1 pinch or more ground allspice**

Whisk together the soy sauce, sugar, ketchup and Worcestershire sauce in a sauce pan. Bring to a simmer and continue cooking for 5 minutes whisking all the while. Then add the mustard and allspice. Remove from heat and cool. Cover tightly and keep in the refrigerator up to one week. Serve cold in small individual bowls.

BEETS

BEET SAUCE

A tasty and colorful sauce which pairs with vegetable and meat dishes equally well. Its flavor accentuates the food it accompanies. Serve it with the Vegetable Terrine (p.39).

Makes abour 2 cups

- **4 medium sized beets, peeled and cut into cubes**
- **1 1/2 cups chicken stock**
- **juice of 1/2 lemon**
- **sea salt and freshly ground pepper**
- **1/2 to 3/4 cup cream**

First cook the beets in chicken stock and lemon juice until quite tender. Add salt and pepper halfway through the cooking process. Purée beets with a hand blender. The purée should have a thickish consistency. Then pass through a sieve for an even smoother texture. Next add the cream and cool to luke warm. If sauce is too thick, thin it down with some milk until a thick pouring consistency is reached. Taste and correct seasoning. Spoon some sauce onto a plate. Spread around with a spoon and place what ever you have planned to serve on the colorful sauce. (Careful – it stains badly!)

About this and that

Curry is a blend of spices. It is not dependant on any one ingredient. It comprises cinnamon, coriander, cumin, turmeric, pepper, cardamom, ginger, nutmeg and cloves.

Curry is the staple spice in Indian cooking. Each cook prepares his or her own blend of spices to produce curry powder. It is advised never to add curry powder to any dish without precooking it in a fat. This brings out its aroma. Curry paste is produced by mixing curry powder with water or broth and is classified as green, red or yellow. The best curry powder and paste are made with whole spices that are first roasted and then ground. If curry powder or paste is seldom used in your kitchen it would be best to keep it in the refrigerator.

BELL PEPPER AND DRIED APRICOT RELISH

BELL PEPPER AND DRIED APRICOT RELISH

This relish perks up any grilled chicken or turkey. Another option is to serve spoonfuls of it with slices of cheese and crusty bread. The spices in the relish accent the flavors that develop during the time it is chilled in the refrigerator.

Makes a bit more than 1 1/2 cups

- **1 large red onion, chopped**
- **1 red bell pepper, seeded, cut into 1 cm wide strips and then cut into cubes**
- **3/4 cup dried apricots, cut into cubes**
- **1/2 cup currants, picked**
- **1/2 cup vinegar**
- **3/4 cup water**
- **1/4 cup brown sugar**
- **1 teaspoon curry powder**
- **sea salt**
- **1/8 teaspoon or less paprika**

Place all ingredients into a saucepan and bring to a boil. Lower heat and simmer, stirring occasionally. Keep pan covered. The relish will thicken in about 45 minutes. Cool completely and then refrigerate until ready to use.

GRAPES

CUCUMBER AND GRAPE SALSA

CUCUMBER AND GRAPE SALSA

Grilled chicken with salsa tastes great. Fresh herbs are natural remedies for many ailments or, just plainly said, herbs are good for us. Luckily it has become easier to obtain fresh herbs nowadays. Look for fresh coriander (cilantro) in the fresh produce section of supermarkets. But I must say parsley can be easily substituted although there would be a distinctive difference in taste and flavor (see page 54). Increase the chilli in the recipe for more kick, depending on how hot you like your food. Cold water may be the best drink to accompany this salsa.

SERVES 4

(Serving size: 1/3 cup)

- **1 cup seedless green grapes, quartered**
- **1 cup red grapes, seeds removed and quartered and each quarter cut in half**
- **1 cucumber, cut in half, seeds scraped with a small spoon and cut into cubes**
- **1 medium onion, finely chopped**
- **a generous handful of coriander leaves**
- **1 fresh red chilli, seeded and chopped**
- **2 tablespoons lemon juice**
- **sea salt**

Soak onion in cold water for 10 minutes. Drain, squeeze all water out and pat dry between paper towels.

Combine all ingredients in a bowl. Cover and chill 2 hours.

Serve with grilled fish or chicken.

SPRING ONIONS

PEACH RELISH

Fresh chutney is great with grilled or poached chicken and fish. The recipe for Poached Chicken Salad with Peaches (p. 55) calls for peach chutney, and I think this no-cook, no-fuss relish (chutney) recipe is the best to use in the dressing. Save what you don't need and use as soon as possible.

Makes 2 cups

- **2 spring onions, finely chopped**
- **2 tablespoons dried currants**
- **1 tablespoon vinegar**
- **1 teaspoon grated fresh ginger or 1/8 teaspoon ground ginger**
- **3 – 4 firm medium peaches, peeled, pitted and cut into tiny cubes**

Combine all ingredients in a bowl and toss gently. Refrigerate covered for a few hours. Toss once in a while to let flavors mingle.

Try this. Add 1 chilli, seeds removed and very finely chopped and 2 tablespoons brown sugar. Then serve the chutney with roasted or poached poultry.

About this and that

Preserve lemons are lemons that have been preserved in a salt-lemon juice mixture for about 30 days. Spices such as cinnamon, cloves and coriander are sometimes added as well. Preserved lemons have a silken texture and a very distinctive flavor. They are an indispensable ingredient in Moroccan cooking and are widely used as a flavoring by many of the leading chefs.

PRESERVED LEMONS

Curing lemons gives the fruit a new dimension and expands its repertoire. Stuff a preserved lemon into the cavity of a chicken to be roasted or add the purée of 1/2 preserved lemon and 1 teaspoon mustard into 2 cups mayonnaise and serve with Roasted Potato Wedges (p.15), or throw in a few slices of preserved lemons into stews or purée just a little bit into a vinaigrette.

- **8 ripe lemons, preferably with thin, shiny and unblemished skin**
- **sea salt**
- **1/4 cup sugar**
- **lemon juice, enough to cover lemons in jar(s)**

Cut lemons lengthwise into quarters but take care not to cut all the way through. Holding the lemon in your hand discard as many seeds as you can and then sprinkle with salt, about 1 1/2 teaspoons for each lemon. Squeeze the lemon closed in your hand and place it into a sterilised jar. You may also choose to divide lemons into two jars. Pack them very lightly. Cover all the way to the top with lemon juice. Sprinkle the sugar into the jar. Secure the lid tightly and store in the refrigerator. In 6 – 7 weeks the lemons will be ready to use with very soft peels. Slice, chop or purée as you like.

L E M O N S

PRESERVED LEMON AND BREAD SAUCE

This sauce brings lemony zing to lamb and poultry dishes. It tastes great on freshly baked crusty bread. It can also be served as a dip for crudities.

Makes about 2 cups

- **4 sourdough bread slices, crusts removed**
- **1 cup parsley leaves**
- **1 1/2 preserved lemons, flesh removed, rinsed, dried and cut to pieces**
- **1/4 cup capers in brine, rinsed well and drained**
- **extra-virgin olive oil**
- **freshly ground pepper**

Blend everything in the food processor. Add enough oil to moisten. Taste and season with freshly ground pepper. Let rest at least 1 hour before serving. Thin sauce with water or lemon juice if too thick.

Tips + Tricks + Techniques

The shells of nuts provide a protective cover that keeps them from turning rancid. Store unshelled nuts in airtight containers. Store shelled nuts in the refrigerator. Unsaturated nut oils oxidize quickly on exposure to heat, light and air and nuts become rancid easily losing their nutrients. LIGHTLY roasting reduces the effect of rancidity and makes them easier to digest. Always toast or grind nuts as you have need for them in your cooking. Toast nuts in a skillet over medium heat tossing them occasionally until they brown lightly. Nuts provide flavor, body and crunch as well as vital nutrients. Use nuts in moderation but do intrigrate them into your cooking.

NUT MILK

I first became aware of a variety of milk options –soy milk, rice milk -- due to a dietary restriction, namely lactose intolerance. I now know that milk is not nature's perfect food. Although it remains to be my favorite, I have to replace it with others in my kitchen. Nut milk is one of them. There are numerous advantages to using nut milk in cooking. There is of course no lactose or casein in it. Furthermore it contains monounsaturated fat instead of saturated. If you are not allergic to nuts, I say, experiment with it.

Grind raw nuts such as blanched almonds or cashews to a fine powder. Use a blender or a food processor. Add water by tablespoons. Process at high speed for a minute or two to ensure that the mixture is thoroughly blended. Start with 2 tablespoons and continue until the desired consistency is reached. The end product can be as heavy as cream or as lean as fat-free milk. For a finer, creamier texture strain the liquid through a sieve. Use it in any recipe you choose. Substitute it for cream in soups or cream based sauces or simply serve it as cream to accompany desserts.

Tips+Tricks+ Techniques

A brief blanching in boiling water for 2-3 minutes often facilitates easy peeling of tomatoes, peaches, and apricots. Although they have thin edible skins, which are also full of nutrients, it is standard practice in the kitchen to peel off the skins of these fruits when a recipe asks for it. The thin skins slip off easily after blanching. Always refresh vegetables or fruits in ice water and peel immediately. The brown hull of almonds is loosened with the same technique. Blanching is required to slip off the skin easily. The removal of skins is necessary for a fine delicate end product.

BASIC TOMATO SAUCE

Tomatoes whether fresh, canned, sun-dried, puréed or turned into a sauce make an important contribution to our daily nutrition. This is my basic tomato recipe which is very versatile because it can be embellished in so many ways with infinite applications -- from gratins, pasta, crepes to chicken and fish, to name but a few. The sauce can be refregirated for up to 1 week or frozen for up to 2 months. End of the summer is a busy time in my kitchen when I make sauces to be frozen with the perfectly ripe and flavorful seasonal tomatoes.

Makes 2 – 3 cups

- **6 large ripe tomatoes, cut in half crosswise, seeded and coarsely grated**
- **3 large ripe tomatoes, skinned, cut in half crosswise, seeded and finely diced**
- **5 teaspoons olive oil** • **1 medium onion, diced**
- **3 – 4 garlic cloves, peeled and finely chopped**
- **3 – 4 teaspoons sugar or more**
- **sea salt and freshly ground pepper**

In a large covered pan sweat the onion and garlic in the olive oil over medium heat about 10 minutes. Stir occasionally. Take care not to brown onion or garlic. If there isn't enough moisture in the pan add 1 tablespoon of boiling water and continue until the onions are translucent. Stir in all of the tomatoes. Add the sugar, salt and pepper. Simmer uncovered for 15 minutes stirring occasionally. By this time the sauce should be thick. If not, then continue cooking until it reaches a thick sauce consistency. Taste for seasoning and add more sugar or salt as necessary. Cool and refrigerate or freeze as needed. Try the variations on the following page.

T O M A T O E S

TOMATO SAUCE VARIATIONS

By adding vegetables, herbs, spices and wine, you can vary the taste of tomato sauce and expand its usage especially with pasta and polenta as well as with fish and chicken. In my opinion, tomato sauce made with Oven – Dried Cherry Tomatoes (p.217) tops the list of any tomato sauce I have tasted. The flavor that comes from roasting gives distinctive fragrance and the sauce hardly needs any additional seasoning. Here are a few more suggestions.

Chunky Tomato – Red Bell Pepper Sauce

Roast 3 bell peppers directly over a flame until charred all around. Place in a paper bag or wrap in plastic wrap. Let cool and then remove all of the charred skin. Remove seeds. Wash and pat dry. Then chop into tiny pieces and combine into tomato sauce. Taste and correct seasoning. This is great on bruchetta and polenta. Add some cream and turn it into a simple yet tasty sauce for pasta.

Tomato Sauce with Herbs

Add herbs to sauce during the last 5 minutes of cooking. Fresh herbs offer the best aroma and flavor. I like to pair thyme, oregano and rosemary. 2 sprigs of each herb is plenty. But remove sprigs before storing or serving.

Tangy Tomato Sauce

Stir in 1 or more minced chillies or add hot pepper sauce (such as Tabasco) to tomato sauce. Add 2 or 3 handfuls of finely chopped parsley as well.

Balsamic flavored Tomato Sauce

Stir in 2 – 3 tablespoons balsamic vinegar during the last 10 minutes of cooking time.

About this and that

Bouquet garni, a French term, describes a bundle of parsley, a spring of fresh thyme and a bay leaf tied together to flavor broths, stocks and sauces. Sometimes peppercorns, a piece of leek or a celery stalk complete this bouquet. Traditionally herbs are wrapped in cheesecloth and secured with kitchen twine. Practically speaking, a coffee filter can easily replace the cheesecloth. Bouquet garni can also be purchased ready-made in the spice section of supermarkets. Dried herbs and other aromatics are packed in bags, ready to be used at the start of the cooking process.

VEGETABLE BROTH

Use this recipe only as a rough guide. Improvise with the vegetables of your choice. Whenever I boil artichokes I use the cooking liquid as the basis for a vegetable broth. And as a rule I add a tiny amount of olive oil to give the broth body, and I never use salt. A great improvisation is to make the broth using roasted vegetables for a richness and debth of flavor. Some of this broth can be used immediately and the rest can be frozen for future use.

Makes a lot (or enough)

- 4 leeks, trimmed, thinly sliced and washed
- 2 celery stalks, chopped
- 2 medium carrots peeled and chopped
- 2 medium onions, peeled and chopped
- 16 cups water
- 1 packet bouquet garni or
- 2 bay leaves
- 1 small bunch parsley
- 1/4 teaspoon black pepper corns
- 2 sprigs fresh thyme
- 1 sprig rosemary

Combine all of the ingredients in a large pot. Bring to a boil. Then turn the heat down and let it SIMMER until liquid is reduced by half. Strain the stock through a sieve into another container. Discard the solids. At this stage you can choose to do one of two things. Either cool broth and use or return it to the pot and boil until it is reduced further more to a desired strength. This is especially worth to do if you are planning to use the broth for risotto or a sauce. The intense flavors enhance the taste of the sauce.

The broth can be frozen up to 4 months and used in a variety of ways – when making soups, sauces, risotto or as poaching liquid for fish or chicken.

CARROTS

CHICKEN STOCK

Making a good stock is not difficult but it is time consuming. The extra effort of making home-made stock is priceless. Stock can be frozen and having some stored away in the freezer yields itself to great options in the kitchen. I freeze stock in ice–cube trays and when they are set I empty them into freezer bags and seal tightly. The cubes of concentrated flavor wait to be used in sauces, gravies and soups. Use the cooked chicken meat in salads, sandwiches or soups.

Makes a lot (or enough)

- **1 whole chicken (about 1 kg), chopped into pieces**
- **16 cups water**
- **1 large onion, peeled and quartered**
- **1 large carrot, peeled and cut into chunks**
- **1 leek, trimmed and chopped**
- **1 packet bouquet garni (p.252) or**
- **2 bay leaves** • **pepper corns**
- **5 – 6 sprigs each fresh parsley and thyme**

Remove the skin from the chicken pieces. Rinse and place in a pot. Pour hot water over the chicken pieces to cover. Bring to a boil and continue cooking for a few minutes. Then remove chicken pieces and discard the water. It is necessary to do this to ensure that the stock is clear. Place chicken pieces back in the pot. Pour in 16 cups fresh water. Bring to a boil and remove all the scum that has accumulated on the surface. Now you are ready to add the rest of the ingredients. Drop them in all at once. SIMMER for another 30 minutes. Remove the pot from the heat and strain the stock.

Cool completely and freeze in portions for up to 4 months.

AND FINALLY...

It has taken me quite a number of years to compile this collection of recipes.
I took my time because the process seemed more satisfying than the end result. It was fun. I had a good time. I am happy with the final product. But now that it is completed, I'm eager for it to reach you.

Our lives are a work in progress and in my progress I have something to share with you.
Through this humble collection of recipes we will develop a bond. You are a part of this book. The collection of recipes is the conversation we might be having.
I would be overjoyed if you thought I was there, in your kitchen, as you cook. Enjoy using the recipes. Enjoy sharing them at your dinner table with those you love.

I think we already know each other.

Until the next collection.....

Take care and happy cooking.

CONTENTS BY RECIPE

ABOUT THIS AND THAT

TIPS, TRICKS, TECH.

TIPS AND TRICKS AND TECHNIQUES

REFERENCES

Bremness, Lesley.
Herbs. DORLING KINDERSLEY, 1994

Davidson, Alan.
The Penguin Companion to Food. PENGUİN BOOKS, 2002

Dries, Jan & Dries, Inge.
The Food Combining Bible ELEMENT, 2002

Norman, Jill.
The Complete Book of Spices DORLING KINDERSLEY, 1990

Kamman, Madeleine.
The New Making of a Cook.
The Art,Techniques,and Science of Good Cooking.
WILLIAM MORROW AND COMPANY,INC, 1997

Pitchford, Paul.
Healing with Whole Foods
Asian Traditions and Modern Nutrition

Spaull, Susan with Bruce-Gardyne, Lucinda.
Leiths Techniques Bible.BLOOMSBURRY, 2003

Roberts, Jonathan.
The Origins of Fruit and Vegetables. UNIVERSE, 2001

Stobart, Tom.
The Cook's Encyclopedia
Ingredients and Processes

Teubner, Christian.
The Vegetable Bible. WHITECAP BOOKS,1998

Tyrer, Polly.
Leiths Vegetarian Bible. BLOOMSBURRY, 2002

Cooking at Home with the Culinary Institute of America
JOHN WILEY and SONS, INC. 2002

The Professional Chef, 7th Edition
Cooking at Home with the Culinary Institute of America
JOHN WILEY and SONS, INC. 2002

Food Lexicon, Das Teubner.

The Complete Cook, Hamlyn.

The Complete Food Guide, Könemann

ACKNOWLEDGEMENTS

This collection could not have been complete without the help and patience of many wonderful people. Words are not enough to express my thanks, but I am going to try anyway...

Heartfelt thanks go to many friends far and near for all the encouragement and genuine support they have offered.

I owe many thanks to Selma Yalter who has read the text from cover to cover. More personal thanks are owed to Adem Şaşmaz who typed each and every recipe and even enjoyed the tedious process of correcting and erasing and changing and rewriting and so on and so on.

Immense thanks go to the creative team at REKLAM MERKEZİ. The following deserve special thanks: Hakkı Sal and Semih Tozlu, for their creative support and dedicated assistance; Nevin Kuloğlu for her art work; Tunç Şardağ, for his painstaiking work in applying my copy editing.

My sincere thanks go to the entire team at Paralel Tasarım in Istanbul with special gratitude to Lâle Apa for her faith in my work and for her superb guidance. Elif Dumanoğlu and Zuhal Aydıncık both deserve special thanks for their professional, administrative and creative support.

Without the harmonious teamwork, this book could not have come alive.

I must express loving gratitude to Sevinç Kocagöz who opened her kitchen and recipe book to me with love and whose Lemon Meringue Pie and Chocolate Cake recipes I first tried baking when I was 13 or 14 (my toddler years in the kitchen) and have proudly used ever since.

More gratitude goes to 'Mama' Elaine Juni who taught me that the heart of a home is the kitchen. And in her kitchen, by watching and trying, I learned to bake and to freeze and more important of all, to cook for a crowd and to pre-plan for meals.

THANK YOU Emin and Selmin, for your dedicated belief in my culinary gift. It underlies all that I have accomplished in the kitchen, including this book. It has been inspirational.

And last but not least, a BIG thank you goes to Gün, my, provider, and enthusiastic recipe-taster. I received generous help. I am grateful.

Thank YOU for sharing this book with me.

If I have forgotten names......I am immensely grateful to you, too. Many thanks, repeatedly and forever.

İNCİ ERKER BİRSEL

İnci Erker Birsel was born and raised in İzmir, Turkey. After completing her education, she returned to her Alma Mater, İzmir American Collegiate Institute (ACI), as an English Teacher. İnci has been a full-time mother and a full-time cook for 38 years. She has always felt very lucky to have been able to combine the three things she enjoys most – bringing up her children, teaching and cooking. This is the first collection of recipes she has compiled after her retirement from teaching. She hopes a new one will follow soon.

NOTES

Gingerbread (Niki's).

25g Demerara Sugar.
75g Butter
50g Golden Syrup
75g Black Treacle.
225g Plain Flour.
$1\frac{1}{2}$ tsp of ground ginger
$1\frac{1}{2}$ tsp of Baking powder
$\frac{1}{2}$ tsp of Bicarb.

$\frac{1}{2}$ tsp of salt.
$\frac{1}{4}$ pint of milk.
1 med size egg beaten.

1. Microwave sugar, bu[illegible], [illegible]reacle & suryp in until melted
2. Stir in sie[illegible] dry ingredients
3. Mix in egg & milk.
4. Beat.
5. Line Tin — 35/40 min. 350°F.
6. Leave to coo[illegible]

NOTES

NOTES

NAVY

NAVAL OPERATIONS IN THE '80s

USN

MICHAEL SKINNER

ARMS AND ARMOUR PRESS

Dedication:

To George Hall
and Michael Whitten
and all the boys of Hobby Night
all around the world.

First published in Great Britain
in 1986 by Arms and Armour Press Limited,
2-6 Hampstead High Street, London NW3 1QQ.

Distributed in Australia by
Capricorn Link (Australia) Pty. Ltd., P.O. Box 665,
Lane Cove, New South Wales 2066, Australia.

ISBN 0-85368-822-2

All photographs courtesy of the United States Navy unless otherwise indicated.

The author's photographs were taken exclusively with Nikon EM Series cameras and lenses.

Cover Design by Bill Yenne
Book Design by C. Swanson

Half-title: "Big John," (*John F. Kennedy*, CV-67)

Title: Guided missile cruiser *England* fires a Standard surface-to-air missile. *Photo courtesy FMC.*

This page: Haddock, Permit-class nuclear submarine, comes under the Golden Gate Bridge.

Contents

The *Enterprise.*

Preface

The USN is a particularly *American* navy. They have their own style, go their own way. No other navy in the world, for example, operates a supercarrier. But big-deck, nuclear-powered carrier fever, along with a similar, unproven faith in nuclear-powered fast attack submarines, dominate American naval thinking.

It's always been that way. The United States Navy has a history of audacious acts. Years before there *was* a Navy Department, years before the new country had proper warships, the colonists twisted the tail of the British lion at sea. The feat was repeated in the War of 1812. America had seventeen ships, the British more than six hundred. But the U.S. won that war, as well.

In fact, the USN has never lost a war at sea. They kept the sea lanes open and the supplies flowing in both world wars, and thrashed the Japanese in the Pacific in an almost unilateral campaign. In Korea, in Vietnam, in hundreds of hotspots since, America's response to crisis has been a *naval* response.

But there's new trouble on the horizon for the American Navy. If the USN is following a different drummer, the Soviet Union steps to the beat of navy marches of the past. As one defense analyst put it, the Russians are hoping to win the next war with the tactics that lost the last one: the Nazi wolfpack concept and Japanese-style kamikaze attacks. Whether or not these concepts can succeed by substituting nuclear attack submarines for U-boats and cruise missiles for kamikaze planes depends on whom you talk with. We'll discuss what the experts are saying. But it's to be hoped that we'll never find out for sure.

The next war at sea holds the potential of great destruction, even without the use of nuclear weapons. I say "potential" because there are a number of scenarios that can be postulated, from an all out, bloody slugfest to a "phony war" in which both sides stay out of one another's way, waiting for an elusive tactical advantage.

Losing means utter destruction. The winner will not be much better off. Ships will run though ammunition at an alarming rate. It could be that the side with the last missile will win the war. The aspects of naval warfare that get the least attention in peacetime—logistics, damage control, training—will be the deciding factors in wartime. Weapons alone are not enough. There are going to be a lot of shiny new ships at the bottom of the ocean at the end of the next war.

This book kicks off the Presidio Seapower series. It is meant to be an overview, an introduction to naval operations and the current issues under debate in the naval world. As such, it is necessarily sketchy at times. Whole books have been written just on naval guns, for example. Later books in the series will cover naval topics in greater depth.

Some subjects have already been tackled. For example, *CV: Carrier Aviation* neatly bridges the gap between Presidio's Seapower and Airpower series. Carriers are also covered in *USN,* of course, but this book concentrates on the ships rather than the planes.

Good Navy data is hard to find. The Navy itself is not that forthcoming, and most of the published material just repeats earlier, often incorrect, reports. There are only a few people doing original work on naval matters in this country, starting with the "two Normans," Norman Polmar and Norman Friedman. Jan S. Breemer's *U.S. Naval Developments* was also helpful, as was the U.S. Naval Institute's *Bluejackets Manual.* Of course, no one can write anything about the Navy without first consulting the Institute's *Proceedings,* the monthly bible of the American naval community. *The Hook* is a similar publication that deals with the world of carrier aviation.

A word of caution: I have never been on a Soviet warship, nor have I been in the combat information center (CIC) of a ship in action, though I write about both topics in detail. Every effort has been made to be as accurate as possible, both in fact and tone, but some things can be known only first hand. Valuable insight was provided by manuscript readers Capt. Richard Phohli, USN Retired, Lt. Mark Nicholson, USNR, and Alan Toon. Still, any errors remaining are my responsibility, and I want to know about them. *USN* will be periodically updated, and any corrections, clarifications, or additions are cheerfully welcomed.

Many thanks this time around to Tom Hall of the Navy's Recruiting Command, Bob Suarez, editor of *Raytheon Magazine* (where some portions of Chapters 3 and 4 first appeared), and the Kaypro Corporation. Thanks also to the officers and men of the U.S.S. *America,* U.S.S. *Barry,* and U.S.S. *Lexington* for their kind assistance, as well as all those crewmen, ashore and at sea, admirals and deck apes, who took the time to try to explain what it's like to spend a life on the Great Ocean.

Michael Skinner
Atlanta, 1986

USN Glossary

Navy talk is Navy talk; nautical lingo, most of it. It also shares a lot of expressions with the military aviation community. The USN's contribution to the vocabulary takes the form of jawbreaking pronouns.

Some of the terms that follow do not appear in the book. They are printed here in the hope that readers who want to research the Navy on their own will not run into the problems the author did, trying to figure out what the anchor-clankers are up to.

ACLS—Automatic Carrier Landing System; radar-directed automated landing system for use in bad weather
AE—Ammunition ship
AEGIS—USN air defense system embarked on Ticonderoga class cruisers
AF—Store ship
AFS—Combat store ship
AGI—Auxiliary Vessel, Miscellaneous type, Intelligence; U.S. Navy designation for small, unarmed Soviet intelligence ships
Air Boss—Primary Air Controller; ship's officer in charge of flight operations
Air Wing—A group of aircraft embarked on a carrier
Alert Five—Aircraft armed and fueled, ready to launch in five minutes
Alfa Strike—An all-out carrier air wing attack on a sea or land target
AO—Oiler
AOE—Fast combat support ship
AOR—Underway replenishment oiler
APU—Auxiliary Power Unit; machinery attached to an aircraft to provide power on the ground
ASM—Air-to-Surface Missile
ASROC—Antisubmarine Rocket; a rocket-boosted torpedo. SUBROC is a similar weapon fired from submarine torpedo tubes
ASuW—Antisurface Warfare
ASW—Antisubmarine Warfare
Autodog—Navy slang for soft ice-cream
Bagel Station—CVBG operating area in the eastern Mediterranean Sea
Barrier—Safety net rigged to snare aircraft unable to make an arrested landing
Battle Group—A task force of Navy warships, usually centered around an aircraft carrier
BB—Battleship
Beam—The widest part of a ship
Big John—The fixed crane on an aircraft carrier
Bingo—The amount of fuel needed to return to base
Blue Shirts—Crewmen charged with moving and spotting aircraft on the flight deck
Blue Water Ops—Carrier flight operations conducted beyond the range of land bases
Boatswain—Pronounced "bo'sun"; an all-purpose seaman's rating
Bolter—A failed landing attempt in which the aircraft fails to hook the wire
Boola-boola—A direct hit in an air-to-air missile exercise
Boomer—Strategic missile submarine
Bow—The front end of a ship
Box—A device used to center the aircraft on the catapult
Bridge—A command center located high in a ship's superstructure
Bridle—An attachment that connects older aircraft to the catapult shuttle
Brown Shirts—Plane captains
Bug Juice—Artificial fruit drink used in place of booze aboard ship
Bulkhead—The wall of a ship's cabin
CAESAR—A network of sonar sensors placed in the Atlantic
CAG—Commander Air Group; a WW II term still used to refer to the air wing commander

CAP—Combat Air Patrol
CAPTOR—Mk-60 ASW mine
Cat—Catapult
CATCC—Carrier Air Traffic Control Center
Centerline—Line drawn down the middle of the flight deck
CG—Guided missile cruiser
CGN—Nuclear-powered guided missile cruiser
CIC—Combat Information Center; command center located inside a ship
CNO—Chief of Naval Operations
COD—Carrier Onboard Delivery
CODAG—Combined Diesel and Gas (turbine) propulsion
Codex—Two-digit number on an aircraft's tail
CODOG—Combined Diesel or Gas (turbine) propulsion
COLOSSUS—A network of sonar sensors placed in the Pacific
Commission—To enter a ship into active service
Corsair II—A-7 attack aircraft
COSAG—Combined Steam and Gas (turbine) propulsion
Cranial—A leather and laminate helmet worn by flight deck personnel
CSGN—Nuclear-powered guided missile strike cruiser (never built)
CV—Aircraft carrier
CVBG—Aircraft Carrier Battle Group
CVN—Nuclear-powered aircraft carrier
CVW—Carrier air wing
Cyclic Ops—An integrated schedule of carrier take-offs and landings
DD—Destroyer
DDG—Guided missile destroyer
DGLN—Nuclear-powered guided missile destroyer leader; original designation for ships later classified as CGNs
DGN—Nuclear-powered guided missile destroyer (never built)
Displacement—The amount of water displaced by a ship
Dixie Cup—Nickname for the traditional sailor's cap
Dodge City—Diego Garcia
Dosimeter—A safety device used for measuring the amount of radiation to which a crewman has been exposed
Draft—The depth of a ship from waterline to keel
Dropline—An orange line down the stern in line with the carrier's centerline
ECCM—Electronic Counter-countermeasures
ECM—Electronic Countermeasures
Elevator—Movable platform used for transferring aircraft between the flight deck and hangar deck
ELF—Extremely Low Frequency
Engine Order Telegraph—A device for transmitting directions between the bridge and engine room
EW—Electronic Warfare
FF—Frigate
FFG—Guided missile frigate
Flight Deck—The open deck of an aircraft carrier where flight operations are conducted
FLOLS—Fresnel Lens Optical Landing system; also called the Light Landing Device, "ball" or "meatball"
FOD—Foreign Object Damage
Foul Line—A line drawn on the flight deck at the boundary of the recovery area
Fouled Deck—An obstructed deck temporarily closed to landings
Galley—Enlisted man's dining area
Gator—Amphibious warfare personnel; a Marine
Gedunk—Ship's snack bar
Gonzo Station—CVBG operating area in the Arabian Sea
Green Shirts—Crewmen involved in launchings and recoveries
Greyhound—C-2 Carrier Onboard Delivery (COD) aircraft
Gunner—Warship not armed with missiles

Handler—Crewman involved with spotting and moving aircraft; also called "mangler"
Hangar Deck—Area underneath flight deck where aircraft are maintained and stored
Harpoon—RGM-84; USN medium-range cruise missile
Hawkeye—E-2C radar aircraft: the "Hummer" or "Frisbee"
Helmsman—Crewman in charge of steering a ship
Helo—Helicopter
Hold—Cargo space in a ship
Holdback—Breakaway link that connects the nose tow to the catapult shuttle
Hook—Tailhook; a steel bar underneath the aircraft that snags the arresting hook
Hook Runner—The Green Shirt responsible for securing the aircraft to the catapult
Hornet—F/A-18 fighter-bomber
Hot Pump—Refueling an aircraft with the engines running
Intruder—A-6 attack aircraft
I/O—Indian Ocean
Island—The superstructure of an aircraft carrier
JBD—Jet Blast Deflector
Knot—Nautical mile per hour; about 1.15 miles per hour

KA-6D tanker, with folded wings.

LAMPS—Light Airborne Multi-purpose System; a shipborne helicopter and its associated electronic systems on board ship, used to prosecute submarines
Langley Stripe—A band of color on either side of the cockpits of some Navy fighters
LCAC—Landing Craft Air Cushion
LCM—Landing Craft, Mechanized; "Mike boat"
LCU—Landing Craft, Utility
Loose Deuce—A Navy tactical fighter formation
LPD—Amphibious transport (dock)
LSD—Landing ship (dock)
LSO—Landing Signal Officer
LVTP—Marines' workhorse landing craft
LVA—Experimental replacement for LTVP
MAD—Magnetic Anomaly Detector
Marshall—The holding pattern behind the carrier
Military—Military power; full engine thrust without using afterburner (also called "buster")
Modex—Three-digit code on the nose of carrier aircraft
Modloc—Modified local operating area; the perimeter of CVBG operations
Mouse—Two-way headsets worn by flight deck crewmen
Mule—Carrier aircraft tug; also called "Stubby"
NavAirSysCom—Naval Air Systems Command
NFO—Naval Flight Officer
Non-skid—Rubber-like coating compound used on the flight deck
Nose Tow—The part of the forward landing gear to which the catapult shuttle is attached
NTDS—Naval Tactical Data System; U.S. Navy voice and data-link network
Nugget—A rookie naval aviator
OOD—Officer of the Deck
Outlaw Shark—USN program for over-the-horizon targeting of cruise missiles
Overhead—The ceiling of a ship's cabin
P-School—A short course in flight ops for new carrier deck hands
P-12—Crash truck
PLAT Channel—Pilot's Landing Aid Television; a closed-circuit TV channel piped through the carrier that monitors the flight deck
Pack—A group of aircraft on deck
Pantry—The ship's food storeroom
Phalanx—Mk-15 CIWS (Close-in Weapons System); a six-barrel, antiaircraft Gatling gun
Phantom—F-4 fighter-bomber
PHM—Hydrofoil patrol boat
Phoenix—AIM-54 long-range air-to-air missile
Pickle—A switch held by the LSO to signal a wave-off to an aircraft attempting to land
Plane Guard—The helicopter or ship assigned to search and rescue during flight ops
Polaris—UGM-27; first generation USN submarine-launched strategic missile
Port—The left side of a ship
Poseidon—UGM-73; second generation USN submarine-launched strategic missile
Prairie Masker—USN ASW countermeasure
Pri-Fly—Primary Flight Control; the carrier's flight control center for launches and recoveries
Primary Air Controller—The Air Boss
Prowler—EA-6B electronic warfare aircraft
Purple Shirt—A carrier crewman assigned to refueling aircraft
Quartermaster—The ship's navigator
RI0—Radar Intercept Officer; the NFO "backseater" in an F-14 or F-4
Rack—Bunk
Ramp—The extreme aft end of the flight deck; also called the rounddown
Rank—Position in the military hierarchy, officer or enlisted man
Rate—The level of a rating
Rating—Occupations in the Navy
Ready Room—Squadron headquarters aboard the carrier
Red Shirt—Flight deck crewman assigned to ordnance handling
Retract Engine—Small motor that lifts the tailhook after landing
Roller—Navy slang for hot-dog

SAM—Surface-to-Air Missile
Scrubber—Vehicle that wipes seawater and fuel off the flight deck
Sea King—SH-3 helicopter
Second Fleet—USN East Coast fleet
Senso—Air crewman charged with ASW search
Seventh Fleet—USN Pacific fleet
Shooter—A warship equipped with surface-to-air missiles
Shuttle—That part of the catapult that attaches to the launching aircraft
Sidewinder—AIM-9 heat-seeking air-to-air missile
Sixth Fleet—USN Mediterranean fleet
SLEP—Service Life Extension Program; an extensive overhaul designed to prolong the use of Navy carriers
Slider—Navy slang for hamburger
Small Boy—Any small warship
Snipe—Engine-room worker
Sparrow—AIM-7 radar-guided air-to-air missile
SSM—Surface-to-Surface Missile
Stack—The ship's smokestack or funnel
Standard-ER—RIM-67 radar-guided, extended-range surface-to-air missile
Standard-MR—RIM-66 radar-guided, medium-range surface-to-air missile
Starboard—The right side of a ship
Stern—The aft end of a ship
Superstructure—The part of a ship above the hull, exclusive of armament
Surface Action Group—A task force organized around surface warships
TARPS—Tactical Air Reconnaissance Pod System; a recce pod slung underneath the F-14
Tacco—Air crewman charged with ASW attack
Tall Moose—Unusually high carrier landing
Tender—A ship that services a group of smaller vessels
Third Fleet—USN West Coast fleet
Three Wire—The third of four arresting cables, counting up from the stern
Tillie—Movable flight deck crane
Tomahawk—A family of USN long-range cruise missiles
Tomcat—F-14 fighter
Towed Array—A group of sonar sensors dragged behind the ship on a long cable
Trap—An arrested aircraft landing on a carrier
Trident—UGM-93; third generation USN submarine-launched strategic missile
URG—Underway Replenishment Group
USS—United States Ship
V/STOL—Vertical/Short Take-Off and Landing
VDS—Variable Depth Sonar
VLS—Vertical Launch System
Vampire—An incoming guided missile
Viking—S-3 ASW aircraft; the "Hoover"
Vulture's Row—The observation deck on the carrier's island
Wardroom—The officers' dining area
Weather Deck—The main deck of a ship
White Shirt—Plane inspector, also called "checker"
Wire—Arresting cable
XO—Executive Officer
Yankee Station—CVBG operating area in the South China Sea
Yellow Shirt—Aircraft movement director
Zone 5—Maximum thrust in afterburner

Chapter One

The Great Ocean

The Great Ocean rolls across more than two thirds of the earth. Six miles of water cover its deepest point; at its shallowest, it is the depth of a droplet vaporizing on a summer's beach. The Great Ocean freezes white at the ends of the earth and nearly steams in the middle. Seven seas, four oceans, countless gulfs, bays, rivers, lakes, and canals all flow into the Great Ocean. It can be blue and featureless, indistinguishable from the darkening sky. Or it can churn into an ever-changing range of white-peaked mountains, a chain of gray-green volcanoes quaking violently under the deck, spewing foam and mist. The Great Ocean is blue, gray, green, white and—if you hold a tiny drop of its 620 million cubic miles in your hand—utterly clear.

The Great Ocean is the highway of the world's commerce. Raw materials sail in, manufactured goods sail out. The actual numbers soon zoom into incomprehension. Sooner or later, coming or going, everything floats across the Great Ocean.

The almost daily advances in military technology have compressed time and space, but they have not lessened the sea's importance as a bulwark for some and an obstacle to others. All but two of America's forty-odd allies lie overseas. American men and equipment must be shipped across the sea to fight, and, once there, they must be supported with more shipping. A contemporary American serviceman in the field will consume his weight in supplies—food, fuel and ammunition—every day. Only the sea can support such a heavy logistical burden. If, in the next war, the battle of the Great Ocean is lost, further battles cannot be won.

America, whether or not it ever realizes it, is a maritime power like virtually every other industrial nation. Western Europe must rely upon shipping to bring in the ten key minerals needed to fire the furnaces of industry. Japan is even more dependent. Neither area has any oil to speak of. The United States is better off only comparatively.

There is only one exception. The Soviet Union, with its vast, rich landmass and restricted economy, is the only major world power whose fortunes do not ride on the tides of the Great Ocean. The implications are complex and enormous.

With the semi-retirement of the Royal Navy, the USN has inherited the responsibility of keeping the Great Ocean open to the West. In peacetime, the American Navy strides across the one sea, showing the flag in countries beyond the compass of land bases and diplomacy. In war, it must keep

New Jersey during sea trials off California.

the sea-lanes open and carry the fight to the enemy's strongholds. And in the war beyond the war, the USN maintains the black watch underneath the Great Ocean, always ready for the final battle.

It is an intricate and imposing mission, one not always understood by either the public or the other military services. Lately, however, the Navy has been caught in the searchlight of publicity. Perhaps more than any other service, the USN has benefited from the fiscal bonanza the Reagan administration has presented to the military. Some of the results are readily apparent—old battleships bristle with new weapons, aircraft carriers are building on the ways, and the superstructures of new warships tower in long dormant shipyards.

But the Navy's build-up is not without its critics. Some question the way the precious resources are being spent. It takes at least ten years for modern ships to make the voyage from the drawing boards to the Great Ocean. The American Navy of the next century is being launched today. Will a battleship built in the 1940s—however modernized—be able to cope with the threats of the year 2000? Even the new ships do not necessarily reflect new ideas. The next nuclear carriers are being built to a twenty-year-old design, though they are not scheduled to be retired until 2040. The latest cruisers boast a new anti-air defense system, but from the hull down, their design goes back nearly fifteen years.

It costs about $35 billion to buy a nuclear carrier battle group—the supercarrier, its aircraft, and its escorts—and run them for thirty years. Could that money be better spent? The tab for the Navy's newest aircraft, the F-18 Hornet, runs about $30 million. Is it worth it? The Navy wants a hundred nuclear attack submarines, at about $700 million a shot. Is it wise to invest that kind of money in a relatively untried weapons system?

The debate over defense costs is a common peacetime theme of the popular press. And certainly the Navy isn't the only service with a fondness for expensive hardware. When the bullets aren't flying, it's a tough call—all weapons are useless in peacetime and priceless in wartime.

But there is a more fundamental reason than dollars and cents to make sure the right weapons are built before the fighting. Long lead times and a vulnerable industrial base virtually ensures that the Navy would fight World War III with the weapons at hand. Is the Navy building the right ships, the right planes? Is the fleet they're building up to the monumental task of controlling the Great Ocean? Everyone has their own answers to those questions. We'll take a look at the modern American Navy—what it is, where it came from, and where it's going.

This would all be academic if it were not for the navy of the Soviet Union. The Soviet Navy has its own problems, but it is the American Navy's only real rival in the battle to control the Great Ocean. Neither Navy has experienced combat on the high seas since World War II, but unlike most Air Force and Army units, American Navy ships confront their Soviet counterparts every day. Each side gets a close-up look at its potential adversary, with the laws of the sea dictating that some of the confrontations fall just short of actual combat.

There is much to admire about the Soviet Navy, including their rapid progress and their willingness to innovate. There is also much to dislike. Contradictory reports of the worth of the Soviet Navy appear constantly in the press. We are concerned when the Soviets build ships similar to ours. We are concerned when they do not. We'll take a look at the Soviet Navy, too. But first, let's define what the navies are fighting for.

The Great Ocean covers 73 percent of the earth, but it is geography that determines which slivers of the sea the Navy is willing to fight and die for. The Great Ocean is vast, but, for the most part, militarily insignificant; oftentimes the sea assumes an importance inversely proportional to the amount of space it occupies between two land masses.

The places where the Great Ocean squeezes strategically are called "choke points". At these points great fleets can be bottled up, and small amounts of firepower can make a big difference. The current naval strategies of both superpowers are drafted around choke points, aimed either at forcing them open or keeping them corked. In the next war, terrible battles will be fought for tiny pieces of the Great Ocean. And the next war at sea will probably be decided there.

The Soviet Navy is particularly ill-placed in relation to choke points. At any given time, less than a quarter of its naval units are at sea. Due to maintenance and operational requirements, most of the Soviet fleet remains tied to the dock. Even the deployed units spend a great deal of time at anchor or under tow. In addition, the majority of Soviet naval units are based so near the Arctic Circle that the path to the open sea is blocked by ice much of the year. Geographically isolated, the Soviet fleets seeking to join up in wartime would have to brave the gamut of allied defenses waiting to mug them at the choke points.

The most important choke point runs from Greenland to Scotland. Called the Greenland-Iceland-U.K., or "GIUK Gap" (or for those who prefer a more mellifluous acronym, the British-Iceland-Greenland, or "BIG Gap"), it covers the area the Soviet Red Banner Northern Fleet would need to traverse to take up station in the Atlantic. Most of the fleet's muscle takes the form of submarines, so the western powers have weaved an underwater trap of sonar sensors, dormant minefields, attack submarine ambush areas, surface ship patrols, and antisubmarine aircraft pickets to bottle up the fleet before it reaches the sea lanes of the North Atlantic.

The Red Banner Baltic Fleet is also fenced in. The only way out is through the Kattegat, between Denmark and the southern tip of Sweden. The Baltic Fleet is not ncarly as powerful as the Northern Fleet—the bulk of its units are small surface combatants and auxiliaries. Its most important function in peacetime is the operational testing of new ships. (The Soviet Union's largest shipbuilding and refit base is off the Baltic Sea at Leningrad.)

The fleet's wartime mission appears to be control of the Baltic Sea and its approaches—choke points swing both ways. The importance Moscow attaches to the mission is evidenced by the almost annual Soviet submarine sighting in Swedish territorial waters; details of the Swedish defenses must be particularly valuable to the Soviets to risk an international incident by getting caught scouting them out in peacetime. Sweden and the navies of NATO's northern tier will fight the bulk of the battle of the Baltic for the West.

The Soviet Pacific Fleet is more dispersed, but no less hemmed in. Its headquarters at Vladivostok and the new installations on Sakhalin Island are poorly placed. Japan's Kuril Islands block the gateway to the Bering Sea. Only the large submarine base at Petropavlovsk, on the eastern side of the Kamchatka Peninsula, is free from waters under Japanese control or observation, but it is also cut off from the rest of the Pacific Fleet's bases on the mainland.

Lately, the Soviet Union has virtually taken control of Cam Rahn Bay, the giant naval base built by the Americans in Vietnam. A number of reconnaissance planes and about thirty Soviet ships are rotated in and out, to provide an almost permanent Soviet presence in the South China Sea.

The Soviet Navy also has a large installation at Sovetskaya Gaven, southwest of Sakhalin Island. One can only guess that the Soviet command thought it was protecting the base from the prying eyes of an American spyplane when it shot down the Korean airliner over Soviet territory in 1983.

There is no hope at all for the Soviet Caspian Sea Flotilla to reach the Great Ocean. The body of water is completely enclosed by the Soviet Union on three sides, and, to the south, the northern coast of Iran. Like the Baltic Fleet, the Caspian Sea Flotilla serves a major role as a center for training recruits and testing naval weapon systems.

The Red Banner Black Sea Fleet is well situated for its primary mission. Headquartered at Sevastopol on the Crimean Peninsula, the fleet should have no trouble controlling the Black Sea—there is a disproportionately large number of ships in its inventory, as well as many aircraft, including Backfire bombers.

However, the reason the Black Sea Fleet is so well equipped is that it is also charged with maintaining the Soviet Mediterranean Squadron. The permanent presence of the Soviet Navy in the Med caused great consternation in the West when the Squadron first began to make its presence felt in the seventies.

However, in wartime, the Soviet Navy would have a tough time breaking out from the Black Sea into the Mediterranean, and an even tougher time should they try to venture out into the Atlantic. First, they would have to force their way through the Bosporus and Dardanelles straits, controlled

Right: An *Aegis* cruiser under construction in Pascagoula, Mississippi. The Navy plans to build three *Ticonderoga* class cruisers a year.

Below: Soviet helicopter carrier *Minsk* in the Med.

by Turkey, a NATO ally. Another bottleneck occurs as the fleet tries to go around the island of Crete through the straits of Karpathos and Kithira.

The Soviet position in the Mediterranean suffered considerably with the loss of Egypt as an ally. Its other friends in the region—Syria and Libya—are not so well-placed or as reliable as Egypt once was. Today, about two dozen ships and submarines are rotated to the Soviet Mediterranean Squadron from other fleets. The Soviet Navy generally confines itself to anchorages in the eastern Med, conducting antisubmarine patrols and keeping tabs on the American Sixth Fleet.

The West has its problems with choke points, as well. Most often mentioned is the Strait of Hormuz, separating the Persian Gulf from the Gulf of Oman and the Arabian Sea. The U.S. imports just a fraction of its oil from the Gulf states. If the pipes were shut off, America could probably get along without it. But our allies could not. Two thirds of the oil that runs the economies of Western Europe flows through the Strait of Hormuz. Almost all of Japan's oil comes from the region.

Iran and Iraq's grudge match has had little effect on the flow of oil from the Persian Gulf. Nearly all the well-publicized attacks on shipping have occurred at the northern end of the Gulf. The total number of ships attacked in the five years of the war barely exceeds the number of tankers that squeeze through the Strait of Hormuz in one day. At times, both Iran and Iraq have hinted at closing the strait, but such an action—if it could be done—would surely bring the hammer of Western military might down on the culprit and tip the balance to the other party. In a global war, however, closing the Strait of Hormuz and bottling up the Gulf's oil would be a major Soviet objective.

Oil on its way to Japan has to pass through another narrow choke point at the Strait of Malacca, between Malaysia and the island of Sumatra in the South China Sea. American naval units on peacetime patrol shoot the straits off Singapore on their way to the Indian Ocean, but there is a growing feeling that Japan should shoulder the responsibility of keeping the straits open in wartime.

Some of America's most vital choke points are right offshore in the Caribbean. The Yucatan Channel, off Mexico, and the Straits of Florida, off the Keys, control the entrance to the Gulf ports of Houston, New Orleans, and Tampa. Both are dominated by Cuba. Cuba also lies to one side of the Paso de los Viantos, off Haiti, the quickest route to the Panama Canal for ships leaving ports on the eastern seaboard. In wartime, of course, Cuba would be isolated and could probably not hold out for long. But the point is, even though the major American naval ports are well placed, the country cannot take its commercial ports for granted, at least in the opening stages of a war.

To keep up with the changing demands of power projection, the Navy has constructed a flexible, if bewildering, command hierarchy. The Navy's organization is tough to follow for two reasons. For one thing, naval units can be under two entirely different chains of command, one for day-to-day operations and another when deployed. And the grouping of units changes constantly.

There are four numbered fleets: The Second Fleet in the Atlantic Ocean, the Sixth Fleet in the Mediterranean Sea, the Third Fleet in the eastern Pacific Ocean, and the Seventh Fleet in the western Pacific and the Indian Ocean. The numbered fleets operate more or less the same types of ships and aircraft, but are quite different in character.

The carriers and their air wings are fairly evenly divided between the Atlantic and Pacific fleets. Although the Pacific fleets have more units, there are more combatants assigned to the Atlantic fleets. This reflects the greater burden of logistics in the Pacific and the greater Soviet presence in the Atlantic. Ironically, even though the newer types of ships and equipment usually make their debut in the Atlantic fleets—especially in the Sixth Fleet—the Pacific fleets enjoy greater prestige. This is because, in Europe, naval operations are

A Mexican patrol boat buzzes around the assault carrier *Tarawa* during exercises off Acapulco. In recent years the Navy has grown increasingly aware of growing threats in waters near the U.S. mainland.

generally subordinate to land operations, but the Pacific theater is essentially a Navy show. The Pacific was also the scene of the Navy's greatest triumphs during World War II. The situation is the reciprocal of the favored status that USAFE (United States Air Forces in Europe) has in the personnel files of Air Force fighter jocks.

The Second and Third fleets have the most ships assigned, but they are considered "non-deployed" fleets and are mainly concerned with training and maintenance. The Navy has gone to a philosophy of "Flex Ops"—instead of sailing circles in the ocean, ships are now usually deployed only for a specific task, usually an exercise. This keeps more units in reserve for crisis and helps the crews get more from each deployment. Ships assigned to these fleets *do* deploy on training cruises, of course, but the units that are rotated from these fleets to the forward fleets see most of the peacetime action.

The Second Fleet is headquartered at Norfolk, Virginia. It is the largest American naval base, and a prime target for a Pearl Harbor-style nuclear attack. Lately, naval planners have become worried about putting so many eggs in one basket, and now plan to base at least some of the carriers normally assigned to Norfolk—and to the naval base at San Diego, nearly as large—to selected ports along both coasts.

Most of the ships assigned to the forward fleets are rotated from the continental fleets for about six months. But the amount of time ships are assigned to the Sixth and Seventh fleets can vary greatly, depending on contingencies and the length of the cruise.

The commander of the Sixth Fleet runs the show from the headquarters in Gaeta, north of

Naples, or aboard his flagship, *Coronado,* a converted landing ship. Ships of the Sixth Fleet make port calls all around the Med. There are a couple of important logistics bases, most of them in the western Med. Naval Air Station Sigonella, Sicily, is a familiar roost for antisubmarine and electronic warfare aircraft. In 1978, Spain asked the United States to cease basing strategic missile submarines at Rota, but the port near Gibraltar is still an important supply point for the Sixth Fleet. The tender that supports the fleet's four or five nuclear-powered attack submarines is docked at La Maddalena, on the island of Sardinia. (The base is ringed by strong defenses manned by Italian troops, but that's as much to keep the sailors in as terrorists out; there is a Club Med on the other side.)

In the eastern Med, the realliance of Egypt to the West has given the Sixth Fleet much needed bases for naval operations near the Middle East. The fleet maintains a strong presence in both Greece and Turkey, although that's a volatile situation politically—both countries are nominal NATO allies, but they hate each other. The USN has grown closer to Israel as the Soviet presence in the eastern Med has increased. The Israeli port of Haifa was particularly busy during the recent crisis in Lebanon.

Carrier *America* (CV-66), in the Med.

The Sixth Fleet used to have two carriers regularly assigned. But since the Iranian hostage crisis and the growing instability in the Persian Gulf, the Sixth Fleet is usually up to strength only during times of trouble, or when another carrier transits the Med on its way to the Indian Ocean. This changes as events warrant, however. The Navy managed to put three carriers off Beirut for a brief period in 1984.

The need for a permanent American naval presence in the Indian Ocean has also stretched the resources of the Navy's Pacific fleets. The Third Fleet provides the bulk of the forward-based Seventh Fleet, as well as support for Task Force 70, the Navy's Indian Ocean (I/O) detachment. The Indian Ocean, and especially the Persian Gulf, has drawn a lot of attention from the Pentagon lately, due to the mismatch of American strategic interests and American military muscle in the region.

The United States has worked hard to get bases in the area. They've had no luck in the Persian Gulf, where the sultan of Oman has turned down a request to base the headquarters of the new Central Command. He's worried that a permanent American presence would stir up Islamic fever among the population. The U.S. is hoping to establish a base on the island of Masirah, where American servicemen would be less visible, but still in position to move quickly in a crisis. Until then, the U.S. headquarters in the region operates out of a ship at sea, cutting circles in the water.

The Navy is also looking for friends in Africa. The U.S. has secured base rights in Kenya, Somalia, and Djibouti. Perhaps "secured" isn't the right word. Nothing is permanent in that part of the world, except, perhaps, hunger and revolution. The Navy is hedging its bets and holding onto Diego Garcia.

The little horseshoe-shaped spit of land at the end of the Indian Ocean doesn't look like one of

The new rocket cruiser *Slava*, one of many new warship types entering Soviet naval service.

the most important military bases in the world. Indeed, until the mid-seventies most people could be excused for thinking Diego Garcia was just a figment of the English imagination. The United States leased the base from the British after realizing that America's lack of bases anywhere near the scene of potential conflict in the region would make military intervention almost impossible.

This was in the days of the old Rapid Deployment Force (RDF), a unit that existed mainly on paper and was neither rapid nor deployable, and not much of a force (although the name was certainly less contentious than its original designation, the Unilateral Intervention Force). All of the units assigned to the RDF were actually based somewhere else, and most had other commitments, usually to the defense of NATO. Until the beginning of the annual Bright Star exercises, only the Navy had ever *seen* the Indian Ocean, and it's still the only service that maintains a permanent presence there.

Diego Garcia is five days steaming from the Persian Gulf, but it's brought logistical support a lot closer to the ships on Gonzo Station in the Arabian Sea. If the island is hard for Navy ships to reach, it's also out of the range of most adversaries. P-3 recon and antisubmarine aircraft stage out of "Dodge City," Navy slang for Diego Garcia, on their seventeen-hour patrols. The new landing strip can also accommodate Air Force B-52s. And in the newly dredged harbor there is enough room for ships packed with all the equipment needed by a Marine amphibious brigade.

The western Pacific is familiar territory to old Navy hands. In particular, the eastern coast of Asia is of vital interest to the Seventh Fleet. Although the Air Force has a few bases in South Korea and Japan, the Navy is the real American power in that part of the world.

The Pacific is huge. Even though the Navy is only concerned with tiny parts of it, the great expanse of the Pacific Ocean still plays a major part in Seventh Fleet operations. Most of its ships are logistic runners. They are on the move all the time, keeping the task forces thousands of miles from the nearest base supplied. A large part of each deployment is spent just getting to and from station.

To cut down on transit time, the Navy has stationed a carrier forward in Japan, at Yokosuka (pronounced "yoh-KOOS-kah"). Currently, *Midway* is so deployed, with its air wing stationed at nearby Atsugi. A number of ships operate from Subic Bay, an important American naval base in the Philippines.

Growing global commitments and block obsolescence of a number of ships built just after World War II has caused the Navy to clamor for more ships and more money. The Navy had more than a thousand ships in 1970. Ten years later, it was down to less than half that number. Significantly, the USN had lost more than half its aircraft carriers, as a number of World War II–era carriers reached the end of their service lives. But the Navy's commitments—and the size of the Soviet Navy—increased during the same time period, necessitating a major rebuilding program.

You hear a lot about the 600-ship Navy these days. Navy Secretary John Lehman set this number as one of his goals when he took office. Although it sounds like a nice round number conjured up to justify more shipbuilding, the number is actually the result of thousands of hours of computer time. The study took into account the Pentagon's impressions of the next war, the Navy's missions, and the Soviet threat. The needs and projected losses were fed in one end, and the number 600 came out the other.

It is important to keep in mind exactly what ships are included in the "600-ship Navy." After all, the Navy has more than that now. The 600-ship goal, however, doesn't include many types of auxiliaries (although it does include fleet oilers and ammunition ships that will go in harm's way to replenish the combatants at sea). Using the "battle forces" criteria, the Navy currently has just over 530 ships in commission.

The 600-ship Navy concept shouldn't be taken too literally. What the Navy really wants is enough ships-of-the-line to make up eight carrier battle groups (with two carriers in every group but one), four surface action groups centered around battleships, and enough escorts to protect one-and-a-half Marine amphibious forces, seven convoys, and ten underway replenishment groups. The figures actually add up to considerably more than 600 ships. But who's counting?

The Soviets, maybe. They've got three times as many hulls as the USN, but the numbers are skewed by a collection of old diesel attack submarines and the kind of small surface combatant ships the U.S. Navy doesn't want to build. The USN doesn't seem to know what to do with their *Oliver Hazard Perry* class frigate, the low end of Adm. Elmo Zumwalt's "high-low mix." The Navy considers it too slow and too lightly armed to take part in carrier battle group operations. But the *Perry* is a heavyweight compared with most warships in the Soviet Navy.

On the other hand, the Soviet Union has a very small number of very large ships, and the number is growing as the Russian Navy wades out from its coasts into deeper water. As its missions change, the design of its ships changes as well. For years, the Soviet Navy was built for a one-shot war. Its mission was to deny the West control of the sea by ambushing its ships with quick, devastating attacks. Soviet maritime design reflected this by building ships with few, if any, main armament reloads, little damage control capability, and spartan crew quarters.

Now, as the Soviets move from sea denial to sea control, their fleet is growing up. It's no coincidence Russian ships are starting to resemble their Western counterparts; the difference has always been mission-oriented, not national. Their new *Udaloy* class destroyers are strikingly similar to the American *Spruance,* for example. It's not a question of imitation. The Soviets have always displayed a willingness to go their own way on ship design. It's just that both ships share the same mission—open ocean antisubmarine warfare (ASW).

The Russians may have bitten off more than they could chew in their hurry to join the big leagues of blue water ops. Despite the construc-

The F/A-18 Hornet is slated to replace both the F-4 and the A-7 on carrier flight decks.

tion of new, dedicated underway replenishment ships and an intense study of how the experts in the U.S. Navy do it, the Soviets may find that keeping their big new ships sailing will be a big headache. And if shooing submarines away from the carrier battle group on the high seas is tough for the USN, it's bound to be a nightmare for the Soviets, with their less sophisticated ASW systems.

But the biggest problem the Russians face is lack of air power on the Great Ocean. They're trying to remedy that by building a new carrier, which we'll take a look at later. Now let's look at the principal warships in the American fleet.

First, a word about nomenclature. Navy ships are all assigned a name and a hull number. Ships used to be christened according to set guidelines. For example, all battleships were named after states. This procedure is no longer followed with any regularity. After the U.S. stopped making battleships, cruisers were named for states. Carriers used to be named after ships that were named after famous Revolutionary War battles. Now cruisers are named after carriers that were named after ships that were named after Revolutionary War battles. And ballistic missile submarines are named after states. You get the idea. If it sounds confusing, it's because it is.

Hull numbers are straightforward only by comparison. The designation consists of a type —cruiser, destroyer, whatever—and a series number. The designation contains the first letter of the type as its first letter, plus other letters denoting special characteristics and abilities. CGN 38, for example, is the thirty-eighth modern cruiser (C), which happens to be able to launch guided missiles (G) and is nuclear powered (N).

CGN 38 is the U.S.S. *Virginia,* usually called simply the Virginia or just *Virginia* (the Navy has a thing against articles). *Virginia* is the lead ship of the *Virginia* class. That is, it's the first of that design built. The other three ships built to that design are said to be *Virginia* class cruisers (or CGN 38 class cruisers).

The roles of modern warships have changed since World War II, and the distinctions between types of warships have been blurred. For example, most American cruisers seem small compared to their World War II counterparts, but they are huge for frigates, which is how most of them started life.

The ships didn't grow, but their role did. With the swipe of a pen on June 30, 1975, the USN lost a bunch of DGLN's (guided missile light destroyers or destroyer leaders) and gained the same number of cruisers. The move was taken to more accurately reflect the capability of the ships, especially compared to the relatively lightly-armed warships the Russians were calling cruisers. A similar threat inflation took place when, at the same time, some frigates were promoted to destroyers. Well, it's one way to improve your order of battle.

The American Navy seems, at first, to contain almost as many classes as ships. But closer examination shows that most of the later classes are merely improvements on a previous design.

For example, even the latest American carriers can trace their design back directly to *Forrestal,* the first of the supercarriers (whose design, in turn, borrowed heavily from the *United States,* an ambitious post-war carrier canceled one day after construction began). There are four carriers in the *Forrestal* class, the others being *Saratoga, Ranger,* and *Independence.* All were built before 1960. Their nominal service lives run out at the end of this decade, but all are undergoing extensive rebuilding that will allow them to sail in the next century.

The earlier *Midway* class carriers have long since reached the end of their projected time in service, but soldier on regardless. Laid down on battleship hulls during World War II, they were the first American warships too big to slip through the Panama Canal. Six were ordered, but only three were built. *Franklin D. Roosevelt* was retired after being grounded, leaving only *Midway* and *Coral Sea.*

Both *Midway* and *Coral Sea* have been extensively modernized, but neither can operate the big F-14 Tomcat fighters or S-3 Viking ASW aircraft. With a smaller flight deck and only three arresting cables and two catapults, they just don't have the room to operate the large aircraft safely. Both will receive the new F/A-18 Hornet to replace the F-4 in the fighter role. *Midway* is in better shape; based forward in Japan, it spends more than two thirds of its time at sea. *Coral Sea*—the "ageless warrior"— has already undergone refit to operate Hornets.

The four ships of the *Kitty Hawk* class are almost identical to the *Forrestals,* although somewhat larger. The port lift was repositioned aft from the end of the flight deck, where it was useless much of the time. In addition, the island was also positioned farther aft, with two of the three starboard elevators forward. The other *Kitty Hawks* are *Constellation, America,* and *John F. Kennedy* (although the Navy officially considers *JFK* a separate class).

The design was retained for the *Nimitz* class carriers, although, since the ships are nuclear powered, there is more internal storage space for fuel and ammunition. There are four *Nimitz* carriers—*Nimitz, Dwight D. Eisenhower, Carl Vinson,* and *Theodore Roosevelt*—with two more, *Abraham Lincoln* and *George Washington* building. They are the largest warships in the world.

The Navy pioneered the concept of the nuclear-powered aircraft carrier with the *Enterprise.* Six were planned, but, as is so often the case, the ship proved too expensive and only one was built. Originally fitted with a distinctive pineapple-shaped island with built-in "billboard" radar aerials, the design proved a maintenance nightmare. *Enterprise* was rebuilt with a more conventional island during her last major refit.

The cruiser *Long Beach* was given a similar facelift during her recent modernization. The careers of *Long Beach* and *Enterprise* have been intertwined from their conception. Built to test the

Nuclear-powered attack submarine *La Jolla* passes the nuclear-powered guided missile cruiser *Long Beach* in San Diego harbor.

concept of nuclear power at sea, the two ships, along with the nuclear-powered *Bainbridge,* took off on a round-the-world cruise in 1964, without once stopping to refuel.

Long Beach has a history of being armed with phantom weapons systems. The ship was originally designed to carry Regulus cruise missiles. When that program was canceled, the intention was to arm *Long Beach* with Polaris ballistic missiles. That plan was scrapped also, and the cruiser entered service without any antisurface armament whatsoever. It was the first warship ever built armed only with missiles, although two 5″ guns were later added amidships. In the same refit in which her "billboard" radars were replaced, *Long Beach* received two Phalanx antiaircraft guns and two quad launchers for the Harpoon cruise missile.

Although *Long Beach* was basically a one-off design, the rest of the Navy's cruisers can trace their design back to *Leahy.* The two ships were built almost simultaneously in the early sixties, a time when the Navy was convinced that the gun was an anachronism at sea. The ships were built with two 3″ gun mounts, poorly placed amidships. (The guns are now being removed to make way for Harpoon launchers). The nine *Leahy*s were built for antiair carrier escort, and are "double-ended" —that is, they have guided missile launchers fore and aft. At congressional insistence, one of the *Leahy*s was nuclear powered. *Bainbridge* is distinguished by her lack of "macks"—the combined mast and stack arrangement introduced in *Leahy.*

The subsequent nine-ship *Belknap* class is very similar in design. Its members differ from the slightly smaller *Leahy*s in that they have full helicopter support facilities (the *Leahy* class cruisers have a helicopter pad, but no hangar) and a 5″ gun in place of the aft missile launcher.

Once again, Congress directed that one of the ships be driven by nuclear power: *Truxtun* is *Belknap's* nuclear-powered half sister. Slightly larger, *Truxtun* also has the missile and gun mounts reversed.

With the building of the *Nimitz* class nuclear-powered aircraft carriers, the Navy set about to construct a new class of nuclear-powered cruisers to protect them. Once again, the basic *Leahy* design was used, with major modifications. *California* and *South Carolina* are much larger, with two 5″ guns, as well as missile launchers fore and aft.

The four cruisers of the *Virginia* class are similar in design, with *California's* ASROC mount replaced by multi-purpose missile launchers. The *Virginia*s also carry a helicopter elevator and hangar aft, although the chopper is not usually embarked when the cruiser is on its primary mission of carrier escort.

Critics have attacked the Navy for building cruisers whose only job is to defend aircraft carriers from air and submarine attacks. They say the ships cannot operate independently, as cruisers have traditionally done, and, in fact, are helpless outside the protection of a task force.

But the criticism fails to take in several points. The first is, *no* ship can operate independently today. Every surface warship depends upon the layered defense of the task force to survive. And, though it's true that the cruisers, as originally built, sacrificed antisurface weapons in favor of AA and ASW systems, the ships are being refit with Harpoon, and, in some cases, Tomahawk cruise missiles for anti-ship punch. They're also being back-fitted with Phalanx antiaircraft guns for close-in protection, another much-needed capacity. With the addition of the new systems, the Navy's cruisers have matured into well-balanced fighting ships, easily the equal of any at sea today.

The Navy has closed the book on the *Leahy*-style cruisers. The newest cruisers sliding down the

Standard ER (extended range) surface-to-air-missile fired from the cruiser *Wainwright* off San Juan, Puerto Rico. *General Dynamics photo.*

Spruance class destroyer *Elliot* in mirror-like seas.

ways are the *Ticonderoga* class. Built around the *Aegis* integrated combat system, the *Ticonderoga* cruisers are built primarily to defend the carrier battle group against cruise missile attacks. But the *Ticonderogas* also have a potent antisubmarine and antisurface capability. We'll discuss the *Tico* and its *Aegis* weapons system in detail later in this book.

The *Ticonderoga* is built on the hull of the *Spruance* class destroyer, the Navy's premier sub-hunter. *Spruance* is *not* a well balanced ship. Although they carry the Harpoon anti-ship missile, the thirty-one *Spruances* must depend on short-ranged missiles for air defense (though two Phalanx mounts are being added during refit). The Navy has announced plans to refit the *Spruances* with Tomahawk cruise missiles. Some will be backfit with eight Tomahawks in a cannister launcher, but most will get a vertical launching system capable of holding a mix of sixty-one missiles. But the ships are very good at what they do. Big and roomy, they are excellent helicopter platforms, even in rough weather. They are also fast enough to keep up with the carrier battle group, yet quiet enough to hear subs without making too much noise themselves.

Some of the *Spruance's* shortcomings were

U.S. Navy's newest guided missile cruiser, *Arkansas* (CGN-41), underway.

Oliver Hazard Perry (FFG-7), lead ship of the Navy's newest and largest class of frigates, undergoes a shock test.

remedied in the *Kidd* class destroyers. The ships fairly bristle with weapons, including the long-range Standard surface-to-air missile system. In fact, all the *Spruance*s were supposed to have been built to this design, but as the program grew more costly, the antiair role was de-emphasized. The four *Kidd*s were originally built for the Shah of Iran, but were snapped up cheap by a grateful Navy when the Shah fell from power. The *Kidd*s are thus known, unofficially, as the "Ayatollah" class destroyers.

The rest of the Navy's destroyers are "shooters"—antiaircraft escorts for the carrier battle groups. The ten *Coontz* class and twenty-three *Charles F. Adams* class guided-missile destroyers were built in the early sixties, and their old-fashioned separate masts and funnels make them look even older. But these are very capable ships, with firepower equal to many Navy cruisers.

The Navy is building a new class of destroyers to replace these ships. The *Arleigh Burke* will be equipped with a version of the *Aegis* combat system now fitted to the *Ticonderoga* cruisers. *Burke* seems to have qualities of "Stealth" embedded in her design: with sleek lines and contoured stacks, the ship appears to have been built with a low radar signature in mind from the beginning. As with later ships in the *Ticonderoga* class, *Burke* will do away with conventional missile launchers in favor of a vertical launching system. The VLS will allow the ship to put more missiles in the air, as well as allowing the skipper more flexibility in the types of missiles launched. But the casual observer will see yet more empty deck space, and wonder why Navy ships are progressively disarming themselves.

The Navy's frigate programs have always been controversial. The problem, it seems, is that these ships, built for convoy escort, are at a loss during peacetime when there are no convoys to protect. The Navy keeps trying to force the frigates into carrier battle group escort duty, but the little ships, built to do everything reasonably well, can't do anything well enough to fit into any of the specialized roles needed in a battle group.

The *Oliver Hazard Perry* frigates, in particular, have gotten a bad rap. The purpose of the program was to put a large number of hulls in the water in a short period of time. This was accomplished; the *Perry* is the largest class of warships in the Navy's inventory. But it was built with cost-effectiveness in mind, and to Navy brass, this translates into "cheap." The *Perry*s have been called the "Chevettes of the Navy." It is ironic that the USN, which is constantly clamoring for more ships, is doing all it can to get rid of the *Perry*s. They've already transferred some to the

Knox class frigate *Pharris* participating in Unitas exercises off the coast of South America.

Naval Reserve, and there's talk of shuffling others off to the Coast Guard.

What's wrong with the *Perrys*? On paper, they are very formidable warships for their size. They carry Harpoon, ASROC, and Standard missiles, and a 3″ gun. But in order to save money, many critical systems, such as LAMPS helicopters and a Phalanx gun, were to be backfit later on. And they are susceptible to critical hits; all the missiles are fired from a single, one-armed launcher. If that goes, the ship is virtually defenseless. The same is true for the *Perry*'s single screw, although a pair of retractable bow thrusters can be used to get the ship home in an emergency.

The ten *Garcia* class frigates are also powered by a single propeller, the only thing keeping them from being classified as destroyers. They are certainly as large and capable as many destroyers, with two 5″ guns and full ASW helicopter facilities. The six *Brooke* class frigates are identical, with the exception of a Tartar missile launcher installed in place of the aft gun mount.

The forty-six *Knox* class frigates are good ASW ships, which is their primary function. They are almost helpless against air threats, with only a single, short-range missile launcher (once again, Phalanx will be backfit into these ships). The *Knox* frigates are distinguished by their circular mack, which looks like a castle turret rising amidship.

But hardware is only half the story. Ships need crews to sail and fight them. Let's take a look at the men who make up the American Navy.

Chapter Two

The Tick of a Ship

The Navy is run by one man. Not the chief of naval operations, or the secretary of the Navy, or even the president. The Captain runs the Navy, as he has since men started sailing on the Great Ocean. There are as many captains as there are ships, but—and this is important—only one captain on each ship.

He may not even wear the four stripes of a captain's rank. On Navy ships smaller than a cruiser, a commander, a lieutenant commander, or even a lieutenant may be in charge. But although the man in charge isn't always a captain, he *is* always the Captain.

Captains are individuals, certainly, with different leadership styles. But when command falls on a person's shoulders, something strange happens. Nice guys get a little meaner. Tough guys soften around the edges. The individual's personality becomes absorbed by the archetype.

No one knows exactly what makes a good captain, but everyone recognizes it. He is consistent in a changing world. He is calm when others are not. He is kind when the situation calls for it, stern when he has to be, fair only in the sense that nature is fair.

Yes indeed, he moves in mysterious ways. The captain never seems to *do* anything. Perched on his high chair in the highest part of the ship, he spends the day like one of the ancient gods. Individuals and incidents are brought to him for judgment. He dispenses justice with a nod of the head or a flick of the pen. He is always right, because he is the captain. How could he be wrong?

The captain has his military superiors, of course. Enlisted men say it hurts their eyes to look at admirals. More than any other service, Navy brass favor themselves with perks of office. Even within the spartan confines of a warship, ranking officers have their own staterooms, sometimes two—a sea cabin *and* an in-port cabin for entertaining.

The admiral eats alone, if he wants. Alcohol is forbidden on Navy warships—even such party animals as fighter pilots have to content themselves with weak fruit juice (called "bug juice") at sea. But no one's going to report the odd toast in the flag quarters. And while everyone else has to climb ladder after ladder, there is an elevator on most aircraft carriers reserved solely for the brass. The elevator, and the heights it rises to, are considered "Flag Country." Any mere, unauthorized mortal who dares approach is likely to get bounced out on his aft end by the marines of the admiral's private Praetorian Guard.

But even the bigwigs envy the ship's captain. Although there are many exceptions, the Navy

New Jersey's exec, the captain's right-hand man.

usually allows only one major at-sea command in each person's career. That tour is cherished, and while many enlisted men spend most of their time trying to figure out how to get off the ship, high-ranking naval officers spend the rest of their careers scheming to get back to sea.

But absolute power has its price. Let the captain screw up just once—even if it isn't remotely his fault—and he'll finish his career on shore somewhere counting widgets. The Navy giveth and the Navy taketh away.

If the captain seems to have one foot on Mount Olympus, the executive officer has both feet firmly on earth. The XO is to the CO as the agent is to the Hollywood star. The captain cannot be bothered with details and petty discipline. That's the exec's job. The executive officer translates the captain's will into action. A good one will anticipate the captain's orders before they're given. Good execs are rewarded with a command of their own. Bad ones will not be execs for very long.

The captain and the exec run the ship through departments, some of which are broken down into divisions. These are the basic working groups of the Navy. The officers and men on board the Navy's ships often seem to be merely along for the ride, but each person on board has a definite job to do, much like the crew of an aircraft.

At the heart of a fighting ship is the Operations Department, headed by the ship's ops officer. On most warships, this department is broken down into several divisions. For example, the OC division handles communications (and, on an aircraft carrier, the control of air traffic). OA division is responsible for intelligence, while the OI division mans the combat information center.

The CIC (combat information center) is where the captain will fight the ship. On older warships, it's located behind the bridge, but on newer ships, the CIC is buried below for more protection. The Tactical Action Officer is the captain's representative in the CIC, just as the Officer of the Deck is his man on the bridge. The TAO stands his watch in the CIC, sometimes assisted by special deputies responsible for particular types of combat.

The OOD is the man in charge on the bridge. In most cases, he has the watch and the "conn," which means, in nautical terms, that he is in charge of the ship and its direction. The conn is an old Navy term for control of the ship (this explains the old submarine term "conning tower," which is now usually referred to as the submarine's sail). A slang term for the conn is the "bubble." On sailing ships the only instrument was a carpenter's level, and the pilot was obliged to keep the bubble in the middle (and the ship upright). The opposite of "having the bubble" is, of course, "losing the bubble"—losing control of the ship's movements. This could have disastrous consequences, both for the ship and for the careers of the men involved.

What sort of things can go wrong? To start with, there are the all-too-common navigational accidents. For the layman, it's hard to understand how ships can collide in the middle of the ocean —for sailors, it's hard to understand why it doesn't happen more often.

It's a matter of physics. It takes a lot to get a deep-draft ship moving, and, inertially speaking, even more to stop it. Turning the ship is easier, though not by much, but sometimes you don't have that option. The laws of the sea are very specific about rights of way, and often the only thing a crew can do is stay the course and hope the other ship lives up to its responsibility. The situation is made worse by the fact that communication with the oncoming ship is frequently impossible, either in English, or with code flashes or flags.

The other ship could be a supertanker with no one alert on the bridge. With such small crews these days, it's not uncommon for commercial vessels to cruise at night on "Iron Mike" —automatic pilot. Or the oncoming ship could be a drug-runner or smuggler. Navy men see some strange sights on the Great Ocean. But unless they are specifically ordered to interdict—as part of a blockade, for example—the USN gives a wide berth to even the most suspicious looking craft. It's none of their business.

Probably the biggest menace to navigation, for the USN, is the Soviet Navy. The superpowers rub elbows every day on the high seas, and they used to scrape a lot of paint. But things have improved since the "Incidents at Sea" talks in the seventies. Actually, it's the intelligence trawlers that really get to American sailors. The Soviet intelligence ships know the laws of the sea and use the letter of the law, if not the spirit, to their advantage. The nimble AGI craft can maneuver into the path of an oncoming carrier and then legally force the flattop to change course. Many a carrier skipper has wanted to ram the little trawlers, and there have been several close calls. Some USN officers think the rest of the Soviet Navy is ashamed of the tricks practiced by the spook fleet, but even American sailors offer grudging respect for the seamanship of the trawler skippers.

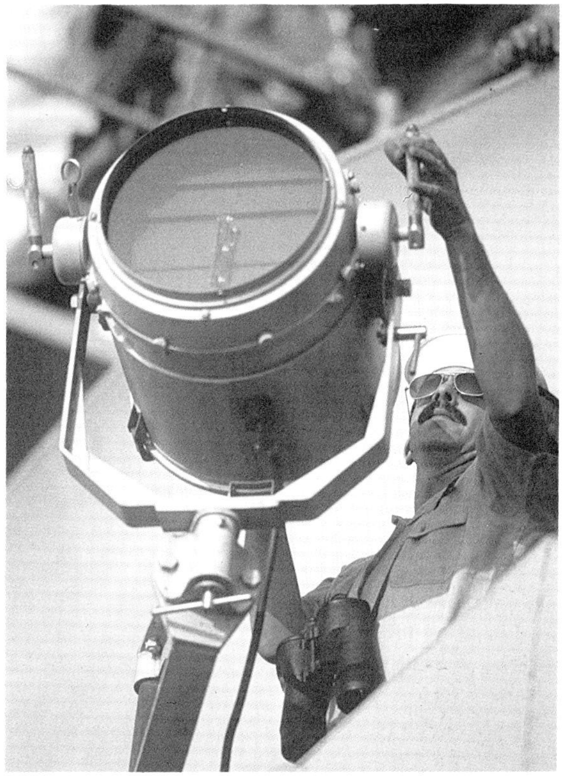

A signalman aboard the battleship *New Jersey* communicates with another ship during an EMCON environment.

In the event of trouble, the ship's log acquires life-and-death importance. Actually, there are several logs. There's the main one, kept on the navigation bridge. There's also a log in the combat information center, another in the engine room, and so on. Any changes have to be initialed. The logs are archived, and any time there's an incident they are collected and locked up for safekeeping till they are handed over to the board of inquiry. On at least one ship a brush and a can of shellac were kept handy so important pages could be shel-

The bridge crew mans the watch.

lacked to prevent tampering.

To help him con the ship, the officer of the deck has a number of helpers. Although the names may change, the duties are the same throughout most navies. The most important enlisted man on the bridge is the Boatswain's Mate of the Watch. A petty officer, the BMOW makes sure all watch stations are manned and ready. He's the "strawboss" on the bridge, and, as one of the more experienced men on the navigation watch, oversees the work of the other enlisted watch standers.

The man with his hand on the wheel is the helmsman, or steersman. He steers the course given him by the OOD, using a compass repeater —the ship's main gyrocompass is usually located well below. The master compass drives most of the other compasses on board, to make sure all the departments are, literally, heading in the same direction. Navy ships still use a big wheel to direct the angle of rudder deflection, but instead of being spoked like a riverboat wheel, the inside of the wooden helm is filled in with a solid piece of polished brass.

The lee helmsman is a second steersman, in charge of transmitting speed and rpm changes ordered by the OOD to the engine room. In older ships, this is done by means of the engine order telegraph, another antique-looking brass affair that uses pulleys connected to bells to communicate speed and rpm changes to the sailor standing watch in the engine room. The engine room watch adjusts the speed and notifies the bridge that it has complied with the order by setting the answering pointer on *its* engine order telegraph to the same sector, from flank speed (fastest) to full speed astern (for a crash stop). The ship can be steered from aft steering in an emergency. In newer ships, speed can be controlled directly from the bridge, by means of a mechanism that increases or decreases propeller shaft revolutions per minute.

The quartermaster makes sure the ship is on the course set by the navigator. Along with the OOD, the quartermaster sets the ship's course and keeps the log on the navigation bridge. He works in the charthouse, which is usually just a section at the rear of the bridge with a large flat table cluttered with charts and drafting instruments. At night, the charthouse is curtained off to keep the light from ruining the night vision of the rest of the bridge watch.

On larger warships there is also a Plan Position Indicator. This is a large sheet of glass etched with the ship's position at the center of a circle showing the relative bearings of the other ships in the task force. The positions are updated by a sailor, as directed by the quartermaster or the OOD.

Ships are guided by a variety of navigational aids. Loran (long-range navigation) depends on a chain of radio transmitters set up by the Coast Guard. Omega is an expansion of the Loran system worldwide. Shoran is a variation of the Air Force's beacon bombing system, and uses transmitters placed on shore for triangulation of position. Radar and the sonar signals of a fathometer are also used to determine the ship's position.

These systems are accurate, but might not be available in wartime. Broadcasting stations can be destroyed and radar transmissions can be jammed or used to betray the ship's position to the enemy. The Navy prefers to use self-contained navigation-

Above. A snipe among the boilers. In an emergency the ship can be steered from the engine room.

al systems that are likely to survive after the shooting starts.

Satellite navigation data is highly accurate and almost impossible to jam. Older systems had their drawbacks. Often ships had to wait more than two hours for a satellite pass, especially near the equator. But when the new NAVSTAR global positioning satellites are fully deployed, instant directions from the heavens will become a reality for most warships.

But ships that will play a role in the black

Right: Launch control console aboard the submarine *Ohio* on patrol under the Atlantic.

"Holystoning" *New Jersey's* teak deck. So far the Navy has had no trouble finding crews for the battlewagons.

theater of nuclear war cannot depend upon satellites, which are prime targets in an all-out conflict. Ballistic missile submarines and aircraft carriers have SINS, an inadvertently appropriate acronym that stands for Ship's Internal Navigation System. This is similar to an aircraft's inertial guidance system. All the navigator needs to know is the longitude and latitude of the port as the ship gets underway. The system's gyros and accelerometers keep up with every movement of the ship from then on. In ballistic missile subs, the missiles' guidance systems are patched into SINS, and that position is referenced so the birds can hit their targets from any point under the ocean.

To keep in practice—and to check the accuracy of the electronic guidance systems which no one in the Navy seems to trust fully, anyway—most navigators still use the ancient ways of finding one's way across the Great Ocean. Navy navigators are still adept at dead reckoning and taking star sightings with a sextant. And all the high-tech gear in the world won't help in getting a huge whale of a ship safely into harbor. Entering and leaving port is one of the trickiest evolutions in a ship's cruise, and one in which accidents are common.

Although today's sailors don't have to contend with mainsails and flying jibs, there is still a lot of seamanship involved in the contemporary Navy. It is, if anything, harder to operate modern ships because, in addition to routine nautical jobs like weighing the anchor and securing the deck, there are technical tasks that would baffle even World War II seamen.

The Deck Department is in charge of most duties one associates with the operation of a ship at sea. The "deck apes" haul the lines, swab the deck, man the boats, stow the cargo, and provide the muscle for the dozens of dirty little jobs that have to be done. The Deck Department is where most seamen start their careers. It gives them incentive to strike for a less strenuous rating.

The Engineering Department keeps the ship moving. In larger ships, it's broken down into several divisions—B division for boilers, M division for main engines, and so forth. The life of a "snipe" is not too much fun, either. In the hot climates—that is, where most of the Navy's ships tend to linger for months on end—temperatures down below can reach 120 degrees. And stay there. For months on end.

It's no wonder the snipes often envy the Weapons Department personnel. Oh, some of them, such as the poor saps doomed to handle ordnance, sweat as much as anyone on board. But the "twidgets" are another story.

Twidgets are fire control technicians who cruise across the ocean high and dry in the air-conditioned comfort of the F-division spaces. The twidget is a nautical version of the civilian "computer nerd." A twidget is seldom without his "tweaker"—a small, clip-on screwdriver used to make minor adjustments to equipment. To a real twidget, it's a badge of office. The rest of the ship's company have other names for it.

The weapons spaces are not cooled for the technician's benefit. Ships built before the widespread use of solid-state electronics carry a giant vacuum tube called a magnetron. When it works, the magnetron powers the ship's search radars. But the magnetron is high-strung and delicate, much like the twidgets who handle it. At high temperatures, the magnetron is prone to melt down, taking the ship's eyes and ears down with it. After a great many awkward—and expensive—magnetron blow-outs, even the U.S. Navy got the message. Now those spaces are air-conditioned, a rare luxury at sea. The twidgets say it's a lucky coincidence. The deck apes sniff a plot.

There is at least one other air-conditioned space on most ships. The crypto room is usually located between the bridge and the CIC. Access is restricted to a few officers and enlisted men. Most crewmen consider the Navy's fascination with codes and ciphers a real pain. Except in warmer climates. There, the air-conditioned crypto room is usually staffed around the clock.

In nuclear-powered ships, there is another department responsible for keeping the reactors running smoothly and safely. The Navy has not been very forthcoming concerning press accounts of alleged nuclear reactor incidents at sea. Such episodes appear to have been confined to nuclear-powered submarines and probably took place long ago. At any rate, the Navy is certainly much more careful with their nuclear power plants than the Soviets. Tales of hairless submariners and jokes about crewmen who glow in the dark are commonplace in the Soviet services. Admiral Hyman Rickover, the father of the American nuclear navy, says he received more radiation during a short tour of a Russian submarine than he did in all his years around the U.S. Navy's nuclear power plants. In contrast, Rickover says no American sailor has exceeded the maximum allowable dosage since 1967.

USN ships are generally much safer than Russian vessels. It's a combination of their design and the people who run them.

The Soviet Union does not have a great seafaring tradition. Generally, the Soviet sailor is a conscripted peasant who has never seen the ocean before being drafted. Their navy is especially weak in the petty officer corps, a rank whose experience, it is widely felt, is what really keeps the American Navy afloat. For the coronation of Queen Elizabeth II in 1953, the Soviet Union dispatched the cruiser *Sverdlov* to Great Britain. The English were very impressed by the seamanship displayed by the crew, as well they should have been; it was

later discovered that every man on board was an officer, hand-picked for the occasion.

Cramped as they are, American ships are luxury liners compared to Soviet vessels. Russian warships look more formidable, but it is an illusion created by putting all the weapons above deck on a very small hull. Although the ships are comparatively smaller, they are less automated than American ships, so more crewmen have to be crammed into smaller spaces. Doubling up is common practice; it is a rare sailor who has his own bunk aboard a Soviet ship. Space below is so crowded and stifling it is not uncommon to see Russian seamen sacked out on deck in the warmer latitudes.

Soviet ships are also lacking in compartmentalization and damage control. The two factors could spell disaster in battle. The effects are felt even in peacetime: In 1974 the destroyer *Otvazhny* suffered an explosion, burned to the waterline, and sank in the Black Sea with almost all of its three hundred men on board, while the captain waited for permission to flood the hold.

The USN has had its peacetime accidents, as well. For example, nearly *every* American aircraft carrier has figured in at least one major accident:

**Nimitz* suffered a major tragedy at sea in 1981, when an aircraft missed a night landing and plowed into a pack of parked aircraft—fourteen crewmen were killed and nearly fifty injured.

**Forrestal* went through a series of fires, including a major conflagration, while on station off North Vietnam (and was instantly dubbed the "Forest Fire" by Navy wags).

**Constellation* had a fire while under construction in the New York Naval Shipyard in 1960. *(Connie* was built at the same time as *Enterprise,* the Navy's first nuclear-powered carrier; since then, the ship has been disparagingly called the *Constellation Prize.)*

Opposite: The "twidgets" of the ship's weapons department let one fly. *General Dynamics photo.*

Fantail of a Soviet destroyer. Crew quarters aboard Soviet ships are much more cramped than those of American counterparts.

**John F. Kennedy* collided with the cruiser *Belknap* off Sicily in 1975. *Big John* escaped pretty much unharmed, but *Belknap* underwent reconstruction so extensive that it's now considered a separate class.

**Ranger* had an engine room fire off Central America not too long ago.

**Coral Sea* suffered damage in a collision with an Ecuadorian tanker in the Caribbean. Ironically, the *Coral Maru* had just emerged from an extensive refit in Norfolk.

**Kitty Hawk* had to undergo repairs after a Soviet submarine tried to surface with the *Hawk*'s 80,000 tons on her back.

**Enterprise* had a fire in 1969 that set off nine major caliber bombs on the flight deck.

**Franklin D. Roosevelt*—the third *Midway* class carrier—was grounded so badly she was soon retired (although the Navy, which was lobbying for nuclear-powered flattops at the time, probably gave *Roosevelt*'s skipper a medal for giving them a reason to replace it).

The Navy likes to point to these accidents as evidence that the carriers are tough enough to take it. Sure, they'll take hits, say Navy brass, but the

Timing is critical in the dangerous business of carrier ops: crewmen crowd around an F-14 about to be launched; as soon as that plane is airborne, they prepare immediately for the next launch. *Photos by Michael Skinner.*

armored flight deck, side armor protection, good compartmentalization, and efficient damage control measures will enable the supercarriers to keep on fighting.

On the other hand, aircraft carriers, with their volatile fuel lines and ordnance exposed on deck while air operations are conducted, are particularly susceptible to catastrophic peacetime accidents. Other types of surface warships have much better safety records. But every ship practices damage control measures constantly. It's one of the things that sets the USN apart from the Soviet Navy, whose sailors have neither adequate training nor adequate equipment. It could make a big difference when the missiles start flying.

The Damage Control Assistant is attached to the engineering department. He supervises the training of the crew in damage control measures and checks the ship's emergency preparations. In battle, he mans Damage Control Central, keeping track of casualties, damage to the ship, and corrective measures taken. The information is provided by at least eight repair parties, each responsible for different sections of the ship.

All seamen are trained in damage control. A course in firefighting is given to every recruit in basic training. Most are also introduced to at least the basics of first aid. In the battle drill, every crewman on board has a station, and a part in damage control operations.

The ships are built to minimize battle damage, and keep fire and flooding from spreading. Compartmentalization is vital to counter damage and to keeping the ship afloat. Navy ships are divided into watertight and airtight compartments by bulkheads and decks. Connected by secure hatches, the compartments can be sealed off to prevent flames or toxic gas from spreading. They can also be flooded to put out fires and provide ballast to keep a damaged ship from tilting over.

Compartments of ships built after 1949 are given a four-part alphanumeric code according to deck, frame, side, and type of space. This

"address" is similar to the way rooms in the Pentagon are designated, and is just as confusing to anyone who has never served in the military. On destroyers and smaller ships, it's not difficult to get around after a couple of false starts. But on larger ships, which seem *so big* on the outside, winding your way through endless cramped passageways and dead-ends can be a frustrating experience.

The decks are numbered from the main deck down. The main deck is the large, open part of the ship. Along with any raised, open platforms, the main deck is also called the weather deck. The superstructure is the part of the ship above the main deck. The "floors" of the superstructure are numbered, beginning with the 01 level (lowest), on up to the highest. However, on aircraft carriers, the hangar deck is considered the main deck, with three others (01 through 03) separating it from the flight deck. Decks below the main deck are numbered in descending order—that is, the second deck is just below the main deck, the third deck is under that, and so on.

It takes a while to get the lingo down. Men have been sailing the Great Ocean for thousands of years, so the new recruit has some catching up to do before he understands what the old salts are talking about. He will learn fast, if the chief has anything to say about it. He will learn his room is actually a berthing compartment, with bulkheads, an overhead, and a deck instead of walls, ceiling, and floor. He will not go upstairs to take a walk outside, he will used the ladder to go topside. Left and right will disappear from his vocabulary, to be replaced by the greater port and starboard, which is the ship's left and right, respectively, whether the sailor himself is facing forward (to the bow) or aft (to the stern).

The Plan of the Day is issued by the executive officer. It is, in effect, a "script" for the ship; it tells what will happen and when, from meals to movies. The POD is usually standard at sea, with some exceptions for out-of-the-ordinary events such as exercises and liberty call.

The plan will dictate the uniform of the day. The traditional "Cracker Jack" outfits with the Dixie Cup sailor's hat are actually dress uniforms, and are worn only on special occasions. At sea, most sailors dress in dungarees, work shirts, and "watch caps"—navy blue baseball caps with the ship's name and designation stitched across the front. The dress uniform looks outdated, but the sailors love it. There was a minor revolt in the ranks when it was briefly ordered out of existence in favor of a nondescript doubleknit uniform that made sailors look like bus drivers.

Most PODs call for a day split into seven sections. The two "dog watches"—four to six in the afternoon and six to eight in the evening—are two hours instead of the usual four-hour watches. This splits up the day so that the men who draw the first overnight watch aren't stuck with it for the duration of the cruise.

Time at sea takes on a strange elasticity, in which the days seem endless, but the tour is over rather quickly. Most time is spent sleeping or at work. On aircraft carriers there are all sorts of diversions, such as boxing exhibitions, basketball games, and "steel beach," a barbeque on the flight deck, complete with steaks, volleyball, and a band flown in for the occasion. On the few times in the past when crews have spent more than a hundred days at sea, the Secretary of the Navy granted each man two cans of beer for his effort.

But such treats are few for crewmen on most surface ships, although, to be fair, they tend not to spend as much time at sea as carrier sailors. Carrier duty is not welcomed by most seamen. The ship is too big and impersonal, thcy say. Liberty, if you get it, is apt to be cut short when someone in the Middle East sneezes. Plus, there's the arrogance of the air wing personnel, universally referred to as "Airedales" by the ship's company, although the term "aircraft characters," a personal favorite, is gaining some usage. Let's take a close-up look at an aircraft carrier—and some aircraft characters.

Sailors in formal dress whites line the deck of *New Jersey,* as it approaches *Enterprise* during VJ Day ceremonies on San Francisco Bay. *Photo by Bill Yenne.*

Chapter Three

Carrier Ops

There *is* a door leading directly onto the flight deck. But rookies on their first visit to the aircraft carrier are never led through it. Here's why.

First, assuming your guide could find it—never a good bet given the fun-house nature of aircraft carrier interiors—the hatch is almost always secured during flight operations. And if it isn't locked, and you aren't stopped by the gang of deck dogs lounging in perpetual exhaustion near the exit, you are likely to walk out the door and into the whirring blades of two E-2C radar planes (and underneath the sign that said "Beware of Props and Rotors"). Or get clotheslined by the wingtip of an F-14 being slingshot off the waist catapult at more than a hundred miles an hour. Or be sucked into the intake of the voracious A-7. Or be blasted off the deck by a passing A-6, or blown off by an idling SH-3 chopper, or squashed like a roach by an S-3 slamming down for a landing.

No, too much mayhem. The flight deck crews live with such danger as a routine, but for a first-time visitor death is *not* a good introduction to life on an aircraft carrier. It tends to spook the surviving members of the media party.

Better to take them the long way around. They

Opposite: U.S.S. *Nimitz* (CVN-68).

Ear protectors and "cranials" — a leather and plastic safety helmet. *Photo by Michael Skinner.*

might have sneaked a peek at the flight deck as they disembarked from the COD plane or the helo, but to tell the truth, most people are so damned happy to be out of the noisy, stifling logistics bird you could lead them overboard and they wouldn't care, as long as they got rid of the cranial. The Navy says the cranial is a safety helmet, but in reality, the segmented leather and plastic thingamabob is a torture device to test how bad you really want to see an aircraft carrier.

Their first real look at the carrier comes after the cranials are pried off, noses are counted, and a short briefing is conducted. (Stay away from anything moving, humming, or squatting menac-

Spiral trim of the E-2C's radome is reflected in the bridge windows. *Photo by Michael Skinner.*

ingly on deck! Empty your pockets and sign this release! And don't look so worried—we haven't lost anyone in the three days we've been out of Norfolk!)

So the tourists step out of the hatch on the starboard side. Their first impression is how *high up* they are. The ocean seems to hiss miles below. It's as if they were looking down on the East River from the porch of a New York co-op. Their second impression is that the carrier is even bigger than they first thought. The island towers over them. That too would resemble a high-rise, if it were not for the antiaircraft guns sprouting from the second story.

But that's nothing compared to the shock the uninitiated get when they round the island. First, there's the smell. There is nothing quite like it. The scent of saltwater and JP-4 steam off the deck, a low, foul-smelling cloud that follows the carrier everywhere.

Then there's the noise. The place is absolutely screaming with jets. The roar of a cat-shot is more felt than heard. When an F-14 blasts off the sound pries through your open mouth and tickles your stomach. A carrier landing is almost as loud. Old hands say they can pick out the steel against steel as the hook hits the deck, but to most people a trap is just one big bash. It sounds as if the aircraft has crashed, which, in a way, it *has.*

Nothing prepares you for your first sight of a carrier during flight ops. Young men in wild-colored shirts scurry everywhere, barely avoiding taxiing planes, which, in turn, narrowly miss *other* aircraft, parked on every square foot of empty deckspace. Suddenly, the crewmen clear the deck, scattering like deer to hide among the huge planes that have somehow arranged themselves into neat rows. Their eyes turn to the stern, to a barely perceptible speck suspended on two columns of faint smoke. The moment is suspended in time. The whir of turbines fades into the background. You are dimly aware of some movement on the deck forward, but all eyes are turned toward the sky behind the ship, to the tiny, winged dot, barely getting larger as hours seem to pass.

Suddenly, the plane's shadow covers the deck. Then shadow and aircraft meet in a deafening smash. The plane tries to roar away, but is caught by its tail. There is a tense moment as the aircraft tries to escape, but it can't break the bond. Finally, the beast surrenders, the snare is released, and the ferocious fighter is led docilely back to the pack by the deckhands.

The drama is cut short by a new commotion, this one on the forward deck. Huge steel plates spring up behind another fighter. Steam is rising from a long cut in the deck. Workers are frantical-

Diamondback F-14 Tomcat launches off one of *America's* waist cats in the Caribbean. *Photos by Michael Skinner.*

ly trying to fasten the big plane to the flight deck. The deckhands run for their lives as flames sprout from the engines and the catapult engages. From a standing start, the aircraft blurs out to the edge of the deck and struggles into a starboard turn.

To the uninitiated it's pandemonium, complete chaos, but the flight deck has rules and rhythms more rigid than most human endeavors. Flight deck workers attend a short course called "P School" to find out how to keep from getting killed while they do their specific jobs. Here's a bit of what they learn, from the deck up.

The flight deck appears to be a solid, unbroken stretch of asphalt. Closer inspection shows it is actually steel, coated with a rubber-like material called "non-skid." Occasionally some of the grooved non-skid will work loose and find its way into the intakes of a jet engine, causing a major and expensive problem called "Foreign Object Damage." To guard against this, the entire deck crew musters in the morning, line-abreast, to march the length of the deck for a "FOD walkdown."

The flight deck is studded with white tie-downs, metal disks sunk into the non-skid about a yard apart used for securing aircraft on the flight deck. The white tie-downs are too small to be seen in most pictures of aircraft carriers, but on the deck they become the most prominent feature.

There are several other breaks in the seemingly unbroken deck. Several APU pits provide auxiliary power for aircraft on alert. There's an ordnance elevator near the island, used to bring weapons up on deck, and, of course, there are the Jet Blast Deflectors (JBDs), arresting cables, and catapults. More on those later.

There's also quite a fleet of vehicles zooming around on carriers. Some of them are quite large, but they tend to get lost on the five acres of flight deck. "Tillie" is an enormous movable crane.

Crewman's eye view of a fouled forward deck. During Cyclic Ops, launches and recoveries must be synchronized to the second. *Photo by Michael Skinner.*

(There is a hoist that is even larger called "Big John," fixed to the ship aft of the island, used to load and unload boats and aircraft when the carrier is berthed.) The "scrubber" is the carrier's equivalent of the type of machine used to smooth ice rinks; when the mixture of saltwater and JP-4 makes the deck too slick for safe landings, the scrubber is called in to clean off the ramp. P-12 is the latest, cut-down version of the carrier's crash truck. But the most common vehicle on the flight deck is the ubiquitous "stubby" or "mule," the squat aircraft tow-tug.

The flight deck is surrounded on both sides by a catwalk. There are seventeen fueling stations on the catwalk. Even-numbered fueling pits are on the port side, odd on the starboard. At the extreme bow and on the end of the angled flight deck there are extensions to catch the bridle attachments used by older aircraft for catapult launching. At the stern the flight deck slopes slightly. This is called the ramp, or rounddown. The dropline is a strip of brightly colored metal that extends from the ramp down the stern. It is lit at night to help aircraft find their way to the centerline.

The centerline does not run down the center of the carrier, but down the center of the angled flight deck, which veers to port of the carrier's stern. Like the steam catapult and V/STOL "ski jump," the angled flight deck is a British invention, designed to allow the safe launch and parking of aircraft forward while recovery operations are conducted aft.

The orange and white centerline extends down the length of the landing area, bordered on either side by the doubled white stripes of the safe launch line. Not coincidentally, the safe launch line is exactly as wide as the wingspan of the old A-3, the largest aircraft ever launched on a carrier. Starboard of the landing area there is a winding red and orange boundary called the foul line. Crewmen must stay behind the foul line during recoveries. Dashed lines by the forward catapults serve the same purpose.

Some carriers carry other markings as well. Helicopter spots are marked with circles divided by a line with a dot in the center. Spots one and two are forward, three and four are near the end of the angled flight deck. There is also a long, white arrow leading from the middle of the centerline to the bow to guide pilots to the correct taxiing angle after landing.

The centerline, dropline, and foul line are lit at night. The whole ship is bathed in sodium vapor lights mounted on the island. These "crime lights" illuminate the carrier without producing shadows. They outline the ship in three dimensions to prevent the flat, often vertigo-inducing "postage stamp" image of the carrier during night landings.

The most important features on the flight deck are the elevators, wires, JBDs and catapults. They come in fours, but that is where the resemblance ends.

The four elevators are the same size and power, but elevators 4 and 2 are used most often. EL-4 is the only lift on the port side (although the *Forrestal*'s port elevator is at the very end of the flight deck, a bad place for it). EL-2 is the middle elevator on the starboard side, near the island. EL-1 is forward, but isn't used as often; it's frequently packed with aircraft during recoveries when the planes are stacked forward after landing. EL-3, aft of the island, is usually "tipped"—overhung with F-14s on alert.

There is a method in the seemingly haphazard way aircraft are arranged on deck. A seasoned carrier crewman can look at a picture of a flattop and tell exactly what was going on the instant the picture was taken.

"Cyclic Ops" is the name given to the schedule of synchronized launches and recoveries that enable the carrier to keep its planes in the air around the clock. It takes a lot of planning. Aircraft must be ready to go and arranged so that they line up on deck in the right order. Time must be set aside for refueling and rearming. The slightest delay can throw off the entire schedule.

The problems inherent in maintaining such a schedule are compounded by the peculiarities of the ship. Some of the older carriers have just two catapults. Even on the new supercarriers, with four catapults, Cyclic Ops can be stalled by bad planning or bad luck. For example, only cats one and three—the starboard catapults fore and aft—are watercooled. Only they can take the heat of an aircraft taking off in afterburner. In addition, cat four—the port catapult on the angled deck—cannot be used to launch S-3s and other large aircraft because the jet blast deflector is too small.

The Air Boss is the one who orchestrates the carrier's flight operations and must keep all these important details in mind. The "Boss"—or Primary Air Controller, to use his proper name—is the head of the ship's Air Department and in charge of flight ops. From his throne in the Pri-Fly tower, the Air Boss is the absolute ruler of everything that flies within five miles and three thousand feet of the carrier.

Crewmen called "handlers" help the boss shuffle the aircraft. From a room inside the island, the handlers, or "manglers," flock around a large drawing of the carrier's flight deck. Using metal models of the aircraft, the handlers keep track of the status of the planes on the flight and hangar decks. They keep in touch with the crewmen who do the actual moving via a two-way radio headset called a "mouse."

In his Pri-Fly, the Air Boss is lord of all he surveys. *Photo by Michael Skinner.*

The carriers are plastered inside and out with "winged keys," the mark of the aviation boatswain's mate. These are the young men who labor on the flight deck and hangar deck to keep the carriers running. The hours are long, the work is hard and dangerous. These crewmen—most of them barely old enough to shave—are entrusted with a great deal of responsibility.

Winged keys are the symbol of the aviation boatswain's mates. *Photo by Michael Skinner.*

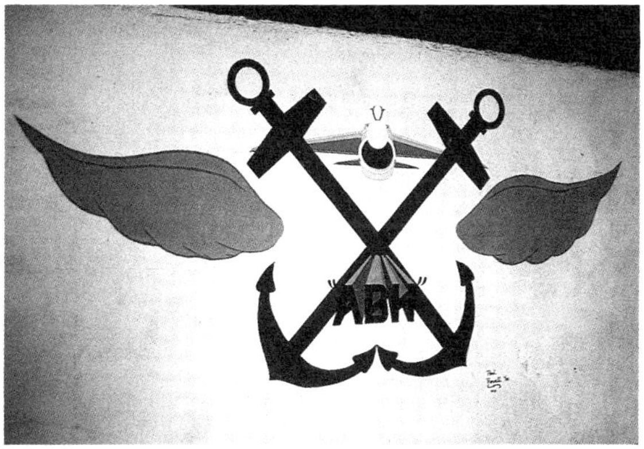

The Alert Birds. Pilots on Alert spend the afternoon in the cockpit. *Photo by Michael Skinner.*

The aviation boatswain's mates work for the Air Department, that part of the ship's company that supports the air wing's flight ops. The Air Department is divided into four sections: V-1 handles the planes on the flight deck, V-2 mans the catapults and arresting rear, V-3 is in charge of the hangar deck, and V-4 refuels the aircraft.

The flight deck personnel are further distinguished by the colors and trim of the jerseys they must wear on duty. The color scheme is so much a part of carrier ops that the flight deck workers are usually referred to as "shirts."

Hornet driver pre-flights F/A-18. The absence of a back seat and a naval flight officer has been just one source of controversy throughout the Hornet program.

Blue shirts are in charge of shuffling the planes on deck. Chockmen weighed down with chains and yellow wooden chocks trudge behind aircraft and tie them down once the planes are spotted. "Wing walkers" march alongside taxiing planes to watch for obstacles. "Plane pushers" do not push the planes by themselves; the white "T" on their jerseys signifies their status as tractor drivers. They man the tugs that tow the aircraft around on deck. A blue jersey with white trim indicates an elevator operator.

Aircraft captains wear brown. They work with the blue shirts, riding the brakes in the planes as they're moved around the deck. Helicopter captains wear brown shirts with red trim.

Visitors to the flight deck wear green jerseys. So do Marine guards and manufacturers' representatives (who have their own offices aboard ship). Plane inspectors—called "checkers"—wear green jerseys with white trim. Squadron maintenance officers wear green shirts plastered with squadron numbers. Most of the green shirts on the flight deck work on the catapults and arresting gear. They wear a black letter on their jerseys corresponding to the particular gear they're responsible for.

Crewmen in charge of the wires, cats, and plane handling wear yellow jerseys. Red shirts with black stripes handle ordnance on the flight deck. Red shirts with black letters are damage control crewmen. Purple shirts take care of refueling the aircraft.

The flight surgeon wears a white tunic. Medical corpsmen also wear white, with a red cross. Messengers wear a white jersey with blue trim. The crewman in the silver suit leaning on the crashtruck is the "Hot Suit" man. His only job is to walk into the flames of a burning aircraft and rescue the crew.

The aircraft on the flight deck have their own personalities. The F-14 Tomcat is the undisputed top cat on the deck. Even with its wings pinned back over the horizontal stabilizers, it is a huge airplane. The two dozen F-14s of the wing's two fighter squadrons are usually spotted aft on both the hangar decks and flight decks. The "Alert Birds" are parked behind the island. The two Tomcats are armed and fueled. F-14s on Alert Five are ready to go on five minutes notice. Alert Fifteen fighters take fifteen minutes.

Sometimes an alert aircraft called the "Deck Launch Interceptor" is parked on the catapult, its idling engines connected to the fuel pits. The DLI is ready to launch instantly, to back up other aircraft on CAP (combat air patrol) or scramble to intercept new threats.

The smallest aircraft on the carrier is the A-7 Corsair II. It's also the last single-seat plane left on deck (although its replacement, the F/A-18 Hornet, is also flown by a single crewman). There are a dozen A-7s in each of the wing's two light attack squadrons.

The A-7 is an aberration in the trend of heavier, more complicated carrier aircraft. The A-7E flown by the fleet does have a "cosmic" bombing system—there is an apocryphal story of a Pentagon study that showed it takes one-and-a-half people to operate the Echo's complex electronics, but otherwise, the straightforward "disposable bomber" is considered a real gentleman's airplane.

The carrier's main battery is the medium attack squadron of ten A-6 Intruders. The A-6 is constantly underrated by everyone but the Navy. Like the A-7, it is subsonic and not very maneuverable, especially when loaded with ordnance and fuel tanks. But the Intruder's ability to fly long distances at low level in bad weather with a big bomb load makes it one of the most valuable planes on the flight deck.

Tales of the A-6's bombing accuracy are legendary (but stories of Marine Intruders dropping eleven of twelve practice bombs in a Dempster Dumpmaster from three thousand feet should be taken with a gram of saltwater). At any rate, although the A-6 first flew in 1960, the design has been constantly upgraded. The A-6 is still in production, with the new ones soon to be coming off the line boasting a series of major improvements, including the same engines used in the F/A-18. *John F. Kennedy* took an experimental all–A-6 attack wing to sea in 1984. The results were good. Look for A-6 squadrons to replace some of the A-7 squadrons that were supposed to be replaced by the expensive, complex, and short-ranged Hornet.

The A-6 design has led to a couple of highly successful spinoffs. There are four KA-6D tankers attached to the wing's Intruder squadron. These are regulation A-6s with navigation beacons and hose

A-6 Intruders provide the real offensive punch of the carrier battle group. *Grumman photo.*

E-2C Hawkeye traps aboard *America. Photo by Michael Skinner.*

SH-3 Sea King is spotted on deck. Rotors and rear fuselage are stowed to take up less room on the deck. *Photo by Michael Skinner.*

reels in place of the night and bad weather bombing electronics.

The EA-6B doesn't fire bombs, bullets, or missiles, but it's an integral part of the carrier's defense. And offense. The Prowler sniffs out and jams enemy communications. The EA-6B

The large S-3 Viking has an elaborate wing-folding mechanism. *Photo by Michael Skinner.*

is stretched to carry a four-man crew and sports more powerful engines to lift its huge bulk into the air. There are four EA-6Bs in each carrier air wing.

The E-2C Hawkeye functions as the carrier's AWACS, and is, in fact, used in that role by Israel over the Middle East. The wing's four Hummers are hard to fit on the hangar deck. They're usually spotted next to the island with the SH-3 helos.

The six Sea Kings, along with the ten wing's S-3 Vikings, make up the carrier's antisubmarine force. The S-3 has the same engines as the Air Force's A-10. Turbofans give the Viking the power to push through the thick air at low altitude (as distinct from the E-2C's twin turboprops, designed to help the Hawkeye claw through the thin atmosphere at high altitudes). The peculiar vacuum-cleaner sound the S-3 makes around the ship has earned it the nickname "Hoover."

Critical parts and people are flown in and out by the "COD-bird" (carrier onboard delivery). These are Grumman C-2 Greyhounds, the basic version of the E-2C Hawkeye with all the electronics removed. A similar stripped-down version of the S-3 Viking was used for COD duty between

Diego Garcia and the carriers off the Persian Gulf. The US-3, as it was designated, was never built, but the prototype still makes the run from Dodge City to Gonzo Station.

Carrier pilots adopt a superior attitude, not just towards the snipes and ship's boys below decks, but to everyone else in the sky as well. Air Force pilots are not known for their humility, but they are saints compared to the "boys on the boat." (The air wing always refers to the carrier as a "boat," which never fails to get a rise out of the ship's company. That's why they do it. The ship's crew can't complain—the carrier's skipper is always a pilot.)

The difference, carrier pilots say, is that USAF pilots are mere jet-jocks while *they* are Naval Aviators, scientists of the air. True, naval air training goes a little further into aeronautics than the other services, but the real difference is that USN pilots possess special flying skills because they are carrier pilots.

Consider the complicated and dangerous ritual Navy pilots have to go through just to get in the air. They emerge from the island, usually in pairs, chatting calmly, as if they could be heard above the crash and din of flight ops (style is important!). The crew has brought the aircraft up from the hangar deck, in a sort of naval version of valet parking.

After a cursory pre-flight—attention to detail would imply a lack of confidence in the flight deck workers—the pilot nonchalantly swings a leg into the cockpit and leans his elbows on the canopy rails. This is really to show plane handlers that he isn't going to hit some button that will let something dangerous fly in their direction, but the casual pose only adds to the naval aviator's image of icy-veined coolness in the face of coming danger.

The crew lines the plane up on the catapult with a metal device called a box. Once in position, the jet blast deflectors rise in sections behind the aircraft. The huge steel plates are designed to direct the engine's thrust up and away from the flight deck. There are four JBDs on most carriers, one for each catapult.

The cat officer gives the signal to run up the engines; one finger for a single-engined aircraft, two for a twin, slowly rotated. He checks forward and aft to clear the aircraft. A high-performance aircraft running up its engines is dangerous to be around. Wandering too close to the aircraft's snout will cause the poor unfortunate to be sucked into the intake and ground into sailor-burger (the A-7 is notorious for this).

And despite the JBD, anyone caught directly behind an engine running up will be blown off the deck like foam off a wave. Deckhands like to rehash the stories of comrades who have been chewed up, spit out, blown away, whacked in two, run over, decapitated by a passing wing, chop-blocked by a runaway cable, or any of the thousands of ways death and/or dismemberment lie in

Positioning marks for aircraft are spot-welded on the cat track. *Photo by Michael Skinner.*

S-3 takes off on patrol. Carrier battle groups keep at least one Viking airborne at all times. *Photo by Michael Skinner.*

wait for the careless on the flight deck. It may be the giddiness of the survivor or the exaggeration of the young adventurer, but deckhands figure they lose at least one man a cruise. And this is *peacetime.*

The catapult shuttle—a device that looks like a roller-skate riding in the groove of the cat slot—is brought to the aircraft. Earlier carrier jets used a bridle attachment to hook up to the catapult. On later aircraft equipped with the nose-tow system, the shuttle is attached directly to a hook on the nosegear.

The catapult crew's hookup man jams the forward nose gear extension into the lip of the shuttle. There is another extension on the rear of the nose gear for the catapult "holdback." Holdbacks are color-coded according to aircraft type and weight. They are designed to break away at a certain level of force and keep the aircraft from launching without enough thrust to get airborne.

When the "hook runner" is satisfied with the setup, he pumps his fist up and down, a signal for the catapult officer to bring the aircraft under tension. When the pilot feels the nosegear stretch under pressure from the catapult, he shoves the throttles up to full military power—maximum thrust without using afterburner.

The force of the catapult is adjusted to the weight of the aircraft; a catapult set to launch a fully-loaded Tomcat would probably fling an A-7 off the bow, never to be seen again. The more sophisticated cats on the newer boats use a computer to adjust the catapult pressure to the weight and type of aircraft, but on the older boats it must be dialed in by hand.

The weight is checked several times, although the aircraft is never actually weighed. Rather, the weight of the dry aircraft is added to whatever fuel and stores have been loaded on. The weight is important, not only to the catapult officer, but to the aircrew as well. If an F-14, for example, weighs out to over 60,000 pounds, it must use afterburner to get airborne. A cat officer holds the weightboard up to the cockpit for a final check. The pilot (or backseater in a Tomcat), gives a thumbs-up signal if the weight is correct.

When the pilot is ready for launch, he salutes. This is not always a regulation salute. Sometimes he only uses one finger. At night, the pilot turns the aircraft's lights on and off to signal he's set. A kneeling crewman windmills his arm and touches the deck in an exaggerated, theatrical motion.

That signals the monkey on the catapult, who puts up his hands (to show *he* hasn't touched anything yet), to check around the aircraft one last time. The pilot comes off the brakes and shoves the throttles out and up, into afterburner. The cat officer punches the button.

Nothing happens. The monkey doesn't actually fire the catapult. The button just signals someone below deck to fire the thing, so there's a three-second delay, the longest three seconds in aviation. In less time than that, the aircraft accelerates to 150 knots and is flung into the air.

Or not. If the catapult has not built up sufficient pressure to launch, or a nose gear collapses, or any number of likely accidents occur, the plane will dribble off the deck and disappear beneath the waves. This can happen in a blink. The crew—braced against the instrument panels with their fingers near the ejection rings—is often the last to know. The air boss is the first, and when he says "Eject!", the air crews eject.

Landing is no easier, or any less dangerous. In fact, "trapping" aboard an aircraft carrier is generally considered the toughest trick in aviation. Naval aviators like to think so, anyway. Zooming in faster than most motorists will ever drive, slamming down solidly on a space smaller than most suburban houses, snagged, and stopped. Suddenly. It's what separates the Navy men from the fly boys.

To help the planes get back aboard, the Navy has come up with a number of devices, none of which the pilots trust completely. The primary landing aid is a group of instruments—the Light Landing Device, the Fresnel Lens Optical System, and the Manually Operated Visual Landing System. Pilots just call the whole assembly the "meatball" because that's what it looks like. In simple terms, the pilot lines up the "ball" on his landing approach; the lights show if he's high, low, or in the groove.

There are also various electronic gizmos beckoning planes back to the carrier that account for a portion of the forest of aerials on the island of an otherwise lightly armed warship. And then there's the ultimate, the Automatic Carrier Landing system, a completely automated contrivance that will land the plane on the carrier all by itself in the worst weather. Even the pilots who trust it hate it. Nothing makes a naval aviator more uncomfortable than having no control, even if a machine can do a better job.

But the pilot's biggest landing aid is another human, the Landing Signal Officer. The LSO is always a squadron pilot, experienced in flying the type of aircraft he's guiding aboard. The LSO stands on a little platform aft of the port elevator, surrounded by safety nets. There's always a crowd on the LSO platform. Except during a bad landing. Then the air is filled with flying bodies diving for the safety net, a horizontal nylon fence that surrounds three sides of the LSO platform.

The LSO talks with the pilots via a headset. In his hand, held high, is a little switch called the "pickle." The LSO studies the pilot's approach. If he doesn't like what he sees, the LSO hits the pickle, the lights on the meatball flash, and the pilot has to go around again. This is called a "wave off."

A plane that attempts to land but fails to catch the arresting cable is a "bolter." The pilots aim for the third of four steel cables strung across the deck forty feet apart (although the older boats have only three wires to make it *more* sporting). The LSO grades each landing. An "Okay Three Wire" (with an underlined "Okay") is the highest compliment he can give. A "C" is the worst; the pilot barely got back aboard and perhaps should have kept going, had he known what was good for him. Somewhere between the two poles are "Tall Moose"—where the plane seems to slam vertically onto the deck, rather than gliding in on a slant—and "Into the pick-up," where the plane seems to climb *up* on deck from under the ramp.

Like the catapults, the arresting cables are set for individual aircraft and weights. The wires are connected to clever machinery below deck that manages to stop a screaming plane safely, without tearing its tail off or letting it slide off the deck. The inch-and-a-half-thick cables are checked carefully each day. A worn cable could snap in two under the terrific stress, and thrumble across the deck to injure or kill a crewman. If any flaw is detected, the wire is unhooked and thrown overboard. Even perfectly good cross-deck pendents are flung into the sea after a hundred traps, just to make sure.

The line between offense and defense is becoming blurred on the Great Ocean. The best way to defend against cruise missile attacks is to attack their launch platforms. And to do that, the carrier air wing mounts an Alfa Strike.

An Alfa Strike is an all-out attack on enemy ships or land-based installations. It is the carrier's —the fleet's—knockout punch. With the exception of the ASW aircraft and the minimum number of planes needed to defend the carrier, every available aircraft in the wing takes part.

Mounting an Alfa Strike is a monumental task. Just getting the planes off on time is difficult. Tactical aircraft can stay in the air for a mere hour and a half without refueling. If it takes too long for the strike to launch and form up, the whole mission is in jeopardy.

The flight deck is even more tense during an Alfa Strike; the pace is a little more frantic. Noise and stress are cranked up a notch. Loaded with fuel and weapons, the aircraft are more sluggish, harder to handle. They must be launched in a precise order. They must be launched without delay.

There are three groups in an Alfa Strike. The fighter escort will clear the way of enemy fighters and CAP the target. They may be directed by E-2Cs farther back or by a controlling agency aboard a Navy cruiser. On MIGCAP, the Tomcats will carry shorter-ranged missiles, the radar-directed Sparrow and remarkable heat-seeking Sidewinder. Navy pilots are proud of their reputations as dogfighters and are fierce foes in air-to-air combat.

The suppression group goes in first to soften up the defenses. The EA-6B leads the way, jamming radars on the ground as well as communications between enemy fighters and their controllers. A-6s and A-7s armed with long-range anti-radiation missiles try to pick off surface-to-air missile batteries. Their goal is to keep the defenders' heads down, to keep the enemy from firing at the strike group following.

The strike group is the carrier's Sunday punch. There aren't enough stand-off weapons to go around. Once the suppression group has fired their Harpoons into the target, the strike group goes in to finish the job. They can carry fragmentation bombs—which riddle the enemy's radar dishes and effectively blind him—and fuel-air explosives, which can create a monstrous fire storm and decimate lightly armored ships.

Usually, the strike group will carry ordinary "iron" bombs. The planes come in low and then pop up, to confuse the radars and give the crews a better look at the target. They'd better not miss; the low speed of the carrier's attack aircraft is a real drawback when trying to get away.

On the return flight, the aircraft will pass over a friendly ship. The ship will "delouse" the Alfa Strike, making sure no enemy aircraft are following the planes back to the carrier. Planes still carrying bombs will dump them into the sea rather than try to land aboard the flattop with live ordnance on board.

Of course, our ships can also attack their ships. And our ships can defend themselves against cruise missile attacks without the help of aircraft, although it's a tricky proposition. We'll find out just *how* tricky in the next chapter.

The "meatball" — a group of landing aid devices that are the pilot's best friend and worst enemy. *Photo by Michael Skinner.*

Chapter Four

War at Sea

When Lord Nelson sailed into harm's way off Trafalgar, he had no reason to fear anything above the sea or beneath it. Even as the French *Fouguex* appeared on the horizon, the admiral had half an hour to reconsider his bold plan. There was no need for rapid, secure command of the English fleet from *Victory*'s deck. The signal flags were sent aloft. The message was simple: "England expects every man to do his duty."

Nowadays, Nelson would not even have time to shake out his famous telescope. By the time today's threats appear, it's often too late to do anything about them. What would the admiral think of twentieth century war at sea, where missiles boil out from under the ocean, scream from the troposphere, or fly hundreds of miles under their own power?

Today's commanders don't even have the luxury of seeing their opponents. Even if the enemy were within sight—a possibility that grows progressively more unlikely as weapons' ranges reach out over the horizon—the captain no longer commands in battle from the bridge. Tactical decisions nowadays are made from deep inside the ship, in the combat information center. There, in the reddish glow of battle lamps and the ghostly green phosphorescence of data screens, modern skippers call the shots.

A salvo from *New Jersey*'s 16-inch guns.

The shift from standing tall on the bridge to hunkering down over the video screen is indicative of the change in surface combat actions since World War II. The modern warship sails two seas: the Great Ocean, with its waves and currents, and the Sea of Beams, with its radio waves and electric currents. Like Nelson's wind, electromagnetic radiation cannot be seen. But it is the key to winning today's war at sea. Just as the ancient mariners used the wind to their advantage, contemporary warriors must ride the Sea of Beams to survive and win.

Modern ships attack and defend, for the most part, with guided missiles. Consequently, most space is given over to missile launchers and the electronic equipment needed to direct the ship's own missiles or confuse the "vampires"—incoming hostile missiles. Electronic warfare is important in land and air combat as well, of course, but it is vital in naval operations. Today, most of the ships' systems use the airwaves as their battlefield. "Hard-kill" weapons—guns, torpedoes, and depth-charges—are fewer in number but more lethal, as a result of electronic guidance.

An aircraft carrier's island bristles with aerials and antennae. Electronic warfare is the key element in modern naval engagements. *Photo by Michael Skinner.*

The Soviet Navy is very interested in electronic warfare. The superstructure of Russian ships bristle with aerials, antennae, receivers, transmitters, bulges, screens, and various protuberances designed to fill the airwaves with signals that will find hostile targets and guide missiles toward them while simultaneously denying the enemy the communications he needs to press home an attack. The USN is also ready to wage warfare in the ether, but instead of relying exclusively on powerful transmitters and raw radiant force, as the Soviet Navy does, American ships tend to use deception and finesse.

The change from brute force to electronic firepower has changed the look of most navies. Gone is the heavy armor, the batteries of huge guns and smaller caliber weapons that characterized the old dreadnoughts. Post-war Navy ships carry only light composite armor to protect against fragmentation. Modern warships are bigger than their World War II counterparts, but the absence of great numbers of recognizable weapons systems make them appear less impressive. With their empty decks and sheer superstructures, they look like floating office parks.

But make no mistake. Today's surface warships are deadly killers. Even a World War II heavy cruiser would have its hands full battling a modern frigate. Miniaturization has given naval architects the capability of putting the same amount of firepower in a much smaller package. And automation has shrunk the size of the crew, with the space saved given over to more fuel, ammunition, and electronics.

The 5-inch gun is the largest on modern Navy warships. The Navy's lack of shore bombardment firepower was one of the arguments for bringing back the battleships and their big guns.

The nuclear-powered guided missile cruiser *Virginia* is one of the U.S. Navy's most formidable warships. But casual observers are often disturbed by the apparent lack of weapons on the deck.

The higher rate of fire and better accuracy of modern naval guns has done away with the need for large numbers of duplicate weapons. Surprisingly, even in World War II engagements in which aircraft were not a factor—night actions, for instance—the smaller-caliber guns, with their high rate of fire, were more useful than the big-bore monsters (although it was the torpedo that usually decided the outcome).

With the exception of those on the recommissioned battleships, there are no guns larger than five inches in the modern Navy. And the majority of those guns are severely limited in their capabilities. *Perry* frigates—the most common class of warships in the Navy—mount a single 76mm.

An experiment that failed—an 8-inch major caliber lightweight gun being tested aboard the destroyer *Hull*. The gun proved too inaccurate and expensive, and the plan was scrapped. *(USN Photo)*

gun, useful for some antiair and short-range surface actions, but of no use in shore bombardment. And the *Spruance* class destroyer's lone 5″ gun lacks the electronics and elevation to fire at air targets.

The Navy experimented with a larger gun for a while, installing an 8″ gun in the forward turret of the destroyer *Hull.* The Mk-71 Major Caliber Lightweight Gun was intended to give smaller ships the punch of a World War II cruiser. The first large-caliber gun designed by the Navy in twenty-five years, the Mk-71 was operated by a single crewman. It fired six different types of shells at the rate of a dozen rounds a minute. The

Phalanx 20mm gun firing aboard *America.* The six-barrel Gatling gun provides close-in antiaircraft on most modern Navy ships.

gun would have been useful in shore bombardment, but proved too inaccurate and expensive for Navy ships. The program was cancelled and the gun removed.

Surprisingly, with the rise of anti-ship missiles, some types of guns are making a comeback. Spewing out huge numbers of relatively inexpensive shells, modern rapid-fire naval guns can put up a "curtain of steel" between the target ship and the incoming missile, something surface-to-air missiles, with their limited numbers and slow rate of fire, could never do.

The Navy's Close-in Weapons System, the Mk-15 Phalanx gun, can put out up to 3,000 rounds a minute, using a six barrel "Gatling gun" arrangement. The 20mm shells are made of depleted uranium to give them heavy hitting power. The self-contained fire control radar is protected by a white dome. The resulting appearance, plus the gun's penchant for jerking into action seemingly without provocation, has earned Phalanx the nickname "R2D2" on board ship (although aboard *Enterprise,* which has three Phalanx mounts instead of the usual four, the guns are called "Huey, Dewey and Louie" after the robots in the Bruce Dern movie *Silent Running).*

Missiles are the main battery now, but guns are still useful for combatting the fast patrol boats that provide the bulk of Third World fleets. They're also good for "power projection"—electronic warfare antennae and missile containers impress naval experts, but there's something about gun barrels bristling on deck that makes people want to see things your way. Besides, as one naval writer points out, sometimes you need to fire a shot across the enemy's bow, and that's kind of hard to do with a cruise missile.

Modern warships cost more, certainly, but size has little to do with it. HY-80 steel is cheap, compared to the electronics that really drive up the price of ships these days. The cost of the hull is less than a tenth of the total price of today's ships. And America's role as keeper of the Great Ocean dictates that even the smallest ships in the fleet must be capable of blue water operations. A bigger ship makes for better seakeeping, as well as providing more comfort for the crew. As the Soviet Navy moves out into the deeper waters, they are discovering that the great many smaller ships they have built—though they may be the darlings of some members of the U.S. Congress—just aren't up to sustained operations far from port.

Paradoxically, bigger ships are, generally speaking, faster ships. In terms of speed, a large hull is much more efficient than a small one. In any case, speed is not the tactical advantage it once was. No ship can outrun a helicopter, much less a cruise missile. The Navy has settled on a speed of about thirty knots for entry into the carrier battle group. Carriers need a wind speed of about thirty knots across the deck to launch aircraft. In a dead calm they must provide that speed themselves, and the rest of the task force must be able to keep up.

Sustained speed is useful for steaming to trouble spots in a hurry. Rapid acceleration is useful for quick course changes in station-keeping and defensive maneuvering. Unfortunately, most marine power systems are good for fuel-efficient sustained speed or quick bursts of speed, but not both.

Conventional oil-burning steam turbines are reliable and efficient, up to a point. But to coax the last 10 percent of speed from the engines, an oil-burner will use the same amount of fuel as it does getting up to 50 percent power from a standing start. Since nuclear-powered ships also use steam turbines, they have the same drawbacks, as well as suffering from the poor acceleration rates of pure oil-burners. Smaller ships may use diesel engines, which are quick to start and quick to accelerate, although, as with steam turbines fuel consumption tends to go up geometrically with increases in speed.

On the other hand, there is the gas turbine,

which is really just a navalized version of an aircraft's jet engine. Gas turbines are enormously powerful and brisk. They can hustle a ship from zero to top speed in sixty seconds. Unfortunately, they are not fuel efficient, gobbling prodigious amounts of fuel, no matter what speed the ship is going.

To give ships some flexibility (and to give the world what it doesn't need—another set of naval acronyms) many modern warships are built with *two* sets of engines: steam, nuclear, or diesel turbines for fuel efficiency, and gas turbines for high speed, high acceleration maneuvers. COSAG stands for "combined steam and gas propulsion." The gas turbines are switched on to boost speed only when needed. This may seem wasteful, but it's actually more efficient than trying to run the oil-burners flat-out.

Some ships use different engines exclusively for different speeds. CODOG (combined diesel *or* gas) ships, for example, switch off the diesel engines and turn on the gas turbine for high speed operations. *Spruance* class destroyers feature a novel COGAG arrangement, using two gas turbines—one for high speed and another gas turbine engine geared for cruising.

Spruance destroyers need the extra speed for sub chasing. In itself, speed is not that important in antisubmarine warfare. Most modern attack subs can outrun all but the fastest surface craft, and at high speed the ship's sonar can't hear a damn thing but its own noise anyway. But at a dead stop, the sonar operates most efficiently, and the hunter doesn't give itself away. So ASW pickets use "sprint and drift" tactics, steaming far ahead of the main battle group, then crashing to a stop to listen for subs.

The *Spruance* is a good example of a modern, purpose-built warship. The trend toward specialized design was evident even in World War II, but most post-war Navy ships are built primarily to perform a specific role in a task force. *Spruance* is perhaps the best surface platform in the world for the prosecution of hostile submarines, but with a single 5″ gun and very limited antiaircraft capability, it depends on other members of the battle group to defend it from aircraft and enemy ships, just as the rest of the task group members depend upon *Spruance* to protect them from submarines. Critics can always find something lacking in every Navy ship, but the ships can really be judged only in the context in which they are designed to operate—as part of a carrier battle group.

The CVBG (aircraft carrier battle group) is more than the sum of its parts. Nominally, the battle group consists of at least one aircraft carrier and its escorts (although the Navy would prefer to go to war with two carriers in each group, to provide more flexibility in cross-deck operations). Usually a couple of cruisers stay close to the carrier. If the flattop is nuclear powered, the accompanying cruisers will be nuclear powered as well. About half a dozen destroyers and frigates—called "small boys" by carrier sailors—will surround the nucleus. They will be scattered for miles around in seemingly random positions, always moving. The exact locations of the escorts will depend upon the nature and direction of the potential threat.

Most important is the posting of the "shooters" —those cruisers and destroyers with long-range antiaircraft missile capability. If the axis of the threat is known, some CGs (guided missile cruisers) or DDGs (guided missile destroyers) will be positioned in that direction to provide a "missile trap." They'll shoot down as many oncoming aircraft and cruise missiles as they can, while giving a "heads up" to the ships at the center of the battle group to look out for any "leakers" that get through the outer defenses.

Some of the ships out on the perimeter can employ electronic warfare against the incoming missiles, to try to jam or confuse the radar seekers in the missiles' noses. Smaller ships can electronically enhance their radar image to appear the size of carriers to the incoming missiles. This is called

One of four gas turbine engines being installed in a *Spruance* class destroyer.

Canisters containing chaff, metal foil strips used to confuse enemy radars. Chaff tuned to the proper frequency can simulate an entire aircraft or flight of aircraft.

"banzai jamming," and is, understandably, not too popular with the crews.

Most ships also carry other countermeasures to thwart cruise missile attacks. Heat-seeking missiles can often be decoyed by flares. Radar-guided missiles can be misled by chaff—strips of aluminum foil ejected from cannisters that form a dense cloud to hide the ship from the incoming missile.

The Navy's primary electronic warfare suite is the AN/SLQ-32 (pronounced "slick thirty-two"). There are four different versions. SLQ-32(V) is the minimum EW (electronic warfare) set, designed to warn minor logistic and amphibious ships of the launch and tracking of hostile anti-ship missiles. SLQ-32(V2) provides additional coverage of weapons control radars for frigates and most destroyers. SLQ-32(V3) has the same capabilities, but gives the option of jamming the enemy radars. It's fitted to cruisers, some destroyers, and principal amphibious and logistics ships.

Antisubmarine defense of the CVBG follows a similar, layered pattern. Although the Navy doesn't publicize the fact, there is usually at least one nuclear-powered attack submarine in each battle group. The fast attack sub prowls ahead of the task group to clear out any hostile subs lying in wait for the carrier. The attack subs operate more or less independently of the rest of the battle group. The surface ships would like more direct support from the hunter-killer submarines, but sub skippers are afraid close communication with the task group would betray their position and leave them vulnerable to counterattack. ASW planes from the carrier and ASW ships guard the battle group's flanks against sub attack, while ASW helicopters from the carrier and choppers from the ships in the inner defense ring keep watch close in.

The ships communicate with each other through radio, or, in an EMCON (emissions controlled) environment, through flags and signal lights. In a fight, the most important communications network is NTDS (Naval Tactical Data System). NTDS consoles are connected via data link, so each ship or plane so equipped sees the big picture. NTDS allows ships positioned on opposite ends of the battle group to exchange information. It's a real force multiplier, allowing each unit in the task group to see on its consoles what all the other units are seeing on their radar and sonar displays.

Guided missile destroyer stands plane guard duty during flight ops. About a half dozen surface war ships accompany each carrier in the battle group. *Photo by Michael Skinner.*

NTDS-equipped ships use a high-speed data link called Link-11. Ships that aren't patched into the NTDS network can still share in the information net using Link-11, but the data must be transmitted slowly via teletype, rather than appearing instantaneously on the consoles in the CIC. Large planes, such as the E-2C and the S-3, can use Link-11, but smaller fighters and attack aircraft are usually patched into NTDS by an ultra-high frequency voice link called Link-4A.

Depending upon the situation, the messages may or may not be encrypted. Data link is pretty secure, anyway—point-to-point microwave communication is hard to disrupt. But Link-4A could present a problem. The U.S. has put a lot of effort into scrambling communications between hostile aircraft and their controllers, and it's reasonable to assume the Soviets are also working on ways to jam or spoof such communications between our carrier fighters and their handlers.

To defend the battle group, the Navy has gone to a sophisticated air defense system based on vector logic. The outer zone is patrolled by F-14 fighters armed with the very long range Phoenix missile. With its sophisticated AWG-9 weapons system (pronounced "aug" as in "dog"), the Tomcat can track two dozen targets and guide as many as six AIM-54 missiles at targets up to sixty miles away. Midair refueling by carrier-borne KA-6 tanker planes enables the F-14s to stay on station for hours, or push their orbits out hundreds of miles away from the battle group. The E-2C directs the intercept, passing information one-way through the data link so both the carriers and the fighters can run silent.

In the vector logic system, single planes are assigned patrol areas. For every two fighters forward, there is another in reserve, ready to take up the battle if the planes on station are shot down, or run out of fuel or ammo. Behind that, there is *another* back-up plane on the carrier, in "Deck Launched Interceptor" mode. In DLI status, the aircraft is armed, manned, and standing by on the catapult, with fuel hoses connected and the engines running.

The vector logic system works better than the old outer defense systems, which were basically freelance set-ups, easily saturated. But unless the threat axis is well defined, vector logic takes a lot of planes, which is one reason the Navy wanted the Hornet so bad. The F/A-18 was sold as an attack aircraft, but its big improvement over the A-7 is its ability to contribute to the CVBG's air defence grid as a fighter.

Even in peacetime, carrier skippers put a lot of planes up in the air. There is usually at least one S-3 aloft, buzzing around the battle group snooping for subs. There is also an E-2C on perpetual patrol, even in the most benign environments. The Navy is *very* nervous about anyone getting close to the carriers. Task force commanders on Gonzo Station in the Arabian Sea have made it clear that they will open fire on any unidentified aircraft that come within five miles of the carrier at an altitude lower than 2,000 feet.

Any strange aircraft within hundreds of miles are intercepted, identified, and escorted out of the area. The carrier keeps two fighters, called "Alert Birds," armed, crewed, and fueled at all times for this purpose. F-14s on Alert Fifteen status are ready to scramble on fifteen minutes notice; Alert Five birds can get airborne in just five minutes. And in a really touchy situation, the Alert fighters will be constantly ready to launch in DLI mode.

The typical supercarrier air wing consists of about a hundred aircraft. Like the ships in the battle group, the carrier aircraft are specialized machines and depend upon one another for survival. In addition to the two squadrons of twelve F-14 fighters on board, each big-deck carrier totes

F-14 Tomcat refuels from one of the air wing's KA-6 tankers.

punch out. There is also a plane guard ship, usual-twenty-four A-7 attack aircraft (in two light attack squadrons), a medium attack squadron of ten A-6 bombers, four KA-6 tankers, four EA-6B electronic warfare aircraft, four E-2C radar and control aircraft, ten S-3 ASW aircraft, and six SH-3 ASW helicopters.

During air operations, at least one of the carrier's choppers will be airborne on "plane guard" duty. The SH-3 circles one side of the ship during launches and recoveries to get a head start on rescuing any crewman who may have to ditch or

Forward missile launcher fires a Standard antiaircraft missile.

ly one of the battle group's destroyers or frigates, on duty during flight ops. It may keep station anywhere around the carrier—except right in front—but it usually steams about a mile behind. The plane guard ship backs up the helicopter on rescue duty, and, once the crew is fished out of the water, circles over the spot where the plane went down to prevent the wrong parties from mounting salvage operations.

The small boys help the carrier in other ways, as well. They tow spars behind the stern for target practice. They try to put themselves between Soviet trawlers and the carrier. Sometimes a surface ship—usually a cruiser—will go in close to shore to direct flight operations ("Red Crown" was the controlling agency aboard various cruisers off the coast of North Vietnam during the war in Southeast Asia).

In fact, until the rise of the modern cruise missile, most Navy ships were relegated to protecting the carrier from other ships and planes. But the cruise missile has made just about every surface ship an aircraft carrier in its own right, and given offensive punch back to the black shoe Navy.

Cruise missiles are the contemporary equivalent of the Japanese *Kamikaze* planes of World War II. Each one is a small aircraft, carrying a warhead instead of a pilot. The USN pioneered the use of modern cruise missiles in the fifties with the Regulus program. But the Navy bit off more than it could chew with these early strategic cruise missiles—they were expensive and, ultimately, technologically unworkable. The programs were easily killed by the jealous carrier aviation lobby, who saw a potential threat in pilotless aircraft.

But the Soviets saw something different in surface-to-surface missiles: a way to get tactical air power at sea without aircraft carriers. The Soviet Navy went for these missiles in a big way and, after some notable failures, developed the weapon to a point that made even the USN take notice.

The Navy was late getting back into the surface-to-surface missile business. But unlike the Soviets, they've managed to come up with a workable weapon on the first try. American superiority in microcircuitry and small engine technology has made Harpoon one of the best anti-ship missiles in the world. The Navy now has more than 3,000 of them. It's an important program, but it hasn't received much publicity, probably because it has gone well.

Harpoon started development in the late sixties when the Navy needed something to defeat subs that might pop up close to the carriers and launch cruise missiles from the surface. But the missile has evolved into a potent anti-ship weapon, used by seventeen nations on a variety of launching platforms.

Since its introduction in 1977, Harpoon has been furiously backfitted to just about every USN weapon system on, above, and beneath the Great Ocean. On larger ships it's fired from ASROC or Standard missile launchers, although most skippers prefer the integrated container/launchers system in order to reserve more space in the ship's surface-to-air missile magazines. Submarines launch Harpoon from torpedo tubes in watertight containers. As it breaks the surface, the missile's first stage fires and it streaks to the target. Harpoon has been fired from nearly every combat aircraft in the Navy inventory, from the little A-7 to the big P-3. Even Air Force B-52s can carry Harpoon.

The secret to such easy installation is the missile's "fire and forget" quality. A smart weapon, Harpoon doesn't need an associated fire control radar of mid-course guidance from another platform. Give it a rough idea where the target is, and Harpoon follows a course set by its on-board computer until the target is close enough to be sniffed out by the active radar seeker in the missile's nose.

Harpoon has a range of more than sixty miles. To save fuel, it cruises at about twenty-five-hundred feet at slightly less than the speed of

Harpoon anti-ship cruise missile fired from canister launcher. Harpoon has emerged as one of the Navy's most successful programs. *McDonnell Douglas photo.*

sound. When the target is detected, the missile drops down to just above the waves. On its final approach, Harpoon pitches up sharply, making it difficult for opposing fire control radars to achieve tracking solutions. The altitude gain also lines the missile up for a near-vertical attack on the most vulnerable part of the ship. Harpoon's 500-pound warhead is set to explode only after the missile has penetrated the hull.

The much larger Tomahawk anti-ship cruise missile follows a similar course, but comes straight in without popping up. TASM, or Tomahawk anti-ship missile, is just one of a family of sea-launched cruise missiles that also includes the conventionally armed land attack missile (TLAM/C) and the nuclear armed land attack version (TLAM/N). With their long ranges—250 miles for the anti-ship missile and more than twice that for the land attack versions—the Tomahawks open up a lot of options for the Navy. But the opportunities are not without cost.

Tomahawks are expensive, technologically ambitious (more than half the initial test flights were failures) and potentially destabilizing. Although less than a quarter of the 4,000 Tomahawks scheduled for production will carry nuclear warheads, only the Navy will know which ones. The Pentagon thinks this is good because the Soviets will never know which ships are the real threats, and will have to defend against just about every Navy vessel as if it were a Trident submarine. But this could also tend to lower the nuclear threshold, if the Soviet Union decides to shoot first—with *their* nuclear weapons—and ask questions later.

The cruise missile has given the battleship a new life. Armed with thirty-two Tomahawks and sixteen Harpoons, the battlewagons return as more formidable opponents than they were in World War II. Armor makes them slow, but it also protects them against the relatively puny warheads on most cruise missiles, which are often no more powerful than an 8″ shell. Phalanx antiaircraft guns and a helipad were also included in the retrofit.

But the main reason behind the comeback of the battleship is its nine 16″ guns, which give the Navy a much needed capability for shore bombardment. Each is capable of hurling a shell the weight of a Volkswagen more than thirty miles inland, although the old silk bags of powder charges threw off the aim of the big guns in Lebanon. The battleship can put 22 tons of high explosives on the beach with one salvo. It would take an hour for all the A-6s in a carrier's air wing to deliver as

Tomahawk cruise missile fired from armored box launcher. *McDonnell Douglas photo.*

Tomahawk long-range cruise missile during test flight. The long-range Tomahawk with its conventional or nuclear warhead has added great capabilities to the fleet, but has brought with it some disturbing political questions. *McDonnell Douglas photo.*

much firepower.

The reactivation of the *New Jersey* cost about $330 million, or about the price of a new *Spruance* destroyer. So far the Navy has gotten its money's worth, if only in publicity. Of course, it takes a lot less to run a destroyer than a battleship. *Spruance* needs about three hundred officers and men to sail. Automation has reduced the *New Jersey*'s complement by nearly eight hundred, but the ship still requires a crew of more than sixteen hundred men, or about the same number as all the players and coaches in the National Football League.

But the Navy has found no shortage of volunteers to man their "new" dreadnoughts. The ship is not hard to run. Most of its systems are common throughout the naval surface warfare community. It uses standard electronic equipment, and its propulsion system is the same as that of the *Midway* class aircraft carriers, and the *Sacramento* class oilers.

Of course, battleships were not built with fuel economy in mind. The smudge rising from *New Jersey*'s stack represents a lot of money going up in smoke. And even with all the huffing coming from the battleship's smokestack, the ship lugs too much heavy armor around for its old power plant to keep up with nuclear-powered carriers. Instead, the Navy plans to use the battleships in a task force called the "Surface Action Group."

The SAG is a throwback to the days of great—and flightless—fleets. The Surface Action Group (sometimes called the Surface Strike Group) would operate either in loose coordination with a carrier battle group or to escort an amphibious force or an underway replenishment group. Or the SAG could hunt other warships on its own, perhaps under the cover of land-based airpower or outside the range of enemy aircraft. With a battleship as the centerpiece, the SAG would operate with destroyers and frigates for antisubmarine and limited antiair protection. Armed with the mighty Tomahawk, the battleship could be used to strike hostile targets far inland. Such a mission could complicate life for enemy planners. But it presents some problems for its users as well.

Perhaps the toughest problem with using Tomahawk—and all cruise missiles, for that matter—is targeting. The cruise missile's biggest asset is its range. But that could also be its biggest liability. Targeting is not much of an issue in the land attack versions. Even the conventionally armed TLAM/C will be aimed at ports, airfields, depots—targets that aren't likely to go anywhere. Both land attack versions use internal guidance, constantly checking the terrain below against electronic maps stored in an on-board computer. And as for TLAM/N, well, as they say in the strategic services: A nuclear warhead tends to solve a lot of targeting problems.

But ships move, and knowing where your enemy is is just as important now as it was in Nelson's day. If anything, it's tougher to locate the enemy these days, because, with long-range, relatively slow-flying cruise missiles, you not only have to know where the enemy is, you also have to have a pretty good idea of where he'll be when the missiles arrive.

Target detection is perhaps the most difficult and most critical stage of modern naval combat. The side that gets the first shot has an overwhelming advantage. The days of ships lining up to exchange broadsides is gone forever. Warfare on the Great Ocean has become a series of ambushes, and the side that doesn't achieve surprise will most likely retire quietly. If they can.

There are two types of ocean surveillance: strategic and tactical. Strategic systems are concerned with the big picture. Both sides use satellites to keep an eye on naval bases and fleets at sea. American satellites are usually more accurate; intelligence snobs call Russian satellites "blob detectors." Satellites are still relatively invulnerable, despite a growing interest in antisatellite warfare on both sides.

And the data must still get from space to ships at sea. In the old days—say, five or ten years ago—satellite data had to be relayed from ground receiving stations to the fleet. By the time the commander at sea got the information, it was often tactically useless. Now, most major Navy warships can get satellite information beamed down directly. The Russians can do it too, but not as well.

Satellites have their drawbacks. They are scarce, fragile, expensive, and they can't be everywhere at once. Some in permanent orbit can be positioned to cover the globe, but it takes a while to complete the circuit, and they're apt to be out of position a great deal of the time. Some short-lived satellites can be launched for special contingencies, but they have to know where to look in the first place. In addition, the picture from space can be obscured by clouds and bad weather, and the enemy usually knows what the other side's satellites are seeing every minute.

Although the superpowers are working hard to improve their capabilities, so far there is no evidence that the systems have been refined to the point that enemy forces at sea detected from space can be *targeted* from there—that is, that the satellite itself can operate as part of a weapon's fire control system. So although satellites give navies a head start, they cannot be relied upon to pinpoint the targets. That's a job for tactical surveillance systems.

The USN has given the grandiose title "Soviet Ocean Surveillance System" to the rather motley collection of converted trawlers, aging bombers, ships, and subs enlisted to keep track of American forces at sea. The laws of the sea allow the AGI vessels to hound—and even disrupt—American naval movements in peacetime. And in the first stage of a surprise attack, the Russian warships shadowing U.S. Fleet movements might even get off the first shot. A nuclear attack by such a ship could have serious consequences, and it might as well be a suicide attack. As one naval officer puts it, Soviet ships will lead a "short, exciting life" in the next war.

But after the opening shots, Soviet naval intelligence would probably deteriorate drastically. Based on human observation and interpretation, the Soviet Ocean Surveillance System is likely to be overwhelmed by the sheer amount of data coming in, even as its sources of data quickly disappear.

The USN also relies on spy ships, among other

The Soviet Bear D, naval reconnaissance aircraft, shadows an American carrier battle group in the Pacific. The TU-95 is a common sight in the "Bear Box," west of Hawaii.

means, to gather intelligence. It used to depend on AGIs a lot more, but a number of American intelligence ships have been involved in rather ugly international incidents, which has inclined it towards more high-tech means of keeping track of Soviet naval movements: *Pueblo,* captured by North Korea in 1968, *Mayaguez,* seized by Cambodia in 1975, and *Liberty,* attacked by Israel in 1967 are examples. Some USN ships are still drafted into shadowing Russian exercises at sea. In fact, a guided missile destroyer, *Harold E. Holt,* did perhaps *too* good a job observing a Soviet V/STOL carrier dead in the water in the South China Sea—the Russian skipper fired flares at the destroyer's bridge in an effort to scare it away.

But the Navy prefers to use submarines for long-term snooping. There are nine fast attack subs fitted out for intelligence gathering, with extra sensors mounted on periscopes. The "Holy Stone" submarines are especially adept at keeping track of port movements and naval evolutions, but just about any American attack sub can be detailed to keep watch on the Soviets at sea.

The Russians also like to use subs for surveillance, but for tactical targeting, the Soviets, like the Americans, prefer airborne platforms. The mainstay of the Soviet naval reconnaissance forces is the TU-95 Bear, a huge, four-engine turboprop with long range and lots of room for electronics and fuel. In the war in Southeast Asia, TU-95s used to fly over American task forces as they crossed the International Date Line in the Pacific, just to let the U.S. Navy know they were not alone out there. It was a neat trick, but much easier to do in peacetime than in wartime.

The American equivalent of the Bear is the P-3 Orion. Designed as an antisubmarine aircraft, the P-3 has proven itself invaluable in the maritime reconnaissance role. It can also be armed with bombs, torpedoes, or Harpoon missiles, to attack the targets it has sniffed out. The P-3 is another example of a highly successful—and important—naval program that has not received much publicity because of its success.

But land-based aircraft have their limitations. They can travel long distances, but because it takes them quite a while to get to station they are not good for quick response. And, despite their long range, they have to be based *somewhere.* If there's no base nearby, they're useless; if there *is* a base close by, it can be attacked. The planes themselves are relatively defenseless against modern fighters and surface-to-air missiles. In fact, the only reasonable role for the Soviet Forger V/STOL aircraft is to chase away allied maritime reconnaissance planes.

Although land-based recce aircraft are generally more capable than their ship-borne counterparts, carrier reconnaissance planes are much better than

nothing, outside the range of land bases. This is why the aircraft carrier is considered the weapon of decision on the Great Ocean. With its fleet of aircraft and helicopters, the carriers can search hundreds of thousands of miles, above and beneath the sea, and they have the muscle to sink anything they find, at ranges far beyond the reach of surface ships.

The E-2C Hawkeye has no equal in the middle of the ocean, keeping an eye out for long-range hostile airborne threats without revealing the carrier's position. The S-3 pushes the carrier battle group's ASW barriers out hundreds of miles. The Viking also has a secondary surface search capability that is getting more attention.

Most surface ships must rely on helicopters for over-the-horizon protection. Choppers have found a permanent home on all but the smallest ships. Their ability to take off and land vertically means they can be accommodated on board in very little space. And helicopters can hover, which is vital for prosecuting subs and spotting targets.

On the other hand, they are easily destroyed, slow, and short-ranged. They are no match for fixed-wing aircraft, but in the absence of carriers and land-based aircraft they can hold their own, as long as they stay low and out of the reach of enemy antiaircraft systems.

Target identification and acquisition is the most difficult problem facing naval officers today. The Navy is depending on helicopters for over-the-horizon targeting data, because cruise missiles have no conscience. It's possible to get a fleeting contact, feed the bearing into the Harpoon and let it fly. Its terminal guidance will give it a good chance of destroying the target. Unfortunately, however, the target could be a neutral ship or another U.S. Navy vessel.

A P-3 Orion, the primary American ASW plane, returns from a mission keeping tabs on Soviet submarines. *Photo by Hans Halberstadt.*

Sea weapons have gotten so sophisticated and long-ranged that positive target identification is a must. "Blue-on-blue" engagements—in which Navy ships mistakenly attack other, friendly units—are a common occurrence in naval exercises. This gives rise to a situation similar to air warfare rules of engagement, in which targets have to be positively identified before thay can be fired upon.

The new LAMPS chopper, the SH-60B Sea Hawk.

Helicopters can provide that ID, as well as mid-course guidance information for cruise missiles. But the chopper pilot must be careful not to make himself a target for the ship he's trying to identify.

The Navy is betting that a new system will help sort out some of the identification and targeting problems, as well as solve the big problem of how to protect the carrier battle group from attack. The Navy is betting a lot on *Aegis.*

In Greek mythology, Aegis was Zeus' magic shield, symbolizing his power and authority over the rest of the ancient gods. In the modern naval pantheon the carrier battle group is supreme—powerful, movable, and versatile. But not invulnerable. For the first time the carrier battle group—the Navy's Zeus—is itself in danger of being knocked out. *Aegis* is designed to shield the carrier and its escorts from saturation attacks by hostile cruise missiles.

Like Zeus' shield, the modern *Aegis* is built to dazzle and frighten its enemies. But it works by electronics, not the supernatural. *Aegis* is the culmination of nearly thirty years of tactical thought, naval doctrine, and high-tech engineering.

Aegis began life in 1957, in a converted garage outside Washington, D.C., where a research team from Johns Hopkins University's Applied Physics Laboratory was assigned to predict what war at sea would be like in the late twentieth century. This APL was the country's leading authority on naval surface-to-air weapons systems, having conducted the Bumblebee project to find ways to knock down the crude German anti-ship missiles late in World War II. That program led to the Talos, Terrier and Tartar missiles, and ultimately to the Standard series of missiles on Navy warships today.

The scientists dreamed a nightmare world, where hostile cruise missiles bore down on the carrier at all speeds and from every direction, converging on the battle group and overwhelming its defenses. But although APL's predictions have been proven correct, its first solution to the cruise missile saturation problem was a failure.

Typhon was their first attempt to thwart the

To silence criticism of its maneuverability, *Ticonderoga* cuts circles in the Gulf of Mexico.

notional cruise missiles of the eighties with actual fifties technology. *Typhon* was an awkward air defense system with a 150-ton radar array connected to banks of rather dim computers. Named after the ancient Greek monster with a hundred heads, *Typhon* was designed to counter an attack by up to two hundred cruise missiles. It was an ambitious program. Too ambitious, given the state of the art in electronics at the time; after three years of testing, APL concluded that Typhon wouldn't work.

But the Navy still had to find a way to protect its carriers from cruise missile attacks. In 1963, it came back with the Advanced Surface Missile System. And APL came up with a way to make it work.

Sea-skimming cruise missiles present a worse case scenario for most older antiair warfare systems. The missiles zoom in below the radar horizon, leaving the ship with less than three minutes to track, classify, aim, launch, and intercept an incoming threat. Much of that time is wasted as the radar antenna revolves—at least half the time it's looking 180 degrees in the wrong direction. More time is wasted as the air search radar data is handed off to the target illuminator, another radar with a shorter range but higher target resolution.

To deal with this, APL designed a prototype of the slab-like planar arrays that would eventually provide the eyes of the SPY-1 radar system. The arrays don't revolve the way conventional radar aerials do. They "stare" constantly, tuning thousands of time receivers to scan their sectors with a pencil-thin beam precise enough to pick up targets well beyond the resolution of conventional shipboard systems.

Critics suggested the Advanced Surface Missile System program was just *Typhon* in disguise, a feeling that grew stronger in 1970, when the program was given another name: *Aegis*.

It was obvious from the beginning that *Aegis* was going to be an important—and expensive—program, but the system had a long way to go before it would put to sea.

Congress and the Navy could not decide the best platform for *Aegis*. It was originally planned to mount the system on the forthcoming *Virginia* class nuclear-powered destroyer escorts, with a specially designed *Aegis* DGN to follow. Later, it was decided that the system was to sail on a conventionally powered destroyer. Two years later, plans were changed once again. *Aegis* would be installed on a nuclear-powered strike cruiser. The CSGN never materialized, and a year later an *Aegis* conversion of the cruiser *Long Beach* was put forward. The idea went nowhere, and in the late seventies, *Aegis* had come full circle, with a proposal to mount the system on a redesigned *Virginia* (which had since been upgraded in class from destroyer leader to cruiser).

A purpose-designed, nuclear-powered *Aegis* cruiser still has support in some quarters. It's probably not a bad idea, although an expensive one. Ultimately, it was decided to put the high-risk technology into a low-risk hull. The system was crammed into a *Spruance* hull, giving it excellent ASW capability, but the cramped design meant four arrays were needed for complete coverage instead of the two originally envisioned. The ship was top-heavy, despite Navy claims to the contrary. Eighty tons of lead were added to the keel and more fuel tanks were laid in the hull.

The resulting ship, much heavier and more capable than a *Spruance* destroyer, was reclassified a cruiser in 1980. *Ticonderoga* is the lead ship. The Navy hopes to build three *Aegis* cruisers a year for a total of twenty-seven.

Compared to most Navy warships, *Ticonderoga* is well balanced and packs quite a punch. Besides the two twin SM-2 missile launchers, the cruiser is armed with two 5″ guns, two Phalanx close-in Gatling guns, six torpedo tubes, eight Harpoon cruise missile launchers, two LAMPS helicopters, and state of the art, antisubmarine sonar equipment. All the systems are routed through *Aegis*, which automatically picks the best weapon for the target and the optimum attack pattern. The longer-range Tomahawk cruise missile and a vertical launching system will be included in future *Ticonderoga* class cruisers.

A similar version of the *Aegis* system will sail aboard the Navy's new *Arleigh Burke* class destroyers. *Burke* and her sister ships will perform for surface action groups and underway replenishment groups the same role the *Ticonderoga* performs for the carrier battle group. The *Burke* is a wholly new design, the first for the USN in more than a decade.

The *Aegis* ships will form the heart of the defense of the carrier battle groups. Its SPY-1 radar can track hundreds of contacts, with data so precise that the target need be handed off to a fire control radar only in the very last seconds of the intercept. Where older systems were limited in targets to the number of channels of fire control radar (usually two or four), *Aegis* is limited only to the number of missiles in its large magazine (and a further development will allow other ships to fire at threats *Aegis* has targeted).

The data from SPY-1 is processed automatically by the fifteen on-board computers that form the heart of the *Aegis* system. In fact, *Aegis* can be programmed to fire automatically when certain threat criteria are met. In the so-called "Armageddon mode," all the crew has to do is turn *Aegis* on. They can even leave the control room; *Aegis* will automatically shoot down anything traveling above a certain speed within ten miles of the ship.

Aegis uses a new missile, the SM-2ER (Extended Range). It's an upgraded version of the Navy's Standard surface-to-air missile, with some important improvements. It's a solid-propellant weapon, with an added fuselage section for extended range. The SM-2ER is also improved electronically, with mid-course guidance capability.

Combined with the *Aegis* system the missile can fly maximum energy trajectories, to get the most from its fuel load. Guided by *Aegis,* the SM-2ER doesn't always have to keep its nose pointed at the target in a lead intercept course. It can "cruise" at the most efficient speed and altitude while *Aegis* keeps track of the target. When *Aegis* works as advertised, the ships aren't waiting for the cruise missiles; the ship's missiles are waiting for the target.

Since *Aegis* ships are designed to be the antiair command center of the modern carrier battle group, the combat information center on board is much more elegant than other contemporary CICs. The captain and other battle group commanders use four large multicolored consoles. The displays can be programmed to show an area more than two thousand miles from the ship, using information fed to the *Aegis* system from satellites, aircraft, or other ships. Normally, however, the displays are set at either 64 or 32 nautical miles, with another programmed at 230 nautical miles, the theoretical limit of the ship's radar range.

The highly detailed displays are just the visible part of the *Aegis* command and decision system. Using NTDS, data gathered by *Aegis* is instantly microwaved to all other units. They need not turn on their own radars and betray their position. The same is true of aircraft. *Aegis* can control a number of intercepts, relaying and processing information to and from carrier aircraft while the flattop itself runs silent.

Aegis has gotten a lot of publicity, most of it bad. The controversy stems from a series of early tests conducted on *Ticonderoga.* Their purpose was to wring the system out to its limits, and so to find potential problems before they arise. The Navy went looking for trouble and they found it; *Aegis* missed more than two-thirds of its targets.

The Navy attributed the problems to three causes: personnel inexperience, missile failure, and software bugs. The first of these was remedied as the crew became more familiar with the system—after all, nothing as complex as *Aegis* has ever sailed before. The missiles used in the tests were

The business end of the *Aegis* antiair warfare system: *Ticonderoga* lets a Standard ER (extended range) missile fly.

earlier versions of the Navy's Standard missile. They simply were not good enough to keep up with *Aegis*. And the Navy says the last problem —software glitches—was easily fixed with a change in programming.

When the system was tested again, *Aegis* knocked down ten of eleven targets with the first missile fired. Even Pentagon officials say privately that those tests were little more than firepower demonstrations, but it's nice to be favorably misunderstood for a change.

The Navy is satisfied with *Aegis;* pleased enough, in fact, to gamble a great deal of prestige, money, and manpower on the most complex and expensive weapons system ever to sail aboard a surface warship. They say it proved its worth in Lebanon, where *Ticonderoga*—fresh from its shakedown cruise—accurately kept tabs on half the surface traffic and nearly all the air activity around Beirut. Task force commanders who had first been suspicious of the much-heralded capabilities *Aegis* brought to the fleet, eventually had so much confidence in the system that *"Tico"* was put in charge of the antiair protection of the American embassy and of the Marines stationed by the Beirut airport.

But the system's performance in the dangerous and confused situation off Lebanon is just a small part of *Aegis'* potential. Even the men who fought the ship off Beirut say they don't really know its limits. The Navy is only beginning to understand how to use the system to its full advantage.

Aegis has had to weather some rough seas. And it may turn out the system *is* a lemon. On the other hand, maybe *Aegis* will revolutionize war at sea. *Aegis* thinks fast, never blinks, and is always looking several moves ahead. Who knows? Maybe the Navy has an electronic Nelson on its hands.

The *Los Angeles* class nuclear-powered attack submarine *Salt Lake City*.

Chapter Five

Boomer's World

SLAP-slap-slap-slap . . .

It makes sense in a way.

Slap-slap-SLAP-slap . . .

After all, it's a big boat, but it's not *that* big. The Navy wants its men fit. And submariners are the most Navy of Navy men.

Slap-SLAP-slap-slap . . .

Okay, so he feels funny the first couple of laps, maybe. Or maybe not. By the time crewmen set out on patrol any moral scrimmage they may have felt about rubbing elbows with weapons of mass destruction has been securely settled. The Navy sees to that.

Slap-slap-slap-SLAP . . .

So around and around he goes, the soft-soled shoes smacking a rhythm on the hard, shiny floor. People on shore might grasp the instant irony of a man jogging to prolong his life around weapons capable of incinerating two hundred cities. But to the boys on the boat, the Trident missiles, slumbering in the twenty-four huge cannisters amidships—called the "tree farm" by crewmen—are just part of the furniture. He jogs on and on, past the weight pulleys attached to the launch tubes, past the exercise bicycle; sixteen laps to a mile in the underwater nuclear gymnasium.

Although the Trident is the biggest submarine the U.S. Navy has ever built, it is so compartmen-

The lower ballistic missile compartment is called the "tree farm" by crewmen.

talized that crewmen see very little of it at one time. The crowded lower missile compartment would be claustrophobic to most people, but to the boys on the "boomer"—the Navy's nickname for nuclear-powered strategic missile submarines—the "tree farm" seems as wide open as a Kansas prairie.

Of course, the scenery is much better outside. Three hundred feet below the surface, the sub churns at an easy three knots through giant canyons of breathtaking beauty. The pressure of the Great Ocean presses against the submarine, holding it suspended in the liquid blue sky. The underwater weather changes constantly. Great clouds of different temperatures roll across the depths. The sub banks gently, changing heading almost imperceptibly to take advantage of the cover the temperature layers provide against sonar detection. Still, he jogs on.

For getting away from it all, there is nothing like a nuclear submarine. Nobody on the outside knows where they are. Nobody. Not the Navy, not the National Command Authority, and certainly not the Russians. In the States, boomers leave port on the surface. Overseas, they leave submerged, with a tug riding shotgun on the surface to keep merchant shipping from bumping into the underwater sea-monster. The Soviet Union keeps watch on the sub pens around the clock; the Navy keeps twenty-four-hour tabs on the Russians monitoring the American subs. The game is soon finished. With a little electronic help from its friends, the submarine quickly disappears.

The routine of life on a boomer descends as soon as the ballast tanks are vented. The sub says goodbye to the world with a pair of claxon blasts and a brief bubble on the Great Ocean. For the next couple of months or so, the men rotate through a familiar cycle of standing watch for six hours and standing down for twelve.

Most of their time off will be spent in one of the fourteen "rack rooms" squeezed in among the missile tubes amidships. There, in one of nine bunks stacked three high in a U-shaped design, an enlisted man can draw the brown curtain and shut out the rest of the undersea world. It's not much privacy by civilian standards, but to most submariners, sharing a room with just eight other men is living high—in some older boats, for instance, men sleep with torpedoes.

The officers sleep forward, in staterooms that are more luxurious only by comparison. All but the most senior officers must double up; some have two cabinmates. There is room for a desk and a washstand. As in the rack rooms, the officers' cabins are decorated with pictures of wives and children, girlfriends, or other remembrances of the world above the waves. But there is none of the permanent sprawl sometimes found in surface ships. There is room only for neatness.

Time sails by on patrol. Crewmen can plug into music pumped through the sub on an airline-style system that plays a variety of continuous programs

Exercising in "Sherwood Forest" aboard *Ohio*.

on four different channels tailored to tastes from Tschaikovsky to Cyndi Lauper. Videotape players have been welcomed aboard by submariners—*Das Boot* is a big hit with the crew.

Little things take on a lot of importance underneath the ocean. Meals are the major social events of the day. The Navy tries to keep its elite sub crews happy and, despite expectations, submarine food is surprisingly good, in fact has a reputation for being the best in the Navy.

Submarine life has some limitations, of course. Theoretically, a nuclear submarine could sail for years without returning to port. In reality, the length of the voyage is constrained by the crew's nerves and the amount of food they can lay in. The old World War II–era diesel submarines could carry, at most, three weeks of supplies. In some of the Navy's older attack boats, it's not uncommon for a sailor to have to inch through a passageway filled with crates of food during the first leg of the patrol.

The *Ohio*'s pantry is as big as the galley in some of those older boats. There's enough room for four months of supplies. The mess resembles a highway diner, but it is a palace compared to other subs. It seats forty-two in plastic and formica luxury. Cooks try to serve square meals, but if a sailor wants rollers and sliders—hotdogs and hamburgers to earth people—he can get them. Another gedunk favorite, soft ice cream, called "autodog," is a welcome addition underneath the sea. But the favorite meal among submariners is the Monte Cristo sandwich, in all its deep-fried variations.

Although there are a surprising number of diversions on the boat, most of the crewman's waking hours will be spent at work, on watch at his station. There is some physical labor on the Trident subs, but just about every one of the 16 officers and 137 enlisted men could rightly be called technicians. In some ways, these subs are more like an aircraft than a ship.

The operations compartment bears more resemblance to a B-1 cockpit than to an older warship. In the sonar and radar rooms men stare at glowing scopes twenty-four hours a day. In the control room, the submarine's nerve center, the two helmsmen guide the boat with airline-style yoke controls. Back-seat driving is encouraged—there's even a metal bar between the helmsmen for the officer of the watch to lean on.

The men on board America's submarines are all volunteers. After passing rigid academic tests and security checks, they attend a two-month course at the Enlisted Basic Submarine School at New London, Connecticut. Most stay at New London for further training in their specialties before being assigned for a tour of at least a year's duty.

Crewmen responsible for keeping the submarine's nuclear reactor humming undergo even more training. Candidates for the Navy's nuclear field are picked out of basic training. They must be U.S. citizens between the ages of seventeen and twenty-four and willing to spend at least six years in active service. After passing the entrance exam and security checks, the candidate will spend well over a year in training at various bases around the country before he submerges for his first tour.

A lot of things the rookie submariner needs to know can't be taught in schools. The officers on board can help guide him, but the department heads are usually too busy to help with the day-to-day instruction; besides, in many cases, they are pretty new on the boat themselves. The responsibility for maintaining "the Navy way" underneath the sea falls on the Chief of the Boat.

Because of space limitations, the COB must perform functions that are shared among several chiefs on surface ships. He teaches the finer points of seamanship, keeps an eye on safety, and acts as the executive officer's right-hand man. He also assigns bunks and lockers and is in charge of supervising the cooking and cleaning details. Perhaps even more important, he monitors special leave and liberty, as well as supervising on-board training and enforcing discipline. The chief of the

boat wields a lot of power; a bad one can make for a miserable cruise, but a good one keeps things running smoothly as the time flies by.

There is hardly time to miss the people on shore. Civilians may tend to think that nuclear submariners spend their two- or three-month patrols loitering under the ocean, waiting for the word to push The Button. But there are a lot of things to do on patrol. The missile boats have two often contradictory objectives of patrol: stay hidden, and stay in touch.

The first part is easy. Modern submarines are big, but the Great Ocean is bigger. Strategic missile submarines are considered the strongest leg of the nuclear triad. The land-based silos are now vulnerable to attacks from new, highly accurate missiles tipped with huge warheads. Modern antiaircraft missile systems make bomber strikes an iffy proposition. But the submarine, moving silently through millions of square miles of dark ocean, is relatively invulnerable to attack.

Once an American submarine disappears beneath the waves, it is virtually impossible to track. Both superpowers are working furiously on methods to reliably detect submerged submarines, but the oceans are likely to remain opaque for a long while, and to nuclear warfare theorists, this is a good thing. American antisubmarine warfare is far from perfect, but it is so much better than Russian means of detection as to approach destabilization of the balance of power.

There is even talk in the naval press about establishing "bastions" for Soviet strategic missile submarines, allowing them free passage through American antisubmarine defenses and establishing zones where they are declared immune from attack. The reasoning behind such a peculiar move is simple: the Soviets would be less compelled to *use* their submarine-launched ballistic missiles rather than risk losing them to the more sophisticated U.S. ASW patrols. But there must be a better way.

Both sides are looking to outer space for more accurate and secure methods of strategic submarine detection. Infrared satellites could sniff the heat from nuclear reactors, or the hot exhaust from a conventional attack sub. Satellites sensitive to magnetic disturbances could pick out large metal objects, such as submarines, that disrupt the earth's natural magnetic field. Some could use an even more esoteric means of detection, measuring the almost-unmeasurable bulge a submarine makes on the ocean's surface as it cruises far below.

Despite the prospects of escalating the antisubmarine war to the heavens, sonar is likely to remain the principal tactical means of detecting subs. Some ships still use hull-mounted sonar, but most modern warships employ bow-mounted sonar, or the more advanced version, variable-depth sonar (VDS), to help isolate their own noise from that of the target. VDS is towed behind the ship, and is also useful for delving under temperature layers where subs hide. Most Navy attack subs are equipped with bow-mounted sonar, as well as towed sonar arrays, perhaps the most formidable form of tactical sonar. Dipping sonar used by helicopters is a form of VDS.

Maritime patrol aircraft drop "sonobuoys" —remote sonar sensors that relay their signals back to the aircraft via data link. Aircraft drop a pattern of buoys and work them for hours, as a hunter works a field of traps. They may also use MAD booms—magnetic anomaly detectors—for close-in work. With their mobility and relative invulnerability, aircraft are the best sub-chasers around, short of a dedicated hunter-killer submarine.

There are two types of sonar, active and passive. Active sonar is similar to radar. Sound pulses are transmitted through the water and those reflected back to the receiver expose the target. Active sonar does not depend on noise generated

Planesman and chief of the watch sail *Ohio* underneath the ocean.

Michigan leaves Bangor, Washington, for a Pacific patrol.

by the target, and is sometimes the only means to detect very quiet subs, such as modern diesel-electric boats lying low. It also gives range and bearing information accurate enough to launch an attack.

On the other hand, active sonar, like radar, tends to betray the hunter to the hunted long before the target is spotted. For this reason, active sonars are hardly ever turned on by Navy submarines. Passive sonar is much more widely used. Passive sonar is little more than a microphone stuck in the water. The ocean is a noisy place, so the microphone is connected to a computer, which compares the samples taken with a library of sounds stored in its memory bank.

American computer technology has allowed the USN to take the lead in ears in the ocean. The U.S. has a network of underwater passive sensors, called SOSUS (Sound Surveillance System), placed on seabeds around the world. CAESAR is the SOSUS installation based off the East Coast. COLOSSUS is a similar system off the West Coast. Other SOSUS sites are located in the GIUK Gap, the western Pacific, and the Azores.

SOSUS is a valuable part of the Navy's ASW effort. Although it is apparently not accurate enough to pinpoint hostile submarines exactly, it drastically cuts down on the area antisubmarine assets must search, giving them a headstart in finding the needle in the underwater haystack. Some estimates say SOSUS can narrow down a search area to as little as thirty miles. The Soviets realize the value of the SOSUS systems. They've even started to deploy a similar, though not as capable, system of their own. But in a war with the U.S. they'd be more concerned with disabling the fragile American system.

The Navy is building a back-up for the SOSUS system. SURTASS (Surveillance Towed Array System) is an array of acoustic sonars hauled around by a tugboat. In peacetime, SURTASS fills gaps in the SOSUS systems and provides a closer look. In war, it could replace "permanent" sites that prove less than permanent.

Sonar systems, especially the new American versions, are growing ever more complex. Connected to giant computers, they can instantly match noises and targets, sometimes to distances ranging hundreds of miles. But there are a number of factors that can seriously degrade sonar performance. And sub skippers use every trick in the book to stay hidden.

Since sound vibrations, like radar waves, travel in a straight line, subs hide among underwater mountain ranges and ice packs to put a barrier between themselves and the sensor. As we have mentioned, they can hide in layers of water that are colder or warmer than the surrounding sea, causing a distortion of the sonar waves. Temperature variation is most pronounced when surface water is heated by the sun. The so-called "afternoon effect" drastically reduces sonar range by bending the sound waves downward.

Salinity and water pressure affect sonar performance as well. Knowing the underwater weather forecast is important enough for the sub captains to risk detection by sending a thermobuoy to the surface. The buoy sends the temperature of the various layers back to the sub. On its way up, the thermobuoy could very well pass another thermobuoy on its way down sent by a surface ship.

Perhaps the most effective means of escaping detection is not to make any noise. This is more difficult than it sounds. Even nuclear submarines can be betrayed by the noise made by water being pumped through the reactor cooling system. Subs powered by diesel-electric power make no such noise operating on batteries. For this reason, they are very, very quiet, skulking at the bottom with all power stopped.

Of course, the faster a submarine travels, the more noise it makes. This is not only due to the racket of the engines, but to a phenomenon known as "cavitation noise", the circular wake of air bubbles and disturbed water churned up by the sub's propeller. So although modern submarines are easily as fast as most surface ships, they use their top speed only in emergencies.

Whenever possible, the subs try to mask their noise through proximity with other, louder sounds. Submariners love whales; ASW hunters do not. Whales can be heard for hundreds of miles, especially when they're in a romantic mood. Offshore oil rigs are also favorite noisemakers. And subs will often hide underneath noisy freighters, especially when they must traverse busy sections of the Great Ocean.

Once they reach their patrol area, the boomers usually cruise about as fast as a man can walk. They're in no hurry. They've got nowhere to go. Besides, the quieter they are, the better they hear. They are silent, listening very hard. They hear the hunters hundreds of miles away, scrambling through the underwater underbrush. They slip silently away, like Indians.

In fact, if the nuclear subs didn't have to communicate with the outside world, they could probably never be found. But it is vital that they stay in contact to accomplish their mission. Sub skippers are very careful how they touch base—it's the touchiest part of any patrol. The boomers have a variety of methods to stay in touch. Unfortunately, none of them is foolproof, and all of them drastically increase the danger of detection.

Subs hardly ever use periscopes anymore. A periscope-mounted radar is sometimes useful to spot ASW search planes, but if the aircraft spots the antenna on his radar, it just makes his job easier (radar-absorbing materials reportedly used in the Stealth projects were pioneered as coatings for sub periscopes). Spy submarines have various electronic warfare antenna mounted on periscopes

Ohio prior to precommissioning ceremonies.

to snoop on enemy exercises, but it's usually too risky for regular subs to come to periscope depth just for the luxury of visual sightings.

Subs also have a microwave dish that receives messages from defense satellites. It's the best way to pick up complex messages, but since at least part of the sub has to break the surface to use it, microwave communication is also asking for it. In peacetime, though, peeking out from the waves for a brief burst of satellite telemetry is not so critical. The fifty-word coded messages for each crewman on patrol are probably transmitted via satellite. The eight "family grams" are their only contact with the outside world.

The Navy has tried a number of schemes using extremely low frequency waves to communicate with their missile boats. ELF systems set up a giant radio circuit using the earth to complete the loop. The resulting waves are powerful enough to cover the globe, even to great underwater depths. They are also slow. It takes an hour to send a dozen letters, an hour and fifteen minutes just to say "Trident Submarine."

Or the subs can send up a radio buoy. This is no more than a tape recorder and a transmitter sent to the surface. Of course, the radio buoy's transmission would reveal its position, but a time delay could be introduced so that by the time it started broadcasting, the sub would be long gone. The problem is that the message only goes one way, and the captain can't be sure it's been received.

The sub can receive messages from NEACAP (the National Emergency Airborne Command Post, or "Flying White House"), or, as a last-ditch maneuver, the Emergency Rocket Communication System, a Minuteman missile armed not with a warhead, but a radio transmitter. If all other command centers have been decimated, ERCS will screech through the sky, beeping its doomsday launch message to anyone still alive to hear it.

But if worse comes to worst, the boomers will probably get The Word from TACAMO, the "Take Charge and Move Out" aircraft constantly aloft over the Great Ocean. The old TACAMO birds are highly modified C-130s, but the Navy is getting a new burglar alarm in the form of the E-6, yet another variation of the Boeing 707/C-135 airframe. The E-6 trails an antenna five miles long, communicating with the submerged sub, trailing a long antenna of its own. The messages cannot be too complicated. But then, they don't have to be.

The press was shocked recently when a Navy admiral revealed that, under certain circumstances, submarine crews can launch their missiles without confirmation from the outside world. But given the difficulty inherent in communicating with submerged submarines and their role as a last resort, it would be surprising if they could not. However, any launch requires the cooperation of nearly all the one-hundred-fifty-odd men on board, all volunteers, constantly checked for cracks, so a renegade launch is not a likely event.

Still, it is an enormous responsibility. The gold and blue crews of America's silent service have conducted more than two thousand strategic deterrent patrols since the introduction of the Navy's first ballistic missile submarine nearly twenty-five years ago. Their record is unblemished. Working autonomously in a high-pressure world where so many things could go seriously wrong, nothing

Here's Boomer! *Ohio* (SSBN-726), lead ship of the class of largest American submarines ever built.

has. Ever. It's a tribute to the more than two thousand naval officers serving aboard submarines at sea.

The order to launch would come in the form of an Emergency Action Message. The captain checks the coded transmission with a message stashed in his safe. If it matches, it's a go launch.

The crew constantly practices launches. In the mission control room, enlisted men lean over consoles with row after row of brightly colored buttons. But the button that really counts is kept locked; it's on a pistol grip at the end of a long, coiled cord.

If the weapons officer pushes that button, gas and steam will fill the launch tube. The missile will be punched out by enormous pressure until it breaks the surface, where the first stage will fire and send the missile on its way. Meanwhile, the tube will fill up with water, providing ballast to steady the sub. The next missile is now ready to fire. The whole operation takes less than a minute.

The two dozen Trident C-4 ballistic missiles wait in suspended animation, each tipped with eight nuclear warheads that can be targeted individually. With the touch of a button, each Trident submarine can wipe out nearly two hundred targets four thousand miles away. But the Trident C-4 is not the last word in submarine-launched ballistic missiles. Beginning in 1989, the new *Ohio*s will carry the even more potent Trident D-5, with all subs in the class eventually slated for the upgrade.

Lafayette class ballistic missile sub *James K. Polk* (SSBN-645). The *Lafayette* boats are still the largest class in the strategic missile deterrent force.

Los Angeles class nuclear-powered attack sub *Birmingham* surfaces for the camera. While on patrol, nuclear-powered subs surface only for emergencies.

695

In the metaphysics of nuclear warfare, the D-5 is a more "humane" weapon. More powerful and more accurate than the old "city-busters," the D-5 can be used in pinpoint attacks against targets such as hardened missile silos. That also makes it more destabilizing. Up till now, submarine-launched ballistic missiles have been too short-ranged and inaccurate to be considered "first-strike" weapons. They lacked the third stage of land-based intercontinental missiles. Moreover, the movement of the submarine—and thus the missile's launch point—introduced an element of uncertainty into the missile's inertial guidance system.

But the Trident D-5 is the first submarine-launched missile that can be called a "counter-force" weapon. The largest such missile ever fielded by the U.S., the three-stage D-5 has a range of more than four thousand miles. And it can hit targets within a twelve-hundred-foot circle, owing to a new guidance system that checks the warhead's position against stars in space.

The $2 billion *Ohio* subs are as big as cruisers. Construction of a dozen of the giant strategic missile subs has been authorized. More are probably on their way. The ships are built at the rate of about one a year, to avoid block obsolescence.

Along with thirty-one older *Lafayette* class Poseidon subs, the *Ohio* boats form the undersea leg of the American nuclear triad. The Navy's boomers carry five thousand warheads, more than half the nuclear warheads in the American strategic arsenal. Although the terms Trident sub and *Ohio* class sub are usually considered synonymous, the last dozen *Lafayette*s have also been converted to fire the Trident missile.

Displacing more than eighteen thousand tons, the 560-foot-long *Ohio* is the largest American submarine ever built. But it is not the largest submarine in the world. That distinction belongs to the Soviet *Typhoon* class ballistic missile submarine, reportedly nearly ten thousand tons larger than the *Ohio* class subs.

Typhoon is larger than the Washington Monument. Although it carries fewer missiles than the *Ohio* subs, it represents a dangerous development in Soviet strategic missile submarine warfare. *Typhoon* skippers can jam the sub up against an ice pack, hiding among the floe's downward peaks in a maneuver called the "ice pick." The submarine can skulk there, motionless, for months at a time. There is even evidence that the new Soviet submarines can launch their missiles *through* the ice. If this is true, it is bad news for the Navy. If *Typhoon* doesn't have to come out to fight, it might not be found until it's too late.

The Soviet Navy is very much a submarine force. Their impressive new surface ships get a lot of attention, but the Russians have always concentrated on submarines. They already outnumber the United States three-to-one under the Great Ocean. But their underwater order of battle contains a great many diesel-electric patrol submarines, a type of U-boat the USN says it has no use for. Furthermore, Soviet subs are no match for American boats, one-on-one. They're noisy, relatively unsophisticated, and don't carry a great number of weapons reloads.

Nevertheless, in terms of sheer numbers, the Soviet Navy is the world's most powerful submarine force. They've got almost twice as many strategic missile submarines, and nearly three times as many attack boats. And in the last decade, the Soviets have introduced a dozen classes of submarines, including two brand-new nuclear attack boats, the *Mike* and *Sierra* classes.

To counter growing Soviet strength under the ocean, the USN is relying more and more on its fleet of nuclear attack submarines. In time of war, the attack boats will operate independently, against both surface and sub-surface targets, either clearing a path for carrier battle groups and convoys or striking out on their own on hunter-killer missions deep in enemy territory. There has been a recent emphasis on coordinating the operations of the Navy's attack submarines more

Soviet *Alfa* class nuclear-powered attack sub in icy waters.

closely with the carrier task forces, but they share the boomers' problems with secure, two-way communications.

The backbone of the American attack sub fleet is the *Los Angeles* class submarine. The Russians have some subs that dive deeper or go faster. But in the qualities that really count in an attack submarine—stealth, endurance, and firepower—the *Los Angeles* class sub is the best in the world. The Navy has more than forty of them, and with plenty more called for in Navy plans, the *Los Angeles* class is the largest class of nuclear submarines built by any nation.

The *Los Angeles* subs are two hundred feet shorter and nearly ten thousand tons lighter than the *Ohio*s. With only slightly fewer men on board, they are more crowded. The layout is roughly the same. The bow is taken up by the huge sonar dome, connected to the rest of the boat by a passageway that runs through the forward ballast tanks. Next come the four torpedo tubes, canted outward, followed by the adjacent torpedo room. Above are crew's quarters and, below the sail, the attack center, with sonar and radar rooms. Underneath are storage batteries and auxiliary machinery. The rest of the boat is taken up by the reactor and the engine room, with the aft ballast tanks surrounding the propeller shaft.

Navy attack submarines get the drop on their prey through information gathered by SOSUS or defense satellites that monitor Soviet subs as they leave port. Sometimes the subs are part of the information net themselves, lying low in waters close to the Soviet Union, cataloging the acoustic signatures of boats passing by. A boomer will sneak away silently if it detects someone in the neighborhood; the captain of an attack submarine will probably close with the intruder for an unscheduled (and rather one-sided) war game.

The attack submarine's principal weapon is the Mk-48 torpedo, a twenty-foot long, 3,500 pound,

olive drab monster guided to the target by signals generated by the Mk-117 fire control system. The Mk-117 takes fixes from the bow-mounted sonar and the towed array. The triangulation helps pinpoint the target. Target information is fed to the torpedo via a long, thin strand of wire. The Mk-48 bangs out of the tube and heads for the target at speeds up to a mile a minute. Long before it reaches the limits of its advertised range of over thirty miles, the wire will snap and the torpedo will guide itself to the target using its on-board sonar.

A typical tactic is to fire torpedoes in salvoes of two. One fish runs at top speed, noisy and easily detected. The other torpedo runs quietly at slower speed. As the enemy sub turns to avoid the first torpedo, the other Mk-48 bores in undetected.

More than likely, the attack submarine skipper won't know if the torpedo hit the target. He's got to go. The noisy torpedo, screwing through the ocean, has announced his presence. Everyone now knows where he *was*. Now he's got to be somewhere else, or *he'll* be the target.

The Navy has recently expressed some concern over the effectiveness of their torpedoes. Specifically, it's thought that the Soviet *Alfa* class submarine could, in some cases, outrun or outfox the Navy's current inventory of undersea weapons.

The *Alfa* is an ambitious design, with no equal in the West. It is extremely fast, once clocked at forty-three knots by an American attack submarine that was attempting to trail it underwater. The *Alfa* has a revolutionary titanium hull that allows it to dive deeper than other subs, and use deeper temperature gradients and ocean floor topography for concealment. The hull is coated with a Clusterguard anti-sonar coating that makes it difficult to detect.

On the other hand, as is the case with most dreaded Russian hardware, there is evidence that the *Alfa* boats are not the sea monsters first feared

Attack center of *La Jolla, Los Angeles* class attack sub.

by Navy planners. The subs have never been put in serial production. There could be problems in producing the ambitious design. Or it could be the *Alfa* is merely a technology demonstrator. There are reports of serious problems concerning the sub's nuclear power plant. And the much-vaunted Clusterguard coating tends to come unstuck, flapping in the water, making the sub easier, not harder, to detect.

Still, the Navy is worried about the *Alfa*'s potential, if nothing else. The Mk-48 is undergoing an advanced capability program (ADCAP), that will improve its depth and speed performance. The Mk-46 lightweight torpedo, carried on some ships, aircraft, and helicopters, is being upgraded to make its sonar guidance system less susceptible to countermeasures. In the long run, the Mk-46 will be replaced by a new, lightweight torpedo, the Mk-50, which will reportedly use a directed-energy warhead and will be effective against surface ships and even diesel subs in shallow waters.

Some U.S. attack subs also carry SUBROC, a rocket-powered depth charge similar to the ASROC carried by surface ships. SUBROC will be replaced by the new ASWSOW (antisubmarine warfare stand-off weapon) under development, with improved range and guidance. The whole family of depth charges is armed with nuclear warheads, which makes them very effective when hunting high-value targets such as enemy ballistic missile submarines. But they raise some problems of their own. Nuclear weapons require the type of authorization not easily transmitted to submarines trying to keep a low profile.

Nevertheless, many naval experts feel the first use of nuclear weapons will be at sea. They're the best way to bag a carrier (or sneaky submarines). Saltwater is an excellent medium in which to diffuse radiation. And there are no civilian targets in the middle of the Great Ocean, hence no collateral damage. Or, as one Navy man puts it: "You can't blow a hole in the ocean."

Navy attack submarines aren't built for attacking surface ships. Russian boomers are their primary targets, plus any enemy attack boats that get in the way. Their weapons are primarily designed for ASW. In fact, the Argentine cruiser

Soviet Oscar-class nuclear-powered cruise attack sub.

sunk by the British nuclear sub in the Falklands was sent to the bottom by World War II–era torpedoes.

The Navy is now re-thinking the role of nuclear attack subs against surface ships. They're putting new missiles in the subs. Both the Harpoon and Tomahawk cruise missiles were designed to be fired from torpedo tubes. Each is capable of surface attack, although over-the-horizon guidance will be a problem with the Tomahawk, as it is with all long-range cruise missiles.

Another problem is weapons load-out. The subs are crowded enough as it is, and there's not much room for more weapons in the torpedo rooms. Even the biggest boats can't carry more than twenty Mk-48s. Also, there are only four tubes, so the skipper has to anticipate which weapons —torpedoes, SUBROC, Harpoons, Tomahawks, or mines—will be needed, and in which order. Some of these problems will be resolved when *Los Angeles* class subs are built with a dozen dedicated Tomahawk vertical launch tubes installed outside the pressure hull.

The *Los Angeles* class will be America's primary attack submarine until the turn of the century. But looming block obsolescence of the earlier *Permit* and *Sturgeon* attack submarine classes, as well as the relentless pursuit of submarine technology on the part of the Soviet Union, has led Navy brass to investigate the design of a new nuclear attack submarine for the twenty-first century.

Dubbed the SSN-21, the new sub, in the words of a senior Navy official, will be "the most heavily armed, the fastest, the deepest-diving, most combat-capable submarine ever built." The first SSN-21 will sail in about ten years.

American control of the under-oceans should survive until then. The Soviet Union is working hard to close the gap, putting forth great technical effort of their own, in addition to "borrowing" the best from the West. But the Silent Service remains silent where it counts. Says a high-ranking naval officer, "We can detect their submarines before they detect ours." And that's what it's all about.

12
5
6
7

Chapter Six

The Other U.S. Navies

It's no secret that the Navy is divided into three "unions": the surface warfare, submarine, and naval air communities. Isolated training tracks begin the division. Competition for funds available in a limited budget accentuates it. Each community is all for a combined arms approach in the abstract, but when it comes down to it, they feel *theirs* is the decisive weapon in combat. And they're not shy about letting everyone else know.

What gets lost in the shuffle of the brown shoes versus black shoes (and aviation boots) is all the vital, but little publicized, missions a modern Navy must carry out.

First of all, a modern Navy must be supplied. This is hard enough in port, but when ships stay on station months at a time, supply lines must be extended to the ships at sea. The Navy does this with underway replenishment. The majority of ships in the Navy are such supply vessels and their bodyguards. Some are detailed for convoy protection—one *Spruance* destroyer and nine frigates are the usual convoy escort force. Underway Replenishment Groups (URG) are guarded by three frigates and a guided missile destroyer (the new *Arleigh Burke* is slated to perform this role).

Opposite: Inchon, an amphibious assault ship.

An underway replenishment group usually consists of three types of ships: oilers, ammunition ships, and stores ships. Oilers are tankers that carry ship and aviation fuels. Some of the AOs—fast combat support ships and underway replacement oilers—have been lengthened to carry other stores. Ammunition ships (AEs) haul reloads of guided missiles in containers that can be directly transferred from ship to ship. These AEs are nervously named after volcanoes. The stores ships (AFs and AFSs) carry food, water, and spare parts. Some sections of the store ships are refrigerated.

One or two AOs, an AE and an AF or AFS

Fleet oiler *Kalamazoo* shuttles from port to battle group.

make up a typical underway replenishment group. It cycles back and forth from port to station. Sometimes the URG ships deliver their loads directly to the battle group. Usually, however, they transfer their load to a multi-product ship and then head back to base to load up again.

One or two multi-product ships travel with the battle group. The giant *Sacramento* class support ship is built to keep up with the fast carriers. The AOE (fast combat support ship) can make twenty-six knots and is armed with short-ranged missiles and guns. The smaller replenishment oilers (AORs) are somewhat slower. Built as an alternative to the expensive AOE, the AOR can still carry enough for two refuelings of a conventional aircraft carrier and its escorts. Nuclear-powered carriers need not be refueled, of course. In fact, they carry extra fuel for their escorts, as well as missile reloads and other supplies for the rest of the battle group.

Some of the replenishment ships are manned by the civilian crews of the Military Sealift Command. The Navy is responsible for all U.S. military equipment shipped overseas, but most of it is shuttled by civilians, using chartered merchant ships. In addition, MSC crews man freighters, tankers, and replenishment ships. Such ships are considered active Navy ships and are given the prefix "T" (for example, an MSC-manned ammunition ship of the Naval Fleet Auxiliary Force is designated T-AE).

The MSC crews may be civil servants, but they are not post office workers. They know what they're doing. A great many of the MSC hands are ex-Navy men. Underway replenishment is tricky business. Even in these days of automated systems, it takes a lot of know-how to pull it off safely. A lot of old-fashioned seamanship sails with the ships of the underway replenishment groups.

Underway replenishment is one of the most exciting sights on the ocean, especially at night. The oiler, surprisingly large, moves up slowly through the task group. It takes up station starboard of the black bulk of the aircraft carrier. Because of the restricted vision from the bridge, the flattop is the only ship the oiler approaches. All other ships must come to it.

Flashing lines shoot from the tanker. The crew on board the receiving ship catch the shot-line and rig a network of cables between the two ships. There are a variety of ways to get the 230-foot, 6″ fuel line from ship to ship. In the close-in method, ships steam about sixty feet apart. That's a dangerous distance, and doesn't allow the use of anti-aircraft guns. The span wire method gives a little more breathing room—the ships steam about 150 feet apart—and since the hose is carried higher over the waves, it's the method most frequently used in rough seas.

Most modern ships use a probe—or the older Robb coupling—at the end of the fuel line. Both methods are faster than the old "pigtail," which is simply a soft rubber hose shoved into the fuel tank and lashed into place. Most ships take fuel in more than one station, and there is often a spirited competition to see which one can get rigged and pumping first.

Even with the most modern methods, it takes an awfully long time to refuel at sea. Ships are particularly vulnerable during such an operation, which is why most refueling is done at night, with ships often serviced two at a time. It's the receiving ship's responsibility to keep station with the oiler. Mistakes happen.

Cargo is sometimes transferred in a similar manner, using lines and winches. The Navy has a completely mechanized system called FAST, or Fast Automatic Shuttle Transfer. FAST was designed to transfer missiles from the UNREP (underwing replacement) ship's cargo hold directly to the magazine of another ship. The system is also used for the movement of conventional cargo.

A great deal of freight also moves through the air, via vertical replenishment. The Navy's

VERTREP workhorse is the UH-46 Sea Knight. The choppers from the replenishment vessel flit from ship to ship like bees in a flower field, bringing spare parts, mail, cargo, and even people. Usually, the helicopter doesn't land. It hovers over the receiving ship's flight deck, while a crew unhitches the load slung in nets underneath. VERTREP is fast and efficient, but will never replace UNREP for transfer of bulk products.

The expansion to fifteen carrier battle groups will stretch the replenishment forces pretty thin. And the Navy pays the price for American presence around the globe with supply lines that often stretch thousands of miles in peacetime, and would most likely stretch even farther in war. A modern war at sea would consume supply at a ravenous rate as ships steam faster, stay longer, and fight day and night.

The Navy has recently come under criticism for its lack of war supply. A congressional study contended that the fleet could not participate in contemporary combat for a month, even a couple of weeks, before it ran out of missiles. Even if the supplies were handy, the far-flung bases are less than secure. And even if the bases escape attack, the fragile underway replenishment groups are tempting targets. Any way you look at it, supply could prove to be the fleet's Achilles' heel in the next war.

The Navy is getting a head start on supply by pre-positioning ships packed with equipment in hard-to-reach places. That's why the heavy stuff of a Marine Amphibious Brigade is bobbing on four ships in the Indian Ocean off Diego Garcia.

The Marine Corps muscle rests in three Marine Amphibious Forces. An MAF consists of a reinforced Marine infantry division and a Marine air wing. With about fifty thousand men, the MAF is the Marine's largest self-contained landing force. There is an MAF on each coast and a third scattered through the Pacific.

But the Navy has only about sixty amphibious ships, enough to transport one MAF at best. About 10 percent of that MAF is permanently embarked, in the form of a Marine Amphibious Unit. There are two MAUs constantly afloat, one in the Mediterranean with the Sixth Fleet, and one with the Seventh Fleet in the western Pacific. These groups of about twenty-five hundred men, along with some light armor and air elements, are used as peacekeepers and a quick reaction force.

The MAU sails in an Amphibious Ready Group, a Navy unit consisting of about half a dozen small landing craft, a couple of ships to carry them in and a helicopter carrier. Several MAUs combine to form a Marine Amphibious Brigade (MAB). Because of sealift restrictions, logistics, and the necessity of tactical surprise, the MAB, with some elements of a Marine Air Wing, is the most likely candidate to attempt opposed landings in combat.

This is not enough force to open up a second front, of course, but that's not the Marines' job. They're used as shock troops to open up a beachhead, or to move quickly to seize territory and wait for reinforcements. The bulk of the manpower will come later, when the Army arrives. The Marines do the dirty work, then move on.

The Marines are the ultimate rapid deployment force, at least on paper. They are a mobile, well-trained, integrated combined-arms team, ready, willing, and able to tackle the toughest jobs. The Marines say men, not machines, make the difference in combat. The story is, if it doesn't leak oil, shed parts, self-destruct, or smoke, it doesn't belong in the Marine Corps.

Sometimes they *do* get new equipment, whether they want it or not. The Marines saw the future in V/STOL (vertical/short take-off and landing); the Navy saw a threat to their carriers. The Marines wanted the Harrier; the Navy wanted them to buy the Hornet instead, to keep the costs down on the F-18 program and keep the lid on a technology that competes with the conventional carrier aircraft the Navy has staked *its* future on. The Marines went to the mat to get the AV-8B, but they wound up buying the F/A-18 as well.

Underway replenishment in the Pacific: *New Jersey* (BB-62), *Kansas City* (AOR-3), and *Buchanan* (DDG-14).

Underway replenishment, Soviet style.

Both new planes, as well as the Marines' A-6 and EA-6, are designed to operate from both land and sea, even though the USMC has no ships of its own. Marine squadrons regularly fill in for Navy units on conventional carriers. The AV-8B is a different story. The Navy is building a brand new ship just to take the Harrier II to sea.

LHD-1 is the first of four new sea control ships built the way the Marines want them. *Wasp* and her three sister ships will carry twenty AV-8Bs and a half-dozen new SH-60B Sea Hawk helicopters. The design is based on the *Tarawa* class helicopter

A rare photo of both Navy amphibious command ships — *Blue Ridge* and *Mount Whitney* — together off Norfolk, Virginia. The ships were built for use by Marine assault force commanders but were commandeered by the Navy.

carriers, with a larger well deck and a hundred-foot ski jump on the bow. The ski jump was invented by the British and tested in the Falklands. It allows the jump-jets to carry heavier loads by giving them a headstart in the air.

The Navy has toyed with the idea of V/STOL carriers for years. Back in 1973, as the Harriers were introduced in Marine Corps service, tests were conducted on the assault carrier *Guam*. Eight years later, further tests on the *Tarawa* class *Nassau* confirmed the V/STOL carrier concept. And with three new supercarriers authorized, the Navy could at last loosen up and allow a Harrier carrier to be built.

Although technically an amphibious assault ship, *Wasp* is more than just another "gator freighter." The Harriers can operate in conjunction with the Sea Hawk helicopters to protect the rest of the amphibious force, especially close to the shore. At sea, the AV-8Bs provide an always-welcome addition to the battle group air defense grid. They are particularly good at low-altitude and fast surface threats in the middle defense zone, where protection is sometimes lacking. And after the landing, when the big carriers have steamed away, *Wasp* and her aircraft can provide close air support and air cover for the invasion forces until an airstrip can be seized or built. In addition, with the helicopters on board connected to the LAMPS ASW system, the ship can provide some of its own antisubmarine support, something the amphibious forces have always had to depend upon other ships for.

Wasp and her successors will carry up to three Landing Craft Air Cushions (LCAC), a new type of landing craft that promises the biggest revolution in amphibious assault tactics since the helicopter. In fact, the LCAC resembles an aircraft in many ways. Riding on a cushion of air, the LCAC is pushed along by huge propellers on the bow, much like an airboat in the Everglades.

Up to a point, the LCAC is truly amphibious. It can negotiate swamps, marshes, mud, wet sand, and a lot of other terrain types that are neither earth nor water. Air cushion technology has opened up more than two-thirds of the world's beaches as possible landing sites, as opposed to the 17 percent that can be reached by other types of landing craft. It is also very fast—fifty knots, tops—with a two-hundred-mile radius of action. The LCAC's speed, range, and landing site versatility combine to put surprise and maneuver back into amphibious warfare.

It's taken two decades for LCACs to get to the fleet. The Soviet Navy has had them for years. Theirs aren't as good as ours, maybe, but they're *there*. The Navy plans to buy about half a dozen a year for the next ten years.

But there are drawbacks. LCACs are expensive —at least $10 million apiece. Both noisy and fragile, LCACs are also big, taking up a lot of room in the few ships large enough to carry them. A lot of that size is due to the large power plants that enable them to do what they do. LCACs are not that big inside. Although they can carry sixty tons, there's only enough room on deck for one main battle tank.

For those reasons, there aren't going to be enough LCACs to go around. The Navy could come up with a way to integrate them with older landing craft, but the prospect of integrating long-range, high-speed LCACs with short-range, low-speed traditional landing craft presents major tactical problems. More than likely, the limited numbers of LCACs will be grouped together in a special force and used for pre-invasion raids or as a first-wave assault leader.

Most of the Marines will come ashore in the older LCMs and LCUs. The "Mike Boat" is the traditional landing craft, only slightly changed from the ones in which John Wayne hit the beach in countless World War II movies. The LCU is larger, capable of ferrying three M-60 main battle tanks ashore. There are several sub-types of both landing craft, but all share the same design. The boat is beached, the armored bow ramp slams open, and assorted gyrenes, grunts, jar-heads and anchor-clankers come boiling ashore like a bunch of maniacs.

Some of the Marines will come directly on shore in amphibious tractors. The problems involved in building a truly amphibious infantry fighting vehicle have yet to be resolved. The Corps' thirty-knot LVA program was canceled in 1979 as too complex and expensive. A new program, the LVT (X) has run into delays. In any case, its eight-knot water speed won't offer much improvement in that respect. The Marines have decided to rebuild their ageless LVTPs and run them until something better comes along.

The Marines have nearly a thousand vehicles of the LVT-7 series. All share the same deficiencies. They can neither dish it out nor take it. Armed with only a machine gun, the LVTP is thin-skinned and vulnerable to hostile fire. Big and boxy, it presents quite a target.

As a landing craft, the "Superhog" also has problems. Although it boasts an advertised range of fifty-five miles in the water, the way the LVTP is used in combat severely restricts the distance it can travel to the beach. The Marines make the approach to the beach buttoned up. The noise, smoke, heat, and fumes inside the vehicle make it impossible for even the hardiest leatherneck to stand a cruise that lasts more than half an hour (although it does make them eager to get out!). At a maximum speed of eight knots, a thirty-minute ride means the LVTPs must be launched about three miles from the beach. Even if the amtracs are spewed from a moving ship—an operation that presents its own problems—the fleet is brought dangerously close to enemy defenses.

Usually, the fleet forms up for a landing about twenty-five miles offshore, over the horizon. The enemy knows something's up; friendly aircraft have swept the skies, reconnaissance planes drone overhead, and minesweepers are constantly sweeping the coast. It's unavoidable—landings can only take place in conditions of absolute air, sea, and

Spiegel Grove, a landing ship dock, off Hampton Roads, Virginia. An LTU assault craft returns to the ship's well deck.

subsurface superiority. Besides, in an era of spy satellites, it's almost impossible to hide something as big as an invasion fleet.

But even if strategic surprise is impossible, *tactical* surprise is not. The enemy may know an amphibious assault is coming, but he doesn't know where. In theory, the fleet can steam nearly five hundred miles a day, although this may be a bit optimistic. ("The true speed of the twenty-knot amphibious force," says one naval observer, "is sixteen knots.") In any case, out of hundreds of miles of coastline, the defender is never quite sure which two or three miles the Marines will choose for a beachhead. The mobility of LCACs makes amphibious surprise attacks possible. But even with ordinary landing craft, it's possible to achieve some level of surprise, using diversionary raids, electronic discipline, night landings, and helicopter encirclement.

A full MAF landing will use more than two hundred landing craft. An assault by an MAB will use a fraction of that, ferried to the line of departure by fifteen or twenty amphibious warfare ships. Helicopter carriers can transport landing craft underneath the flight deck, but the bulk of the assault boats will be carried by LSDs and LPDs (which also carry personnel).

The LVTPs will go in first. If surprise is lost, or

not deemed as important as softening up the defenses, the beach will be pounded with naval gunfire and air strikes. Minesweepers will have cleared lanes leading to the beachhead. (The LCAC makes a good minesweeper because of its low displacement and rubber "hull.") The wave-guide commander will be in one of the two primary control ships that mark the boundaries of the landing zone.

The LVTPs go in line-abreast, carrying assault troops and combat engineers. More light infantry move in on the second wave. They have no heavy weapons. If their mission is a success, the tanks and artillery will arrive on LCUs on the third and fourth waves. The whole thing takes less than ten minutes.

Or at least, that's the plan. But amphibious landings are tricky. There is no such thing as a "classic" amphibious assault. There are too many variables; something always goes wrong. The

Marines know this. To paraphrase the common wisdom, the things that make Marines difficult to deal with in peacetime make them invaluable in wartime. They improvise, they take their lumps, and if there's a way it can be done, they'll do it.

Like the Marines, the Coast Guard is controlled in wartime by the Navy. But in peacetime, the Coast Guard is under the orders of a civilian agency, the Department of Transportation. The two masters give the Coast Guard a dual personality as it performs its usual tasks in peacetime while preparing for war.

Coast Guard *Hamilton* class cutter *Sherman,* en route to Alaska for ten-week law enforcement patrol. Although thought of only as life-saving vessels, the high-endurance cutters are equipped for combat missions. *Photo by Hans Halberstadt.*

Combat is nothing new to the Coast Guard. Since its formation nearly two hundred years ago, Coast Guard personnel have taken part in nearly

F-5 and A-4 "adversary" aircraft from Top Gun, the Navy Fighter Weapons School at NAS Miramar, California.

every war the U.S. has fought. The service conducted ASW patrols in both world wars, search and rescue in Korea, and Market Time warfare (coastal patrol) in Vietnam. Most recently, Coast Guard ships took over protection of Grenada after the Navy invasion fleet steamed away.

The Coast Guard has seen a lot of wartime action, but there is perhaps more danger in carrying out its peacetime patrols. At least in war, one knows who the enemy is. Imagine what a young guardsman must go through, calling a boat to heave to in the middle of the night, not knowing if the people on board are panic-stricken vacationers or heavily armed drug runners. In fact, the Coast Guard has seen more real action lately than the Navy has. The crackdown on drug runners has produced some tense moments on the high seas, especially in the Caribbean.

The Coast Guard is charged with a number of other, less dangerous missions. In addition to their well known role in search and rescue, the Guard is also responsible for safety inspections of ships, ports and bridges, and the maintenance of navigational aids. One aspect of the Coast Guard's mission that doesn't get much publicity is the resupply of American military installations near the North Pole and civilian installations in Antarctica. The Coast Guard uses five icebreakers for the lonely voyages to the top and bottom of the world.

The Coast Guard fleet would be the envy of many navies. Among its larger vessels are a dozen *Hamilton* class high endurance cutters. Armed with a 5″ gun, torpedo tubes, and full helicopter facilities, the *Hamilton*s are powerful enough to take their place, in wartime, with the carrier battle group or as a convoy escort. The same role is planned for the new *Bear* class cutters, which carry a 3″ gun and ASW systems (and may even get Phalanx and Harpoon later on). Critics say the *Bear* is too slow and lacks range, but the Coast Guard is happy to get the new ships. They've also got their eye on the Navy's *Oliver Hazard Perry* class frigates. The Navy seems to want to get rid of them. If that's the case, the Coast Guard would love to have them.

The Naval Reserve has already gotten some *Perrys*, the first new equipment they've received in years. For a long time, the regular Navy wasn't getting many new ships, so the Reserve had it even rougher. Now, they're getting brand new equipment, including the F/A-18. A Reserve outfit in California was among the first to receive the Hornet. The Navy hopes to be able to continue the trend.

Like the Air Force and Army reserves, the Naval Reserve is far from being the group of "weekend warriors" often pictured in the press. Much of the nation's combat skill is vested in the reserves. In many exercises, they come out ahead of their active duty counterparts. There's no substitute for experience, and the Reserves train enough to be ready should they be called up.

In particular, the Naval Air Reserve is a valuable national asset. There are two Reserve carrier air wings, CVWR 20 on the East Coast, and CVWR 30 on the West Coast. Although, in general, they fly hand-me-downs from the fleet, the Reserves make a good showing in fleet exercises. The Reserve air wings sometimes deploy to a carrier for practice workups. There's even been talk about carrying a composite Reserve squadron aboard for an entire cruise, although it would be tough for the pilots, many of whom fly for commercial airlines, to get away for any length of time, short of a national emergency.

The USN has a number of relatively small, but interesting organizations that also bear mention, as long as we're on the subject of *other* U.S. navies.

The SeaBees are the Navy's master builders on shore. The original SeaBees were a group of civilian construction workers who volunteered during World War II. They were organized into construction battalions (hence the name). In the Pacific, the SeaBees built airstrips and port facilities. Today, they play a major role in screening foreign contractors building American facilities abroad. They also perform some minor construction themselves, for American embassies and bases around the world.

The SEALS are the Navy's commandos. The name stands for Sea-Air-Land teams, and that's exactly what they are. Trained in a variety of war skills, they can parachute in, drop from helicopters, row in silently on rafts from a submarine offshore, or swim in using scuba gear. A big part of their job is scouting ahead of an amphibious invasion, perhaps even planting electronic beacons to guide aircraft and direct shore bombardment. But they won't clear obstacles on the beach; that's the job of the UDT (Underwater Demolition Teams). The SEALS were the first Americans on shore during the Grenada invasion.

The Blue Angels are the Navy's flight demonstration team. There are a great many aerobatic teams in the world, but the Blues are something special. If they are not the best, they are certainly the best known. From their base at NAS Pensacola, Florida, the Blue Angels have traveled around the world. Their blue and gold jets are a familiar sight to most aviation enthusiasts. The Blues' performances will take on a new dimension soon when they trade in their A-4s for brand new Hornets.

If a tour with the Blue Angels looks good on a naval officer's record, it's nothing compared with a degree from the Naval Academy. The academy at Annapolis, Maryland, takes only the best; high school and prep school candidates must be nominated by their congressmen before they'll even be considered (although a few Navy enlisted men are also admitted each year). The Naval Academy is a good school, academically, but what is really taught is an attitude. Midshipmen leave as boomer ensigns, complete with a gold ring, a feeling of invincibility, and a set of preconceptions that may or may not prove true in the real world. We'll discuss some of those in the next chapter.

Chapter Seven

Seapower and the State

All hail Sergei Georgiyevich Gorshkov, Admiral of the Fleet of the Soviet Union, Naval Thinker, Consummate Politician, Civil Servant, and First Class Production Hero!

Gorshkov does not look like the Governor of the Great Ocean. He's retired now; after all, he was born in 1910, the year of the first flight of an aircraft from the deck of a ship. And without his glasses, Gorshkov would resemble Rodney Dangerfield, were it not for that cold fish stare common to big-time Soviet leaders.

But make no mistake, Gorshkov is still a real heavyweight. He has single handedly led the Soviet Navy out onto the Great Ocean, as surely as if he'd grabbed his boats by the bow and waded out into the blue water himself. And he's done it pretty much alone, through bluffs, intimidation, skillful political maneuvering, and unwavering dedication. He is very much the father of the modern Soviet Navy, and that fleet resembles the man in all respects: ambitious, innovative, and aggressive, stumbling at times, but always ready for the next step.

Gorshkov was not only commander-in-chief of the Soviet Navy, he also served as Deputy Minister of Defense and a full member of the Communist Party's Central Committee. That made him equivalent to both the civilian Secretary of the Navy and the uniformed Chief of Naval Operations. Gorshkov could dream things up and then make sure they came true. Of course, that enormous power could have led to unchecked failures, of which he had plenty, trying to move too fast too soon. But Gorshkov's administrative muscle, coupled with his experience on the job—he'd been running the Navy since 1956—and not a little help from his unsung predecessor, allowed him to translate his vision of a Russian fleet fit for the Great Ocean into steel and steam.

What, then, is Admiral Gorshkov's ultimate goal for his Navy? That is hard to figure. You can't really go by what he says. His book, *Seapower and the State,* is remarkable only for its ability to mean different things to each reader. Even his clear statements are not often reliable. In 1967 he wrote that the aircraft carrier was finished; since then, the Soviets have built half a dozen.

On the other hand, one can argue—as Gorshkov has no doubt done before the politburo—that the Soviet carriers and his other shiny new ships are built to hunt down American ballistic missile submarines and keep the USN off the backs of the

Destroyer *Preble* caught between A-6 fuel tanks. *Photo by Michael Skinner.*

Soviet *Kiev* class guided missile VSTOL aircraft carrier *Kiev*. The Soviet Navy has always shown a willingness to go its own way in warship design.

Red Army, two goals very much in line with Kremlin thinking. But Gorshkov seems to have something bigger on his mind—a fleet that can challenge the mighty USN on the Great Ocean.

For years now, the prying eyes of American spy satellites have been staring at Nikolayev Chernomorskij on the Black Sea. There, in Shipyard 444, the Soviet Union has built its first real aircraft carrier.

Estimated to weigh 65,000 tons and measure 1,000 feet, the ship is still not quite as large as the newer American behemoths. But it's a big step up from the relatively dinky helicopter cruisers and antisubmarine carriers that have characterized the first steps of the Bear into the deeper waters of carrier aviation. (Ironically, the Soviet Union's first real aircraft carrier may be classified as an "aviation battleship" to permit passage through the Straits of Turkey, prohibited to carriers by treaty.)

Unfortunately, despite what you have read, that is all we really know about Black-Com-2, the U.S. Navy's sinister code name for the new carrier. (Actually, the proper designation is Bal-Com-2, for the second surface combatant building in the Baltic. But the other name sounds so much more menacing that no one uses the correct one anymore.) Satellites cannot peek into people's heads. The Russians aren't talking about their new carrier, but everyone else is. This is what they're saying:

The new carrier is almost certainly nuclear powered, a trend begun with the *Kirov* battle cruiser. It may also borrow some of *Kirov*'s weapons systems, including the vertical launch tubes, for its *Kiev*-like bow, although some reports suggest the new ship will have a through-deck similar to American carriers, with the hatches of the vertical launch tubes mounted flush on the forward flight deck.

Most estimates say the new carrier will embark around seventy-five aircraft, although reports differ on the type. The new Helix naval helicopters are sure bets, and navalized versions of the swing-wing Su-24 Fencer strike aircraft and MiG-27 Flogger fighter-bomber are often mentioned. But *Jane's* says the emphasis will be on "fixed-wing interceptor-attack aircraft," even though no likely candidates for this role are yet apparent. Given the Soviet penchant for electronic combat and their need for over-the-horizon targeting, other types of support aircraft are likely to be carried, although, again, there is no evidence of any such aircraft being tested.

No one even knows the truc name of the new carrier. *Leonid Brezhnev* came and went (although the name was bandied about for the second *Kirov* before that ship was known to be christened *Frunze)*. The new carrier was also called *Sovetskiy Soyuz* (Soviet Union), but now the press seems to have settled on *Kremlin* as the best guess.

One thing *is* certain. Although Black-Com-2 has been launched, it will be a long time before it poses a real blue water, blue sky threat to the USN. Even if it were to set sail tomorrow with all the aircraft on board, it would still take years before the carrier could become operational. For the Soviets, *Kremlin* is not just another ship. It's another world.

Carrier ops is a folk art. The U.S. Navy, which is built around the supercarrier, has a cadre of officers and men who have learned the lessons of the flight deck the hard way. The knowledge is passed from sailor to sailor. But even though American carrier crews are recognized as the best in the world at what they do, mistakes still happen. Given the generally poorer skill level of Soviet sailors, their new carrier will have to weather a series of long and difficult shakedown cruises before reaching smooth sailing.

The Soviet Union is preparing as best it can. Russian ships shadowing American task forces have been very interested in launches and recoveries as of late. And for years, Soviet pilots have reportedly been practicing on a full-scale outline of the carrier's flight deck sketched out on concrete at Saki naval air base off the Black Sea. The Soviets are also working on catapults and arresting gear there, although, even at this late date, some experts believe the ship will use a ski jump in place of steam catapults. All the newest Russian aircraft, including the Su-27 Flanker, the MiG-29 Fulcrum fighters, and the Su-25 Frogfoot ground attack aircraft have rolled off the ski jumps at Saki, although it's difficult to say if this is just pure research or if the aircraft are actually destined to sail on the new carrier.

The U.S. Navy is flattered by the attention, but they have mixed feelings about Black-Com-2. The idea of Soviet attack carriers prowling the Great Ocean—and there are reports that as many as seven more *Kremlin*s will be constructed—does not sit well with American naval planners. Even if only one is completed, and the Russians suffer the problems expected learning the fine art of flight ops, *Kremlin* will usher in a new era of warfare on the Great Ocean. U.S. naval aviators will no longer be alone in the sky over the blue water. The spectre of supercarrier battles in mid-ocean will demand a significant change in American maritime strategy.

On the other hand, the first reports of a new Soviet carrier building couldn't have come at better time for the U.S. Navy. The news from Shipyard 444 arrived just as the Navy was trying to push three new supercarriers through Congress. The *Kremlin* served the lobbyists well, both as a threat and proof that the carrier was *not* just an American anachronism.

Aircraft carriers have an impact greater than any other weapon system. They also have a greater number of advocates—and detractors.

The modern nuclear supercarrier is no doubt a powerful military asset, able to sail for thirteen years without refueling, carrying an armada of versatile tactical aircraft that can reach targets just about anywhere on the globe. A carrier battle group can theoretically control six hundred miles of ocean, above, beneath, and on the surface. They are movable, and cannot be overrun, which is not true with land bases—of the dozens of air bases built by the U.S. on the Asian mainland *not one* remains available to American forces today.

On the other hand, aircraft carriers are tremendously expensive. A conservative estimate of the cost of a *Nimitz* class supercarrier is around $3 billion. That's a pretty big chunk in itself, but with its air wing, submarine, and surface escort, the modern carrier battle group costs at least 17 billion not even counting operating costs. That's the biggest price tag in the entire defense budget, more than a hundred B-1 bombers, or seventy-five MX missiles. Carriers are also a huge drain on the Navy's dwindling manpower, especially in the critical nuclear engineering field.

And worse, they can be sunk. The question of the extent of the carrier's vulnerability to modern cruise missiles is still being debated. Both sides point to the Falklands war to support their arguments, but the fact is the war in the Malvinas was too limited in scope to garner any hard evidence. Still, it is hard to ignore the image of sixteen British ships damaged or sunk, burning in the freezing waters at the bottom of the world.

The truth is probably somewhere between the two poles. The carrier is much more difficult to bag than the critics would have us believe. Defense analyst Jim Dunnigan figures that less than 3 percent of the Soviet cruise missiles fired at Western task forces would get through. He bases the estimate on World War II Kamikaze warfare—if anything, the suicide planes were more accurately guided than today's weapons—and American versus Russian technology. (Dunnigan says Western cruise missiles could be as much as ten times more accurate than Soviet weapons.)

There *will* be hits—up to a dozen if the Soviets manage to get off the estimated four hundred cruise missiles potentially aimed at each carrier group. The supercarriers are built to take up to four hits and keep functioning, although the small boys in the task force could be sunk or disabled after just one hit. However, it's doubtful the USN would put its precious carriers in a position in which they would suffer the onslaught of a complete Soviet attack, or that the Russians would be able to get off a fraction of that number of missiles in the face of an American counterattack.

But some Navy skippers are more than a little concerned about Navy Secretary John Lehman's talk about sailing up the Kola Peninsula to keep Soviet subs bottled up at their bases in the Arctic Sea. As a civilian, Lehman has no direct control over American naval operations, and perhaps this is a good thing. Although Lehman argues that land-based air power would help the battle groups pull it off (contradicting his arguments that land-based air power is obsolete and carrier battle groups can protect themselves independently), most naval experts consider an attack against four hundred Soviet ships, subs, and countless aircraft at the main-force Soviet bases in the early stages of a conventional war a suicide mission. As for Lehman, an A-6 bombardier-navigator in the Naval Reserve, should he somehow point a carrier towards the Barents Sea in wartime, he is likely to find himself, helmet in hand, alone on deck with just a single pilotless Intruder running up on the catapult.

Even without sailing into the Bear's mouth, carriers are not likely to survive long in a nuclear war. We said before that weapons are useless in peacetime and priceless in war, but the supercarriers are the exception. They are an invaluable asset for force projection in peace and tactical support in limited war, but in an all-out global nuclear conflict most are likely to be eliminated at their bases in the first wave.

For all the Navy's talk about the carrier's mobility and global range, the fact is that aircraft carriers spend most of their time in port or traveling to and from station. This is more of a support problem than any fault of the carriers' design, but it is still a big headache for Navy planners.

At any given time, about one-third of the Navy's carriers will be in port, refitting for the next voyage. One of the carriers will be undergoing a major overhaul called the Service Life Extension Program, or SLEP. A carrier put to SLEP will be out for a long time, perhaps two years or more. The program gives the Navy more carriers in the long run, but puts pressure on an already tight deployment schedule. Another third of the USN carrier force is out of action while steaming to station or returning to port after being relieved. The Navy likes to keep four carriers on the Great Ocean and another in reserve, ready to sail.

The recent commitment to keep a naval presence on station in the Indian Ocean has stretched the Navy thin at a time when many older ships are due for retirement or are undergoing extensive refit. The USN, as the saying goes, has become "a one-and-a-half ocean navy with a three-ocean commitment." That's why they need the new carriers.

The new American supercarriers will be built, but the issue was touch and go for a while. Many

Coral Sea, "The Ageless Warrior," in the Sea of Japan. The *Coral Maru* has recently undergone SLEP refit.

congressmen fought desperately for an alternative to the huge, expensive, and increasingly vulnerable nuclear-powered supercarrier. And during the reign of Elmo Zumwalt—the first surface Navy man to become chief of naval operations after a long line of carrier admirals—critics of the supercarriers found an ally.

Zumwalt thought the USN's preoccupation with the war in Southeast Asia—essentially a carrier show, from the Navy's standpoint—had led to a decline in surface warfare capability. Numbers were what was needed in NATO. Zumwalt's "Project 60" called for a "high-low" mix of ships that would supplement the Navy's few and expensive modern warships with a large number of relatively cheap ones.

Several proposals were put forth, ranging from a conventionally powered carrier almost as large as the *John F. Kennedy* class to a much smaller sea control ship. Many recommended the U.S. follow the Soviets and the British in building a V/STOL carrier. Some even suggested America had enough carriers and no further building was necessary.

With Zumwalt's retirement in 1974, the carrier Navy counterattacked viciously. Defense is never cheap, they said, but the smaller carriers were no bargain. Nuclear carriers carry nearly twice the aviation fuel of a conventionally powered carrier, and 50 percent more ammunition. A smaller carrier, such as the Navy's Design Study 45—a 44,000-ton sea control ship with less than half the aircraft of a *Nimitz* class carrier and very little battle damage protection—would still cost about two-thirds the price of a new supercarrier.

Not only was the CVLX-45 less than cost-effective, said the Navy, it was not a viable weapons system. To carry the interceptors, airborne warning aircraft, subchasers, and electronic warfare platforms needed to survive in modern sea warfare, CVLX-45 would have to give up its attack squadrons, its offensive punch. As for the carrier concept being obsolete, the Navy said, the aircraft carrier will be obsolete only when aircraft are obsolete.

So the Navy will get its three new supercarriers. *Theodore Roosevelt* is undergoing trials, while work is well under way on both *Abraham Lincoln*

Enterprise, with its rebuilt island, returns to port. Controversy follows the carriers wherever they sail.

and *George Washington* in Newport News. And it looks like the Soviet Union will get its new carrier too, but the debate is far from over.

There's a new storm brewing on the horizon for the supercarrier. This time, the criticism comes not from outsiders, but from the heart of the Navy itself. And the debate isn't about the carriers as such—to these naval officers, the utility of the modern supercarrier is beyond question—but with the way they are used.

Weapons and strategy are interlocked. New technology affects strategy, certainly, just as strategy plays a major part in the kinds of weapons that are developed. The Navy's crush on the aircraft carrier is a perfect example of this. Is current naval strategy built around the supercarrier, or is the supercarrier built to carry out current naval strategy? It is a moot point. Barring catastrophe or loss in combat, the USN's new carriers will be sailing at least until today's Annapolis graduates take over the helm.

Naval planning takes years to develop. Today's world can change in the flash of an explosion. It may already be ahead of current American naval thinking. The Navy prides itself on being the first, and often only, U.S. service on the scene at hotspots around the globe. But the days of presidents dispatching an aircraft carrier as if it were an angry letter to the editor may soon be over. A growing number of voices in the Navy's professional press say that if the carriers continue to park off the scene of world crisis spots they are headed for trouble.

The Navy has a philosophy called "modified local operations," or ModLocs for short. At the first sign of trouble, the carrier battle group is dispatched to the scene, where it sails around in circles. The area described by the circle is a ModLoc, an imaginary tract drawn on the water that defines the operating perimeter of a carrier battle group. Perhaps the most famous ModLoc is Yankee Station, off the North Vietnamese coast. There are others: Gonzo Station is off Oman in the north Arabian Sea; Bagel Station is in the Eastern Med, off Israel. Other ModLocs include Kermit Station, Parrot Station, and dozens of other points familiar to most carrier sailors.

There are good things about ModLocs. They simplify the huge logistics problems that follow carrier battle groups around the globe. Since rapid communications are imperative in the sensitive areas bordering most ModLocs, they help make sure the carriers don't wander off where they can't be reached rapidly. And, again, since the carriers are operating where a false move could have international repercussions, ModLocs keep the task force grouped where the commander can keep a close eye on every part.

There are bad things about ModLocs, as well. With their familiar supply lines, they don't help train our sailors in the improvisation of logistics that will be a vital part of any war. Since everyone knows where the carrier battle group is, there's no sense in maintaining electronic silence, another crucial wartime skill that needs constant practice.

But the most dangerous part of the ModLoc philosophy is that, in addition to not serving the purpose it's intended to, it leaves the precious carrier group open to attack. With today's long-range weapons and often irrational adversaries, a battle

Bainbridge (CGN-25) and a *Knox* class frigate operate on Gonzo Station in the Indian Ocean.

group steaming off a hostile coast is not a threat, it's a target. The carriers and their escorts, tied in nets of political, logistical, and tactical restraints, are sitting ducks cutting circular grooves in the waters off the most dangerous parts of the world. And it won't be long before someone decides that the battle group, filling the air with radar beams, radio waves, sonar soundings, smoke, and noise, is too easy a shot to pass up.

The Navy is slowly beginning to realize this. In the eastern Med off Lebanon, it was not uncommon to see crews mounting fifty-caliber machine guns and Marines on guard with Stinger shoulder-launched missiles on the catwalks of American ships. The irony of men defending America's most technologically advanced warships with relatively primitive weapons could not have been lost on Navy brass.

As a modern version of gunboat diplomacy, the ModLoc concept is rapidly going out of date. Intimidation needs the threat of force behind it. The idea of offering an American supercarrier as hostage isn't going to solve anything. It worked well for a while because it was expedient. It didn't really involve American troops in combat on foreign soil—the president's greatest worry—and it satisfied the modern American penchant for substituting technology for manpower.

But what if the bad guys aren't afraid of machines? What if the bad guys aren't afraid of anything? What if the floating diplomats have to fight to make their point?

Navy carriers on Yankee Station continuously pounded North Vietnam for years, but, in the end, it didn't make any difference (although, to be fair, nothing else the U.S. did in that war seemed to work either). More recently, two carriers off Lebanon sent a twenty-eight-plane Alfa Strike against three antiaircraft sites that had fired on F-14 reconnaissance planes. The Pentagon says the raid was "very successful" although detailed results were not released. And the Navy says the raid put a stop to further attacks on American recon aircraft. It *is* known that the U.S. lost two aircraft; one pilot was rescued, another was killed, and a third crewman—Lt. Robert Goodman—was at the center of an international incident when he was captured, and later released through the efforts of the Rev. Jesse Jackson.

No one really knows if an American fleet in the window has ever prevented a war, or helped cause one. The USN has intervened on more than two hundred occasions since World War II, but these days, with the troublemakers seeking to draw the U.S. into conflict, not keep it out, a carrier pacing off the world's hot spots is a dangerous temptation. Even an attempted suicide attack on the carriers could lead to serious trouble for everyone concerned. The Libyans have bought some fast Swedish powerboats that would be perfect for a Kamikaze run at an American carrier. (The carriers off Bagel Station were expecting a similar attack by private aircraft packed with explosives.)

Does this mean the Navy should give up its coveted role as America's peacetime policeman? Of course not. But the carriers' new critics say the Navy should change its tactics; come in silently, hit hard, and get out quick. Hanging around the ModLoc doesn't do anything except increase the carrier's vulnerability.

The Navy has worked hard to make the carriers viable. They have filled the flight decks with expensive, long-range interceptors to knock down bombers and long-range cruise missiles. They've built early warning radar planes to guard over the carriers and antisubmarine aircraft to keep watch underneath them.

It is an intricate, expensive, and imposing defense. It might work. But it is a *defense.* It is not the Navy way. The USN can argue that the best offense is a good defense, that the only way to sucker the Soviets into coming out to fight is to offer the carriers as bait. But the idea of the Navy leading with its jaw is disturbing to a lot of critics, not all of them out of uniform. As one authority puts it: "If you're going to be a duck in the shooting gallery, then you've got to design a very, very invulnerable duck."

The carriers have seen plenty of peacetime action, but never against the Soviet Union. Perhaps it's time to realize that the enemy doesn't always wear a red star and start building for the types of actions the carriers have actually been fighting since World War II—the projection of power on land. This is what the Marines have been saying all along, of course. But the Navy rarely listens to what the Marines have to say.

The critics claim that too much of the supercarrier's flight deck is taken up with defensive aircraft, and that too many of the Navy's ships are designed with only carrier air defense in mind. The great carrier battle groups *may* turn out to be as invulnerable as the Navy advertises, but they lack offensive punch.

Carrier supporters counter with this line: The Navy is not alone in this design philosophy. Even the mighty Soviet cruiser *Kirov* carries only twenty cruise missiles for offensive attack. The rest of its huge hull is filled with defensive antiair and antisubmarine weapons, systems and electronics. And after the Backfires are neutralized and the subs sunk on their way back from patrol, then the carriers become an unchallenged instrument for power projection. An Alfa Strike from a single aircraft carrier could deliver more than half a million pounds of bombs. And the planes will be back for another airstrike the next day, while the missiles would be lost forever.

There is a third possibility beyond the annihilation of either fleet. It could be that both sides, reluctant to expose their precious fleets unless they have a clear advantage, will circle one another endlessly on the Great Ocean, like boxers waiting for an opening that never comes. It could be that the next war at sea will resemble the first world war on land, a kind of trench warfare on the high seas in which no one gets to the carriers, but the carriers can't get to anyone else, either.

In the supercharged atmosphere surrounding the supercarriers, it's tough to get a reasonable dialogue started about the carriers' role now and into the next century. The supercarriers have taken on an importance even beyond their expense and importance in the Navy's order of battle. They have become floating icons. Zealots instinctively move to smite down blasphemy against the supercarrier and its floating and flying vassals. Carrier iconoclasts will hear nothing good about the obviously useful ships; they are devils and must be done away with without any thought of what could take their place.

Although the role of the carrier—or the attack submarine, or any other naval weapons system—is constantly being debated, the worth of the Navy itself is beyond question. There was a time, in the dawn of the atomic era, when analysts felt sea power, like so many other military endeavors, had been rendered superfluous by the bomb. Now it's recognized that just the opposite is true: the nation that controls the sea controls the world. And despite a growing threat from the Soviet fleet, the USN still rules the waves.

Above: Carriers have been described as sitting ducks. Here ordnance men install a fifty-caliber machine gun on the starboard island. *Photo by Michael Skinner.*

Below: "Wings over America." A pair of Black Lions from VF-213 overfly CV-66.

Perry class frigate, *Halyburton*.

Appendix I

U.S. Navy Organization Chart

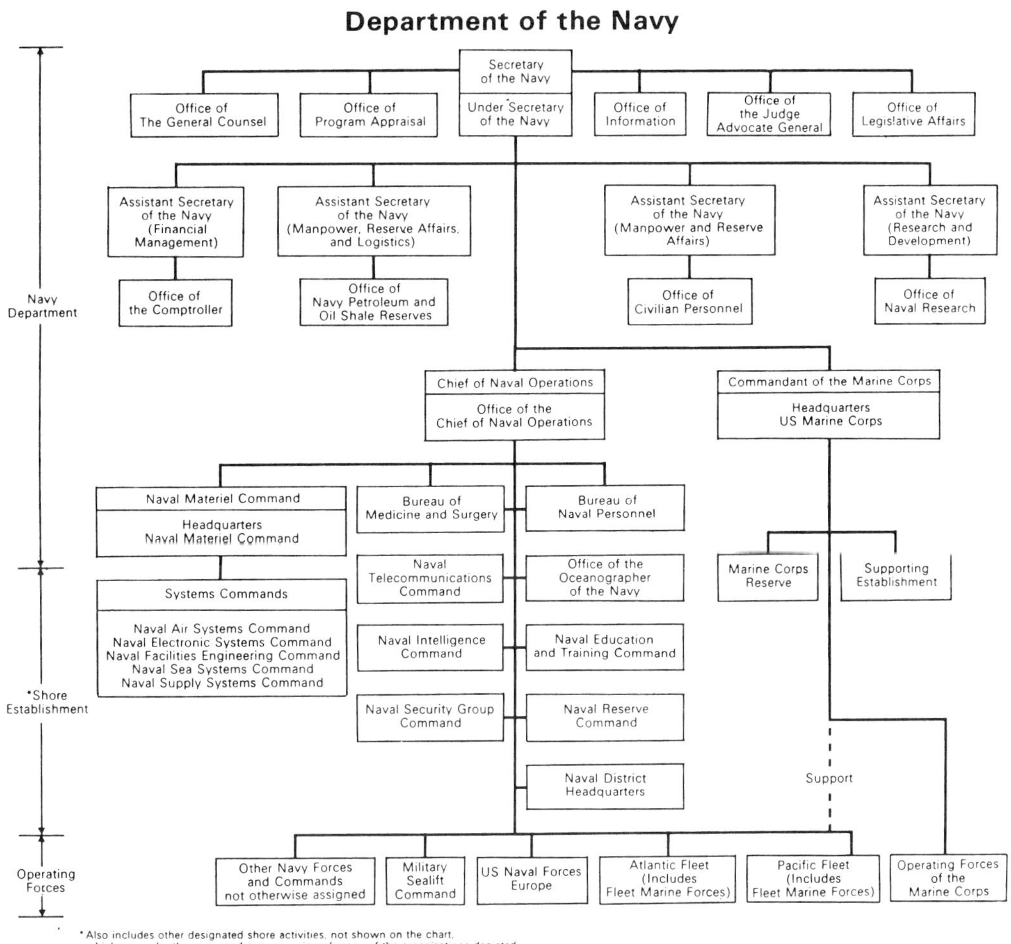

*Also includes other designated shore activities, not shown on the chart, which are under the command or supervision of many of the organizations depicted.

Note: Chart is current as of 1985. Ongoing reorganization will result in changes during 1986.

Appendix II

U.S. Ranks and Ratings

A Comparison

While ranks are fairly comparative throughout the other services, the Navy has chosen, once again, to go its own way. This chart, reprinted with the kind permission of the U.S. Naval Institute from their invaluable *Bluejacket's Manual,* may help clear up some confusion. And explain, once and for all, the big difference between a captain in the Air Force and a captain in the Navy.

By the way, the USN has recently brought back the rank of Commodore. Formerly used merely as an honorific for any naval officer in command of a group of ships in wartime, the *rank* of Commodore has now been institutionalized, if only because it sounds so much more classy than Rear Admiral.

Guided Missile destroyer.

NAVY	MARINES	ARMY	AIR FORCE	
MASTER CHIEF P.O.	SGT. MAJOR; MASTER GUNNERY SGT.	SERGEANT MAJOR; COMMAND SERGEANT MAJOR	CHIEF MASTER SGT.	E-9
SENIOR CHIEF P.O.	1ST SGT.; MASTER SGT.	FIRST SERGEANT; MASTER SERGEANT	SENIOR MASTER SGT.	E-8
CHIEF P.O.	GUNNERY SGT	SGT. 1ST CLASS	MASTER SGT.	E-7
P.O. 1ST CLASS	STAFF SGT.	STAFF SGT.; SPEC. 6	TECHNICAL SGT.	E-6
P.O. 2ND CLASS	SGT	SGT.; SPEC. 5	STAFF SGT.	E-5
P.O. 3RD CLASS	CORPORAL	CORPORAL; SPEC. 4	SENIOR AIRMAN	E-4
SEAMAN	LANCE CORPORAL	PRIVATE 1ST CLASS	AIRMAN 1ST CLASS	E-3
SEAMAN APPRENTICE	PRIVATE 1ST CLASS	PRIVATE	AIRMAN	E-2
SEAMAN RECRUIT	PRIVATE	PRIVATE	BASIC AIRMAN	E-1

NAVY	MARINE CORPS	COAST GUARD	ARMY	AIR FORCE
W-2 CHIEF WARRANT OFFICER	GOLD SCARLET W-1 WARRANT OFFICER; GOLD SCARLET W-2 CHIEF WARRANT OFFICER	W-1 WARRANT OFFICER; W-2 CHIEF WARRANT OFFICER	SILVER BLACK WO-1 WARRANT OFFICER; SILVER BLACK CW-2 CHIEF WARRANT OFFICER	GOLD SKY BLUE W-1 WARRANT OFFICER; GOLD SKY BLUE W-2 CHIEF WARRANT OFFICER
W-3 CHIEF WARRANT OFFICER; W-4 CHIEF WARRANT OFFICER	SILVER SCARLET W-3 CHIEF WARRANT OFFICER; SILVER SCARLET W-4 CHIEF WARRANT OFFICER	W-3 CHIEF WARRANT OFFICER; W-4 CHIEF WARRANT OFFICER	SILVER BLACK CW-3 CHIEF WARRANT OFFICER; SILVER BLACK CW-4 CHIEF WARRANT OFFICER	SILVER SKY BLUE W-3 CHIEF WARRANT OFFICER; SILVER SKY BLUE W-4 CHIEF WARRANT OFFICER
ENSIGN	(GOLD) SECOND LIEUTENANT	ENSIGN	(GOLD) SECOND LIEUTENANT	(GOLD) SECOND LIEUTENANT
LIEUTENANT JUNIOR GRADE	(SILVER) FIRST LIEUTENANT	LIEUTENANT JUNIOR GRADE	(SILVER) FIRST LIEUTENANT	(SILVER) FIRST LIEUTENANT
LIEUTENANT	(SILVER) CAPTAIN	LIEUTENANT	(SILVER) CAPTAIN	(SILVER) CAPTAIN
LIEUTENANT COMMANDER	(GOLD) MAJOR	LIEUTENANT COMMANDER	(GOLD) MAJOR	(GOLD) MAJOR
COMMANDER	(SILVER) LIEUTENANT COLONEL	COMMANDER	(SILVER) LIEUTENANT COLONEL	(SILVER) LIEUTENANT COLONEL

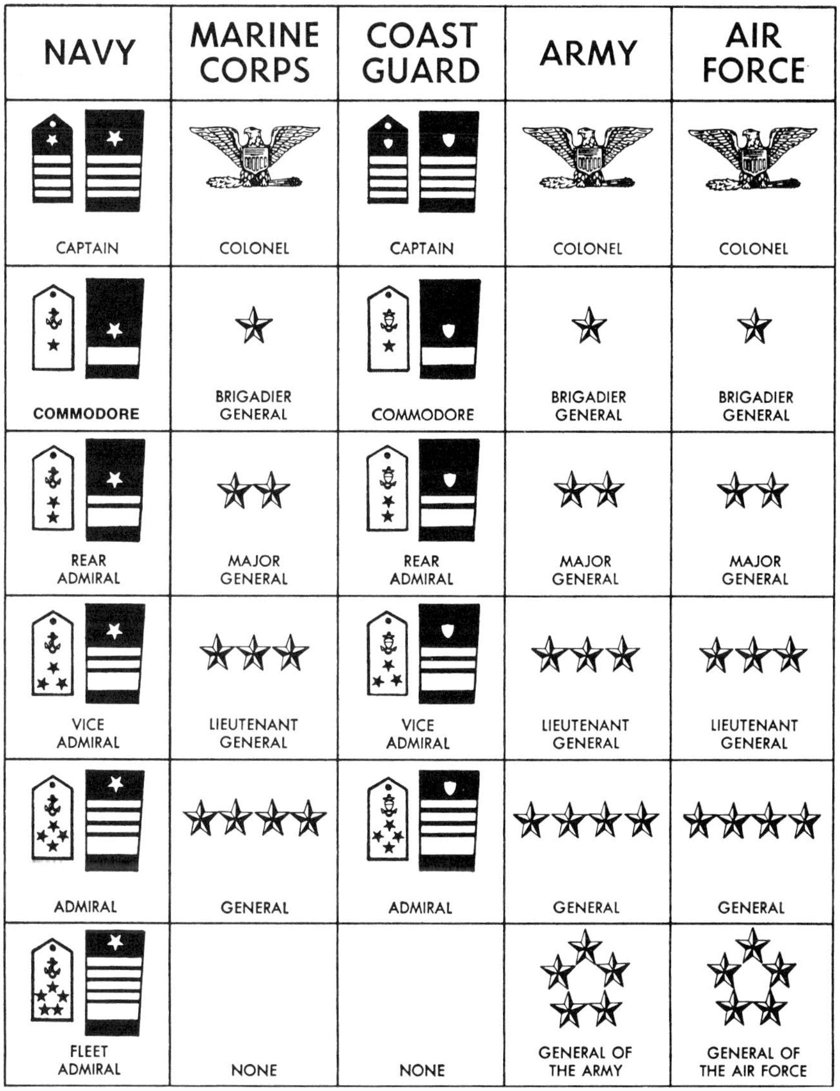

NAVY	MARINE CORPS	COAST GUARD	ARMY	AIR FORCE
CAPTAIN	COLONEL	CAPTAIN	COLONEL	COLONEL
COMMODORE	BRIGADIER GENERAL	COMMODORE	BRIGADIER GENERAL	BRIGADIER GENERAL
REAR ADMIRAL	MAJOR GENERAL	REAR ADMIRAL	MAJOR GENERAL	MAJOR GENERAL
VICE ADMIRAL	LIEUTENANT GENERAL	VICE ADMIRAL	LIEUTENANT GENERAL	LIEUTENANT GENERAL
ADMIRAL	GENERAL	ADMIRAL	GENERAL	GENERAL
FLEET ADMIRAL	NONE	NONE	GENERAL OF THE ARMY	GENERAL OF THE AIR FORCE

From *The Bluejackets' Manual,* 20th ed., revised by Bill Bearden and Bill Wedertz.

Appendix III

U.S. Navy Organization and Deployment

American combat sailors belong to two navies. For training and major maintenance, it's convenient to organize ships of similar types into units called groups and squadrons. Generally, even-numbered units are based on the East Coast, and odd-numbered units on the West. This is a listing of major USN homeports, along with the types of ships and organizations based there.

I have taken the liberty of translating the unit designations into plain, non-acronymic English. The "correct" Navy title for a submarine group, for example, is "SubGru"; a destroyer squadron is actually a "DesRon." You get the idea. (My favorite is CruDesGru, which sounds like an industrial solvent but is actually a Cruiser/Destroyer Group.) I have also combined some different ship types together, such as CGNs with CGs and DDGs with DDs. This was done to save space, but in the squadrons and groups, different subtypes of ships are lumped together anyway. Also to save space, amphibious ships, minesweepers, and auxiliaries have been omitted.

Sailors belong to a different type of organization afloat. When deployed, ships are assigned to groups called Task Forces. These are often broken down into their component parts, called Task Groups, and identified by the initials "TG," a dash, and a series of numbers denoting, in order, the numbered fleet in operational command, the primary mission of the group, and, if there's more than one such unit in the fleet, a decimal followed by an identifying number. Thus, TG-60.2 is the second battle group in the Sixth Fleet Task Force (and can also be referred to as simply "Battle Force Bravo").

The whole thing is actually even *more* complicated than it sounds here. There are major organizational differences, for instance, between the chains of command in the Pacific and Atlantic fleets. And there's a similar schizophrenic chain of command for naval air units. But this list should give you a quick look at where the Navy's muscle is.

Atlantic Fleet

Second Fleet

HQ Norfolk, VA

Portland, ME	2 Destroyers
	2 Frigates
	Surface Squadron 2 (Naval Reserve Force)
	Destroyer Squadron 8

New London, CT	7 Attack Submarines Submarine Group 2 Submarine Squadron 10
Groton, CT	8 Ballistic Missile Submarines 16 Attack Submarines
Brooklyn, NY	1 Destroyer 1 Frigate
Philadelphia, PA	2 Destroyers
Newport News, VA	4 Ballistic Missile Submarines
Norfolk, VA	6 Aircraft Carriers 1 Battleship 9 Cruisers 19 Destroyers 9 Frigates 19 Attack Submarines Carrier Groups 4 and 8 Cruiser/Destroyer Group 8 Destroyer Squadrons 2, 10, 22, 26, and 32 Submarine Squadrons 6 and 8
Charleston, SC	2 Cruisers 10 Destroyers 12 Frigates 11 Attack Submarines 18 Ballistic Missile Submarines Cruiser/Destroyer Group 2 Destroyer Squadrons 4, 6, 20, and 36 Submarine Squadrons 2, 4, and 18
King's Bay, GA	Submarine Squadron 16 (new East Coast SSBN unit)
Mayport, FL	1 Aircraft Carrier 1 Cruiser 4 Destroyers 24 Frigates Carrier Group 6 Cruiser/Destroyer Group 12 Destroyer Squadrons 12, 14, and 24
Key West, FL	6 PHMs (hydrofoil patrol boats) PHM Squadron 2
Pascagoula, MS	1 Destroyer

Sixth Fleet

HQ Gaeta, Italy
(Sixth Fleet ships operating in the Mediterranean are rotated forward from the Second Fleet. But some organizations are permanent, and here they are.)

Holy Loch, Scotland	Submarine Squadron 14
Naples, Italy	Carrier Group 2
La Maddalena, Italy	Submarine Group 8

Pacific Fleet

Third Fleet

HQ Pearl Harbor, HI

San Diego, CA	2 Aircraft Carriers 11 Cruisers 22 Destroyers 20 Frigates 14 Attack Submarines Carrier Groups 1 and 3 Cruiser/Destroyer Groups 1, 3, and 5 Destroyer Squadrons 5, 7, 9, 13, 17, 21, 23, and 31. Submarine Group 5 Submarine Squadron 3
Long Beach, CA	1 Battleship 1 Destroyer 12 Frigates Surface Squadron 1 (Naval Reserve Force)

Alameda, CA	2 Aircraft Carriers 2 Cruisers
Vallejo, CA	6 Attack Submarines
Bangor, WA	4 Ballistic Missile Submarines 1 Attack Submarine
Bremerton, WA	1 Aircraft Carrier 1 Cruiser 3 Attack Submarines Submarine Group 9
Pearl Harbor, HI	1 Cruiser 3 Destroyers 9 Frigates 18 Attack Submarines Destroyer Squadrons 25, 33, and 35 Submarine Squadrons 1 and 7

Seventh Fleet

HQ Yokosuka, Japan

(As in the Sixth Fleet, most elements of the Seventh Fleet are forwarded from U.S.N.-based units, in this case, the Third Fleet. However, the Seventh Fleet does have some units assigned on a permanent basis.)

Agana, Guam	Submarine Squadron 15
Yokosuka, Japan	1 Aircraft Carrier 1 Cruiser 3 Destroyers 4 Frigates Destroyer Squadron 15 Submarine Group 7
Cubi Point, RP	Carrier Group 5
Subic Bay, RP	1 Cruiser

Crew falls in in dress whites as *Joseph Strauss*, an *Adams* class guided missile destroyer, returns to its home port, Pearl Harbor.

16

Appendix IV

Warships of the USN

Ohio Class Ballistic Missile Submarines

SSBN 726 *Ohio*	Bangor, WA	P
SSBN 727 *Michigan*	Bangor, WA	P
SSBN 728 *Florida*	Bangor, WA	P
SSBN 729 *Georgia*	Bangor, WA	P
SSBN 730 *Henry M. Jackson*	Bangor, WA	P
SSBN 731 *Alabama*	Bangor, WA	P
SSBN 732 *Alaska*	Bangor, WA	P
SSBN 733 *Nevada*		

Lafayette Class Ballistic Missile Submarines

SSBN 616 *Lafayette*	Groton, CT	A
SSBN 617 *Alexander Hamilton*	Groton, CT	A
SSBN 619 *Andrew Jackson*	Groton, CT	A
SSBN 620 *John Adams*	Charleston, SC	A
SSBN 622 *James Monroe*	Charleston, SC	A
SSBN 623 *Nathan Hale*	Charleston, SC	A
SSBN 624 *Woodrow Wilson*	Charleston, SC	A
SSBN 625 *Henry Clay*	Charleston, SC	A
SSBN 626 *Daniel Webster*	Groton, CT	A
SSBN 627 *James Madison*	Charleston, SC	A
SSBN 628 *Tecumseh*	Newport News, VA	A
SSBN 629 *Daniel Boone*	Charleston, SC	A
SSBN 630 *John C. Calhoun*	Charleston, SC	A
SSBN 631 *Ulysses S. Grant*	Portsmouth, NH	A
SSBN 632 *Von Steuben*	Charleston, SC	A
SSBN 633 *Casimir Pulaski*	Charleston, SC	A
SSBN 634 *Stonewall Jackson*	Charleston, SC	A
SSBN 635 *Sam Rayburn*	Groton, CT	A
SSBN 636 *Nathanael Greene*	Groton, CT	A
SSBN 640 *Benjamin Franklin*	Charleston, SC	A
SSBN 641 *Simon Bolivar*	Charleston, SC	A
SSBN 642 *Kamehameha*	Groton, CT	A
SSBN 643 *George Bancroft*	Charleston, SC	A
SSBN 644 *Lewis and Clark*	Charleston, SC	A
SSBN 645 *James K. Polk*	Charleston, SC	A
SSBN 654 *George C. Marshall*	Groton, CT	A
SSBN 655 *Henry L. Stimson*	Newport News, VA	A
SSBN 656 *George Wash. Carver*	Newport News, VA	A
SSBN 657 *Francis Scott Key*	Newport News, VA	A
SSBN 658 *Mariano G. Vallejo*	Charleston, SC	A
SSBN 659 *Will Rogers*	Newport News, VA	A

Los Angeles Class Attack Submarines

SSN 688 *Los Angeles*	Pearl Harbor, HI	P
SSN 689 *Baton Rouge*	Norfolk, VA	A
SSN 690 *Philadelphia*	Groton, CT	A
SSN 691 *Memphis*	Norfolk, VA	A
SSN 692 *Omaha*	Pearl Harbor, HI	P
SSN 693 *Cincinnati*	Norfolk, VA	A
SSN 694 *Groton*	Groton, CT	A
SSN 695 *Birmingham*	Norfolk, VA	A
SSN 696 *New York City*	Pearl Harbor, HI	P
SSN 697 *Indianapolis*	Pearl Harbor, HI	P
SSN 698 *Bremerton*	Pearl Harbor, HI	P

SSN 699 *Jacksonville*	Norfolk, VA	A
SSN 700 *Dallas*	Groton, CT	A
SSN 701 *La Jolla*	San Diego, CA	P
SSN 702 *Phoenix*	Norfolk, VA	A
SSN 703 *Boston*	Groton, CT	A
SSN 704 *Baltimore*	Norfolk, VA	A
SSN 705 *City of Corpus Cristi*	Groton, CT	A
SSN 706 *Albuquerque*	Groton, CT	A
SSN 707 *Portsmouth*	Groton, CT	A
SSN 708 *Minneapolis-St. Paul*	Groton, CT	A
SSN 709 *Hyman G. Rickover*		
SSN 710 *Augusta*		
SSN 711 *San Francisco*	Pearl Harbor, HI	P
SSN 712 *Atlanta*	Norfolk, VA	A
SSN 713 *Houston*	San Diego, CA	P
SSN 714 *Norfolk*	Norfolk, VA	A
SSN 715 *Buffalo*	Norfolk, VA	A
SSN 716 *Salt Lake City*		
SSN 717 *Olympia*		
SSN 718 *Honolulu*		
SSN 719 *Providence*		
SSN 720 *Pittsburgh*		
SSN 721 *Chicago*		
SSN 750 *Newport News*		

Sturgeon Class Attack Submarines

SSN 637 *Sturgeon*	Charleston, SC	A
SSN 638 *Whale*	Groton, CT	A
SSN 639 *Tautog*	Pearl Harbor, HI	P
SSN 646 *Grayling*	Charleston, SC	A
SSN 647 *Pogy*	Vallejo, CA	P
SSN 648 *Aspro*	Pearl Harbor, HI	P
SSN 649 *Sunfish*	Charleston, SC	A
SSN 650 *Pargo*	New London, CT	A
SSN 651 *Queenfish*	Pearl Harbor, HI	P
SSN 652 *Puffer*	Pearl Harbor, HI	P
SSN 653 *Ray*	Charleston, SC	A
SSN 660 *Sand Lance*	Charleston, SC	A
SSN 661 *Lapon*	Norfolk, VA	A
SSN 662 *Gurnard*	San Diego, CA	P
SSN 663 *Hammerhead*	Norfolk, VA	A
SSN 664 *Sea Devil*	Charleston, SC	A
SSN 665 *Guitarro*	San Diego, CA	P
SSN 666 *Hawkbill*	Pearl Harbor, HI	P
SSN 667 *Bergall*	Norfolk, VA	A
SSN 668 *Spadefish*	Norfolk, VA	A
SSN 669 *Seahorse*	Charleston, SC	A
SSN 670 *Finback*	Norfolk, VA	A
SSN 672 *Pintado*	San Diego, CA	P
SSN 673 *Flying Fish*	Norfolk, VA	A
SSN 674 *Trepang*	New London, CT	A
SSN 675 *Bluefish*	Norfolk, VA	A
SSN 676 *Billfish*	New London, CT	A
SSN 677 *Drum*	San Diego, CA	P
SSN 678 *Archerfish*	Portsmouth, NH	A
SSN 679 *Silversides*	Norfolk, VA	A
SSN 680 *William H. Bates*	San Diego, CA	P
SSN 681 *Batfish*	Charleston, SC	A
SSN 682 *Tunny*	Pearl Harbor, HI	P
SSN 683 *Parche*	Vallejo, CA	P
SSN 684 *Cavalla*	Pearl Harbor, HI	P
SSN 686 *L. Mendel Rivers*	Charleston, SC	A
SSN 687 *Richard B. Russell*	Vallejo, CA	P

Narwhal Class Attack Submarine

SSN 671 *Narwhal*	Charleston, SC	A

Glenard P. Lipscomb Class Attack Submarine

SSN 685 *Glenard P. Lipscomb*	Norfolk, VA	A

Permit Class Attack Submarines

SSN 594 *Permit*	Vallejo, CA	P
SSN 595 *Plunger*	San Diego, CA	P
SSN 596 *Barb*	San Diego, CA	P
SSN 603 *Pollack*	San Diego, CA	P
SSN 604 *Haddo*	San Diego, CA	P
SSN 605 *Jack*	Portsmouth, NH	A
SSN 606 *Tinosa*	Portsmouth, NH	A
SSN 607 *Dace*	New London, CT	A
SSN 612 *Guardfish*	Vallejo, CA	P
SSN 613 *Flasher*	Vallejo, CA	P
SSN 614 *Greenling*	New London, CT	A
SSN 615 *Gato*	New London, CT	A
SSN 621 *Haddock*	San Diego, CA	P

Skipjack Class Attack Submarines

SSN 585 *Skipjack*	Groton, CT	A
SSN 588 *Scamp*	Groton, CT	A
SSN 590 *Sculpin*	Groton, CT	A
SSN 591 *Shark*	Groton, CT	A
SSN 592 *Snook*	Groton, CT	A

Skate Class Attack Submarines

SSN 578 *Skate*	Pearl Harbor, HI	P
SSN 579 *Swordfish*	Pearl Harbor, HI	P
SSN 583 *Sargo*	Pearl Harbor, HI	P
SSN 584 *Seadragon*	Pearl Harbor, HI	P

Seawolf Class Attack Submarine

SSN 575 *Seawolf*	Sasebo, Japan	P

Barbel Class Attack Submarines

SS 580 *Barbel*	Pearl Harbor, HI	P
SS 581 *Blueback*	San Diego, CA	P
SS 582 *Bonefish*	Charleston, SC	A

Darter Class Attack Submarine

SS 576 *Darter*	Sasebo, Japan	

Midway Class Aircraft Carriers

CV 41 *Midway*	Yokosuka, Japan	P
CV 43 *Coral Sea*	Norfolk, VA	A

Forrestal Class Aircraft Carriers

CV 59 *Forrestal*	Norfolk, VA	A
CV 60 *Saratoga*	Mayport, FL	A
CV 61 *Ranger*	San Diego, CA	P
CV 62 *Independence*	Norfolk, VA	A

Kitty Hawk Class Aircraft Carriers

CV 63 *Kitty Hawk*	San Diego, CA	P
CV 64 *Constellation*	San Diego, CA	P
CV 66 *America*	Norfolk, VA	A
CV 67 *John F. Kennedy*	Norfolk, VA	A

Enterprise Class Aircraft Carrier

CVN 65 *Enterprise*	Alameda, CA	P

Nimitz Class Aircraft Carriers

CVN 68 *Nimitz*	Norfolk, VA	A
CVN 69 *Dwight D. Eisenhower*	Norfolk, VA	A
CVN 70 *Carl Vinson*	Alameda, CA	P
CVN 71 *Theodore Roosevelt*	Alameda, CA	P
CVN 72 *Abraham Lincoln*		
CVN 73 *George Washington*		

Iowa Class Battleships

BB 61 *Iowa*	Staten Island, NY	A
BB 62 *New Jersey*	Long Beach, CA	P
BB 63 *Missouri*	San Francisco, CA	P
BB 64 *Wisconsin*		A

Ticonderoga Class Guided Missile Cruisers

CG 47 *Ticonderoga*	Norfolk, VA	A
CG 48 *Yorktown*		
CG 49 *Vincennes*		
CG 50 *Valley Forge*		
CG 51 *Thomas S. Gates*		
CG 52 *Bunker Hill*		

Virginia Class Guided Missile Cruisers

CGN 38 *Virginia*	Norfolk, VA	A
CGN 39 *Texas*	San Diego, CA	P
CGN 40 *Mississippi*	Norfolk, VA	A
CGN 41 *Arkansas*	Alameda, CA	P

California Class Guided Missile Cruisers

CGN 36 *California*	Alameda, CA	P
CGN 37 *South Carolina*	Norfolk, VA	A

Long Beach Class Guided Missile Cruiser

CGN 9 *Long Beach*	San Diego, CA	P

Belknap Class Guided Missile Cruisers

CG 26 *Belknap*	Norfolk, VA	A
CG 27 *Josephus Daniels*	Norfolk, VA	A
CG 28 *Wainwright*	Charleston, SC	A
CG 29 *Jouett*	San Diego, CA	P
CG 30 *Horne*	San Diego, CA	P
CG 31 *Sterett*	Subic Bay, RP	P
CG 32 *William H. Standley*	San Diego, CA	P
CG 33 *Fox*	Long Beach, CA	P
CG 34 *Biddle*	Norfolk, VA	A
CGN 35 *Truxtun*	Bremerton, WA	P

Leahy Class Guided Missile Cruisers

CG 16 *Leahy*	San Diego, CA	P
CG 17 *Harry E. Yarnell*	Norfolk, VA	A
CG 18 *Worden*	Pearl Harbor, HI	P
CG 19 *Dale*	Mayport, FL	A
CG 20 *Richmond K. Turner*	Charleston, SC	A
CG 21 *Gridley*	San Diego, CA	P
CG 22 *England*	San Diego, CA	P
CG 23 *Halsey*	San Diego, CA	P
CG 24 *Reeves*	Yokosuka, Japan	P
CGN 25 *Bainbridge*	Bremerton, WA	P

Charles F. Adams Class Guided Missile Destroyers

DDG 2 *Charles F. Adams*	Mayport, FL	A
DDG 3 *John Keene*	Norfolk, VA	A
DDG 4 *Lawrence*	Norfolk, VA	A
DDG 5 *Claude V. Ricketts*	Norfolk, VA	A
DDG 6 *Barney*	Norfolk, VA	A
DDG 7 *Henry B. Wilson*	San Diego, CA	P
DDG 8 *Lynde McCormick*	San Diego, CA	P
DDG 9 *Towers*	Yokosuka, Japan	P
DDG 10 *Sampson*	Mayport, FL	A
DDG 11 *Sellers*	Charleston, SC	A
DDG 12 *Robison*	San Diego, CA	P
DDG 13 *Hoel*	Long Beach, CA	P
DDG 14 *Buchanan*	San Diego, CA	P
DDG 15 *Berkeley*	San Diego, CA	P
DDG 16 *Joseph Strauss*	Pearl Harbor, HI	P
DDG 17 *Conyngham*	Norfolk, VA	A
DDG 18 *Semmes*	Charleston, SC	A
DDG 19 *Tattnall*	Mayport, FL	A
DDG 20 *Goldsborough*	Pearl Harbor, HI	P
DDG 21 *Cochrane*	Yokosuka, Japan	P
DDG 22 *Benjamin Stoddert*	Pearl Harbor, HI	P
DDG 23 *Richard E. Byrd*	Norfolk, VA	A
DDG 24 *Waddell*	San Diego, CA	P

Coontz Class Guided Missile Destroyers

DDG 37 *Farragut*	Philadelphia, PA	A
DDG 38 *Luce*	Mayport, FL	A
DDG 39 *MacDonough*	Charleston, SC	A
DDG 40 *Coontz*	Norfolk, VA	A
DDG 41 *King*	Norfolk, VA	A
DDG 42 *Mahan*	Charleston, SC	A
DDG 43 *Dahlgren*	Philadelphia, PA	A
DDG 44 *William V. Pratt*	Charleston, SC	A
DDG 45 *Dewey*	Charleston, SC	A
DDG 46 *Preble*	Norfolk, VA	A

Arleigh Burke Class Guided Missile Destroyers

DDG 51 *Arleigh Burke*

Kidd Class Guided Missile Destroyers

DDG 993 *Kidd*	Norfolk, VA	A
DDG 994 *Callaghan*	San Diego, CA	P
DDG 995 *Scott*	Norfolk, VA	A
DDG 996 *Chandler*	San Diego, CA	P

Spruance Class Destroyers

DD 963 *Spruance*	Norfolk, VA	A
DD 964 *Paul F. Foster*	Long Beach, CA	P

DD 965 *Kinkaid*	San Diego, CA	P
DD 966 *Hewitt*	San Diego, CA	P
DD 967 *Elliot*	San Diego, CA	P
DD 968 *Arthur W. Radford*	Norfolk, VA	A
DD 969 *Peterson*	Norfolk, VA	A
DD 970 *Caron*	Norfolk, VA	A
DD 971 *David R. Ray*	San Diego, CA	P
DD 972 *Oldenford*	San Diego, CA	P
DD 973 *John Young*	San Diego, CA	P
DD 974 *Comte de Grasse*	Pascagoula, MS	A
DD 975 *O'Brien*	San Diego, CA	P
DD 976 *Merrill*	San Diego, CA	P
DD 977 *Briscoe*	Norfolk, VA	A
DD 978 *Stump*	Brooklyn, NY	A
DD 979 *Conolly*	Portland, ME	A
DD 980 *Moosbrugger*	Charleston, SC	A
DD 981 *John Hancock*	Charleston, SC	A
DD 982 *Nicholson*	Charleston, SC	A
DD 983 *John Rodgers*	Charleston, SC	A
DD 984 *Leftwich*	San Diego, CA	P
DD 985 *Cushing*	San Diego, CA	P
DD 986 *Harry W. Hill*	San Diego, CA	P
DD 987 *O'Bannon*	Charleston, SC	A
DD 988 *Thorn*	Charleston, SC	A
DD 989 *Deyo*	Charleston, SC	A
DD 990 *Ingersoll*	San Diego, CA	P
DD 991 *Fife*	San Diego, CA	P
DD 992 *Fletcher*	San Diego, CA	P
DD 997 *Hayler*	Norfolk, VA	A

Brooke Class Guided Missile Frigates

FFG 1 *Brooke*	San Diego, CA	P
FFG 2 *Ramsey*	Long Beach, CA	P
FFG 3 *Schofield*	San Diego, CA	P
FFG 4 *Talbot*	Mayport, FL	A
FFG 5 *Richard L. Page*	Mayport, FL	A
FFG 6 *Julius A. Furer*	Charleston, SC	A

Oliver Hazard Perry Class Guided Missile Frigates

FFG 7 *Oliver Hazard Perry*	Mayport, FL	A
FFG 8 *McInerney*	Mayport, FL	A
FFG 9 *Wadsworth*	Long Beach, CA	P
FFG 10 *Duncan*		
FFG 11 *Clark*	Mayport, FL	A
FFG 12 *George Philip*	San Diego, CA	P
FFG 13 *Samuel Eliot Morison*	Mayport, FL	A
FFG 14 *Sides*	San Diego, CA	P
FFG 15 *Estocin*	Mayport, FL	A
FFG 16 *Clifton Sprague*	Mayport, FL	A
FFG 19 *John A. Moore*	San Diego, CA	P
FFG 20 *Antrim*	Mayport, FL	A
FFG 21 *Flatley*	Mayport, FL	A
FFG 22 *Fahrion*	Mayport, FL	A
FFG 23 *Lewis B. Puller*	San Diego, CA	P
FFG 24 *Jack Williams*	Mayport, FL	A
FFG 25 *Copeland*	Long Beach, CA	P
FFG 26 *Gallery*	Mayport, FL	P
FFG 27 *Mahlon S. Tinsdale*	San Diego, CA	P
FFG 28 *Boone*	Mayport, FL	A
FFG 29 *Stephen W. Groves*	Mayport, FL	A
FFG 30 *Reid*	San Diego, CA	P
FFG 31 *Stark*	Mayport, FL	A
FFG 32 *John L. Hall*	Mayport, FL	A
FFG 33 *Jarrett*	Long Beach, CA	P
FFG 34 *Aubrey Fitch*	Mayport, FL	A
FFG 36 *Underwood*	Mayport, FL	A
FFG 37 *Crommelin*	Long Beach, CA	P
FFG 38 *Curts*	Long Beach, CA	P
FFG 39 *Doyle*	Mayport, FL	A
FFG 40 *Halyburton*	Charleston, SC	A
FFG 41 *McCluskey*	Long Beach, CA	P
FFG 42 *Klakring*	Charleston, SC	A
FFG 43 *Thach*	Long Beach, CA	P
FFG 45 *De Wert*	Charleston, SC	A
FFG 46 *Rentz*		
FFG 47 *Nicholas*	Charleston, SC	A
FFG 48 *Vandergrift*		
FFG 49 *Robert C. Bradley*		
FFG 50 *Taylor*		
FFG 51 *Gary*		
FFG 52 *Carr*		
FFG 53 *Hawes*		
FFG 54 *Ford*		
FFG 55 *Elrod*		
FFG 56 *Simpson*		
FFG 57 *Reuben James*		
FFG 58 *Samuel B. Roberts*		
FFG 59 *Kauffman*		
FFG 60 *Rodney M. Davis*		

Glover Class Frigate

FF 1098 *Glover*	Norfolk, VA	A

Knox Class Frigates

FF 1052 *Knox*	Yokosuka, Japan	P
FF 1053 *Roark*	San Diego, CA	P
FF 1054 *Gray*		
FF 1055 *Hepburn*	San Diego, CA	P
FF 1056 *Connole*	Newport, RI	A
FF 1057 *Rathburne*	Pearl Harbor, HI	P
FF 1058 *Meyerkord*	Long Beach, CA	P
FF 1059 *W. S. Sims*	Mayport, FL	A
FF 1060 *Lang*		
FF 1061 *Patterson*		
FF 1062 *Whipple*	Pearl Harbor, HI	P
FF 1063 *Reasoner*	San Diego, CA	P
FF 1064 *Lockwood*	Yokosuka, Japan	P
FF 1065 *Stein*	San Diego, CA	P
FF 1066 *Marvin Shields*	San Diego, CA	P
FF 1067 *Francis Hammond*	Yokosuka, Japan	P
FF 1068 *Vreeland*	Mayport, FL	A
FF 1069 *Bagley*	San Diego, CA	P
FF 1070 *Downes*	San Diego, CA	P
FF 1071 *Badger*	Pearl Harbor, HI	P
FF 1072 *Blakely*		
FF 1073 *Robert E. Peary*	Pearl Harbor, HI	P
FF 1074 *Harold E. Holt*	Pearl Harbor, HI	P
FF 1075 *Trippe*	Charleston, SC	A
FF 1076 *Fanning*	San Diego, CA	P
FF 1077 *Ouellet*	Pearl Harbor, HI	P
FF 1078 *Joseph Hewes*	Charleston, SC	A
FF 1079 *Bowen*	Charleston, SC	A
FF 1080 *Paul*	Mayport, FL	A
FF 1081 *Aylwin*	Charleston, SC	A
FF 1082 *Elmer Montgomery*	Mayport, FL	A
FF 1083 *Cook*	San Diego, CA	P
FF 1084 *McCandless*	Norfolk, VA	A
FF 1085 *Donald B. Beary*	Norfolk, VA	A
FF 1086 *Brewton*	Pearl Harbor, HI	P
FF 1087 *Kirk*	Yokosuka, Japan	P
FF 1088 *Barbey*	Long Beach, CA	P
FF 1089 *Jesse L. Brown*	Boston, MA	A
FF 1090 *Ainsworth*	Charleston, SC	A
FF 1091 *Miller*		
FF 1092 *Thomas C. Hart*	Norfolk, VA	A
FF 1093 *Capodanno*	Newport, RI	A
FF 1094 *Pharris*	Brooklyn, NY	A
FF 1095 *Truett*	Norfolk, VA	A
FF 1096 *Valdez*		
FF 1097 *Moinester*	Norfolk, VA	A

Garcia Class Frigates

FF 1040 *Garcia*	Charleston, SC	A
FF 1041 *Bradley*	Long Beach, CA	P
FF 1043 *Edward McDonnell*	Mayport, FL	A
FF 1044 *Brumby*	Charleston, SC	A
FF 1045 *Davidson*	Pearl Harbor, HI	P
FF 1047 *Voge*	Mayport, FL	A
FF 1048 *Sample*	Pearl Harbor, HI	P
FF 1049 *Koelsch*	Mayport, FL	A
FF 1050 *Albert David*	San Diego, CA	P
FF 1051 *O'Callahan*	San Diego, CA	P

Bronstein Class Frigates

FF 1037 *Bronstein*	San Diego, CA	P
FF 1038 *McCloy*	Norfolk, VA	A

Blue Ridge Class Amphibious Command Ships

LCC 19 *Blue Ridge*	Yokosuka, Japan	P
LCC 20 *Mount Whitney*	Norfolk, VA	A

Wasp Class Amphibious Assault Ship

LHD 1 *Wasp*		

Tarawa Class Amphibious Assault Ships

LHA 1 *Tarawa*	San Diego, CA	P
LHA 2 *Siapan*	Norfolk, VA	A
LHA 3 *Belleau Wood*	San Diego, CA	P
LHA 4 *Nassau*	Norfolk, VA	A
LHA 5 *Peleliu*	Long Beach, CA	P

Iwo Jima Class Amphibious Assault Ships

LPH 2 *Iwo Jima*	Norfolk, VA	A
LPH 3 *Okinawa*	San Diego, CA	P
LPH 7 *Guadalcanal*	Norfolk, VA	A
LPH 9 *Guam*	Norfolk, VA	A
LPH 10 *Tripoli*	San Diego, CA	P
LPH 11 *New Orleans*	San Diego, CA	P
LPH 12 *Inchon*	Norfolk, VA	A

Raleigh Class Amphibious Transport Docks

LPD 1 *Raleigh*	Norfolk, VA	A
LPD 2 *Vancouver*	San Diego, CA	P

Austin Class Amphibious Transport Docks

LPD 4 *Austin*	Norfolk, VA	A
LPD 5 *Ogdon*	Long Beach, CA	P
LPD 6 *Duluth*	San Diego, CA	P
LPD 7 *Cleveland*	San Diego, CA	P
LPD 8 *Dubuque*	San Diego, CA	P
LPD 9 *Denver*	San Diego, CA	P
LPD 10 *Juneau*	San Diego, CA	P
LPD 12 *Shreveport*	Norfolk, VA	A
LPD 13 *Nashville*	Norfolk, VA	A
LPD 14 *Trenton*	Norfolk, VA	A
LPD 15 *Ponce*	Norfolk, VA	A

Thomaston Class Landing Ship Docks

LSD 28 *Thomaston*	San Diego, CA	P
LSD 30 *Fort Snelling*	Norfolk, VA	A
LSD 32 *Spiegel Grove*	Norfolk, VA	A
LSD 33 *Alamo*	San Diego, CA	P
LSD 34 *Hermitage*	Norfolk, VA	A
LSD 35 *Monticello*	San Diego, CA	P

Anchorage Class Landing Ship Docks

LSD 36 *Anchorage*	San Diego, CA	P
LSD 37 *Portland*	Norfolk, VA	A
LSD 38 *Pensacola*	Norfolk, VA	A
LSD 39 *Mount Vernon*	San Diego, CA	P
LSD 40 *Fort Fisher*	San Diego, CA	P

Whidbey Island Class Landing Ship Docks

LSD 41 *Whidbey Island*
LSD 42 *Germantown*

Newport Class Landing Ship Tank

LST 1179 *Newport*	Norfolk, VA	A
LST 1180 *Manitowoc*	Norfolk, VA	A
LST 1181 *Sumter*	Norfolk, VA	A
LST 1182 *Fresno*	San Diego, CA	P
LST 1183 *Peoria*	San Diego, CA	P
LST 1184 *Frederick*	San Diego, CA	P
LST 1185 *Schenectady*	San Diego, CA	P
LST 1186 *Cayuga*	San Diego, CA	P
LST 1187 *Tuscaloosa*	San Diego, CA	P
LST 1188 *Saginaw*	Portsmouth, VA	A
LST 1189 *San Bernardino*	San Diego, CA	P
LST 1192 *Spartanburg County*	Norfolk, VA	A
LST 1193 *Fairfax County*	Norfolk, VA	A
LST 1194 *La Moure County*	Norfolk, VA	A
LST 1195 *Barbour County*	San Diego, CA	P
LST 1196 *Harlan County*	Norfolk, VA	A
LST 1197 *Barnstable County*	Norfolk, VA	A
LST 1198 *Bristol County*	San Diego, CA	P

Charleston Class Amphibious Cargo Ships

LKA 113 *Charleston*	Norfolk, VA	A
LKA 114 *Durham*	San Diego, CA	P
LKA 115 *Mobile*	Long Beach, CA	P
LKA 116 *Saint Louis*	Sasebo, Japan	P
LKA 117 *El Paso*	Norfolk, VA	A

Avenger Class Mine Countermeasures Ships

MCM 1 *Avenger*
MCM 2 *Defender*
MCM 3 *Sentry*
MCM 4 *Champion*
MCM 5 *Guardian*

Cardinal Class Minesweeper/Hunter

MSH 1 *Cardinal*

Aggressive Class Ocean Minesweepers

MSO 443 *Fidelity*	Panama City, FL	A
MSO 448 *Illusive*	Charleston, SC	A
MSO 490 *Leader*	Charleston, SC	A

Suribachi Class Ammunition Ships

AE 21 *Suribachi*	Earle, NJ	A
AE 22 *Mauna Kea*	Vallejo, CA	P

Nitro Class Ammunition Ships

AE 23 *Nitro*	Earle, NJ	A
AE 24 *Pyro*	Vallejo, CA	P
AE 25 *Haleakala*	Concord, CA	P

Kilauea Class Ammunition Ships

TAE 26 *Kilauea*		
AE 27 *Butte*	Earle, NJ	A
AE 28 *Santa Barbara*	Charleston, SC	A
AE 29 *Mount Hood*	Concord, CA	P
AE 32 *Flint*	Concord, CA	P
AE 33 *Shasta*	San Diego, CA	P
AE 34 *Mount Baker*	Charleston, SC	A
AE 35 *Kiska*	Concord, CA	P

Mars Class Combat Stores Ships

AFS 1 *Mars*	Oakland, CA	P
AFS 2 *Sylvania*	Norfolk, VA	A
AFS 3 *Niagara Falls*	Guam, HI	P
AFS 4 *White Plains*	Yokosuka, Japan	P
AFS 5 *Concord*	Norfolk, VA	A
AFS 6 *San Diego*	Norfolk, VA	A
AFS 7 *San Jose*	Agana, Guam	P

Improved Cimarron Class Oilers

AO 98 *Caloosahatchee*	Norfolk, VA	A
AO 99 *Canisteo*	Norfolk, VA	A

Cimarron Class Oilers

AO 177 *Cimarron*	Pearl Harbor, HI	P
AO 178 *Monongahela*	Norfolk, VA	A
AO 179 *Merrimack*	Norfolk, VA	A
AO 180 *Willamette*	Pearl Harbor, HI	P
AO 186 *Platte*	Norfolk, VA	A

Sacramento Class Fast Combat Support Ships

AOE 1 *Sacramento*	Bremerton, WA	P
AOE 2 *Camden*	Bremerton, WA	P
AOE 3 *Seattle*	Norfolk, VA	A
AOE 4 *Detroit*	Norfolk, VA	A

Wichita Class Fleet Oilers

AOR 1 *Wichita*	Alameda, CA	P
AOR 2 *Milwaukee*	Norfolk, VA	A
AOR 3 *Kansas City*	Alameda, CA	P
AOR 4 *Savannah*	Norfolk, VA	A
AOR 5 *Wabash*	Alameda, CA	P
AOR 6 *Kalamazoo*	Norfolk, VA	A
AOR 7 *Roanoke*	Alameda, CA	P

Rigel Class Stores Ship

TAF 58 *Rigel*

Sirius Class Combat Stores Ships

TAFS 8 *Sirius*		
TAFS 9 *Spica*	Oakland, CA	P
TAFS 10 *Saturn*		

Mispillion Class Oilers

TAO 105 *Mispillion*
TAO 106 *Navasota*
TAO 107 *Passumpsic*
TAO 108 *Pawkatuck*
TAO 109 *Waccamaw*

Neosho Class Oilers

TAO 143 *Neosho*
TAO 144 *Mississinewa*
TAO 145 *Hassayampa*
TAO 146 *Kawishiwi*
TAO 147 *Truckee*
TAO 148 *Ponchatoula*

Dixie Class Destroyer Tenders

AD 15 *Prairie*	Long Beach, CA	P
AD 18 *Sierra*	Charleston, SC	A
AD 19 *Yosemite*	Mayport, FL	A

Samuel Gompers Class Destroyer Tenders

AD 37 *Samuel Gompers*	San Diego, CA	P
AD 38 *Puget Sound*	Gaeta, Italy	A

Yellowstone Class Destroyer Tenders

AD 41 *Yellowstone*	Norfolk, VA	A
AD 42 *Acadia*	San Diego, CA	P
AD 43 *Cape Cod*	San Diego, CA	P
AD 44 *Shenandoah*	Norfolk, VA	A

Ajax Class Repair Ships

AR 5 *Vulcan*	Norfolk, VA	A
AR 6 *Ajax*	San Diego, CA	P
AR 7 *Hector*	Oakland, CA	P
AR 8 *Jason*	Pearl Harbor, HI	P

Fulton/Proteus Class Submarine Tenders

AS 11 *Fulton*	Quincy, MA	A
AS 18 *Orion*	La Maddalena, Italy	A
AS 19 *Proteus*	Agana, Guam	P

L.Y. Spear/Emory S. Land Class Submarine Tenders

AS 36 *L. Y. Spear*	Norfolk, VA	A
AS 37 *Dixon*	San Diego, CA	P
AS 39 *Emory S. Land*	Norfolk, VA	A
AS 40 *Frank Cable*	Charleston, SC	A
AS 41 *McKee*	San Diego, CA	P

MK-54 five-inch gun.

Appendix V

U.S.N. Carrier Air Wings

The Typical Carrier Air Wing

To begin with, there is no such thing as a typical carrier air wing. The present standard has been around for a while, but the numbers and types of aircraft on the carriers are constantly changing as planes age and new ones come into fleet service. For example, the older carriers—*Coral Sea* and *Midway*—cannot handle F-14s and S-3s. And the types of aircraft on the ship can be shuffled to account for various contingencies; *John F. Kennedy,* off Lebanon, carried an experimental attack component comprised solely of A-6s.

That said, here's a look at a "typical" USN air wing:

Modex	Designation	Type	Number Carried	Trim Color	Notes
100	VF (fighter)	F-14	12	Red	Also Marine F-4s to be replaced by F-18s.
200	VF (fighter)	F-14	12	Yellow	
300	VA (light attack)	A-7	12	Blue	To be replaced by F-18s.
400	VA (light attack)	A-7	12	Orange	
500	VA (medium attack)	A-6	10	Green	Also 4 KA-6Ds
600	VAW (airborne early warning)	E-2	4	Black	
	VAQ (electronic warfare)	EA-6	4	Black	Also EA-3s on forward carriers
700	VS (fixed-wing antisub)	S-3	10	Black	
	HS (helicopter)	SH-3	6	Black	

Current Carrier Air Wings

Navy carrier air wings are hard to pin down. Some squadrons stay together constantly through deployments (and often with the same ship—CVW-8 is the only wing *Nimitz* has ever had). Others, such as the Navy's precious electronic warfare assets, flit from ship to ship seemingly without a rest.

This list is a representative sampling from early 1985, seeking to match carriers to CVWs. Not all these wings were embarked then. Some had just returned from deployment. Others were getting ready to sail. There are also two reserve carrier air wings, CVWR-20 on the East Coast and CVWR-30 on the West Coast. Reserve squadrons do not normally embark as a wing and are not included here.

CVW-1/AB
USS *America* (CV 66)

VF-33	Tarsiers
VF-102	Diamondbacks
VA-46	Clansmen
VA-72	Bluehawks
VA-34	Blue Blasters
VAQ-136	Gauntlets
VAW-123	Screwtops
VS-32	Yellow Tails
HS-11	Dragon Slayers

CVW-2/NE
USS *Ranger* (CV-61)

VF-1	Wolfpack
VF-2	Bounty Hunters
VA-146	Blue Diamonds
VA-147	Argonauts
VA-145	Swordsmen
VAQ-130	Zappers
VAW-116	Sun Kings
VS-38	Red Griffins
HS-2	Golden Falcons

CVW-3/AC
USS *John F. Kennedy* (CV-67)

VF-11	Red Rippers
VF-31	Tomcatters
VA-75	Sunday Punchers
VA-85	Bombing Buckeyes
VAQ-137	Rooks
VAW-126	Seahawks
VS-22	Checkmates
HS-7	Shamrocks

CVW-5/NF
USS *Midway* (CV 41)

VF-151	Vigilantes
VF-161	Chargers
VA-93	Ravens
VA-56	Champions
VA-115	Eagles
VAQ-136	Gauntlets
VAW-115	Liberty Bells
HS-12	Wyverns

CVW-6/AE
USS *Independence* (CV 62)

VF-14	Tophatters
VF-32	Swordsmen
VA-87	Golden Warriors
VA-15	Valions
VA-176	Thunderbolts
VAQ-131	Lancers
VAW-122	Steeljaws
VS-28	Hukkers
HS-15	Red Lions

CVW-7/AG
USS *Dwight D. Eisenhower* (CV 69)

VF-142	Ghostriders
VF-143	Pukin' Dogs
VA-66	Waldos
VA-12	Clinchers
VA-65	Tigers
VAQ-132	Scorpions
VAW-121	Bluetails
VS-31	Topcats
HS-5	Night Dippers

CVW-8/AJ
USS *Nimitz* (CV 68)

VF-41	Black Aces

VF-84 Jolly Rogers
VA-82 Marauders
VA-86 Sidewinders
VA-35 Black Panthers
VAQ-135 Ravens
VAW-124 Bear Aces
VS-24 Scouts
HS-9 Sea Griffins

CVW-9/NG
USS *Kitty Hawk* (CV-63)
VF-24 Fighting Renegades
VF-211 Checkmates
VA-192 Golden Dragons
VA-195 Dam Busters
VA-165 Boomers
VAQ-138 Yellowjackets
VAW-112 Golden Hawks
VS-33 Screwbirds
HS-8 Eight Ballers

CVW-11/NH
USS *Enterprise* (CV-65)
VF-114 Aardvarks
VF-213 Black Lions
VA-22 Fighting Redcocks
VA-94 Mighty Shrikes
VA-95 Green Lizards
VAQ-133 Wizards
VAW-117 Night Hawks
VS-21 Redtails
HS-6 Indians

CVW-13/AK
USS *Coral Sea* (CV-43)
VFA-131 Wildcats
VFA-132 Privateers
VMFA-314 Black Knights
VMFA-323 Death Rattlers
VA-55 Warhorses
VAQ-139 Cougars
VAW-127 Seabats
HS-17 Neptune's Raiders

CVW-14/NK
USS *Constellation* (CV-64)

Crewmen on a carrier line up another cat shot.

VF-21 Freelancers
VF-154 Black Knights
VFA-25 Fist of the Fleet
VFA-113 Stingers
VA-196 Milestones
VAQ-139 Cougars
VAW-113 Black Eagles
VS-37 Roostertails
HS-8 Eightballers

CVW-15/NL
USS *Carl Vinson* (CV-70)
VF-51 Screaming Eagles
VF-111 Sundowners
VA-27 Chargers
VA-97 Warhawks
VA-52 Knightriders
VAQ-134 Garudas
VAW-114 Hormel Hawgs
VS-29 Dragonfires
HS-4 Black Knights

CVW-17/AA
USS *Saratoga* (CV-60)
VF-103 Sluggers
VF-74 Be-Devilers
VA-83 Rampagers
VA-81 Sunliners
VMA
(AW)-533 Hawks
VMAQ-2 Det
VAW-125 Tigertails
VS-30 Diamond Cutters
HS-3 Tridents

America (CV-66).

Air Wing Crew

On board the carrier, the crew is divided almost equally between the ship's company and the air wing. The air department—the part of the ship's company that works on the flight and hangar decks —is grouped into four divisions:

V-1 handles the planes on the flight deck.
V-2 mans the catapults and arresting gear.
V-3 handles the planes on the hangar deck.
V-4 is in charge of refueling the planes.

The flight deck personnel can be distinguished by the colors and trim of the jerseys they must wear on duty:

Blue—Plane pushers, chockmen
Blue with white "T"—Tractor drivers
Blue with white trim—Elevator operators
Yellow—Plane handling officers, arresting gear and catapult officers
Green with black letter—Arresting-gear and catapult crewmen
Green with squadron numbers—Maintenance personnel
Green with white trim—Plane inspectors
Green—Marine guards, flight deck visitors
Red with black stripe—Ordnance personnel
Red with black letter—Damage control crewmen
Purple—Fueling crews
Brown—Plane captains
White—Flight surgeon
White with red cross—Medical corpsmen
White with blue trim—Messengers
Silver—"Hot suit" fire rescue personnel

Appendix VI

Birdwatchers' Guide: Navy Camouflage and Aircraft Markings

Navy Camouflage

The new gray-on-gray Navy camouflage gives new meaning to the phrase "ton of bricks"—planes slamming on the decks now look as if they're molded from solid concrete. Although some Navy pilots resisted the change, they were converted after seeing how the new schemes worked out in mock combat. Then they couldn't wait until their own aircraft received the new toned-down look, thus proving the old fighter pilot admonition: "Never fly in an aircraft that isn't camouflaged!"

The new color schemes are the first real change in naval aircraft finishes since the Navy switched from blue to gull gray with light undersides, although the fleet *did* switch from flat gull gray to glossy gull gray in 1971. Big deal. The light gray finish was a good compromise between the high visibility needed for carrier ops and the lower visibility needed for war at sea. But for air-to-air fighting and attacks against ground targets, the gray Navy birds with their bright plumage of squadron markings made easy targets.

The Navy experimented with the Air Force-style camouflage for Intruders, Skyhawks, and Vigilantes during the Vietnam war, but the tests conducted on *Kitty Hawk* and *Constellation* in 1966 proved unsuccessful for two reasons. First, as long as the aircraft was right side up, the scheme worked fine. But if the plane was bounced from above, a break turn would expose the aircraft's white belly, easily spotted against the dark earth. Fire from the ground produced similar problems. Evasive action exposed the dark upper surfaces against the lighter sky, making the gunner's job easier.

The Air Force eventually compromised by wrapping the three-tone camouflage around the underside of the aircraft as well. But the darker finish never caught on with the Navy because it increased the danger already inherent in night carrier landings. The fleet continued the light gray scheme well into the seventies, until the now infamous AIMVAL-ACEVAL jousts at Nellis AFB in Nevada.

The exercises, while not exactly no-holds-barred, were quite extensive and proved a number of crucial but long forgotten air combat concepts. One of these was the relationship of size to survivability. Both services' pet fighters, the F-15 and the F-14, were at a disadvantage in close-in dogfights against the smaller F-5s and F-16s.

The Tomcat's bright colors and garish markings only made the situation worse. The Navy showed up with half a dozen F-14s finished in the new Ferris "splinter" camouflage. Developed by aviation artist Keith Ferris from experimental World War II Luftwaffe design, the ragged light-and-dark scheme helped disguise the aircraft's attitude by scrambling the shadows pilots use as visual cues. There was even a false canopy painted over the forward landing gear doors.

The Ferris scheme was not adopted by the Navy or the Air Force. Instead, the fleet adopted the now familiar low-contrast gray and gray scheme introduced by the Air Force. There were a number of "free-lance," low-viz Navy designs in the late seventies, before the Naval Air Systems Command stepped in to standardize a low visibility paint scheme for attack aircraft.

NavAirSysCom's Air Combat Survivability Branch developed the new camouflage using computer modeling techniques and flight tests. The computer predicted the amount of reflectivity needed in the paint to accurately match different backgrounds. Higher-reflectance translates into lighter colors to the eyes, but special qualities in the paint enable the finish to appear to change hue. For example, the underside of low-viz aircraft appears almost white at high noon, but seems to darken to a pearly gray at sundown.

Close attention was paid to lightening the finish where shadows are normally thrown in flight, to give the aircraft an overall solid gray appearance. There are actually four such finishes, optimized for use in central Europe, northern Europe, Southeast Asia, and the Middle East. The scheme adopted for the fleet is a compromised "all-purpose" camouflage, but finishes for specific contingencies have also been developed.

The new tactical paint schemes do work. Prowler drivers, used to having their big EA-6B spotted as far out as thirty miles, now say they can get within five miles of the bad guys without being seen. But there are minor problems. The new faded finishes fade even quicker in the harsh environment of blue water. The multi-million dollar matte jets look pretty washed out at the end of a long cruise.

In contrast, the glossy finish on the E-2s and S-3s keep them looking good. But not for long —low-viz camouflage for the Hawkeyes and Vikings is on its way. In fact, every carrier aircraft in the fleet—except for some helicopters—is scheduled for the new slate-gray paint jobs. The change will come gradually, as the aircraft are overhauled during scheduled progressive air rework at the Naval Rework Facilities. One admiral, exasperated by the disappearance of the beloved squadron markings, proposed painting the full color badges and ribbons on the wing's four KA-6 tankers, but someone—probably the tanker crews—nixed the idea.

The markings aren't gone forever. They're just toned down, along with the aircraft finish. Research found that the bright markings were not just easy for the eye to detect, but that the red ejection triangles and intake warnings also made it easier for today's ultra-sensitive infrared missiles to get an IR "paint" on Navy aircraft. So the warning panels, along with the rest of the flashy fleet markings so dear to the heart of modellers everywhere, are being diminished in size and reduced to shades of gray.

Naval Aircraft Markings

Each carrier aircraft carries a modex, a three-digit number stencilled on either side of its nose. The first number of the modex denotes the squadron. The wing's two fighter squadrons are given 100 and 200 series modexes. The 300 and 400 series is reserved for the A-7s of the wing's two light attack squadrons. The Hornets will probably wear 300 and 400 modexes when they come into the fleet, except on the older carriers, where they will inherit the fighter role, and the 100 and 200 modexes of the fighter squadrons, from the venerable F-4.

The wing's Intruders wear the 500 series modex of the medium attack squadron. So do the wing's KA-6 tankers. The EA-6s and E-2s carry the 600 series modex. The wing's antisubmarine forces—S-3s and SH-3s—wear the 700 series. Training squadrons carry an 800 series modex.

The modexes were once related to colors used to trim the squadron aircraft. The trim codes were never followed consistently throughout the fleet—tradition took precedence even when the squadron was transferred to another wing. At any rate, all colors are currently disappearing from carrier aircraft (see "Navy Camouflage" appendix). If the planes carry any trim now, it's likely to be a washed-out version of the former color, barely distinguishable in flight. But for history's sake, here are the modexes/trim colors: 100/red, 200/yellow, 300/blue, 400/orange, 500/green, 600 and 700/black.

The other two numbers correspond to specific squadron aircraft. By Navy custom, the first aircraft in the squadron (modex X00, called "double nuts") is reserved for the carrier of the air wing. Called the "CAG Bird" (because the CVW commander was formerly called "Commander, Air Group") it features special trim, commonly stars or stripes, in the colors of the various squadrons in the air wing. Less widespread is the custom of reserving modex X01 for the squadron CO and modex X02 for the squadron XO.

F-14 lines up on Cat 3.

Note that even though these particular aircraft may be marked on the canopy rails with the names and rank of the specific officers, any pilot can and does fly them on a regular basis. In fact, the Navy's Vietnam war ace, Lt. Randall ("Duke") Cunningham, was flying *Constellation's* CAG bird when he made his final three kills.

The codex is a two-digit number that repeats the last two numbers of the modex. The codex is put high on the tail to aid the air boss and the deck handlers in sorting out closely packed aircraft when the modex is not readily distinguishable.

The air boss and the rest of the carrier crew use modexes to sort the aircraft, since the number carried on each plane is unique to the air wing. Sometimes they are even used for call signs, but a more widespread practice is to use the squadron's call sign and the codex.

The tails of Navy aircraft also carry an air wing code. This specific two-letter code corresponds to the carrier to which the wing is currently assigned. Air wings based on the Atlantic coast carry codes beginning with an "A." West Coast air wings' codes begin with an "N" and land-based ASW patrol squadrons have a tail code beginning with "P."

The system is similar to Air Force tail codes, but where USAF birds display the last three digits of their serial number beneath the two-letter codes, Navy aircraft carry a "buno," or bureau number, underneath the horizontal tail. The buno is assigned to each Navy aircraft in sequence of procurement. The "Bureau" referred to, the Bureau of Aeronautics, has since become the Naval Air Systems Command.

In addition, each aircraft carries both the name of the carrier upon which it is currently deployed and its squadron designation stencilled on its fuselage. In the Navy, "V" means fixed wing. The letter is combined with others to denote a particular type of squadron. For example, "VF-XX" is a Navy fixed wing fighter squadron, often referred to as "FITRON XX" or sometimes "Fighting XX."

Some fighter squadrons also carry a "Langley Stripe," a band of color on either side of the canopy that reflects the squadron's tail marking motif. Its origin is unclear, but it seems to distinguish the Navy's original fighter squadrons. Some planes also carry a "battle E." This marking, usually carried on the port side of the canopy or intake, denotes a superior record for a type of squadron in a command—the best fighter squadron in the Atlantic Fleet, for example. Battle S's are similar, celebrating a superior safety record. An excellence letter with hashmarks signifies consecutive awards.

Appendix VII

The Soviet Navy

Warships of the Soviet Navy

This is a book about the U.S. Navy, but this listing of the Soviet Navy's ships was too good to pass up. Often, the Soviet Navy is presented as a floating monolith, but their ships have names, too. Good ones. LCMR Charles E. Adams and noted naval authority Arthur David Baker III performed a needed service by digging up the English equivalents of Russian ships' names. Their list was printed in the Naval Institute *Proceedings* in July 1979. I've added later ones, with translations when available.

***Kremlin* Class Aircraft Carrier**

Kreml	Kremlin

***Kiev* Class Aircraft Carriers**

Kiev	Ukranian city
Minsk	White Russian city
Novorossiysk	Black Sea port city
Kharkov	East Russian city

***Moskva* Class Helicopter Cruisers**

Moskva	Soviet capital
Leningrad	Baltic Sea port

***Kirov* Class Battle Cruisers**

Kirov	Ukrainian city
Frunze	Mikhail Vassilyevich Frunze, former Commander-in-Chief, Soviet Armed Forces

***Slava* Class Cruiser**

Slava	Strength

***Kresta I* Class Cruisers**

Admiral Zozulya	Former Head of Naval Staff
Vladivostok	Sea of Japan city
Vitse Admiral Drozd	WW II naval hero
Sevastopol	Black Sea port city

***Kresta II* Class Guided Missile Cruisers**	
Kronshtadt	Baltic port city
Admiral Isakov	Head of Naval Staff, WW II
Admiral Nakhimov	Hero of Russo-Turkish War of 1827
Admiral Makarov	Nineteenth century naval figure
Marshal Voroshilov	WW II Army Commander-in-Chief
Admiral Oktyabr'skiy	Black Sea Fleet Commander, WW II
Admiral Isachenkov	Naval engineer
Marshal Timoshenko	Chairman, Army General Staff, WW II
Vasily Chapaev	Revolutionary and WW II military hero
Admiral Yumashev	WW II Pacific Fleet Commander

***Kynda* Class Guided Missile Cruisers**	
Admiral Fokin	WW II Pacific Fleet Commander
Admiral Golovko	WW II Northern Fleet Commander
Groznyy	"Terrible" (Czar Ivan the Terrible)
Varyag	Norseman

***Kara* Class Guided Missile Cruisers**	
Nikolaev	Black Sea port city
Ochakov	Black Sea port city
Kerch	Black Sea port city
Azov	Sea of Azov city
Petropavlovsk	Northern Kazakhstan city
Tashkent	Uzbek city
Tallinn	Estonian city

***Sovremennyy* Class Guided Missile Destroyers**	
Sovremennyy	Modern
Otchayannyy	
Otlichnyy	

***Udaloy* Class Guided Missile Destroyers**	
Udaloy	Courageous
Vitse Admiral Kulakov	WW II Naval Commander
Marshal Vasilevskiy	WW II Army Commander
Admiral Zakharov	Soviet Naval figure

***Kashin* Class Guided Missile Destroyers**	
Komsomolets Ukrainy	Ukranian Young Communist
Krasnyy Kavkaz	Red Caucasus
Krasnyy Krym	Red Crimea
Obraztsovyy	Exemplary
Odaryennyy	Gifted
Ognevoy	Burning
Otvazhnyy	Valorous

Provornyy	Swift
Reshitel'nyy	Resolute
Sderzhannyy	Discreet
Skoryy	Speedy
Slavnyy	Famous
Smelyy	Audacious
Smetlivyy	Sharp-witted
Smyshlyennyy	Clever
Soobrazitel'nyy	Quick-witted
Sposobnyy	Capable
Steregushchiy	Watchful
Strogiy	Severe
Stroynyy	Gracious

Kanin Class Guided Missile Destroyers

Boykiy	Smart
Derzkiy	Daring
Gnevnyy	Wrathful
Gordyy	Proud
Gremyashchiy	Thunderous
Upornyy	Tenacious
Zhguchiy	Intense
Zorkiy	Alert

Kildin Class Destroyers

Bedovyy	Mischievous
Neuderzhimyy	Irrepressible
Neulovimyy	Elusive
Prozorlivyy	Sagacious

Kotlin Class Destroyers

Blagorodnyy	Honorable
Blestyashchiy	Brilliant
Bravyy	Gallant
Burlivyy	Tempestuous
Byvalyy	Experienced
Dal'nevostochnyy Komsomolets	Far East Young Communist
Moskovskiy Komsomolets	Moscow Young Communist
Nakhadchivyy	Resourceful
Naporistyy	Assertive
Nastoychivyy	Persistent
Nesokrushimyy	Indestructible
Plamennyy	Ardent
Skromnyy	Modest

Soviet *Alpha* class torpedo attack submarine.

A Soviet Yankee class strategic missile submarine takes up station on patrol. Recent espionage scandals in the U.S. Navy may have seriously jeopardized American ASW secrets.

Skrytnyy	Secretive
Soznatel'nyy	Conscientious
Speshnyy	Urgent
Spokoynyy	Tranquil
Svedushchiy	Experienced
Svetlyy	Lucid
Veskiy	Weighty
Vdoknovennyy	Inspired
Vliyatel'nyy	Influential
Vozbuzhdyennyy	Excited
Vozmushchyennyy	Indignant
Vyderzhannyy	Steadfast
Vyzyvayushchiy	Defiant

Skoryy Class Destroyers

Bessmennyy	Permanent
Besstrashnyy	Fearless
Bezuderzhnyy	Impetuous
Buynyy	Violent
Ognennyy	Fiery
Okrylennyy	Inspired
Ostorozhnyy	Wary
Ostryy	Keen
Otchayannyy	Desperate
Otchyetlivyy	Distinct
Otmennyy	Exquisite
Otvetstvennyy	Responsible

Ozhestochyennyy	Violent
Ozhivlyennyy	Animated
Serdityy	Angry
Ser'yeznyy	Earnest
Smotryashchiy	Sharp-sighted
Sokrushitel'nyy	Shattering
Solidnyy	Strong
Sovershennyy	Perfect
Statnyy	Stately
Stepennyy	Sedate
Stoykiy	Hardy
Stremitel'nyy	Impetuous
Surovyy	Stern
Svobodnyy	Free
Vdumchivyy	Thoughtful
Vnezapnyy	Surprising
Vnimatel'nyy	Attentive
Vol'nyy	Free
Vrazumitel'nyy	Convincing

***Krivak I* Guided Missile Frigates**

Bditel-nyy	Vigilant
Bodryy	Cheerful
Deyatel'nyy	Active
Doblestnyy	Valiant
Dostoynyy	Worthy
Druzhnyy	Harmonious
Leningradskiy Komsomolets	Leningrad Young Communist
Letushiy	Volatile
Razumny	Reasonable
Razyashchiy	Combative
Retivyy	Zealous
Sil'nyy	Powerful
Storozhevoy	Watchful
Svirepyy	Ferocious
Zharkyy	Ardent

***Krivak II* Guided Missile Frigates**

Gromkiy	Celebrated
Grozyashchiy	Threatening
Neukrotimyy	Indomitable
Pylkiy	Ardent
Razitel'nyy	Impressive
Rezkiy	Harsh
Rezvyy	Frisky

Destroyer on the horizon.

Soviet Fleets

Soviet naval bases are widely separated and poorly placed. The numbers of units estimated to be stationed at each base vary, but this Defense Department list is as good a guess as any. The Soviet Navy has also taken up semi-permanent residence in the American-built port of Cam Rahn Bay in Vietnam.

Soviet Red Banner Northern Fleet
HQ: Severomorsk
Bases: Motovsky Gulf, Severodvinsk, Polyarny
Warships: 149
Submarines: 151
Auxiliaries: 205
Aircraft: 425

Soviet Red Banner Baltic Fleet
HQ: Kalingrad
Bases: Kronstadt, Talinn, Liepaya, Riga
Warships: 141
Submarines: 32
Auxiliaries: 160
Aircraft: 275

Soviet Black Sea Fleet
(Caspian Sea Flotilla)
HQ (Black Sea Fleet): Sevastopol
HQ (Caspian Sea Flotilla): Baku
Bases: Balaklava, Odessa, Nikolayev, Tuapse, Poti
Warships: 162
Submarines: 24
Auxiliaries: 180
Aircraft: 405

Soviet Pacific Fleet
HQ: Vladivostok
Bases: Sovietskya Gavan, Komsomolsk, Petropavlosk, Magadan
Warships: 89
Submarines: 102
Auxiliaries: 235
Aircraft: 440

Mediterranean Squadron (SOVMEDRON)
Major Ports of Call: Tartus, Syria; Benghazi, Libya
Warships: 12
Submarines: 12
Auxiliaries: 20

Indian Ocean Squadron (SOVINDRON)
Major Ports of Call: Socotra, Democratic Yemen; Dahlak, Ethiopia; Seychelles; Beira, Mozambique; Mauritus; Sri Lanka; India
Warships: 6
Submarines: 1
Auxiliaries: 12

Photo credit: Ian Rutan

Michael Skinner has been a writer and editor for the *St. Petersburg Times, the Washington Star,* and the Cable News Network in Atlanta, Georgia. He is the author of USAFE: A PRIMER OF MODERN AIR COMBAT IN EUROPE and RED FLAG: AIR COMBAT FOR THE '80s (Presidio AIRPOWER books). Skinner is currently at work on a book on USAREUR, the United States Army in Europe.